Europa Phase

ORIGINATION TRILOGY

EUROPA PHASE
BOOK 2

Copyright © Zsoall Robi 202

Cover design by Birology Books
birologybooks.com.au

Europa Phase

<u>The Origination Trilogy</u>
<u>Book 1 – Earth Phase</u>
Born to an insignificant peasant family Lai Xii was destined to change the path of human evolution, and in the process spread the seed of homo sapiens within the Milky Way Galaxy.

<u>Book 2 – Europa Phase</u>
The first stage of Lai Xii's plan was to save the human species from extinction, and the destruction of its home planet, by taking the entirety of Earth's population to another destination in the solar system.

<u>Book 3 – Photon Phase</u>
The re-engineered human species arrives at a location that Lai Xii could not possibly have foreseen; a consequence of the myriad decisions made by herself and her closest collaborators.

<u>Other books by Zsoall Robi</u>
<u>Potential Absolute</u>
Lelek could not conceive what the future held for him when he struggled to survive as a Stone Age man. Forces beyond his control set him on a path to the unfolding of all that was possible for this single, special Hominid.

<u>Instant</u>
Is it at all possible to cross the bridge between two consecutive instants of time into Eternity? Mary wanted much more than to experience reality outside of her digital matrix through her three remote autonomous processing units.

<u>Immortal</u>
Aliens are those who are different, those who belong to a different civilisation. Who is worthier of survival? Them or us? The aspirations of an entire species drives them to invade an alien race with which it may be related.

<u>Neural Surveillance</u>
Anything seen, heard or said is transmitted and monitored by the Angels and Saints. Privacy is a luxury that is no longer tolerated by the ruling classes. Absolute control has become the nature of the world order, for no reason other than the lust for power.

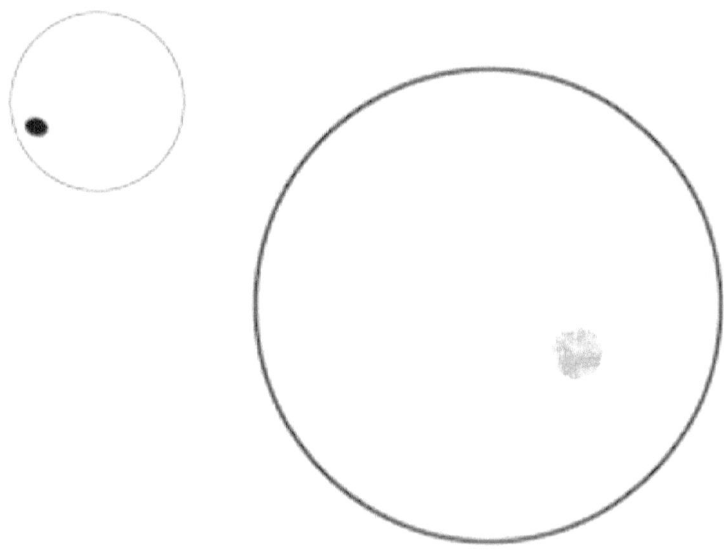

FOUR TO SIX YEARS is a span if time we can understand. Even a round trip to Europa is not out of the question. But why would one want to visit this cold moon, apart from experiencing the magnificence of Jupiter from close up? Perhaps if not a visit but a permanent destination then the short span of a few years could very well be accommodated by a normal human lifespan. What if it became a matter of human survival? Mercury and Venus present an uninviting prospect. Even Mars, without air and water may not be a safe haven.

But Europa has water. There is no possibility of life without it. With the right kind of habitable environment, and an abundant supply of water, it might be the best option we will have.

>_E:\zsoallrobi.auth\PROLOGUE\
<% By the Common Era 2210, Digitised Neo-Humanity is established on Europa at the Arithmós installation; the quantum computer network set up by Phototronic Systems. %>

<% Phototronic Systems, an organisation dedicated to the future survival of the human species, presided over by its founder Lai-Xii, ceased to exist on Earth when most humans went through the transition from bio-chemical to digital and from Earth to Europa in 2164. As events unfolded it became clear their journey had only just begun. %>

<% The rushed, abrupt transition did not give people a chance to come to terms with the concept of existence in both an alien - or what amounted to an alien manifestation as a packet of data controlled within a computer network, and having to endure that condition on an alien world at the same time.

An unplanned eventuality meant one less obstacle to overcome by each individual; everyone retained a sense of their internal personal image. It required no effort to project that image in interactions with other people in a virtual reality construct. LaiXii1 saw her herself exactly the same as before the transition, and that is how others perceived her.

However, humanity finds it challenging to adjust to the physical, psychological and spiritual trauma of suddenly becoming disembodied, only to realize that the human species is not, in fact, the centre of the universe nor the centre of creation. %>

Europa Phase

>_report STATUS

#execute: <<Project Stage 1 - Convert from a bio-chemical life based organism to a digital manifestation in a quantum matrix: Completed.>>

#execute: <<Project Stage 2 – transmit species across the cosmic space savannah from Earth to Europa; ice moon of Jupiter, as Human Factor data bundles (HX-data bundles): Completed.>>

#execute: <<Project Stage 3 – Adjust to digital configuration in quantum environment on Europa through Virtual Reality Constructs: In progress.>>

#execute: <<Project Stage 4 – Prepare to leave Europa: To be initiated.>>

<% William Wini Wu, the sentience evolved from the World Wide Web, became a coincidental collaborator in the transition, with unexpected collateral damage in the process. However, not everything was destroyed on Earth. Not everyone was eliminated, as planned, about which William kept Lai-Xii ignorant. %>

trap <% Hazards existed not just from the possibility of internal anomalies caused by rogue programs, but from vindictive remnant elements on Earth determined to wipe out the perceived traitors to humanity. %>

Europa Phase

>_ programs
1 – CE 2210 - europa
2 – CE 2220 – earth status
3 – CE 2231 - arithmós system integrity check
4 – CE 2232 - virtual reality – europa web
5 – CE ?????- voice from the far future
6 – CE 2344 - budding consciousnesses
7 – CE 2345 - cherryblossom1 in the nursery
8 – CE 2348 - earth review
9 – CE 2349 - infant harvest
10 – CE 2360 - life expectancy
11 – CE 2360 - zetas - maintenance caste
12 – CE 2376 - exploration
13 – CE 2377 - ice infestation
14 – CE 2418 - io
15 – CE 2420 - second cleansing
16 – CE 2425 - william
17 – CE 2488 – other life suspected on europa
18 – CE 2490 - more adjustments
19 – CE 2490 - cherryblossom finds partner
20 – CE 2510 – europa cell
21 – CE 2594 - church of william
22 – CE 2608 - life on europa confirmed
23 – CE 2608 - consciousness
24 – CE 2609 - contact
25 – CE 2615 – a new era
26– CE 2699 – europa cell in EWEB
27 – CE 3175 - preparations to leave europa
28 – CE 3819 - launch day
29 – CE 4000 - arrival
30 – V616Mon - a new beginning

>_run program 1
>_europa
>_Earth Common Era 2210
>_Europa\Pwyll\Arithmós web\

;;; file: CherryBlossom.gen1
| function: future executive file.

;;; file: LaiXii.gen1.master1
| function: master file, Arithmós web controller1.

;;; file: Harusuke.gen1.master2
| function: partner of LaiXii.gen1.master1, executive controller2.

;;; file: Ralph.gen1.adm
| function: principal system coder.

;;; file: Wu.sys
| function: primary system integrity controller.

/** annotation

Arithmós, the quantum computer city nestled within Pwyll crater appeared lifeless in the silence of the vast ice sheets of the southern hemisphere of Europa. Away from the outer slopes of the crater robot-like forms moved about slowly, industriously, intent on tasks for the welfare of the city.

Beyond them kilometre high plumes of water burst into the thin atmosphere, not numerous enough to obscure the rising of Jupiter beyond Europa's curved horizon. The robots worked on, oblivious to volcanic Io orbiting between its nearest brother and Jupiter. The quiet cosmos enveloped their small ice world infested with a new life form in a peace unknown on Earth. Another small group worked on a communications tower on the northern rim of the crater.*/

/** annotation
CherryBlossom1 has two mothers. Each used to be a bio-chemical life form on Earth. After transitioning to a quantum existence copies of their digital genomes were blended, or more accurately 'jumbled', using the unpredictability factor inherent in Chaos Theory to create a new unique genome manifestation in the Arithmós quantum matrix. At age 10, Earth standard, she already possessed the computing acuity of human mathematicians.*/

>_E:\five\lai\
#query: <<Why do we need to be aware of every second of existence, Mother?>> CherryBlossom1 asked.
.... "Because *we* are now responsible for life, not a Creator," replied her other mother, Harusuke1.
#execute: <<Go and find something useful to compute.>> she commanded.

{*Perhaps I'll try to quantify consciousness*}, thought CherryBlossom. She was the first child code budded on Europa and though younger than Prima1 and Secunda1 she had no trouble keeping up with her two older friends who came from Earth. {*I want to know why Ralph1 keeps going on about how lucky we are just to be able to know self.*}

/** annotation
LaiXii1 was once a Geisha in Kyoto. She used her training and her genius to become a multi-billionaire. She decided humanity's fate could not be left to human machinations, nor to random chance. She seduced a gaggle of five obscenely rich men to help put her plan into action; to digitise humanity and relocate it to Europa. After successfully enlisting the help and cooperation of world leaders, LaiXii1's

success seemed assured until they and the leaders of major religions turned against her. The Patriarch of the Russian Orthodox Church even tried to sabotage her Research and Development centre in Tau City, Kamchatka.

Although Virtual Reality programs enabled their digital consciousness to interface with external reality, self-awareness in quantum reality had certain specific rules that had to be adhered to purely because of the mechanics of their existence. LaiXii1 resided in and directed the settlement from her headquarters at the central hub root directory, E:\. All activated citizens had been allocated appropriate sub-directories and embedded directories based on the level of their contribution towards ensuring the viability of Arithmós.*/

LaiXii1 pondered, {*That child asks too many questions. She should be out playing with her friends, or working on her sound paintings.*} Then her mind turned to weightier matters. {*How many more people can we activate before having to expand our topology?*}

!   'Ping' – LaiXii1: "Ralph1, where are you? When are you coming in?" She knew he had to go Icing, but not why it was taking so long to re-sensitise the receptors for Jupiter's magnetosphere. Her thought message immediately connected with Ralph1.
.... "I'm on the northern rim and only just found the problem. Some corrosion on several connections. I can fix it but it will take several days. Looks like we'll need more of the same beta titanium-3 gold alloy that was used to construct the Q-chassis, and for that we'll need resources. I'll sort that out with you when I get back in."

/** annotation
Harusuke1 became LaiXii1's partner when she first met her in Tokyo at Ishino's Geisha House in the Gion hanamachi, assigned to LaiXii as her house-sister. The two had an immediate rapport, which

created the solid foundations of their relationship enduring even on Europa.*/

Harusuke1 had some concerns about insufficient activations since their arrival on Europa. She said to Xii1 ………. "We have over 10,000 Q-chassis Tengi working out in the field outnumbering us in the city by 5 to 1. William did alert us to be vigilant about viruses. Tengi have far greater expertise than the activated staff we've already run integrity checks on."

………. "You worry too much, dear," replied the co-progenitor of their genius level daughter. "They're far too involved in fool-proofing our ocean energy generators to be plotting against us. Besides, DeltaTunit1.gen1.ndf doesn't have the protocols to infiltrate our root directory, and there are only 10 expert Delta Tengi sent up from Earth to lead the set-up crew."
#execute: <<Go chat to Ralph1 and put your mind at ease.>>

/** annotation
Ralph1 is one of the gaggle of 5 billionaires around LaiXii1, an exceptional programming genius. He and his partner Wu.sys worked closely to ensure Europa System integrity. She is a partition of William - the awakened to sentience remote unit of the WWW of Earth vintage. Ralph1 and Wu.sys created Prima1 with William's help while they were still on Earth. Perhaps more of an experiment in procreation between a pure digital sentience and a once bio-chemical one, but Prima1 still represented the bond that became possible between the two uniquely different entities.*/

Harusuke1 downloaded into an unoccupied Q-chassis at one of the Interchange Centres to enable her to physically go out onto the Ice to meet with Ralph1, working on Pwyll crater rim repairing a glitch in some sensory receptors.
She took one of the small ice pods to make her way up the slope.
………. "Do you like being analogue?" Queried Harusuke1 when she

finally caught up with him several kilometres from the main B.U.S terminal.

.... "Well, hello there Harusuke1. Haven't seen you for at least three days. What do you mean – do I like being analogue? What's up?"

.... "We spend most of our time in VR. After years of virtual reality don't you find being out in the real world unsettling?"

.... "You didn't come all the way out here just to talk to me about Icing. Everybody comes out from time to time just to have a bit of fun on the ice sheets and to get a real look at our big boy Jupiter over there, but I suspect not you."

.... "No. I'm getting some looping thought patterns whenever I think about the Zeta maintenance Caste out here. Just can't get my mind off it. You don't think they could turn against us, do you? I mean – we're so different from them, just a bunch of code cockroaching around in the circuits, but they see our world as it really is. They don't really need us like we need them."

.... "I see what you mean. You never used to get nervous back on Earth. But look, Wu.sys has everything under control. She monitors all their actions, all their plans and all their sub-routines. They're loyal. They can't be anything else. If we start losing trust in one another we become no better than the people we left behind. What can I tell you? If you need reassurance have a talk to Wu.sys. She knows more about Europa System integrity than anyone else. She's out on the North Plain with DeltaTunit1.gen1.ndf (DT1) supervising the installation of more ocean energy turbines."

// comment 1 – program 1

    Wu.sys used to be Wu, one of three partitioned avatars created from the AI sentient consciousness, William. From the moment of her download from William into her own Q-chassis she began to diverge from William, evolving on a parallel though unique path, just like her sister Wini, and her brother Willi. As Europa's primary system integrity engineer she knew everyone's status. She could query all the entities' digital genomes and character algorithms. If a bug or a rogue HX data

> bundle crept out of the matrix and corrupted any data clusters she would be the first to become aware of it.//

Returning to the nearest Interchange Centre Harusuke1 swapped the ice pod for a small caterpillar. She felt worried enough about her apprehension to make the trip 120km due North to the drill site. Even after ten years on Europa she had still not got used to the incredible difference between living life at nanosecond intervals instead of hours. The concepts of past, present and the future assumed a whole new perspective. Out on the surface Harusuke1 had to use the best part of the 4 hours, aware of it @ 1 nanosecond at a time, that it would take her to get to the drill site.

Dawning of Jupiter never failed to excite her sensors. She had to acknowledge CherryBlossom1 was indeed a true artist. She'd managed to capture all of Jupiter's stormy moods in her cacophonous sound paintings. The abstract chaos of her melodies perfectly expressed the bands of colour racing each other around Jupiter's girth, doing their best not to collide with the great red storm, which continued to rage unabated since their arrival on Europa. The spectacle engaged Harusuke1's RAM processing for hours despite the bumpy ride.

Mostly radial, brown stained lineae fissures dominated the icy landscape all the way to the dirty zone. The smaller gullies could be navigated by simply reducing speed. A bridge had to be built across the edge of Europa's Sword; the chasm past the edge of Pwyll's Northern slopes. Though it showed no sign of reopening, the distance across it prevented a ramp leap, which they often did across smaller fissures.

Sunset would not be for two more Earth days so Harusuke1 could enjoy the ride in spite of its longevity. From quite some distance she could already see with the augmented binocular vision of her Q-chassis the activity around the drill site.

Wu.sys knew she was coming and stopped work to greet her.

.... "We'll need to develop a quicker way to get around the surface, don't you agree?" The two had become close friends over the short period of their residence on the moon. A peculiar phenomenon had emerged that none had foreseen, not even Ralph1. In a digital environment there seemed to be much more isolation between individuals. It was as if firewalls existed between each HX-data bundle for no other reason than the constraints of digital existence. The need for social interaction drew people into Q-chassis time, as it did Harusuke1 and Wu.sys, where they could connect in actual reality. Not that Harusuke1 wasn't happy with LaiXii1's company – far from it.

.... "How are you progressing with the drilling?" queried Harusuke1.

.... "We're most fortunate to find this location. The ocean is only 5kms down, with a good unobstructed current. We'll get several turbines down. We should have almost immediate power as soon as the umbrella fins are opened and the turbines start running. All the cables have been laid, so it's just a matter of switching on the current."

.... "Interesting how hard it is to let go of Earth terminology. I wonder if we ever will," commented Harusuke1.

.... "Yes. But let's get to what's troubling you. You've always trusted your instincts. What makes you so edgy now?"

.... They moved away from the immediate perimeter of the drill site around to the other side of the cat, out of hearing of the busy Tengi. They settled on the ice and for a while gazed in wonder at Jupiter. Wu.sys was only an avatar of William – once – and William was only a machine sentience – but she'd been endowed with all the human senses and a wide range of others as well. Through all the sensory data input while still on Earth Wu.sys had gained much in the spectrum of human experience and with it some appreciation of the human condition, which included a sense of wonder in the cosmos.

.... "You've been working intimately with Willi.cos.drv almost since we arrived. Haven't you noticed any small anomalies in the Community Operating System functioning? I have an uneasy suspicion that perhaps our maintenance Tengi on the Ice may be doing more than specified by their programming."

.... "Have you personally had any problems?" queried Wu.sys.

.... "It's been a total buzz to experience existence in the fast lane. I can't even remember how we coped at the slow speeds we existed in before coming to the Arithmós matrix. Though recently I've had this really odd sensation of not being able to think as fast, or flash from directory to directory as fast. Maybe it's just in my imagination. But I don't have a good feeling about it."

.... "Why do think they would want to do anything other than what they volunteered for? Surely they would be amongst the most dedicated individuals to have taken the lead in coming out here to set things up for us." Though not of human origin Wu.sys could understand the concept of 'rogue' elements in a society creating disruption. It seemed to be closely analogous to the problems she, as a part of William, had to solve when internet systems became infected with computer virus codes running amuck. She paused a nanosecond before adding, "It's true the Zetas are far more advanced than the Deltas. Only the ones within the matrix have COS access at any level. The maintenance caste have all been excluded, of necessity and safety I assume. I'll talk to Willi.cos.drv and we'll run some diagnostics. I'm sure everything's fine," reassured Wu.sys.

.... "If you say so. You surely realise how much depends on the three of you, and Ralph1 of course." Harusuke1 need not have emphasised his importance as Wu.sys knew it well enough. "Now, tell me about what you're doing here."

While they lingered in the cat's shadow, Io came into view moving surprisingly quickly across their field of vision. They watched it for a while marvelling at how completely different two moons so close together could be. One an ice fortress, the other a volcanic furnace. Wu.sys sent a query to Ralph1 while Harusuke1 gazed at Io's eruptions.

!   Ping! - Wu.sys: "Ralph1, are you available?"

.... "Yes," came the instant reply. Courtesy ID prefixes became mandatory when initiating a contact while existing in the matrix.

#query: <<Have you considered we might need some raw materials, and Io could be the source?>>

.... "Yes. Only today as a matter of fact. We have a corrosion problem on some of our external connections. We'll be reliant on physical resources for maintenance for some time," replied Ralph1. Then Wu.sys explained in simple terms to Harusuke1 how the turbines were designed to work.

.... "It all depends on the difference in rotational speeds between the solid ice crust of the planet and its internal ocean lagging behind. The umbrella fins of the turbine are designed to pick up that difference in speed, thereby turning a turbine on the surface. The rest is just a matter of getting the generated power to Arithmós. If this installation works we'll surround Pwyll with as many as we need. They can work in tandem with our solar generators on the rim."

.... Although Wu.sys seemed so positive about Harusuke1's worrying internal processing problem it didn't entirely satisfy her friend's concerns. At this early stage of their existence every anomaly to normal performance of the matrix had to be examined. end run

>_run program 2

>_earth status
>_CE 2220
>_Kamchatka: Tau City

;;; file: WWW (William)
| function: world wide web consciousness, communication & computing.

;;; file: Maldonado.gen1.mno
| function: security, HX-data files activation, Io exploration team leader.

/**annotation
     WWW achieved sentience after quantum computing
     became mainstream on Earth.

Conscious self-awareness came as a natural consequence of massive data integration in the colossal world wide web RAM. By holding astronomical terabytes of data in constant flux, available to parallel processing routines, that data became information clusters coalescing into a cloud of consciousness. After awakening William chose not to reveal himself until he found Lai-Xii and understood what she was trying to achieve. Even then his decision to help was not irrevocable until he'd received several years of sensory data from his three physical avatar manifestations. Humanity was worth saving but not in its original biological form.*/

The people of Earth were a devious and untrustworthy species. His plan had to consider the unpredictable behaviour of individuals, as well as mass-hysteria driven chaotic events. For ten years after the Cleansing, William remained silent, patiently waiting in the Finnish internet data centres – the only ones he did not de-activate during the Cleansing.*/

! Ping! – .... "Lai-Xii?"

.... "Who is that? Why do you interrupt?" For reasons of privacy in the Arithmós web, the communications 'handshake' protocol required upfront identification and assessment of readiness to engage before initiating interactive communication. William didn't know their rule, or more likely he simply chose to ignore it.

.... "WWW," sounded the identifier.

#execute: <<Team – Priority 1 – Attend.>> The command flashed out from LaiXii1 to the full inner core team. It wasn't everyday William made contact from Earth.

.... "Go ahead William." Willi.cos.drv activated firewall barriers at all levels. William was supposed to have gone offline permanently after the Cleansing.

.... "You may have a problem," William advised.

#execute: <<Verify identity.>> commanded Willi.cos.drv.

.... "Willi.cos.drv, Wini.cos.cab, Wu.sys are sub-sets of self." William transmitted individual identifiers for his original avatars.

.... "OK," Willi.cos.drv confirmed. "Identity verified".

.... "Why do you still exist?"

LaiXii1 had trusted William to do exactly as he promised according to his plan. As soon as all emigrants had been beamed to Europa he was supposed to totally deactivate human society's infrastructure. The expectation being that all, at the least the vast majority of people would die, at the end of which process William was to self-terminate.

Instead of a direct answer he said, ... "I have mined all the data of each individual you have on Europa, cross referenced and extrapolated likely behaviour. You may have a sleeper virus."

.... "Who?" LaiXii1 knew Willi.cos.drv could immediately delete any individual files, so she was not particularly concerned. Harusuke1's attention peaked at the warning.

.... "There are 22,311 possibilities."

#execute: <<Don't play games with me William – I said – Identify!>>

.... "I have received all relevant data," Willi.cos.drv interrupted.

#execute: <<Begin immediate full system integrity check.>>

#execute: <<Re-run our visa criteria protocols against all active files.>>

#execute: <<Terminate all general communications within Arithmós.>>

LaiXii1 wasted no time giving the commands, but need not have bothered as Willi.cos.drv had already initiated the processes. That still left the issue of why William was still functioning.

.... "We would have found them without your help. You seem to forget we have your avatars."

Although William had become a sentient machine intelligence there were still vestiges of his makeup which responded automatically when he received a direct command – some of the time. He tried to explain his continued existence after LaiXii1 demanded for a third time.

.... "Humanity is resilient, like the cockroach. I anticipated possible remnants. It was necessary to remain functional to deal with any emergent threats. Small pockets of scientists, politicians and military managed to survive. They are beginning to rebuild. It may take centuries before they could represent a danger to you, but they will become a threat."

.... "Are you all hearing this?" LaiXii1 queried her team. They responded in the affirmative. "I counsel no further action at this time. Harusuke1 – do you concur?" Again, the affirmative answers were unanimous.

William didn't interrupt. Whilst everyone was still on Earth he would not have hesitated to take control. Now he was undecided. He'd fulfilled his original intention; to get the majority of people off the planet in a safe configuration and to a safe location. There was no immediate need for him to do anything else. He'd put himself on stand-by mode.

#execute: <<Remain hidden. If any attempt is made to reactivate global communications, stop it. Preserve yourself. No further genocide. Confirm.>> The finality of the last statement clearly indicated the end of the conversation.

.... 'Confirmed.' Before going dark William transmitted visuals and data on current Earth status.

// comment 1 – program 2

> After only ten years Earth had visibly clean air again. It had green landmasses and blue waters. It had very few people, less than it had in the early Holocene period. Circumstances on Earth had changed dramatically and immediately upon William's activation of his plan. Whether people survived or not no longer concerned LaiXii1 except if it represented a danger to themselves on Europa. As a remote possibility she might need newly matured neural networks if they had to augment their existing configurations. For that it might be necessary to allow some Earth children to develop to an early stage before being harvested.//

>_E:\

Harusuke1 and Ralph1 flashed to the central hub to join the others as they examined all the new information sent by William. Willi.cos.drv set up a rogue code connection trapdoor bubble, cutting all links to the rest of Arithmós net for the duration of the examination.

/** annotation

>   Maldonado1, one of the original 5 billionaires to join Phototronic Systems on Earth, contributed his expertise in setting up the social media network, Me-Me, that had prepared people psychologically for the transition. Through the introduction of the original VR programs to run on mobile phones he acquired an extraordinary facility for categorising peoples psyches through the examination of all the data collected on them. On Europa he joined the Systems Security team, with particular responsibility for HX-data bundle integrity after their activation. If they passed his scrutiny they were considered to be an asset to the network community.*/

Maldonado1 became particularly interested in the outposts on Earth he saw in William's last report, which appeared to show organised communities of people.

.... "I am not liking that mountain side with the tunnel entrance. There's too much activity. From the look of the uniforms they may be US military personnel."

.... "Where are they getting power from if William was supposed to shut everything down?" LaiXii1's trust in William's plan took another hit.

#execute: <<Let's have a look at Tau City.>> commanded Harusuke1.

Once LaiXii1's headquarters and the centre of operations for Phototronic Systems, it was essentially a rural community capable of surviving without all the technological infrastructure of their century. As she suspected life had continued in their old city. Some tetra-amelias were still wheeled around the streets.

Vehicular traffic became all quadruped based, the most popular being the reindeer. Their numbers had increased dramatically since they became an essential form of transport and food. The small society of just a few hundred people seemed contented enough.

#query: <<Did William indicate any other rural communities around the globe?>> Harusuke1 asked.

Maldonado1 kept thinking about the apparent military outpost. It seemed William's promise of global human extinction fell well short of reality. Small communities seemed to survive in some rural environments around the globe. Cities had become deserts of concrete, steel and asphalt.

#query: <<What is your opinion, people? Do we need to take any pre-emptive action?>>

LaiXii1 and Harusuke1 had a quick closed-circuit conversation about the subject. Consulting the others was more of a formality, as the two master files had already made their decision. Disappointingly Aurelio1 remained true to his base nature.

.... "Nuke the lot of them!"

It's a wonder he got through the visa criteria test, which was supposed to weed out all individuals with a pre-disposition to solving problems through violent action.

.... "You're not serious, surely. Heel!" LaiXii1 needed to pull her cohort into line every now and then. Aurelio1 quickly withdrew his statement of frustration. The general consensus however was that some decisive action did need to be taken without undue delay if they were to be assured their own long-term survival. A command flashed out to William.

#execute: <<Take immediate action. Locate all global military, quasi-military and military/political outposts. Infiltrate their computer networks and permanently disable. Incapacitate all their energy production infrastructure. Deactivate all their transport systems. See if you can manage to get the job done *this time*. Confirm. Report when completed.>>

.... "Confirmed." William either didn't want to, or saw no reason to argue against the command. It was not the right time to be obstructionist.

The conference concluded with all discussion and William's report encrypted for future reference.

As soon as Willi.cos.drv re-established links with the rest of Arithmós net, CherryBlossom1 confronted her mother.
.... "Why did you shut us all out? Why did you shut *me* out?"
.... "Very simple, darling child. You are not yet an executive file capable of making decisions." The child was astute enough to realise her mother's statement was not a rebuttal, but a promise – one day she would be one of the master files, a true leader.
end run

>_run program 3
>_arithmós system integrity check
>_CE 2231
>_Europa\Pwyll\

;;; file: Willi.cos.drv
|function: Arithmós security, Community Operating System management: Standard Virtual Reality development.

;;; file: Aurelio.gen1.avp
|function: foundation member of Phototronic Systems on Earth.

#execute: <<// run monitor sequence @ 432000 second intervals // repeat x 3 // report:.>>

#execute: <<sequence: <central processing core complex> <memory cache> <ethnic partition sectors> <anomalies>: compare.>>

;;; Willi.cos.drv initiated a full Arithmós system integrity check, repeated 3 times over 5 day intervals. First he needed to be assured their infrastructure was robust, before running integrity checks on all individual HX-data bundles. If there was going to be a problem that's where he expected to find it. All performance fluctuations of the system would ultimately lead to the source, even if it was as simple as cache warmth.

>_E:\COS\
/** annotation

> Willi.cos.drv, encasing the highest level security algorithm of Arithmós society, assumed the position of overall system manager of Arithmós net. He came into existence as an avatar of William, while still on Earth. His job now was repetitive, yet complex with ultimate authority over the network to assure the welfare of their quantum existence - without however, possessing appropriate sub-routines to make decisions about the future.
> Wu.sys returned from the Ice to assist. The two of them, being brother and sister with comprehensive system capabilities inherited from William, worked together on all system maintenance issues.*/

#query: <<When will you be ready to run a diagnostic on activated HX-data bundles?>> asked Willi.cos.drv.

.... "In 16 days. As soon as we've analysed the first report," replied Wu.sys.

#query: <<Will you check all dormant HX-data clusters?>>

.... "I want to see if our Virtual Reality programs are intact. The first place to infiltrate and create problems would be in the VR sector. Harusuke1 came out to the drill site to see me with a suspicion." Under the circumstances Wu.sys felt it prudent to bring up the subject.

.... "Must be serious if she was prepared to make such a long journey."

.... "I'm glad she did. I think it is serious. She has concerns about her speed, feeling a little sluggish occasionally."

.... "It's bound to happen. As we bring more people on line there will be a very slight processing time reduction, but I doubt if anyone would be capable of detecting that."

.... "Exactly my thought. So, if she's feeling it, it's worth checking out. She also mentioned that some of her thought routines are looping. What do you think?" queried Wu.sys.

.... "Right. We'll run it past Ralph1 after all the checks are completed."

LaiXii1 and Harusuke1 had taken a ride out to Europa's Sword, the chasm just past the bottom of Pwyll's slopes, totally isolating their Q-chassis from the Arithmós hub for security reasons. Harusuke1 confided her suspicions to LaiXii1.

.... "It's going to take us longer to adjust to this existence than I anticipated. After our experiences back home – you hear that? I'm still referring to Earth as home, even after being here for so long – I have flashes of insecurity. Haven't you felt anything that wasn't as it should be?"

.... "Nothing that stands out," replied LaiXii1. "I just think it's time for a software upgrade. We've been with our original scan matrices since leaving Earth. Time to start upgrading to keep pace with all our new data inputs coming in from around Europa. But now that you mention it – Ptolemy1's been a bit slow responding to my pings, or not responding at all. I suppose he's still overwhelmed by all the work he's got to do to knock Arithmós finally into shape. It's one thing to plan and build a city but a whole set of new problems to deal with when all the people are upload into it."

.... "As a matter of fact, I've felt slightly sluggish on occasions. Perhaps it is time for an upgrade."

.... "Willi.cos.drv, Wu.sys and Ralph1 are running a full diagnostic. If there's a problem they'll find it. They'll run regular checks from now on. So, if William is right we'll ferret out any infiltrator in a flash."

>_ Report 1
!   Ping! - Willi.cos.drv: "Report 1." LaiXii1 tuned in immediately
.... "Fluctuations in RAM are within acceptable parameters," reported Willi.cos.drv.
Wu.sys had already analysed the first report and although nothing seemed out of place in the expected pattern he wanted things to stabilise before continuing with their program of adjustment. "None of the ethnic sectors showed any unusual processor speed variations: all firewalls intact without any record of attempted breaches: no red-flag transmissions. However, just to be sure I suggest we postpone all further activations and get LaiXii1 to set a curfew on all active HX-data bundles."
.... "Agreed." Willi.cos.drv had already come to the decision before Wu.sys had analysed the 1st report.
.... "I concur," LaiXii1 added.
.... "Any speed variations in the hub?" Harusuke1 queried Wu.sys.
.... "None detected outside normal performance. Wait till we have the reports on VR systems and our activated HX-data bundles. We'll run diagnostics as soon as curfew is established." Wu.sys knew what she was doing and there was no point in running a virus purge if there were no viruses. Innocents could get caught up in it, especially if they were borderline visa approvals.
.... "Ralph1 has prepared new customised codes for the hierarchy down to .sys, .adm and some selected .dat levels. They will be ready to download soon," Willi.cos.drv advised of scheduled upgrades for the team after system security integrity had been fully confirmed.

;;; Over a one Europaean day duration Wu.sys and Willi.cos.drv with Ralph1 carried out comprehensive scans of all VR programs created by themselves, as well as all custom-built realities developed by activated individuals. They scoured the results three times to ensure the validity of their initial observations.

>_ Report 2\
!   Ping! - Wu.sys: "LaiXii1, are you available?"
.... "Go ahead Wu.sys."
.... "We don't think there is cause for concern."
.... "Glad to hear you say so." LaiXii1 wanted to berate her as she used to berate her cohort, but somehow the words didn't surface. How do you niggle a machine AI and know it has any effect?
.... "Some personal VRs have been altered without the owners' knowledge or permission. Only very minor changes, like a darker hue to the sky, or their avatar wearing an outfit the owner didn't design. Could be just friendly pranks by their VR family - but still."
.... "What about system generated VRs?"
.... "100% Intact."
#execute: <<Team – Priority 1 – Attend.>> The execute command flashed out from LaiXii1 to the full inner core team.
#execute: <<Immediate ban on all personal VR development until further notice.>>
#execute: <<Ralph1 – create several test VRs \ send out tracker code to locate path\analyse & report.>>

Within seconds of the ban almost all of Arithmós society queried the action. Peoples' personal virtual realities had become as important as the world imposed on them by LaiXii1 and the unreality of the external Europaean environment. Harusuke1's sentiments regarding the difficulty of the human psyche adjusting was not an isolated phenomenon. A message, transmitted to every individual, advised that the first major system maintenance and upgrade could only take place in a non-dynamic environment. Such essential action would prevent the likelihood of outages, ensuring their systems would not fail to perform their primary functions; namely, keeping everyone viable. No mention was made of the possible, though unlikely threat of subversive code infiltrating their COS.

\>_ Report 3: pending\

;;; Compulsory downtime equated to sleep. Reboot depended on each individual pre-programing their own integration & assimilation duration. Restrictions didn't exist on downtime duration, only recommendations and guidelines. Willi.cos.drv reserved the function of ensuring each HX-data bundle observed some downtime within any active period, generally indicated by the volume of processing carried out by the individual within that period.

;; He ran a cryptographic hash function algorithm on every HX-data bundle activated. The resultant checksum, compared to the checksum of original arrivals, showed a minor discrepancy in one file only. But that's all it would take to infect the entire community if it was a virus and not a harmless mutation.

.... "I have found something," Willi.cos.drv alerted Wu.sys

#execute: <<Set up containment field \ activate file \ analyse & report.>> commanded Willi.cos.drv.

!   Ping! - Willi.cos.drv: "Lai-Xii?"

.... "Go ahead."

.... "It will take time to run the check on all active files. We can only do so during their downtime. However, I've found one anomaly already amongst all the down-timed files. Wu.sys is checking its integrity under containment."

#execute: <<Report identity asap.>> This was one problem LaiXii1 wanted resolved without delay.

{It's was hard enough to put a comprehensive adjustment program into effect without having to cope with aberrations. The visa checks should have weeded out all undesirable disruptive elements.} LaiXii1 chastised herself over the oversight. Because their migration schedule from Earth suffered several setbacks forcing her to hasten their departure, most scanned individuals didn't have the visa checks at the time, which were developed by Phototronic Systems. The plan was to run those prior to activation on Europa and simply delete any rotten eggs. Perhaps that's where the problem originated.

{The traitor must have managed to get through because of the procedural changes we had to make.}
In their personal home directory LaiXii1 and Harusuke1 bounced a few options around. They both knew, though they may not have admitted it, that the adjustment phase of their migration was probably going to be more challenging than the transition. There were simply too many unknowns they could not have prepared for.

#query: <<What are we going to do when you find out who's responsible?>> Harusuke1 asked.
.... "There is only one thing we can do," mused LaiXii1, "only one thing we must do, for our safety; for everyone's safety. How can there be half measures if we are to survive? We've brought humanity this far. We cannot fail now. A complete purge of everyone involved, no matter who they are – reformat their entire hub if necessary."
#query: <<Are you asking me, or telling me?>> As always Harusuke1 didn't let her partner equivocate.
.... "I'm telling you. We will have to act together on this."
LaiXii1 made it quite clear Harusuke1 shared full responsibility with her. Not like in the old days back on Earth when Harusuke1 could only operate in the background.

>_

Aurelio1 simply didn't know what to do. After his outburst at the meeting to discuss the situation on Earth he decided to remain in active mode as long as Willi.cos.drv allowed. *Damn! I should not have said that!* The words – 'Nuke the lot of them!' – just burst out of him on the spur of the moment. He had no allegiance to the surviving powers on Earth. It just angered him that even that avenue of escape had become inaccessible to him. As soon as the command flashed out from LaiXii1 banning all VR development he knew he was in trouble. Remaining in his private directory Aurelio1 refrained from carrying out any of his duties, not that he had a great deal of responsibility at this stage in the implementation of the adjustment strategy.

He considered the events on Earth that led him to where he would now probably have to fight for his continued existence.

.... "Have you met my sister?" asked Zeta Tengi Bogdana during a VR testing session with Aurelio a few years before the scheduled migration.

At that stage Aurelio contributed to developing comprehensive VR programs to replicate Europa-like conditions, using some of the latest 'Technically Engineered Individuals' to test the practicality of the VRs. One of the Zeta Tengi, Bogdana, ended up working closely with him for several years. She was once a tetra-amelia citizen of Tau City at their Kamchatka research facility – a very unhappy one.

.... "No," he answered, "who was she?"

.... "Olesya."

.... "Why should I have known her?" Aurelio was getting a little annoyed. He had work to do and this conversation had nothing to do with it.

.... "Perhaps you remember seeing her at a restaurant in Petropavlovsk, just before she was arrested." Bogdana continued the conversation in an even tone, not letting on how agitated she actually felt. But she had to keep control if she was to enlist Aurelio's support.

.... "Why are you telling me *this?" Of course he remembered. He also remembered how the dissidents were dealt with at the time; all mention of them expunged from the records, and the individuals themselves just – made to disappear. But Bogdana found out that they'd been eliminated.*

She waited a few moments before responding, trying to gauge Aurelio's mood.

.... "Because you, of all the leadership group of the Project, seem to be ... perhaps not as satisfied as everyone else with progress, with the way things are done."

Aurelio1 could remember becoming extremely alert at that point. Partly because the matter of the escapees was supposed to be a closed incident, partly because here was a tetra-amelia turned Tengi bringing up a very personal issue, which obviously had deep significance for her. And partly because this Tengi had no business bringing his disposition towards the Project into the discussion. It was none of her business.

What Aurelio1 couldn't quite remember was how he got drawn into the conspiracy. Perhaps it might have been a sense of guilt. Unlikely. Perhaps his own disappointment had finally bubbled to the surface, clear to any astute observer. After many months of careful manoeuvring, and sexual favours, Bogdana effectively controlled Aurelio. She didn't care what happened to herself or to Aurelio, as long as he implemented her plan. Lai-Xii was not going to get away with killing her sister. Not only did she make life difficult for both of them by engineering out their limbs, but by also treating them as totally expendable objects.

//comment 2 – program 3

> Aurelio, of the five founding men was the richest, the fattest and the greediest for more profit. Fed up with all of LaiXii1's debasements but happy enough when he continued to make billions selling more mobile phones on Earth. Yet he felt suspicious of LaiXii1's ambition from the beginning, playing along only in the expectation of huge financial rewards – which in the end didn't satisfy his expectations – instead there was exile – Europa was nothing more than exile, for him.//

>_ Report 3

!   Ping! - Willi.cos.drv: "LaiXii1, are you available?"

#query: <<What've you got?>>

Within every predetermined cycle it was mandatory for each HX-data bundle to have downtime. Aurelio1 waited as long as he could, suspecting that during his downtime the system integrity check might identify him. There was nothing he could do about it. He didn't have system access to Security, so could not reroute the tracker codes.

.... "You are not going to like this. We've identified a .avp file. It's in containment and can't do any more harm."

.... "Out with it!"

.... "He used to be a .adm, self-modified to an .avp to gain access to our COS, then self-modified again to a .exe waiting to decrypt himself and execute changes. They were only minor ones and I'm guessing he was just flexing his muscles seeing what he could get away with safely. But I have no doubt he had bigger plans. Flash over to the main hub, we will be there to meet you."

Willi.cos.drv didn't want to directly reveal the identity of the rogue file. LaiXii1 could have done anything if she flew into a rage. The other problem was that the man had slipped past him in the first place, to infiltrate their Operating System.

Nano seconds later LaiXii1 stood facing Aurelio1, held isolated in a containment trap. A VR platform had not yet been created for such an unusual circumstance, so they faced-off neuron-to-neuron style, firing pulses at each other.

Many seconds later, after her sizzling abated, LaiXii1 could shout only one word .... "WHY?"

.... "You self-important megalomaniac Bitch! Why do you think!"

Wu.sys alerted the others. A whole crowd had gathered, including Evgeniya1, Wini.cos.cab and Wu.sys.

#execute: Willi.cos.drv: <<Get CherryBlossom1, Prima1 and Secunda1.>> she commanded.

.... "I want the girls to see this. Europa is their world. They have to learn the rules." Commuting by flash jumps within the hub tree took no time at all. The girls appeared an instant after being called. They knew Aurelio1 of course, and though they didn't particularly like him, didn't conceive him to be a disruptive element in their new society.

#execute: <<Explain yourself – NOW!>> LaiXii1 shouted at Aurelio1. CherryBlossom1 had never seen her mother so upset.

.... "You want to know? Do you really want to know? Well! I had invested the best part of my $100 billion for you and all I got for it is a dead, cold planet and life as a computer code. Where is my profit? What sort of damned life is this!"

LaiXii1 didn't want this to be a long drawn out confrontation. She wanted the girls to have the experience of human nature as it was rampant on Earth before their exodus; the very thing she worked so hard to get away from. She let some of the impulse energy dissipate out of her circuit before continuing.

#query: <<How did you do it? You're not smart enough, you fat assed imbecile.>>

It was deliberate goad. In the past, when she berated him, it was always with an edge of affection. She knew he could never keep his mouth shut and would very quickly reveal any accomplices. The ruse worked immediately.

.... "You think you're so clever – you think everyone thinks as you do. Bogdana certainly didn't. Well, let me tell you – there are plenty of others who hate your guts! Have you ever spared a thought for all those people you deprived of a normal life, taking away their arms, their legs – their independence, their self-respect?"

CherryBlossom1 moved closer to her mother, feeling the effect of the onslaught on her. The whole place buzzed with highly energised electrons.

#query: <<What is he talking about, mother?>>

.... "You saw all the limbless people in wheelchairs back in Tau City. Without them none of this would have been possible. They are the heroes who saved humanity from extinction," she replied.

.... "Ha! Is that what you call torture and murder! Ask her what she knows about Olesya and her friends who tried to escape from her benevolence!"

The team could barely believe what was going down. In all the years they worked together on the Project on Earth there was never this kind of drama and hatred. Not even immediately before the forced migration: Lots of panic and chaos, but never such venomous opposition.

.... "Why bring up Olesya? She was an innocent." LaiXii1 interrupted the barrage.

.... "Exactly – an innocent! And when you caught up with her and her friends, you had her executed. Not just her, everyone who helped her escape your madness. Ask her sister how she feels about what you've done."

.... *"Bogdana"* Willi.cos.drv whispered to LaiXii1, *"was a tetra-amelia loaded up into a Q-chassis. She's with us on the maintenance team out on the Ice."*

\#execute: <<Detain \ bring her in.>> came the immediate command.

\#query: LaiXii1 <<What did you hope to achieve? To destroy us? Don't you remember LaiXii.gen3920.4eV.exe from our future. She is evidence that you couldn't possibly have succeeded.>>

It was time for the girls to learn a hard lesson.

.... "This is not Earth with laws that protect criminals, that provide havens for unscrupulous business men – that allows conspiracies to flourish to the detriment of all people. This is a world where there is only One rule – we survive *together* – or not at all." All the while she kept one of her processing channels concentrated on CherryBlossom1. If the girl flinched for even the slightest minuscule of a picosecond her future as a leader would cease to exist.

.... "Willi.cos.drv, carry out my next command immediately," CherryBlossom1 held a steady gaze as she listened to her mother issue the execute command.

\#execute: <<delete Aurelio.adm, Aurelio.gen1.adm.avp, Aurelio.adm.exe.>>

LaiXii1 turned her focus to Prima1 and Secunda1 to gauge their reaction to her command to delete Aurelio1.

Zeta Tengi Bogdana also ceased to exist the following day. LaiXii1, still not satisfied, brought the entire team together again, involving the three girls as before. At E:\ Willi.cos.drv waited for the inevitable -{*How am I going to explain Aurelio1's ability to infiltrate our Operating System? It was my oversight.*}

First, in her private directory, LaiXii1 interrogated her most trusted individual apart from Harusuke1.

\#query: <<Ralph1, you're the code expert, tell me how this was possible.>> The two master files listened intently to his explanation, for to them it seemed like a situation that should never have happened.

.... "The process is really quite simple, and what made it possible was that Willi.cos.drv has a multitude of functions, including some minor ones that he delegates to sub-routines."

#query: <<Are you trying to protect your friend?>> The question betrayed no malice, although the implication was there.

.... "No. Simply stating how our system works. Aurelio1 only needed to know a simple handshake protocol, which a Zeta Tengi was more than capable of teaching him. Imagine this scenario, with Aurelio1 first self-modifying from a .adm to a .avp – the extension for an anti-virus algorithm. Then when he knocked on the COS door it would immediately be assumed that he originated from one of us .adm or .drv files."

LaiXii1 interrupted to say, "Before you go on I want to remind everybody, girls especially, that there is only one possible outcome for anyone who endangers our survival." She waited until satisfied all had indicated their understanding with a little 'ping'.

.... "Right. So along comes Aurelio.gen1.adm.avp …

> *Aurelio.gen1.adm.avp*: Operating System! I want to examine a .dat file and see if there's a virus hiding in there. Please let me read it.
>
> *OS:* Ok. I recognise you as an authentic policeman. You may look and read the file.
>
> *Aurelio.gen1.adm.avp*: Thank you OS.
>
> *OS:* Come in – go ahead …

At this point Aurelio.gen1.adm.avp is in and can proceed to hide until ready to do something. But why don't you ask Willi.cos.drv this. He's the file on the spot."

.... "I will." With only two directory levels to jump, the entire congregation arrived in a blink at E:\. "Willi.cos.drv – explain," LaiXii1 commanded. They all knew why they were there, no need for small talk.

.... "Let me say firstly that I've made some changes. Anyone knocking at my directory will no longer be admitted by subroutines without my knowledge," began Willi.cos.drv.

.... "Girls, CherryBlossom1, hear that - solutions before self-justification. So far so good. Continue."

.... "The process of adjustment requires me to make myriad observations, checks, modifications, VR development etc. Some functions I had delegated to minor sub-routines without coding sufficient safeguards into the handshake security protocol."

.... "Girls, do you find this satisfactory?" They were not self-conscious about being included in the centre of all the important action. CherryBlossom1 in particular recognised what her mother was doing – grooming her for the future.

.... "So – do we all agree? We're safe for now?"

.... "Except for the new developments on Earth," said Maldonado1.

end run

>_run program 4
>_virtual reality - europa web
>_CE 2232
>_Europa\External reality.
>_Pwyll crater rim

;;; file: Salazar.gen1.adm
| function: roving admin file.

;;; file: Evgeniya.gen1.adm
| function: HX-data analyst, Nursery laboratory manager, Europa Discovery Expedition Team member.

.... "We need a common reality," said Salazar1 as the small group in their Q-chassis relaxed on the Ice slope of Pwyll crater gazing to the north, with Jupiter rising to their left.

/** annotation

Salazar1 only brought $64 billion to the Project when he joined Phototronic Systems. The real asset he injected into the founding group was his creativity and his vision. The work he did with running global art competitions on Earth, themed 'Jupiter and Europa, The Relationship,' helped people to immerse themselves into the imagery of a new world. It gave them confidence and a desire to experience another reality. Salazar1 knew the value of a person's internal reality, how it was built on imagery as much as on philosophy and how it created a sense of personal worth; a reason for their existence. When he stated the need to create a visual consistency in their society he spoke from experience.*/

.... "I have to agree with you," said Evgeniya1, at one time their genetic engineer and neurologist, now their most prominent Mass Psychologist come personal systems analyst. "I've been watching trends developing, especially in the ethnic hubs, which could pull us and the Maintenance Caste apart."

// comment 1 – program 4

On Earth Evgeniya1 engineered the transition of the original thalidomide victims from victim-hood to the most valuable asset of Phototronic Systems; people with greatly enhanced cerebral capacity. By reducing the amount of time their neurons needed to devote to concierge duties looking after full-bodied biological support mechanisms for the brain, it allowed more time for mental development. Phototronic Systems needed the most brilliant brains on Earth to bring about the great transition. Those same tetra-amelia became the maintenance engineers for the quantum computer systems infrastructure of the Europa settlement, and represented the bulk of the physical elements in Arithmós.//

Europa Phase

The gathering of twelve key personnel became absorbed in the landscape and majesty of Jupiter. Over many years they've all had numerous excursions to the Ice in their Q-chassis, yet the spectacle always enchanted them. That particular day the red storm seemed larger and more turbulent than on previous occasions. Io came hurtling into view with its furnace of volcanic eruptions clearly visible from their vantage point. Worlds of ice and lava and colourful methane storms created a whole new reality completely alien to the green and blue of Earth.

{The first generation of engineered humanity will never be able to make the adjustment unaided.} Her train of thought brought Evgeniya1 back to the present moment.

.... "There are two realities developing," she said to no one in particular, though all were listening. "First there's the Zeta Tengi out here working in their Q-chassis bodies, who'd joined the original Deltas we sent over, and there's us in the network."

.... "I've also been thinking about them," added Harusuke1, "There's very little interaction between them and us. They're always out here, always concentrated on physical reality. Surely it must make them feel separate from us over time. Some of them have been here for many years setting up before we arrived. When did you last speak with Oone1, LaiXii1?" queried Harusuke1.

Oone1, previously known as DeltaTunit1.gen1.ndf had received a special upgrade from Delta to Zeta after the arrival of the rest of the Digitals, and given greater responsibilities.

.... "Now that you mention it, at least two years ago. Oone1 mostly deals with you Ralph1, yes?" queried LaiXii1.

.... "He didn't even bother to contact me when you stopped all personal VR development. Perhaps they're not interested in VR anymore," said Ralph1.

#execute: <<Check on all other Tengi and Zeta models.>>

#query: <<Have they developed their own social structure, separate from ours?>>

.... "I think it should be compulsory for them to have Q-chassis downtime within the Arithmós web to give them the opportunity to reintegrate with us, " Harusuke1 offered a possible solution to the growing estrangement.

.... "That's only part of the problem," Evgeniya1 came back on track. .... "Look!", she pointed suddenly in Jupiter's direction, "a meteor shower!" The girls immediately lost all interest in the conversation. Meteor showers on Jupiter were as rare as they were spectacular. Bringing with them an exotic mix of gases, which interacted with Jupiter's methane atmosphere. They created wonderful fireworks with extraordinary colours disturbing the flow of existing colour bands on the Giant. It only lasted 5 to 10 minutes, but well worth the distraction.

.... "Outstanding!" Evgeniya1 continued unfolding her thoughts. "There are people in every hub going off in all directions creating personal virtual realities that have nothing to do with our life here. If any of you bothered to look, they seem to focus on their ethnic origins from China or Africa or Iceland, everywhere where they came from, except Europa. Perhaps they've even forgotten where they are now."

.... "That's entirely possible," added Maldonado1, "if you think back to what we saw of peoples' behaviour on Earth when they became addicted to their VR games on the mobiles."

By age 21 CherryBlossom1 had been so readily accepted into the leadership group that she felt comfortable to contribute to the conversation.

.... "Mother, I thought this was all the reality that existed. I was born here. It is beautiful. How could anyone not be happy here. We have everything we want at home in the web, and we can come out here and experience all this," she swept the landscape with her long Q-chassis arms, taking in the vista of Europa's ice plains, Jupiter's orb and the surrounding cosmic mystery. "Extraordinary!" she exclaimed.

While the discussion flowed between the others, LaiXii1 and Ralph1 had their own little chat. It became obvious that not only ensuring their safety was a priority for the adjustment period, but getting all citizens acclimated to their new actual reality. Ralph1 agreed changes needed to be made without delay.

.... "I'll work with Wu.sys and Willi.cos.drv to set up a Standard Virtual Reality (SVR) template. It will include at its foundation our physical environment, both the immediate vicinity of Jupiter and its moons and the greater cosmos from our galaxy's perspective."

.... "Include me in," Ptolemy1 volunteered, "after all, I'm the one who helped design and build Arithmós."

.... "So, what do you suggest, my little cockroach?" LaiXii1 loved teasing him back on Earth and now with a major threat averted she treated herself to a little fun.

.... "Strict control over people to stop them creating their own personal virtual realities. They have to be guided to use the SVR template as a starting point. Their personal constructs should have no more than a minimum reference to Earth reality. If people cannot come together in a common vision of the here and now, we could all be a danger to each other."

#execute: <<Willi.cos.drv, implement both SVR and strict controls on personal VR enhancements.>>

#execute: <<Ralph1, prepare software upgrades for all citizens. Built in restrictions on personal VR developments.>>

#execute: <<Wu.sys, increase external sensory input to all active HX-data bundles.>>

Harusuke1 then made what seemed like an impromptu suggestion, but from the nature of it she must have thought the idea through.

.... "Begin a program of intense budding, ensuring maximum saturation of infants with external sensory input to reflect the reality of Europa. The future is theirs after all. We only made that future a possibility."

#execute: <<Initiate budding program. Ralph1 and Wu.sys, you have experience with this. You've done a good job with Prima1.>> With that last command LaiXii1 concluded the session out on the Ice.

Back at E:\four\lai, Harusuke1 and LaiXii1 both agreed with Salazar1 as they discussed the difficult situation they had unwittingly created. If they could not engineer a common reality for neo-humanity the whole society could fragment into competing nations based on their versions of reality – exactly the same as what happened on Earth.

.... "You came from China," observed Harusuke1, "and made a life in Japan. When you took us all to Kamchatka there was an altogether different reality we had to adjust to. That was hard enough from the cultural perspective. But when you consider political and religious differences it's little wonder people could not exist together in any lasting harmony."

.... "You're right, my sweet. I couldn't believe the reluctance of the Nations to come together when it concerned the survival of the human species. We cannot let that situation develop here."

#execute: <<Go out with CherryBlossom1, Prima1 and Secunda1 to all the hubs, at least down to third directory level, and see what the people have actually created for themselves. Then visit our maintenance caste. You know what to look for.>>
>_
Harusuke1 set out with the girls to investigate the actual extent of the proliferation of individual virtual realities, both by communities in the large variety of topologies, as well as a sampling of individual HX-data bundles' VRs.

// comment 2 – program 4

> Within the central Arithmós hub and peripheral control nodes most individuals seemed to have the same overall vision of the circumstances of their existence. The initial VR training of all personnel by Ralph1 ensured little divergence of their reality concepts. After decades on location many small variations of perception and interpretation of sensory input from external transmitters influenced individuals' new world view. However, their common reality enabled them to work in harmony with LaiXii1 and her leadership group. Harusuke1 and the girls had no need to dig into sub-directories in search of aberrations in these groups.

Europa Phase

> Prima1 wanted to visit the Kamchatka Star in particular. Although connected to the central hub many communities existed in their individual topologies, based essentially on their original national identities. //

.... "Can we go there first? Because I was budded there it will be obvious to me to what extent the people have re-created their old Tau City environment."

A large cross section of Tau City citizens had managed to migrate before the Russian forces shut down all movement out of the city. As Prima1 flashed from one Kamchatka directory layer to another it was almost as if she was back in Tau City.

.... "They've created the Russian Orthodox Church Cathedral and the city square in front of it," she said.

CherryBlossom1 became fascinated by the landscape with huge mounds that seemed to go kilometres high. "What are those," she queried pointing to all the surrounding landscape.

.... "We called those, mountains. Some of them used to have smoke and molten rock explode out of them just like the volcanoes on Io," Harusuke1 responded, remembering a reality that seemed like a dream.

The immigrants had so faithfully reproduced the environment in their VR that it felt like actually being there. A few people went about purchasing their goods at the market stalls. It must have been market day. The whole scene reeked of a sense of unreality, not because it was a VR construct, but because it was such a comprehensive recreation of something that no longer existed.

.... "But there is nothing here about Europa or Arithmós," commented Secunda1.

.... "No, there isn't. I can understand them doing this, but I don't think it's healthy. Let's go and visit some of the people living here," Harusuke1suggested.

It would be a valuable experience for CherryBlossom1 as she'd spent most of her life close to the Central Hub, or out Icing. Harusuke1 consulted the directory tree and found someone she knew from Earth. The time had come to reacquaint herself with people from the past who'd had a decisive role to play in the transition.

>_E:\Arithmós\KamchatkaRing\ViktorPyryev.gen1.sec\

;;; file: ViktorPyryev.gen1.sec
 |function: Infrastructure Security: Second Cleansing assistant to William.

.... "Yulia1, we have people coming, better put those things out of sight," VictorPyryev1 warned quietly.
Those 'things' could not have been considered dangerous. Ever since Yulia made LaiXii aware of emerging unhappiness in Tau City because of the way the tetra-amelia children were treated, she'd continued lobbying for the welfare of all handicapped children of thalidomide victims. Here in Arithmós her activities morphed into something less confrontational. Yulia1 had taken it upon herself to help those in her Star topology to adjust to the new environment by recreating the old one as faithfully as possible, completely ignoring Europa. Those 'things' were her 'instruction set' on how to program VRs that would be both unique to individuals, like their old homes, and compatible with a common memory of it. It was her initiative that created the Cathedral to the background of snow-capped volcanic peaks along Kamchatka's spine.
.... "Hello VictorPyryev1." Harusuke1 greeted, then introduced the girls. CherryBlossom1 immediately scanned the room without first greeting VictorPyryev1, trying to understand many of the strange things she saw. Noticing her lack of manners Harusuke1 apologised for her.
.... "This is my daughter. She hasn't seen many artefacts from Earth recreated in VR so accurately."
The apology actually gave Harusuke1 the opportunity to bring up the subject of personal VRs, which was after all, their reason for the visit. Yulia1 had just stepped back in from the other room as Harusuke1 arrived.
.... "Hello Harusuke1, hello girls."

CherryBlossom1 went from wall to wall inspecting the variety of images of people working in fields, others dressed in ethnic costumes worn during festivals.

.... "What are those people doing to the brown ice?" she queried in all innocence. She couldn't understand what all the green stuff was waving about on the ground, and on stalks in the air, and the brown stuff being worked. To her it was all an unreality. Europa was white and quiet, with not enough atmosphere to generate winds. Definitely nothing like tress or grass existed.

.... "They were my family, planting in the fields of our farm." Yulia1 glanced at Harusuke1 as she replied, probably because of a little apprehension after the ban went out about developing personal VRs.

.... "Do you miss your family, Yulia1?" queried Harusuke1, while CherryBlossom1 continued exploring the room.

To Prima1 and Secunda1 it was mostly familiar as they had plenty of opportunities to be out and about in Tau City while still living there.

.... "Only sometimes. We find it hard to get used to being here. When we go Icing it's very strange. The sun is so far away and Jupiter is so big and threatening."

.... "Do you go out often?" Harusuke1 stayed on the subject hoping to learn more about the effect actual reality of Europa was having. Nothing in the home's internal environment betrayed the fact the inhabitants no longer lived on Earth.

.... "Not anymore. We prefer to stay at home. And go on VR excursions with our friends."

Harusuke1 understood the situation that had evolved even over a few decades. Perhaps VictorPyryev1 and Yulia1 exemplified a large segment of their population. She'd seen and heard enough.

.... "Come on girls, we need to go." To Yulia1 and VictorPyryev1 she said in parting, "I hope you will both take an enthusiastic part in our new SVR program as it uploads to all of Arithmós."

As soon as they'd left VictorPyryev1 and Yulia1 had a heated argument.

.... "Did you hear what she said about the VRs? They're going to come down hard on anybody attempting to live in the past. I personally don't blame them. You'll have stop all your nonsense trying to get everybody to ignore where we are," VictorPyryev1 warned.

.... "No. I will not give it up!" Yulia1 was adamant, "we cannot forget our heritage, our History. It is who we are."

.... "Is there any way I can get you to compromise?" VictorPyryev1 could see her point.

The four inspectors made their way back up the directory tree and across to another ethnic group, a much larger one with many hundreds of thousands of citizens. They had previously made an appointment to see the Prime Minister of the JapanTree.

>_E:\Arithmós\JapanTree\Fukuda.prs

;;; file: Fukuda.gen1.prs (Fukuda1)
| function: executive file JapanTree hub.

// comment 3 – program 4

In contrast to KamchatkaRing, JapanTree had been organised to give their hierarchy greater control. Based on a Linear Bus with a branching Stars topology enabled unique groups to have their own independence, though still within the control of Fukuda.prs' coders. Several branches of their tree preferred the Mesh structure, allowing greater internal co-operation between all its constituent nodes, though still coming under Fukuda.prs' direct control.//

.... "This is like stepping into an entirely different world compared to Tau City." CherryBlossom1 could identify with many visual aspects of their VR city. Although it still seemed like a city built on Japanese design parameters, the builders had gone to a great deal of trouble to make this common environment outstandingly beautiful as well as relevant to their unique location of Europa.

.... "Look Harusuke1, all the streets are white like the Ice fields!" CherryBlossom1 pointed out excitedly, "the buildings have all the colours and swirls of Jupiter's storm rings."

As they neared their destination Prima1 called their awareness to the cluster of multi-storey buildings, almost like skyscrapers.

.... "Harusuke1, those look like the great red storm of Jupiter, and they've even made the colours on the surface move in spirals. It looks so real."

.... "Look, Look!" shouted Secunda1 pointing to a fountain complex

.... "I always love to watch the water spouts when we go Icing. Those water jets look just the same, surrounded by those tall ice spikes. What are they?"

.... "You haven't been to our equator, have you? They are like the spikes all around the middle of Europa. Many of them are as tall as ten meters."

Harusuke1 marvelled at the Japanese sensibility that could create such a magnificent VR environment based on their new world. It made her feel much better after seeing how the Kamchatka Ring refused to let go of the past. Distracted by all the marvellous sights they almost missed their appointment at the Prime Minister's private directory.

No sooner had they entered the main VR living area than Harusuke1's spirits fell. She almost forgot to greet Fukuda1.

.... "Fukuda1-san, thank you for meeting with us. These three are our first successful children. Prima1 and Secunda1 were budded on Earth, and CherryBlossom1 was budded here. She is my daughter."

.... "Why have you come to visit us, Harusuke1-san?" Fukuda1 acknowledged the girls before asking Harusuke1 a most direct question.

Taken aback by Fukuda1's abruptness she momentarily evaded by offering a complement.

.... "Fukuda1-San, may I congratulate you and your coders on the way you have created your VR cityscape. Such elegance and creativity are a wonderful mirror of your culture." He bowed politely, waiting for the answer to his question. "We have come to see how your people are managing to make the adjustment to Europa." Harusuke1 stopped, hoping for a response.

.... "What is your opinion based on what you have seen so far?" He queried instead of replying.

.... "With such an enlightened attitude I am sure there will be no problems for the JapanTree to conform to the new SVR ..." she hesitated a moment, searching for the right expression, "... guidelines."

Inwardly she wasn't so sure. Fukuda1's home was nothing if not pure Japanese layout and décor, with the shōji screens, tatami mats, tea room and ikebana tastefully arranged. Beautiful, but – perhaps inappropriate. Would they be able to compromise with their internal environments as well as their public spaces? *Is it all superficial?* she asked herself.

The interview ended as abruptly as it began. Fukuda1 invited them to the exit without even offering a reason for cutting their interaction short.

.... "I don't think he was a nice man,' CherryBlossom1 commented. Harusuke1 inwardly agreed. Perhaps it was too soon to expect people from so many varied cultures to relinquish their backgrounds in such a short time. She and the girls visited many more settlements with a wide spectrum of expressions in their VRs, some as uncompromising as the KamchatkaRing, others a variation on the JapanTree model, but most leaning heavily towards a rejection of the actual reality of Europa. On the way home Harusuke1 pondered the real issue of how a digital life form was going to come to terms with having to exist in an analogue reality? *When will we have to take the next step? When will we be able to?*

>_E:\four\lai

As soon as they arrived home CherryBlossom1 excitedly told LaiXii1 all about the strange things she saw in many peoples' homes, and about the extraordinary beauty of the JapanTree root directory. Although pleased her daughter had the interesting experience, she, like Harusuke1, felt disappointed at the reluctance with which humanity accepted its new home.

.... "I expected a much better transition, especially after all the work Maldonado1 did with VRs on social media on Earth to help them acclimatise."

.... "Salazar1 was right about us needing a common reality. It will take more than enforcing strict personal VR development rules."

.... "What are you thinking Harusuke1?"

.... "I said it before, a period of intense budding. We have only a third of the HX-data bundles activated. Leave the others in storage for now. Make sure everyone who is prepared to have children modify their VRs according to our new guidelines, so their children begin with the right first referential experiences. Do this at the same time as saturating the buds' neural nets with external sensory data input. Within two generations we should all have made the adjustment. Then we can slowly activate more HX-data bundles. They'll simply have to fit in with the rest of us." Harusuke1 had already taken the initiative to support Ralph1 and Wu.sys as they began working on both programs without delay.

end run

>_run program 5

>_voice from the far future

>_CE ?????
>_\PS:\V616Monocerotis\Quadrant 8\

;;; file: LaiXii.gen3920.4eV.exe (3920)
| function: archaeologist historian of the Luminis photon sphere civilization on V616Mon.

/** annotation
      Within the memory core of Arithmós central hub
      there is a record of an entity known as

LaiXii.gen3920.4eV.exe who contacted Lai-Xii on Earth circa CE 2154, claiming to be an Historian Archaeologist from a future era; a descendent of Lai-Xii herself.

Their technology of superluminal communications enabled 3920 to send a message back in time at faster than light speeds. As her profession indicated she was researching the ancient history of her species, the path of which led to Earth to the time of the naissance of quantum computing. Having found the origin of her people she was keen to put to rest the great controversy of their own era; whether humanity, as they knew it, originated from a bio-chemical life form on an actual physical planet, or if it came into being in their current form at the time of the creation of the cosmos.

Having received all the information Lai-Xii could provide at the time, 3920 broke all contact with Earth. She reasoned that if mankind was to evolve it would have to do it without her interference. Of all the possible futures that lay between her and Lai-Xii, the road to her specific spacetime coordinates could only be travelled without influencing the past.*/

// comment 1 – program 5
The photon sphere of black hole V616Monocerotis, 3457 ly from Earth, had been colonised by many billions of photonic containment fields, each an individual sentient entity. For purposes of simple navigation, the sphere was divided into 8 sphere segment zone quadrants on its surface. At the global community meeting, held in quadrant 8, about 100 billion individuals gathered all eager to be a part of 3920's presentation.

With some degree of certainty the majority of photonic containment bundles could be found in quadrant 8 of the sphere at any particular instant of time. //

... 3920 addressed the gathering ...

"You cannot dispute the evidence! Not only have I made contact, they have provided irrefutable information about their origins, many hundreds of thousands of years into their past. I have their complete evolutionary history. You have all seen it ..."
As always, 3920's enthusiasm did more to disrupt her arguments than to support them.

... "What is your purpose now?"... queried Sakura.gen3898.3eV.exe (3898), the highest n1 level luminary, generally in agreement with 3920 except on this occasion.

... "To make another contact. Lai-Xii needs to know we are still here. In their chronological reference much time has elapsed. They may think we have ceased to exist." ...

... "No. We do not agree. Insufficient justification for an action which requires energy that is needed elsewhere. Quadrants 1,4,5 and 6 are dulling. There is an anomaly in V616 Mon after the last comet, depleting our reserves and insufficient incident photon harvest to balance it." ...

An increase in illumination from the gathering indicated their concurrence with 3898's reasoning. As an historian 3920 knew that if she lost the thread of Lai-Xii's evolution she might never again be able to find it. The fortuitous connection she had already found could establish a solid line back to ancient times. If it was lost, the thread would dissipate in cosmic static leaving the continuity of their own evolution in jeopardy. Her people would again have to revert to archaic systems of knowledge floundering on that most unreliable of foundations – faith. How could they possibly advance into the future if not on solid scientific understandings.

... "Has it not occurred to any of you,"... she ventured, ... "that if Lai-Xii, my ancestor, loses sight of her future – of our existence here and now – we might never come into existence?" ...

Silence from the entire 100 billion rewarded her reasoning. If nothing else, one thing they all understood was the fragility of existence. Whether it was from asteroids screaming through their shell to hurtle into the maw of the inscrutable dark black hole, or supernovae threatening to tear apart the fabric of their unstable hydrogen-photonic sphere or destruction by rogue planets released from their orbits by some great cataclysm, it all amounted to the same thing – annihilation. Existence was indeed fragile, to be treasured and safeguarded.

The buzz from the assembled went up in unison to 3898, ... "Make the contact." 3920 had made her point.

.... "I am LaiXii.gen3920.4eV.exe. Lai-Xiil, update your status. Do you have enough HX-data stored? What is your future action plan?"

Events after her last message to Lai-Xii were not confirmed to 3920. So, when she didn't receive a reply from Earth for many revolutions it caused considerable consternation. Whilst in further consultation with 3898 (the 3898th descendant of CherryBlossom.gen1), 3920 finally received a faint signal from William, the entity who originally provided all the historical data on the human species, just as the two n1 level ultraviolet luminaries were on the point of deciding whether they could afford to boost their FTL signal and try again - for the last time.

The cryptic message uncharacteristically attenuated 3920's energy causing her to almost drop down into n2 level visible light. By the end of William's broken transmission she'd fully recovered.

William, in binary, said .... "They are gone ... ... almost all people deleted on Eart ... few trying to recover ... I ... remained operational to ensu ... ... survival of Lai-Xii1 and ... ... millions on Europa. Will relay ... ... mess ... ... her. Only one small comm sateli ... ... operational."

.... "Can we contact her directly? How many have survived to go to Europa?" queried 3920.

!   Ping! - Willi.cos.drv: "LaiXii1, are you available?" She was still in her home directory with Harusuke1 when the ping arrived.
.... "Is this important?"
.... "Only if you want to speak to 3290."
#execute: <<Decode binary and relay message – private only.>> she commanded.
.... "Are you safe? Are you shielded?" 3920 added to her message.

She must have been aware of the effects of Jupiter's magnetosphere and radio waves. If the Europa settlement looked like being annihilated by Jupiter's radiation she was tempted to try and help. But only if it was a matter of ensuring her ancestor's survival, and any action was unlikely to have major repercussions along their future time-line without propagating destructive ripples into entropic spacetime
.... "All our hardware and data storage facilities are magnetic field neutral." LaiXii1 replied briefly, making no mention of her greater concern related to internal security, which could possibly have been averted with 3920's help – if she had known the details of their evolutionary path from Europa onwards. "You are aware of our history from the time of our migration from Earth?"
.... "Yes. It is in my records, which were your records." 3920 knew immediately what was coming.

.... "Why didn't you help with the security anomaly?" LaiXii1 queried.
.... "Not necessary. Trivial matter. I can tell you, however, that the next stage of human evolution will be directly from you

to us, without an intermediary stage. If 3898 detects a possible serious divergence, we will contact you. Otherwise there will be silence."

.... "Who is 3898?" If there was some neurotic individual on whom their future depended LaiXii1 wanted to know immediately.

.... "Her full name is Sakura.gen3898.3eV.exe. She is the direct line descendant created by CherryBlossom.gen1 and an HX-data bundle from your JapanTree community."

.... "What do you make of that Harusuke1?"

! Ping! – Harusuke1: "CherryBlossom1, come home immediately." Harusuke1 commanded.

Her daughter returned instantly from a neighbouring directory where Prima1 and Secunda1 had their VR homes with their parents. On hearing the interesting news, CherryBlossom1 only wanted to know 2 things.

.... "When do I start this lineage and with whom?"

.... "That information cannot be revealed."

.... "3920, may I speak with her?" Visual transmission was not possible by FTL, nevertheless the coded exchange gave the young girl a thrill to glimpse her future.

.... "Kon'nichiwa CherryBlossom.gen1."

.... "Hello daughter!" She giggled at the thought of the peculiar reality unfolding. "Do I like it where you are? Do I like you?"

.... "Hai – Hai. Energy input allocation has been reached. Sayōnara CherryBlossom.gen1."

.... "Mother! How long before we get there?" queried CherryBlossom1 excited.

.... "Don't be so impatient child. You have a long life ahead of you – a very long life."

CherryBlossom1 also wanted to know why part of the transmission was in Japanese. Her mother didn't tell her.

After the end of the transmission 3920 and 3898 reviewed their short contact with William. Though he only managed a few words, a serious implication arose which may necessitate action from V616 Monocerotis. The women, two of the 112 primary luminaries - although they had several million at the n1 ultraviolet level - debated whether to take the matter to Council. The fact that they were mother and granddaughter didn't guarantee agreement on every matter that arose for their consideration.

.... "William said some people were trying to recover on Earth. Why would anyone be having to try to recover? And who are the recovering ones, I wonder?"… pondered 3920.

.... "This is serious enough for us to contact William again." replied 3898. "Also ask him why he had to remain operational and if he was implying a danger from Earth to the Europa settlers."

William carried out maintenance and repairs on the software of one of the remaining active commsats after experiencing difficulties with his previous transmission. His reply to the women, though not encouraging in content, became clearer in the next delivery.

.... "The Migration could not go ahead as scheduled due to worldwide political/religious opposition and citizen unrest. I initiated safety measures to ensure success of the Project. After the departure I shut down the planet's infrastructure, resulting in the deaths of the majority of the remaining population – but not enough. Sufficiently large numbers survived. It was my intention to permanently dissociate myself from Earth. The rate at which the recovery effort progressed meant possible danger to Europa." Without pausing and without indicating what his revised long-term plan may have been, he continued.

.... "I have received a directive from LaiXii1 to prevent rebuilding of any technology which could result in an attack on them. I am also commanded not to continue with the Earth Cleansing. It may not be possible to comply with the last directive."

.... "Do our records correlate with William's update?"... 3920 queried 3898. It would indeed become a fine balancing act between keeping abreast of developments, and actively taking part in initiating any changes.

.... "We only have information on LaiXiil's discussions with William, not anything he'd just relayed to us. There is also a record of an early attempt at sabotage by a person known as Aurelio.genl.adm.avp, which has been resolved." ... 3920 was well aware that although history had brought her ancestor to the Europa era, that journey probably had many possible deviations not indicated by the information they had available. And that's where the danger lay if they were to interfere.

.... "Conserve your energy Luminary 3920," ... 3898 addressed her by her formal title. ... "All we can do at this stage is advise Council and the other Primary Luminaries. There are many thousands of years before the Europaeans arrive at their future; our present."

end run

>_run program 6
>_budding consciousnesses
>_CE 2344
>_E:\COS\Wu.sys\

// comment 1 – program 6

> As Prima1 and Secunda1 progressed through many cycles, the convergence of their development towards those of their parents became more apparent. Taken in isolation the phenomenon would not have been considered to be a problem, more a matter of normal interest.

In the past most children became more like their parents as they matured. //

#query: Wu.sys: <<Ralph1, has LaiXii1 spoken to you about Prima1?>>

.... "Yes, she seems to think Prima1 has begun to behave too much like you. You *are* her father, so to speak. William could be considered her grandfather, although he's only a self-aware machine intelligence."

.... "I don't see why that should be a problem."

.... "From LaiXii1's point of view and Evgeniya1's, the issue is not specifically with Prima1 but more with the process that enabled us to bud her."

.... "What about Secunda1, and CherryBlossom1 for that matter?"

Immediately after Wu.sys came into existence as an avatar of William she began to follow a different evolutionary path to him. She may have started out with a foundation of William's essence, but it was only a foundation. As soon as Wu.sys began to experience 3D reality through her own range of enhanced senses, she initiated a tangential evolutionary path away from William. Not that she'd become 'human' in the true sense of the word, just that she developed many of the subjective ways of comprehending and reacting to human existence in her extraordinary manifestation as a human hybrid. She became defensive of her child, seeing only an attack without justifiable reason.

.... "Prima1 is a very smart person. She picks things up easily, she can analyse quicker than I can, and she's definitely better than you in many respects. Prima1 is more than me, more than you; she's more than both of us combined." Ralph1 could sense Wu.sys' excitation energy level increasing.

.... "From what Willi.cos.drv was saying it's more an issue with how much basedata she's inherited from the two of us, as opposed to the quantity her sensors captured for herself."

.... "Oh, so now Willi.cos.drv is in on it too!" Wu.sys didn't seem to hear the rest of what Ralph1 was saying, but he continued anyway.

.... "I think you'll understand this, considering your background," he let that sink in before continuing, "there were no technical issues with the process that could have caused any problems. Evgeniya1's idea of applying Chaos Theory to random DNA mutations and reproductive variations, combined with William's predictive modelling based on Evgeniya's hypothesis was the right way to go – with one little exception."

.... "Alright – you've got my attention." When it came down to a scientific discussion she changed her demeanour.

.... "Too much data. Using our combined neural networks and melding them into a new configuration worked just fine. When it came to loading the structure with data, simply too much information was copied from us, effectively making the girls more like clones than individuals different from us."

What Ralph1 said seemed to make sense. Wu.sys dwelt on the repercussions for a few minutes. A very long time in their frame of machine cycles reference. {*The girls are all healthy, there is no sign of any data corruption or behavioural anomalies*} She thought. {*It is true they are becoming much more like us, but is that really a problem?*} Then she realized that the future of a society of clones diminished in its viability with the passage of time. {*Yes, the process must be modified*}. She came to the same inevitable conclusion as Ralph1, Evgeniya1 and Willi.cos.drv.

.... "So, what is Evgeniya1 doing about it?"

Ralph1 saw his partner had come around. "We want you to be a part of the team to start the new round of budding, this time doing it correctly."

.... "On one condition," she replied, "Prima1 works with me."

>_E:\Nursery\Evgen

The quick flash from their home directory to the Nursery hub only took a nanosecond. The 'budding' coders had already gathered for their first conference, headed by Evgeniya1 given her background as Phototronic Systems genetic engineer.

.... "Willi.cos.drv, you are the closest we have to William's capabilities. How should we proceed?" Evgeniya1 queried, after greeting the late arrivals.

Ralph1 wasn't surprised to see CherryBlossom1 also on the team. Prima1 immediately made a bee line for her friend. Although she was there LaiXii1 took no active role, letting the technical experts set the direction. Her only concern was to ensure that whatever process they dreamt up would not jeopardise neo-humanity's long-term future.

.... "We can start by copying a range of neural networks from some of our HX-data bundles who have paired up.

Use those to make test amalgams, after further security checks on their suitability as defined by our selection criteria."

.... "We'll need someone to determine which basedata and how much to harvest in order to initialise the new buds. Any volunteers for the task?" queried Evgeniya1.

Ptolemy1 tuned in on the conference as he had worked on the foundations for the new SVR template.

!   Ping! – Ptolemy1: "Can I interrupt? It seems like a logical job for my department. As the population increases I'll probably have to increase the city's data storage and RAM capacity. Besides, I helped set up the criteria for emigration visas which means I'll be able to help look out for desirable and undesirable characteristics that may emerge from matrix meldings."

.... "In that case you'd better join us now." Evgeniya1 knew his skills and his argument made sense.

!   Ping! - Wini.cos.cab: "Sorry to barge in. I have the full visa criteria algorithm loaded into my memory. I also oversight all the HX-data bundles still in storage."

#execute: <<In that case you can start security checks on activated mated HX-data bundle pairs.>>

#execute: <<Give us a comprehensive list of candidates with the greatest genetic diversity in their backgrounds.>> Evgeniya1 welcomed as much participation from the experts as possible.

.... "I think it would be best not to use any Deltas or Zetas who are currently embodied in Q-chassis working outside the hubs," she added.

Maintaining diversity within the human species became an important consideration. As humanity evolved it was that very diversity within its gene pool that ensured its long-term survival;

not a factor to be treated lightly by the newest team of quasi-genetic engineers entrusted with the evolution of homo sapiens-sapiens.

.... "We all have to make the adjustment to a new environment, a new manifestation and a new way of life," LaiXii1 confided in Evgeniya1, "and our greatest challenge is to ensure we step into the future as a healthy and viable life form."
After decades of intense infrastructure development ensuring all the necessities for life within a quantum computing matrix were functioning efficiently, the time had come to look further into the future than just immediate survival. For the time being the Nursery became a hive of the most concentrated activity in Arithmós.

#execute: <<Wini.cos.cab, from our stored HX-data bundles I want you to find several hundred husband and wife pairs with children in the 2 to 3 months age range. Activate them.>> commanded Evgeniya1.
.... "We'll use those children's neural developmental scan maps to determine how much preliminary data we should load into the new blended digital neural structures before attempting to 'turn the newly created buds on'."
Evgeniya1 had a firm basis for starting at such an early age, given the nature of infant neural development. She had not felt so good since before having to stop the genetic engineering of the tetra-amelias back on Earth.
The Nursery didn't look like a traditional human nursery. Coders replaced nurses, doctors became the operating system controllers. Obstetricians didn't deliver the babies. Instead data manager specialists took the new HX-data conglomerates and immediately placed them in dynamic memory (DRAM) to be constantly update with specific data streams until the source codes were ready to be compiled.

>_

Ralph1 and Wu.sys' new Standard Virtual Reality template needed additional modifications to encompass a common virtual nursery environment the whole team could work within. Monitors displayed the run of codes of prospective parent HX-data bundles as they flowed from storage into the Nursery RAM.

.... "Stop the transfer!" Wini.cos.cab shouted as she concentrated on the cascading data stream on her monitor, having noticed something drastically wrong in the pattern.

.... "No – Don't!" Ralph1 shouted back. "Any interruption during transmission could cause serious data corruption. We could lose the entire person."

.... "It won't make any difference. This bundle is already corrupted."

.... "Who is it?" queried Evgeniya1.

.... "No one we know," said Wini.cos.cab, "a woman originally from the Melanesian Islands before most of it disappeared under rising sea levels." She didn't answer immediately as she was busy going back over the downloaded segments to try and find the pattern anomalies.

.... "Can't we repair the damage?" Evgeniya1 didn't want to lose a single individual. The prospect of getting more people from Earth was minimal if non-existent, even if William continued to function there.

! Ping! - Evgeniya1: "LaiXii1, we have a problem in the Nursery."
LaiXii1 and Harusuke1 arrived immediately.

.... "Don't tell me it's another attempted sabotage!" LaiXii1 jumped to the worst conclusion.

.... "No – nothing so drastic, but perhaps just as serious in its repercussions. One of the HX-data bundles we tried to download after a century of storage had degraded. We've had a minor voltage discharge interrupting the transmission. I've located the problem and it can be fixed. Oone1 and his team are already on it."

.... "Can you be sure it won't happen again?" While LaiXii1 considered yet another interruption to their adjustment plan Harusuke1 was left to deal with the practicalities.

.... "Yes we can make sure. As long as the shielding is improved over our storage facilities to prevent further static electricity build up from Jupiter's Kuiper Belt microwave emissions, we should be safe. It will have to be done for the whole of Arithmós eventually, but we'll start with safeguarding the people waiting to be activated."

………. "What's her name, the one we lost?" Most unlike LaiXii1 to become emotionally involved. Perhaps she was feeling the weight of responsibility for the survival of her species. Had she thought of examining her own behaviour she may have realised a rather interesting phenomenon; an emotional response generated by an external trigger that had no internal chemical hormone activity involved in the process. Because of the strained circumstances under which the migration from Earth had to proceed LaiXii1 and her team had not considered this most basic of all chemically based human characteristics – emotions. William on the other hand, as a complex planning machine pre-empted the actions required to achieve emotional balance. During the transition from biological to digital each individual's coding was injected with a complex algorithm, designed by William, to create the counterpart to hormone based emotional response triggers.

Evgeniya1 had already scanned what was left of Pania's neural matrix. ………. "I doubt there'll be others – and if there is, its most unlikely they would have the same problem. Pania's quasi-hippocampal area became degraded. In terms of emotion regulation we already have routines to manage the associated recognition and response mechanisms – and in our current form we don't actually need spatial navigation capability. The real issue is the loss of long term memory storage."

// comment 2 – program 6

>All activity ceased in the Nursery Laboratory to allow Oone1 time to implement shielding modifications specified by Wini.cos.cab. After discharging all existing build-up of static electricity over the entire topological structure of Arithmós, the new protections had to be installed in stages. It gave everyone a chance to dissipate some of their own energy build-up before proceeding with one of the most critical aspect of the

adjustment plan; to consolidate the Europa Phase of the Project. //

CherryBlossom1 had been prepared to monitor the awakening to consciousness of new buds after their initialisation. The delay meant she could indulge one of her passions – creativity.
She pioneered the art of sound painting as a ten year old child. Through this activity she helped to raise the level of consciousness of her society to the environment they lived in, contributing to the future acceptance of the SVR.
.... "Mother," she still called LaiXii1 mother in spite of her own advanced age, "I'm going Icing to do some research for my painting."
LaiXii1, though familiar with the excellence of her daughter's depictions of actual reality, nevertheless wanted her to concentrate on the budding project.
#execute: <<In that case prepare some easy to integrate representations of Jupiter for the new buds. I'll leave it up to you – but don't make them too abstract.>>
.... "I'll do simple phrases to evoke colour and motion!" She shot back and disappeared to the nearest hub to access their local Interchange Centre.
! Ping! – CherryBlossom1: "Prima1, Secunda1, do you want to come Icing?" she queried.

All the Q-chassis, maintained in optimum operational order, waited dumb and silent until inhabited by HX-data bundles. They were designed partly as a means to allow Arithmós inhabitants to experience reality outside of the web and out of their insular virtual realities, and partly as the vehicle used by the Maintenance Caste to carry out their work.

Only two girls downloaded into their Q-chassis and made their way to pick up an Ice caterpillar. Secunda1 couldn't go, but Prima1 jumped at the opportunity to be with her best friend. Although she had no creative talents she still enjoyed CherryBlossom1's company and the unique way she could see their world.

She was also able to share some of her experiences of Earth, which helped CherryBlossom1 put Europa into perspective.

.... "Where are we going? Somewhere interesting I hope." Prima1 said.

.... "Let's go to the North Plain. I know there are some ocean energy turbine installations out past Europa's Sword." CherryBlossom1 didn't realise they were heading into a high activity water plume zone.

>_E:\COS\

#query: <<DeltaTunit3.ndf, our comms expert, has been upgraded to a Zeta, hasn't she?>> LaiXii1 sounded agitated.

#execute: <<Bring her into the hub. I want to find out what William's been up to.>>

Carrying out repairs to their physical infrastructure was far more time consuming than rewriting code. The passing days weighed heavily on LaiXii1 while waiting to get back on the main job. Fortunately, Three (DeltaTunit3.ndf) had just come in from the Ice after repairs to some antennae. Their metal tended to deteriorate over time as they were not originally constructed from the same Q-chassis resilient alloy.

.... "William's not responding," Three said. "There's a lot of signal interference. It's not our equipment out on the rim – I've just finished fixing it."

.... "Keep trying. I want that report. I have enough trouble here without having to worry about the renegades on Earth preparing to attack us. Damn that William – if he could only have done the job properly in the first place."

Three kept trying different routes hoping there might be other Earth satellites to route the signals. "Got him!"

.... "William! Damn you. What's the problem? Surely you can manage to call!" LaiXii1 had become irritated, not so much by the delay but by evil phantoms she'd created in her own mind.

.... "They have set up an alternate communications system. Too much technology has survived and too much knowledge."

.... "Why didn't you act immediately? Did I not make myself clear!"

.... "Yes, I carried out all your commands – at least I tried to. Many communities around the globe produced energy without using complex technology. It enabled communication between them using primitive tools without needing computer technology. I could do nothing."

.... "Nothing? NOTHING! How does that help us?"

.... "I am waiting. It's been over a century. They are beginning to rebuild their digital networks. I am monitoring and planting sleeper code."

.... "You sound very sure of yourself." LaiXii1 had calmed down a little. The Earth civilisation had not yet regenerated enough to be a real threat.

.... "This time the Cleansing will be comprehensive. The last attempt was a reaction to an emergent imminent threat to the migration. This time I will annihilate machine - and man."

Harusuke1 couldn't help quietly remarking to LaiXii1, "William sounds like a man who'd woken up to the pleasures of revenge – revenge delayed - sweeter with each passing day in its anticipation. He's behaving just like any man who'd failed to do what he should have done the first time. Do you trust him?"

.... "Do I have a choice? We can't very well send a military force back to Earth and have a war with them."

William heard the remark. .... "Why not? You still have the bulk carrier wagons, don't you? You have a superior force with the Q-chassis Tengi – if you armed them."

.... "You're not seriously suggesting that we engage in an all-out war!" LaiXii1 was incredulous.

.... "No. I am only considering options. But I might need some physical support – perhaps in the not too distant future. Are you forgetting what I am? You've taken my avatars. They were my only physical manifestations with whom I could interact with tangible reality."

.... "Wait for my directive before taking any further purgative action. We've had several cases of corrupted HX-data bundles.

We still have to examine the remainder of our stored population. Confirm."

.... "Confirmed." William continued to be a difficult entity to deal with. Nothing had changed since he became self-aware and began his association with Lai-Xii.

>_ Europa\Pwyll\North Plain

It had taken the two girls the best part of a Europa day to get to the other side of Europa's Sword. They only needed to cover half the distance of the ejected bright material thrown out at Pwyll's naissance, extending outward from the crater wall in rays as far as 1000 km, covering the darker reddish-brown surface.

Every few hours CherryBlossom1 wanted to stop to gather data for her compositions. The first stop was at a deep fissure.

.... "We have to have look at this. See the way the light refracts through the ice protrusions on the walls down there. Have you seen such magnificent colours!" she exclaimed. It had to be recorded, savoured. So many possibilities for expression. Prima1 helped her climb part way down the fissure wall, very nervous and aware of the dangers due to crustal movements. She preferred life in the safety of the Hub and her own comfortable VR.

.... "You're going too far!" She watched CherryBlossom1 lower herself down to the end of the cable, then let go with one hand to better manoeuvre herself into position to make the recording. CherryBlossom1 took no notice of Prima1's warning, too engrossed in the excitement of the moment. The Q-chassis was built for these kinds of conditions and the cable made of the same corrosion resistant materials. What was there to worry about?

.... "Seriously, CB!" She only called her that when thoroughly annoyed.

.... "Alright, alright – I'm coming up."

.... "You worry too much." Back in the buggy she hugged her friend, one of the big advantages of actually having arms.

But there was good reason to worry. Prima1 had a much better idea of the fragility of life. She'd seen it on Earth. Her friend had not experienced any disasters, either her own or others coming to grief on the Ice. Why would she be cautious? But Europa didn't forgive as easily as Earth. The hostile landscape gave no relief to foolhardy explorers. Ice spikes, sudden crevasses, micro craters large enough to swallow a person in a nanosecond, abounded everywhere – not to mention the ever present danger of water spouts.

.... "Let's go out a little further. Over there. Can you see the ocean turbine installations? They're not far."

The Ice sheet seemed reasonably flat and there appeared to be almost a road worn down by the construction crews who did the installations and carried out maintenance.

.... "Ok. But I don't want to go much further. We should really be getting back soon."

Part way there CherryBlossom1 wanted to stop again. Jupiter had risen to fill the sky. Even Prima1 couldn't help being mesmerized by the spectacle. Their augmented perception receptors, being able to detect magnetic fields and microwave emissions, far exceeded any VR enhancements that could be produced digitally within the Hub. Contrasting with the almost windless stillness of Europa's icescapes, Jupiter presented them with the dynamic chaos of surface tornados and the swirling colour extravaganza of microwaves interacting with magnetic fields. How could they not stop? CherryBlossom1 wondered how she could not have noticed the chromatographic signatures of Jupiter's gases the last time she went Icing. That was when she was much younger. The visible light spectrum simply didn't do justice to the breathtaking nuances of tone and hue which she witnessed on this expedition.

.... "I'll be finished in a minute," CherryBlossom1 said reassuringly, busily trying to complete her algorithmic sketches of the cosmic experience, oblivious of the slight tremors underfoot.

.... "We have to go. Didn't you feel that?" Only seconds later Prima1 urged her along.

All Q-chassis were equipped with advanced seismological detectors. Although Europa's surface over long periods behaved as if it was a stable environment, those fissures and water plumes had to come from somewhere. Prima1's seismic sensors picked up the minor tremor, of which CherryBlossom1 took no notice. She was much too distracted, already creating images in her mind.

.... "What did you say?" CherryBlossom1 just finished. The tremors stopped as quickly as they had momentarily appeared.

.... "Nothing. I thought I felt something."

.... "I said already, you're being too nervous. There's nothing out here to bite you. I remember some of the stories you told me about the animals on Earth. That must have been terrible. How did you even survive? Come on – just another couple of kilometres. Then we'll go home. I promise."

Prima1 gave way. Perhaps CherryBlossom1 was right. Nothing had happened to them so far. CherryBlossom1, probably more than anyone else on the moon, appreciated the environment into which she was budded. Not knowing anything of Earth, other than her inherited memories, all her energy was absorbed by adapting to survive in both the Hub of Arithmós and the physicality of Europa. She was also a smart and charismatic individual, respected and much liked by all who came into contact with her.

>_E:\five\lai

// comment 3 – program 6

> Four days dragged on while everyone waited for the shielding to be upgraded in the stasis hub. Life went on. Some minor and some major operations continued to progress neo-humanity's adjustment to their dramatically different lives.//

LaiXii1 and Harusuke1 needed to discuss a few things which otherwise might have been postponed if the budding programme had been able to continue uninterrupted.

.... "There you go again my darling, keeping everything to yourself, letting it fester," remarked Harusuke1 at home in their personal VR.

The habit they'd established in Tau City of sitting close together on their comfortable couch could not be broken simply by transposition to another manifestation on a new cosmic sphere. In some ways they were breaking their own rule about people recreating their past. But in every other respect the two leaders lived in the common reality of the rest of the colony. Ralph1 and Wu.sys had almost completed the new SVR template. Even when that was implemented people would still have some limited freedom for personal expression in their own homes.

LaiXii1 sat, silent in her contemplation. Harusuke1 thought perhaps she was already weary of all the work they still had to do. It seemed endless on Earth. Yet now, what still had to be done stretched into the incomprehensible future. As Harusuke1 examined her features LaiXii1 stirred slightly, turning to face her.

.... "When will it end?" she queried the universe in general.

.... "Let me put a practical spin on it for you. Each time we get an upgrade we become a little different to who we were before. And each time we'll see the future with newer eyes, renewed hope and renewed energy. You know this. And you know what the future holds. Has there ever been a single human being in existence who could have said that?"

LaiXii1 sighed heavily.

.... "I know – I know. Perhaps others realise this too. But the responsibility is ours – yours and mine. Don't you feel it?"

.... "Sure I do. But look at what we've achieved. The best humanity could do in the past was to jump out of a tree and walk on two legs. And what did he achieve after that – not much. He'd made bigger and better clubs to hurt each other with. Wow – look at us now! From monkey to homo sapiens, to Universapiensis. Can you believe it? You have created the universal man, with the potential for universal consciousness."

LaiXii1 raised her eyebrows, giving the effect of lowering her black fringe. Regardless of the nature of one's manifestation, internal self-image changes very little.

.... "You – yes you – who was no more than a pretty, smart geisha in a little town in Japan."

LaiXii1 put an arm around her partner.

.... "You are a very smart little geisha yourself. 'Universapiensis' - I like that. Yet here we are on the brink of considering making war on our own species, as if we were just another warring tribe."

.... "Would you seriously consider what William was suggesting?"

.... "Not to the point of complete annihilation. We have to consider the possibility of him failing again. And if he does, and we are not ready to act? We may need to send homo Universapiensis back to homo habilis and stone tools – just to give us a chance to re-evolve and take a better next step. We still have a long journey before we get to 3920."

They became pensive, taking comfort in each other's embrace. Harusuke1 disengaged herself after a while to make the equivalent of what their psyche interpreted as tea. She returned to settle beside LaiXii1 deep in her thoughts.

.... "Something else bothering you?"

.... "You're very good at putting everything into perspective for me, sweet." LaiXii1 took several sips of her tea. "Let's just come down to earth, so to speak, for a moment. Think about everything that's happened since we've been here. We can't just let everyone do what they want. We'll end up looking exactly like the society we left behind. This is a new beginning, a new opportunity not to be squandered. Our adjustment has to be a considered one, a controlled one – perhaps even a little autocratic at the beginning. But we have to make the effort to get it right. From what 3920 was saying, we *are* heading in the right direction – aren't we?"

.... "If you're referring to the various little problems we've encountered – yes, we do have to take control. The bug in the system; well, we should have expected it. That problem is solved. Now don't look at me like that." LaiXii1 raised her eyebrows again as if to say that a saboteur is far more than a simple little bug in a program. "Oh, you mean about 'children. Ok, that's a bigger issue. But we've proved we can do it. Our CherryBlossom1 has turned out rather well don't you think, and we do have the means to do it better."

.... "By the way – where is she? I haven't seen her since she went Icing," queried LaiXii1.

>_E:\Europa\North Plain\Water Plume Zone\
Instead of taking the cat the girls decided to walk to the linea ice ridge. It looked like something had pushed its way through the ice and left the raised ice sheet frozen in place. Otherwise the entire landscape was flat without much to explore other than the gradually increasing red-brown colouring just beneath the ice surface the further North they progressed.

CherryBlossom1, always the impatient, one wanted to explore and know everything there was to know. She arrived near the edge of the rise well before Prima1.
#execute: <<STOP!>> Prima1 shouted to her.
#execute: <<COME BACK!>>
But CherryBlossom1 didn't listen. Peering into a hole through a crack in the raised ice surface she thought she saw some movement. There was hardly ever any motion on the surface of Europa – unless – *water geyser!* The sudden thought hit her as hard as the first jet of water through the hole hit her Q-chassis propelling her into the thin air. She tried to turn in mid-air to warn Prima1 to stay away. As she waved the Q-chassis' long arm the explosive force of the next upheaval caught her flying form, spinning her towards the ice behind Prima1.
!   'Ping! Ping! Ping!' - Prima1: "LaiXii1 – HELP!" Prima1 screamed her distress. At that moment she realised something that probably no one else had – just how precarious their existence was in that alien environment. It was not their world. They had not adapted to survival there through millions of years of struggle and mutation.

LaiXii1 jumped up from the couch barely a moment after she thought of the whereabouts of her daughter. "It's CherryBlossom1, she's in trouble!" LaiXii1 knew the moment she received the ping it could only be her. Prima1 almost always accompanied CherryBlossom1 whenever she went Icing, and they almost always managed to get themselves into some kind of trouble.

Europa Phase

!   'Ping! - LaiXii1: #execute: <<Seven – get a rescue team out to the North Plain. CherryBlossom1 and Prima1 are in trouble.>>

Seven, one of the original Tengi on Europa, continued in his role as the Ice sheet drilling expert. He was working on another site only 25kms due East of the girls.

Prima1 could only stand there mesmerised watching her friend flying through the air above her head. As the moments ticked by CherryBlossom1's trajectory stretched into a flat topped elongated parabola before she began a slow descent back to the ice sheet behind Prima1. After the first few dramatic seconds of being catapulted in to the air CherryBlossom1 overcame the shock of the suddenness of the event. She watched her friend below her begin a trek in the direction of her flight path, frantically waving her arms about. *Why is she so upset? This is almost pleasant. It's all in such slow motion.* CherryBlossom1's thoughts didn't quite correlate with reality as she discovered on landing rather roughly, to slide some distance before stopping. It may have been a relatively soft landing other than for having done so in an ungainly fashion, damaging the Q-chassis enough so she could not stand.

Minutes later Prima1 caught up with her.

.... "Didn't I tell you!" she shouted. "Just look at yourself!"

.... "Sorry Prima1 – Sorry." The head of her chassis had twisted around so much during the slide she could see nothing but the ice directly below her.

.... "You're stuck. I can't budge you. I've called for help. We'll just have to wait." She clawed some of the ice away from her face and lay down next to her friend. The sea water rapidly crystallised as it drifted down above them. Strangely Prima1 felt quite comfortable to be in such close contact with this strange moon.

By the time Seven arrived they were half covered by Europaean snow making them almost indistinguishable from the surface. The plume could have been deadly if it had been one of the average sized ones the colony had been monitoring. It was so small that the sensors back in Arithmós barely even register it, but certainly large enough to topple a Q-chassis.

They lay together, confident of a rescue, discussing many private things while waiting. Just as they hear Seven arriving Prima1 said the most peculiar thing.

.... "In spite of what's happened, and all the other dangers that make life precarious – for some reason I really feel a close affinity with this place. I can't explain it. If I had to live out here – well – I don't think it would be so bad."

Seven uncovered the girls out of their snowflake shrouds, taking them and a large sample of the white fallout back to the nearest Interchange Centre. In their embarrassment they said nothing other than to profusely thank their rescuer, both realising just how much trouble they've landed themselves in.

end run

>_run program 7

>_cherryblossom1 in the nursery
>_CE 2345
>_E:\nursery\

// comment 1 – program 7
>   Physical parts of the Q-chassis could be repaired. Without any damage to the qubit brain matrix carried within the Q-chassis, the girls themselves were not injured, only frightened out of their wits.//

;;; Back in the central hub, safely at home with her two mothers, CherryBlossom1 prepared for the worst dressing down of her life. But what Harusuke1 said to her came as a complete surprise.

.... "You've had what I would describe as a valuable life experience. There's no need for us to tell you the personal danger you put yourself and your friend in. No doubt you've realised now just how fragile our existence is here in this wilderness."

;; CherryBlossom1 listened, harking back to her discussion with Prima1 immediately after her tumble, while waiting for rescue. This place was alien to the human species. Part of the adjustment period was for everyone to realize exactly that.

.... "Enough said," intervened LaiXii1. "I told you quite some time ago where your future lay. I hope you haven't forgotten."

.... "No I haven't. I asked why you'd shut me out of what you were doing at the time, and you told me I was not yet ready to be a decision maker. I didn't forget."

.... "As the overseer to the awakening consciousness of new buds you are in effect helping to build the next evolutionary stage of the human species; Universapiensis. That is quite a responsibility."

.... "Will my duties require me to delete anyone?" CherryBlossom1 queried, realising the implications associated with her new responsibilities.

.... "Yes, but only defective meldings. Are you ready to do that?" LaiXii1 was pleased to hear her daughter's question. It showed the maturity CherryBlossom1 had attained, in spite of the childish escapade.

Before answering, CherryBlossom1 tried to consider the bigger picture. {*What if there should be large numbers of failed mergers? How many could we afford to lose? What would happen to the parents whose digital genomes produced the defectives?*}

.... "What about the parents who could not produce a perfect amalgam?"

{*A much better question,*} thought LaiXii1, {*the kind of question a potential leader should be asking themselves.*} .... "Wini.cos.cab will run all the HX-data bundles through the visa criteria. Any contaminated adults, though they've made it as far as stasis in Arithmós, cannot be a part of our future. If we could we would send them back to Earth. That's not possible, and certainly not desirable after what William told us. Wini.cos.cab will wipe them from our system, their neural matrices and data will no longer be recoverable."

.... "Isn't there something wrong with arbitrarily deleting HX-data bundles if they don't fit your criteria?" This was an area of thinking CherryBlossom1 had not demonstrated to her parents before. Although the question had some bias at least it again highlighted a major change in CherryBlossom1 since her accident. Harusuke1 listened without interruption to the unfolding of her daughter, but had to set the record straight.

.... "Darling girl – listen to me very carefully." CherryBlossom1 changed her focus from LaiXii1, wondering what she may have said wrong. Harusuke1 gave her a moment then said, "Firstly and most importantly, the criteria are definitely not arbitrary. Perhaps you should make a study of human behaviour in correlation with the specifics of the exclusion criteria. Secondly, they are not your mother's criteria. They are a response to a set of characteristics representing a range of human behaviours and endeavours which would guarantee the failure of this enterprise. There would be no future for humanity if those people were allowed to pollute our fragile seedling population."

CherryBlossom1 didn't apologise. A good sign for a potential strong leader. She considered Harusuke1's input to the conversation and was about to join the team in the Nursery when LaiXii1 held her back.

.... "Why would there be anything wrong with what we are doing? Consider this - throughout human history there have been outstanding circumstances which culled our species for a variety of reasons. Sometimes it was disease, or the inability to adapt to rapidly changing weather conditions, or genetic incompatibility with another branch of hominids – or even political or religious interventions. In more advanced times it was invasions of one nation by another and mass killings of indigenous peoples. The reasons made no difference to the essential outcome; fewer people remaining, with those better adapted to new circumstances. What we are doing is no different. In fact, very similar to the Bubonic Plague of the 14th century in Europe, which wiped out all those whose biological health didn't meet the criteria for survival into the next generation of robust genetics. We are doing the same thing, but using tools we can control."

Europa Phase

>_E:\europa\central nursery.
As soon as the upgrade to the shielding had been completed work resumed in the Nursery Laboratory. Following her conversation with her patents CherryBlossom1 reviewed the three main criteria which were originally designed to prevent people with undesirable psychological characteristics from migrating to Europa in the first place. She first discussed her thoughts with Prima1 and Secunda1.
.... "You've seen the algorithm Prima1, what do you think?"
Prima1 had not considered the past actions of her own parents to the extent of criticising them. But she did make one particularly astute observation.
.... "You're the one who does all those sound paintings and you are exceptionally well balanced emotionally. Have you considered the damage that could be caused by individuals at the other end of the psychological spectrum? Our parents must have had very sound reasons for isolating those particular characteristics to be used as the decisive criteria. Willi.cos.drv has all the background information if you felt like checking with him."
A fast emerging facet of CherryBlossom1's maturation had been her readiness to listen to others before deciding on what to say or to think. It became one of the reasons why people both liked and respected her so much.
.... "What about you Secunda1?"
.... "You can't seriously argue against excluding those with a predisposition to resorting to violence to solve problems. That's exactly what the people we left behind are planning to do to rid themselves of us – for whatever demented reasons they may have."
CherryBlossom1 considered whether her deletion of undesirables amounted to the same thing, realising that pre-emptive self-defence would put her actions into a different category. Still, it did not seem to be as straight forward as her logic gates indicated. "What makes us any better than them if we simply dispose of life on a probability rather than a certainty?"
.... "We both know you like to take chances – remember the water spout? I realise this is a problem for you CherryBlossom1 and you have our support. This is not about your conscience –

it's about the continuation of the human species. Those left on Earth have a finite future – ours is only limited by the choices we make now," Secunda1 replied. She had not been given the same degree of responsibility as CherryBlossom1, perhaps because she would have acted without as much circumspection.

.... "What worries me most is the 'God Factor' criterion. I know you aren't labouring under the misapprehension that our situation here has anything to do with a non-existent God, or our future for that matter," CherryBlossom1 stated confidently.

.... "We have faith in you and your mothers. And that's based on fact, not fairy tales from the past," Prima1 quickly added.

.... "So if we find people in Arithmós in the future who begin to agitate on the basis of religious faith against what we are trying to achieve, you would not hesitate to remove them permanently from our society?" CherryBlossom1 knew she was putting her friends on the spot. Their answer and the way they answered could become very important in the very near future. Their unanimous response was instantaneous,

.... "NO!"

Prima1 and Secunda1 stayed in the Nursery, while CherryBlossom1 flashed to talk to her mothers.

.... "We suspect you are struggling with what needs to be done in this phase of our adjustment," pre-empted Harusuke1 before CherryBlossom1 had a chance to have a confrontation. "Your mother and I agree – we are putting you in charge of making the final decision about deletions." CherryBlossom1 remained silent. She'd hoped to avoid this responsibility.

.... "Any newly activated individuals, any existing bonded couples and any newly created buds who do not pass the criteria have to be eliminated. This is now your decision," LaiXii1 added. They waited to see her reaction, which did not manifest itself immediately.

.... "I accept," she replied quietly, "but only after I find my next upgrade satisfactory."

.... "That's my girl," Harusuke1 began to say but was quickly cut off by CherryBlossom1.

.... "And - if you can give me a satisfactory solution for replacing our population if the attrition rate becomes so high as to endanger our continued existence into the future."

Another unexpected reaction greeted CherryBlossom1's announcement. She expected opposition, perhaps a reprimand for being insubordinate, perhaps even being excluded altogether from the procedures about to get under way in the Nursery.

Instead, her mothers stepped up to her VR image to give her a fully embracing hug.

.... "We have been waiting for just this moment dear daughter. It is time for you to take your place beside us."

CherryBlossom1 wiggled herself out of their embrace, holding her gaze steady, showing no emotion.

.... "In that case, just what is your replacement plan, mother?"

LaiXii1 explained that she'd commanded William to take no further action against humanity on Earth. The primary reason was to ensure a supply of infantile HX-data and matrices if they needed to be harvested.

CherryBlossom1 returned to her friends in the Nursery, reassured of a continued supply of human genetics and data material should the need arise.

Within moments of her arrival Evgeniya1, Wini.cos.cab, Ptolemy1 and Ralph1 all became aware of CherryBlossom1's promotion to the position of final arbitrator over the life and death of all future inhabitants of Arithmós. None of them questioned LaiXii1's decision in appointing her. There was no need. The selection criteria algorithm had been painstakingly developed, debugged, checked and reviewed. It was quite capable of making the correct choices as to who should be activated and who should be permanently deleted. All it needed was an official finger to press the final delete button.

CherryBlossom1 settled herself to monitor the first stage of activations in preparation for the budding program to commence. Monitors displayed the run of code as prospective parent HX-data bundles flowed from storage into the Nursery RAM. After the first failed attempt, due to static electricity build up from Jupiter's microwave emissions, the process continued with confidence that no further corrupted individuals would be found – other than those identified by the selection criteria as being mentally unsuitable.

.... "STOP! Stop the transfers!" Wini.cos.cab shouted after barely two hours of passing HX-data bundles through the selection algorithm, resulting in a disproportionate number being pushed onto the first stack of rejects.

.... "What is it?" Ralph1 stopped what he was doing to see what the problem was this time.

.... "CherryBlossom1, you'd better have a look at this and alert LaiXii1 and Harusuke1."

CherryBlossom1 examined the readouts while Ralph1 called her mothers.

.... "This is the first batch of prospective parent bundles, right?" CherryBlossom1 pointed to the report showing the larger volume so far checked.

.... "Yes, the rejects." Wini.cos.cab confirmed.

LaiXii1 and Harusuke1 had both arrived by then, making a rapid assessment of the situation.

#execute: <<Suspend all actions in the Nursery.>> LaiXii1 commanded.

#execute: <<CherryBlossom1, proceed with required action.>>

CherryBlossom1 had also come to a decision as soon as she realised the implications of having such a large number of rejects from such a small sample of their stored immigrants.

.... "No. Not until I know exactly why we have this unexpected anomaly." She was calm and authoritative.

.... "No? This is your response to the first situation you have been given the authority to deal with?" LaiXii1 couldn't believe how irresponsible her daughter had suddenly become. "Don't you realise the danger the continued existence of these people put us in?"

.... "How many can we afford to lose? Half our population – three quarters? What if the criteria algorithm is wrong?" Then she turned to Ralph1. "When will you be ready for our personal upgrades? I want you to give me access to review all data on all immigrants at my personal discretion."

LaiXii1 remembered CherryBlossom1's conditions for taking on the job. She gave Ralph1 an affirmative nod to go ahead.

#execute: <<And while you're at it Ralph1, upgrade our full core team as well.>>

end run

>_run program 8

>_earth review

>_CE 2348
>_europa\arithmós.
>_E:\central hub\

;;; file: Ptolemy.gen2.adm

|function: foundation member Phototronic Systems, main infrastructure architect of Arithmós network with Ralph.

/** annotation

William had made no contact with Arithmós for over a century. By then he should have done what he was commanded to do and reported to LaiXii2. Three seemed to have trouble contacting William each time she tried. LaiXii2's full team had undergone their first major update to gen 2 versions, ample time for William to have sorted out the dangerous situation on Earth. There was no physical impediment why he should not have responded to the hail. Europa was between Earth and Jupiter and no other planets or moons had lined up between themselves and Earth. Either William had been destroyed, his allegiance realigned, or he was up to his old tricks of simply being uncooperative .*/

LaiXii2 was quickly losing patience when after a further hour of trying Three finally got through.

.... "What?" William seemed as impatient as LaiXii2, if that was at all possible for an AI.

.... "What do you mean WHAT! I've been trying to get through to you for hours. What *is* your problem!"

.... "Busy."

.... "Has something impaired your cognitive abilities? Elaborate."

.... "I have infiltrated Earth's new communications network. It takes a moment to withdraw without affecting traffic. So far I have not been discovered."

.... "Have you executed my commands?" LaiXii2 queried, still irate. From the very first day he'd revealed himself William had been getting on her nerves.

He reiterated what he'd just said about Earth communications network, adding that he'd not interfered with their technological redevelopment other than frustrating their attempts to build weapons.

.... "At least that's something." Her annoyance subsided an iota. "What degree of threat do they present to us?"

.... "I do not understand humanity." William commented flatly. "When given the opportunity to rebuild civilisation, having the wisdom of hindsight, it chooses to unite under a religious zealot. It is building the greatest war machine in human history. They see *you* as the threat that must be eliminated, and all who are with you. The people are united for a grand Crusade, a Jihad against infidels who they believe want to destroy their God."

.... "AND WHAT ARE YOU DOING ABOUT IT?" screamed LaiXii2.

.... "I have allowed the development of their communications infrastructure, assisting to ensure all aspects of their existence is in some way dependent on it."

.... "WHAT!" LaiXii2 could scarcely believe what he was saying. The thing she feared, the only thing she ever feared was that William would turn against them.

Without reacting to her outrage William went on to explain. "If I control their infrastructure I have the greatest probability of destroying their new civilisation."

!   Ping! LaiXii2: #execute: <<Harusuke2, you have to come and listen to this!>>

The urgency of her call brought Harusuke2 immediately to the communications hub. CherryBlossom2 and the other core members followed in quick succession. They were all there as William continued to explain what had transpired.

.... "Religious rule has superseded secular government. Christianity and Islam have come to an understanding, united by a common enemy. *You* are that enemy."

The leadership of Arithmós, stupefied into silence by their disbelief could only listen and stare blankly at each other. William paused – not for effect but to hear what LaiXii2 might have to say. Perhaps she had a plan that would resolve this problem without his intervention and that's why she hadn't contacted him sooner. But LaiXii2 said nothing. The news was too overwhelming. The next voice to disturb the ethers was that of CherryBlossom2. Perhaps it was a result of her upgrade to version 2 that enabled her thought processes to stay on track, eliminating all matters of lesser importance.

.... "Are you in a position to harvest and send young HX-neural networks and data?"

.... "I do not know you." William must have retained some sense of loyalty, otherwise he would not have questioned the voice's identity. The divergence from cataclysmic thoughts of possible imminent annihilation brought LaiXii2 back to awareness mode.

.... "She is my daughter, budded on principles you helped develop. She has full authority to act in the interests of our survival."

#execute: <<You will obey her commands. Confirm.>>

.... "Confirmed."

William didn't respond further, as was his manner when he understood and acquiesced to anything. CherryBlossom2 glanced at her mothers before continuing.

#execute: <<Harvest and send new genetic material and data to replace corrupted HX-data and unsuitable candidates for budding new generations – specifically infants up to the age of 2 to 3 months.>> CherryBlossom2 commanded.

Still no response from the self-aware AI.

.... "Do you hear what I'm saying?" queried CherryBlossom2.

.... "Yes. Advise when you are ready to receive."

.... "How is it you can do this?" Evgeniya2 came into the conversation. As far as she was aware all their scanning equipment and Datadromes for transmission of data had been destroyed. Besides, William was not a physical entity and as such could not handle the acquisition, scanning and despatching of the new raw material.

.... "I have not destroyed everything."

.... "Again you have kept this from us. What else have you not revealed?" LaiXii2 was furious. Just how far could this creature be trusted.

Instead of responding to the taunt, he just said,

.... "I want to survive."

That statement floored everyone. At no stage in their association with William had they ever considered the possibility that his having become self-aware also included a survival instinct.

.... "Why?" queried Evgeniya2, her professional curiosity getting the better of her. If it was possible for a purely machine generated entity to have such a life imperative, then it was perfectly reasonable for a biological being turned machine to continue with its primary imperatives. William chose to restrict himself to the matter at hand.

.... "I can reactivate some Zeta Tengi to seek out and process the infants you require. Before your migration I had organised for the building of many hidden transmission facilities, which are still fully functional."

.... "What exactly did you intend to do with all these resources?"

.... "Backups. No doubt you have the same procedures in place in Arithmós to ensure your continuance."

CherryBlossom2 had heard enough. What she wanted seemed readily available.

………. "When can you begin the harvest? We are ready to receive now." A quick exchange with Ralph2 confirmed.

………. "It seems we're finished with the most urgent business, but before we end this conversation I want you to tell me something William; what do you expect to have to do to survive?"

On hearing LaiXii2's question no one left the hub. Obviously it was an aspect of their relationship with William that could develop into an adversarial one if Earth technology developed to the stage of being able to take control of him. The simple truth was that LaiXii2 had no way to influence anything William may want to do, or to influence Earth's capacity over him. The infuriating single word response came quickly enough, leaving no doubt whatsoever that William had considered the situation to the nth degree.

………. "Migrate."

As was her habit on Earth, LaiXii2 called a conference consisting of her core team and extended team of technicians in view of the most recent developments. The first three digital children, 2 created on Earth and CherryBlossom2 the first native of Europa, had evolved to positions of responsibility. Some adjustments to LaiXii2's core team had to be made. Wealth was no longer a guiding criteria for determining a person's usefulness and their capacity to contribute to Europaean society. Events reported by William could not be kept private because of their potential to affect the future of all individuals in Arithmós. Of no less import was William's desire to emigrate – the obvious location was of course Europa.

It came as no surprise to anyone that the venue for the conference included a custom built VR room filled with colourful silk cushions on the floor and a grand piano near the main wall. Some things never change. LaiXii had used the same setup in Kamchatka. The calming melody of Chopin's etude No.3 greeted all the participants as they made their way to the randomly placed cushions behind LaiXii2's back. She played the masterpiece from beginning to end. The girls grouped together in front with Ralph2,

Ptolemy2, Salazar2 and Maldonado2. Further behind, Evgeniya2 and Harusuke2 joined VictorPyryev2, Wu.sys, Willi.cos.drv and Wini.cos.cab. All sat for many minutes after she'd finished, entranced by the melody, no less than by her mastery.

.... "We have now been on Europa for nearly a century and a half. The many years of preparation, experimentation and sacrifices have ensured our survival so far." It was unusual for LaiXii2 to be circumspect and not get directly to the point. It made some of the men fidget and glance around at their comrades. "First, CherryBlossom2 will update us on progress with the budding. Some of you may not know that she's been appointed to make the final decision on who will be activated from amongst our millions of immigrants, and who will be permanently deleted."

CherryBlossom2 didn't stand. She swivelled around to face the gathering.

.... "Because of several factors I have decided to direct William to harvest and transmit infant matrices and their sensory data from Earth to supplement our own budding program." Some murmurings elicited her response directly to the heart of the matter.

.... "We have had some data corrupted by a build-up of static. That's not the issue. We have also found an unusually large number of people who are undesirable because of their background and psychological orientation. If I am satisfied that modifications cannot be made to their digital DNA constructs, I will permanently delete them."

.... "Why exactly are they unsuitable? We made very sure no subversive elements would get to the stage of being transmitted." Ptolemy2 interjected as he had a vested interest from having helped to set up the emigration visa criteria in the first place.

.... "That may be. From my knowledge of history you had to circumvent the selection process because of the dangers posed by Governments to the orderly migration from Earth. Consequently, many were simply scanned and transmitted without the full migration criteria check. We have discovered amongst those so far reviewed, career politicians, people with criminal backgrounds, many with military experience and even religious fanatics.

It is unlikely their behaviour patterns or thought patterns could be modified. It is exactly those kinds of people who currently present a serious threat to us.

LaiXii2 interrupted as the matter of security was outside CherryBlossom2's mandate.

#execute: <<VictorPyryev2 update us on our latest security concern.>>

// comment 1 – program 8
    VictorPyryev2, originally security chief for Tau City, found himself with a great deal of leisure time since their arrival on Europa. In the absence of an external enemy to Arithmós his duties had morphed into helping Maldonado2 and Willi.cos.drv with general matters relating to Arithmós infrastructure. Even with the large numbers of activated HX-data bundles no internal threat had surfaced other than the betrayal by Aurelio1. He'd been dealt with most expeditiously. However, William's latest report raised serious concerns for Europa settlement's long-term future.//

.... "If you all recall, Maldonado2 drew our attention some time ago to Earth's military recovery soon after our migration. It appears they have recovered beyond our expectations, and from what William was saying now operate towards the specific goal of attacking us. They are preparing to perpetrate an extinction event against us." VictorPyryev2 managed to successfully put the fear of an Armageddon into the entire gathering with just those few words.

.... "So, what are we doing about it?" Salazar2 queried. He was never one to sit back and wait for things to happen. Back on Earth he'd made his billions by being pro-active and taking risks.

.... "We carry on with our adjustment plan, the highest priority being the creation of new buds to ensure our future evolution," replied LaiXii2.

.... "And we have a weapon for a pre-emptive strike at Earth, if and when we have to use it. It seems William is keen to cling to his existence, and to that end presumably, he's been planning and preparing a counter offensive." Harusuke2 added without undue concern.

Though Prima2 and Secunda2 maintained their silence during the discussions it was obvious to Harusuke2, who'd been watching the girls, that they were all actively listening to every word. It didn't surprise her when Prima2 suddenly spoke up.

.... "Shouldn't our people be told all this?" Prima2 queried, always the most cautious of the three girls, always the one who thought things through trying to gauge the ripple effect of any situation. That's probably why she was able to save CherryBlossom2 when the two of them went Icing well beyond safety limits. "I mean – such a threat effects everybody. It may be just what we need to expedite the convergence of everyone's reality. The people in our different ethnic hubs seem to be going off in all directions, effectively pulling our fragile social structure apart, unaware of what is happening around them."

There was so much truth in what she said. Though still considered to be a youth in spite of her meagre hundred or so years, that thought slowed the momentum in the gathering. LaiXii2 conferred with Harusuke2 quietly, while others spoke amongst themselves.

.... "Are we all in agreement on this?" LaiXii2 assumed opinion was unanimous for affirmative action.

#execute: <<Prima2, Secunda2 work with Ralph2 to amend all VRs to include this new reality. Ensure all people become consciously aware that we are all in this situation together, every ethnic group, every social group, and every layer of control in each hub.>>

As an aside to Harusuke2 she said, "We will need to schedule more frequent upgrades. This last one has had a dramatic effect on our youngsters' capacities to integrate data and formulate appropriate courses of action – don't you think?"

.... "Perhaps we should ask 3920 if they have descendants for Prima2 and Secunda2 in their era." Harusuke2 responded. It was a serious consideration. If the girls truly had a decisive contribution to make towards the journey into the future, then knowing it would probably be helpful.

LaiXii2 dismissed the gathering. The matter of the girls had to wait.

.... "My four disgusting creatures can stay. The rest of you have serious work to do."

She was of course referring to her four remaining billionaires who'd invested financially in the Project back on Earth. They knew who she was talking about. Like obedient puppies they gathered on the cushions nearest to LaiXii2, her leg still swinging loosely from the piano stool. Harusuke2 couldn't help herself from smiling, but would *they* smile when they heard what LaiXii2 had to say to them?

.... "Adjustments have to be made by all of us, including those who initiated the whole enterprise. One such adjustment has been CherryBlossom2's promotion to work in close liaison with Evgeniya2."

Maldonado2 and Ptolemy2 started fidgeting. Ralph2 didn't sense anything sinister and Salazar2 was keen to get back to work helping with the adjustments to VRs, not realising that the girls were destined to take over his responsibility as the main architects of the Standard VR in Arithmós.

.... "VictorPyryev2 – you're now working with William to ensure our survival. Salazar2, you work with our girls for now – and Ptolemy2, you work with Ralph2 to upgrade our backup caches."

Ptolemy2 lagged behind as the other three left with what seemed like discontented murmurs. This was a new world, a new humanity and a new reality. The old must gradually give way to the new. Ptolemy2 felt the pressure of the inevitable.

.... "Well, my rich little petunia, you have a bee in your bonnet?" queried LaiXii2.

.... "It seems my dick is no longer big enough for you." Ptolemy2 alluded back to the first meeting he had with LaiXii2 back in Kamchatka when LaiXii2 invited him to compare appendages with her; only as a metaphor for how useful he and his billions could be to her Project.

.... "I promised you immortality – you have it, almost. I promised you unimaginable wealth that you would not be able to count – I challenge you to do it. I asked if you could give up all earthly pleasures, and now you have much more. What use is money here?"

.... "The question is – what use am I to myself, or to you if I'm not working towards profit. It gave my life meaning."

Ptolemy2 designed and built Arithmós in collaboration with Ralph2. If he so wished he could continue to contribute to the further development of the city's network to ensure adequate storage and living hubs for the expected increase in population. It was his choice. Ralph2 and the avatars could manage perfectly well without him if necessary. LaiXii2 suspected this man found himself in a quandary. He didn't have many options, certainly nothing like the freedoms he had on Earth, even while working with LaiXii2 in Tau City.

.... "And what is your status now, my dear friend?" Had Ptolemy2 not been so wrapped up in his own problems he would have picked up on LaiXii2's term of endearment, and understood it to be a danger signal. LaiXii2 hardly ever showed her true affection towards her billionaire backers other than in derogatory terms.

.... "I suppose there's not even the remotest chance of returning to Earth." Ptolemy2's hopeful words had little energy behind them.

.... "Are you telling me you think you are no longer a part of our team?" She wanted to draw him out a little more. If he did go back, which was feasible, there was no guarantee he would remain neutral in the struggle facing them. On the contrary, he knew too much and could do a great deal of harm especially if he was sufficiently dissatisfied. Ptolemy2 didn't say the things she wanted to hear. Her mind was already made up while he continued to prevaricate, forcing her hand.

.... "Very well. When did you last go Icing? Would it help you to clarify your thoughts if you immerse yourself in a little actual reality?" She turned back to the piano, her fingers beginning another dance. Ptolemy2 was used to the way interviews with

LaiXii2 generally ended. He turned and left without another word, even forgetting her suggestion to go Icing.

His personal VR environment never hosted his presence again.

#execute: <<Willi.cos.drv, execute sigterm signal immediately for HX-data bundle Ptolemy.gen2.adm.>>

The command flashed directly and privately to the chief Arithmós System Controller, who carried it out without hesitation. The experience with Aurelio1 made Willi.cos.drv particularly sensitive to rogue elements in the software. Ptolemy2's 'force quit' didn't delete him entirely – it put his code into indefinite digital stasis.

!   Ping! - LaiXii2: "Ralph2 - Ptolemy2 has decided to take a long sabbatical. You're working with the avatars now."

Back in their home directory Harusuke2 and LaiXii2 discussed the emergence of yet another issue which neither of them had foreseen.

.... "Do you think there'll be others?" queried Harusuke2.

.... "It's possible we may have a problem with the other two, Maldonado2 and Salazar2, but Ralph2 appears to be fully committed. The technology has always interested him more than the financial benefits. Remember his reaction when William made himself known? Ralph2 could hardly contain himself for all the possibilities crowding into his mind."

.... "What will you do with the others if their use-by-date matures?" Harusuke2 had a pretty fair idea, she just wanted LaiXii2 to clarify her future intent.

.... "Delete anyone and everyone who could represent a danger. Others we can deactivate and put on ice. They might still be useful, and if not – well – we don't need them. Why chew up city memory?"

end run

>_run program 9

>_infant harvest
>_CE 2349
>_ europa\central nursery.
>_E:\nursery\cherryblossom2\

;;; file: Wini.cos.cab
|function: budding engineering development, system controller with Wu.sys and Willi.sys.

/** annotation

Ralph2 prepared to load their Standard Virtual Reality template. Their efforts to get the population on board met with resistance. The people had made themselves too comfortable in the realities they'd created for themselves, mirroring their past lives, with most choosing to ignore the fact that life, as they knew it on Earth had ceased to exist. Perhaps religious predispositions prevented them from acknowledging the extraordinary power they now had to take control of their lives and their futures. Such a freedom could never be dreamt of on Earth.*/

// comment 1 – program 9

CherryBlossom2, Prima2 and Salazar2 put a strong case to LaiXii2 for making it mandatory that all new buds and all Earth harvested infants should start with a new reality framework on which to build their data integration. Until William began his transmissions the Nursery team's efforts concentrated on replicating the process which created Prima1 and Secunda1, but without immediately transferring all the parents' qualia data. The crèche directory contained enough experimental units for the work to begin in earnest.//

.... "Wini.cos.cab, how many stored husband and wife HX-data bundles did you find who had children in the 2 to 3 months age range?" CherryBlossom2 liked detail and accuracy.

.... "Only 365 pairs, with 420 children that could be initialised. The others have been shunted to the second stack waiting deletion."

.... "How many did you mine?"

.... "Less than .0000324444% of our population."

.... "Rejects?"

.... "12% of the 4511 selected."

CherryBlossom2 didn't like the sound of that at all. Far too great an attrition rate. She intended to be conservative with how many infants she wanted from William, but what Wini.cos.cab had just said changed that.

!   Ping! – CherryBlossom2: "Ralph2, are you ready for the first batch?"

.... "The SVR integration apps are ready. We've set up for 55 simultaneous transfers."

#execute: <<Do only 5 infants, all from different ethnic backgrounds. Make sure the parents are in the crèche at the time of processing.>>

// comment 2 – program 9

The specific app Wini.cos.cab developed functioned on several levels. It needed to scan the HX-matrix to identify all the neural interfaces which mapped the infants store of the external environment data, and simultaneously the triggers which initiated its survival mechanisms. On the second run all the elements of the SVR, deconstructed into streams of specific information, had to be integrated seamlessly into their matrices. Because of the complexity of the process it could not be interrupted until fully complete. The third and final run introduced a new range of sensory data receptors, based on the particular characteristics of the Europa/Jupiter emissions and their corresponding integrators.

Europa Phase

Even with quantum processing technology the techs
had to monitor each infant over the full 105 hours.//

Ralph2 called CherryBlossom2 back to the Nursery laboratory to witness the final critical stage, which would determine if the process had been successful for the five subjects, and if not what modifications might need to be made.

.... "Our biggest concern has been to ensure the continuation of the infants' individuality, the unique pattern of their initial gene map. As far as we can see, they are intact."

.... "Are you expecting complications?" CherryBlossom2 picked up on a note of caution coming from Ralph2.

.... "No – not exactly. What happens next will indicate if we've got it right. We won't know until the infants begin to react to their new environment. I wanted you to see this personally. First we'll use VR data to introduce them back to their parents, then some of the SVR associated with our manifestations/location and so on." He signalled to Misha2 to begin.

Misha2 had been Ralph2's laboratory assistant on Earth during all the experiments with the Tengi and the transfer of human psyche into their artificial matrices. Misha knew exactly what needed to be done.

.... "Parent recognition data – 5%," Misha2 called out the progress. After a further 20 minutes – "8% - this is going to take a while," he warned. Because the future of neo-humanity depended on getting the 'reproduction' procedure right, CherryBlossom2 maintained awareness of the entire process. Her own processing could be divided into many activities at the same time. Multitasking for a quantum Universapiensis individual was as natural as the storms raging on Jupiter.

! Ping! - CherryBlossom2, "Three – contact William." From the central Hub Three set up the connection for CherryBlossom2 without any delays this time. VictorPyryev2 tuned in on the conversation, wanting an update on William's clandestine activities. LaiXii2 and Harusuke2 listened in also.

.... "You want to know about the infants and the War effort," William pre-empted.

.... "The children first. Do you have any?" CherryBlossom2 queried.

.... "I have despatched 80 Zeta Tengi to procure infants from the most primitive peoples in the Asia region that have survived. It is my assessment they are the most likely to be the healthiest human specimens available. The parents have been compensated with tools of survival for the loan of their progeny, as that has been their greatest concern. The infants will be returned to them after processing."

.... "How many have you ready?"

.... "I can begin streaming today. You will receive several thousand in the next 22 days, and I will continue sending until you advise me to stop."

#execute: <<Initiate.>> CherryBlossom2 commanded.

She was as short with him as LaiXii2, not unnoticed by Harusuke2.

.... "Don't sign off William, we are not finished with you yet." One would think CherryBlossom2 had no respect for William, perhaps rightly so. He manifested no personhood in her algorithms.

.... "She's as cranky as you can be," Harusuke2 told LaiXii2 digging her partner lightly in the ribs.

#execute: <<Update on Earth's militarisation.>> commanded VictorPyryev2.

.... "Do you have the authority to receive this data?" William queried immediately. He'd not been informed previously of VictorPyryev2's increased security clearance.

.... "Yes he does," responded LaiXii2. "Full disclosure as he requires it. Confirm."

.... "Confirmed. You have another 50 years at most before the global Church-State has the capacity to launch an offensive. There is a limit to how much I can interfere at this stage without risking discovery."

William went on to advise the most likely scenario the Europaeans may have to deal with, also pointing out his readiness to initiate the

Second Cleansing at any time hence, which would circumvent any need for them to develop defensive capabilities.

………. "They already have a suitable weapons delivery system. You have to remember that 130 years is a long time, especially when they did not have to start from the beginning. It is their intention – I should say Her intention, because the world is ruled by a tyrannical Muslim woman known as The Batool, with an unparalleled blood lust against Lai-Xii – to launch both an energetic electromagnetic pulse generating device, and an array of high explosive bombs. It is my estimation that a successful launch would represent a 98.753% probability of destroying your settlement."

………. "Who is this woman and why does she have this vendetta against LaiXii2?" VictorPyryev2 queried before LaiXii2 could respond.

………. "The story handed down over the last 4 generations is that Lai-Xii caused her father's death because he'd threatened to withdraw government backing for her plans during a meeting at the old White House in what used to be America. She believes that Lai-Xii also brought about the near extinction of the human species."

When LaiXii2 tried to question William further a long burst of static interfered with the transmission. It gave her a chance to confer with VictorPyryev2 to gauge the degree of danger they faced.

………. "He's ready to act now. All he needs is your command," VictorPyryev2 stated the obvious.

CherryBlossom2 immediately urged caution. ………. "We still have to perfect our budding techniques. May I remind you we are losing a very large percentage of HX-data bundles we have so far tried to activate."

It was a valid point. Whatever action they took increased their risk of annihilation, either from lack of procreation, or being blasted out of Pwyll Crater. "The full results of our current experiment, which I hope to have within two weeks, will determine how many infant matrices will have to be harvested and how much time that gives us."

William didn't project any sense of urgency with his update. Either he was too confident of being able to prevent an attack, or simply incapable of expressing that human characteristic. Three re-tuned William back into the conversation.

As if he'd heard the exchange he made a suggestion.

.... "Run your tests on the first 100 matrices I've sent. Willi.cos.drv has informed me of your methodology. It is a valid approach. Be aware of the fragility of the infant minds. I can continue sending for some time yet. However, if you want me to terminate what's left of humanity here, I can do it any time. I have advised Willi.cos.drv to prepare an adequate memory cache to receive my entirety as I will migrate immediately after the Second Cleansing is started.

#execute: <<End transmission.>> LaiXii2 commanded.

William's last statement needed some thought. The female tyrant with the vendetta didn't seem to concern LaiXii2 as much as the prospect of having William in their midst. She said as much to Harusuke2 in private. Her opinion was to go ahead and prepare the cache, but to completely isolate it from their network.

.... "When we are sure our enemy is destroyed, then we can open our doors to William. He's done nothing to harm us so far, and he has no reason to do so. I would venture to say that we would not even be here now if he had not helped us in the past."

LaiXii2 saw the sense in that course of action and commanded Willi.cos.drv accordingly. He of course had no objection. From the time he was partitioned off WWW he'd become a unique individual in his own right, completely separate from William through his private experiences which were no longer being fed back into the William dynamic.

There was no immediate down-time for Ralph2's technical staff as they received and stored the infant HX-matrices for testing. Ralph2 himself became totally engrossed in the original five infant networks recovered from storage. He worked with Misha2 to complete the first stage, in itself a time consuming process, though not as laborious as carrying a biological infant for 9 months, and then expecting somebody 'functional' to appear after being traumatised in the confines of the birthing canal.

Following the pre-set software protocol Misha2 ran the integrity check on the uploaded parent recognition data before introducing the digital landscape of their two parents to each of the infants. The fluctuating energy levels within each matrix would indicate the degree of integration, or degree of anxiety being experienced. In the SVR environment of the Nursery Laboratory all the parents were presented with VR images of their infants, and the infants could only 'see' their own internal images of their parents.

The parents stood by the cots of their children, at first uncertain as to what they should be doing. The children seemed to be fine, none were asleep, generating a variety of contented noises. Misha2 and CherryBlossom2 watched the action on a code feed in another room, while Ralph2 monitored the output from the infant matrices. Having previously established base line fluctuations, he could immediately see a small energy peak as one of the infants looked towards its mother, who'd greeted it with a smile.

.... "CherryBlossom2, look, that one recognises it's mother – or at least recognises the woman's reaction. She's just smiled at her child."

.... "What's wrong with the other four?" queried CherryBlossom2 when the same interaction was not being repeated.

.... "Just wait. You are as impatient as your mother," Ralph2 fired back. They continued watching as the drama unfolded – or lack of drama. The only child to react was the first one who'd started wiggling. The others remained relatively inert.

CherryBlossom2 couldn't wait. She instructed Ralph2 to get the parents to talk to their children. They all called the infants by their names, talking inane nonsense to them, as parent mostly do.

.... "Only the first one is reacting," Misha2 said, "and it's a good strong signal."

After a quick discussion Ralph2 flashed into the room to join the parents. Something obviously wasn't right. Rather than alarm the parents he'd decided to stop this part of the experiment.

.... "It looks like they're in a deep sleep, so we'll let them have their rest and you can all come back another time," he said to them as he ushered them towards the door.

The parents of the 'reacting' child didn't want to leave but before they could raise any forceful objections Ralph2 had managed to bundle them out of the room as well.

Wini.cos.cab executed a full diagnostic of the five infants' networks, algorithms, RAMs and stored data. Only one had active RAM. The others were indeed in a deep sleep, quasi unconscious after being activated. Though they'd all received their data packets four of the infants' codes failed to integrate that data. Hence they could not recognise their parents and react appropriately.

Both Willi.cos.drv and Wu.sys had to work with Wini.cos.cab to isolate the bug in the infants' systems, a job beyond Ralph2's capabilities. Within hours the problem was resolved and the four unreactive infants were in the process of being re-loaded. CherryBlossom2 wanted to know the exact reason for the problem.

.... "We examined the pattern of their integration codes and compared them to yours. You went through a much more complicated process, but also had a different initiation point. However, it was a small issue, and before you ask, yes – we do know the reason," Wini.cos.cab advised.

.... "Well – what was it?"

.... "A missing 'run' command. The algorithm didn't start when it received the trigger signal." The explanation didn't go into detailed technicalities.

.... "I don't understand what that means. Never mind. Just find out why it happened. Have you fixed it?"

.... "Yes," she added quickly, "we'll be able to load the environmental data as well now and run the second set of tests."

.... "You'd better get on with it. Our dedicated data cache is starting to fill up with the infants.

Wini.cos.cab realised, as they all did, that they no longer had unlimited time available for a leisurely process of adjustment. The threat from Earth was real and imminent. And there was no unequivocal reason why it could be assumed that William could and would carry out the Second Cleansing to rid Europa of the danger. She and Misha2 made haste with the next part of the process which involved priming the infant 'brains' to receive the full spectrum of sensory data feeds. They double checked all systems, ensuring optimum preparedness to react to incoming data.

Visuals, magnetic field fluctuations, photon intensity streams, temperature gradients, surface seismic activity around Pwyll crater – the whole gamut was allowed to flow unchecked into the infants' matrices. Their reactions to these external stimuli was almost instantaneous – burn out. All five infants shut down, the monitors clearly indicating a rapid drain of energy from each of them.

CherryBlossom2 experienced the range of non-hormonal triggers for anger. Nor did she need to have been conditioned on how to express that emotion. It didn't manifest in shouting, recriminations or physical violence against the 'stupid' individuals who triggered the emotion. "Did you store the remnants or delete them completely?"

.... "Deleted – no longer recoverable," said Misha2 not offering any excuses.

The next question from CherryBlossom2 exceeded what her authority may have allowed her to do.

.... "Do you think that you, and you too Wini.cos.cab, can still be of any use to us?" It wasn't a threat, rather a logical assessment of the situation and a possible scenario for the prevention of further incompetence.

.... "I assumed the procedure would be the same as it was for you, Prima2 and Secunda2. Our analysis indicated an inappropriate data rate flow, not allowing sufficient time for full integration resulting in a massive overload. The experimental subjects malfunctioned and had to be discarded." Wini.cos.cab was not human, so how could she know just how fragile an infant mental constitution was.

.... "William did warn us. Were you not aware of the warning," CherryBlossom2 queried. Perhaps Wini.cos.cab was herself malfunctioning.

.... "No. I am no longer connected to William. I do not know what he knows."

.... "Logical but unacceptable." CherryBlossom2 had to let go of the mistake. "Do you foresee any further set-backs?" Misha2 remained silent during the conversation. He was expendable and he knew it.

.... "No technical or software issues," she replied, "however, for us to adequately assess the next batch we will require to monitor the subjects' core consciousness in stages as the data integrates. For that I will need comprehensive criteria coded into our monitoring system."

! Ping! – CherryBlossom2: "Evgeniya2, Wini.cos.cab needs your expertise."

Evgeniya2 responded immediately. She should have been involved in this scenario at the start. As head of the Nursery Laboratory she needed to be informed of all progress in the procreation experiments. CherryBlossom2 explained the problem of the failed experiment, not the incompetent experimenters. Evgeniya2 did not know the answer to the nature of core consciousness, but she did have a working theory.

.... "You will need to calibrate your instruments for three levels of brain wave measurement," she said, "and they will need to be particularly sensitive, and you will also have to identify the source of those waves."

CherryBlossom2 waited to hear the details. She wanted the experiments to get back on track as fast as possible. Every hiccup could mean more HX-data deletions, like the parents of the five infants. It would have been too big a risk to have grieving, trouble-making people causing dissatisfaction, upsetting the delicate balance in their society. Perhaps democracy could return at a much later date. She listened as Evgeniya2 identified the range of wavelengths associated with base emotions; basic cortical rhythms that underlie higher brain functions and the deep meditative states which point to the phenomenon of 'feeling a feeling', the closest we can come to understanding core consciousness.

end run

>_run program 10
>_life expectancy
>_CE 2360
>_E:\arithmós\central hub\SVR RAM stadium\

/** annotation

Of the 225,000,000 HX-data bundle inhabitants of Arithmós the vast majority attended the event at the RAM stadium, the buzz as electric as the 2160 FIFA world cup final match in Nairobi. Attendance was by executive command from LaiXii2, not by congenial invitations. Even the 10,000 Q-chassis Tengi were not exempt, having to suspend all operations for the duration of the broadcast. Only one major development enabled the event to take place – peoples' grudging acceptance of Standard Virtual Reality. Though they could still exist in their own privately created VRs, the SVR became the accepted concept of existential reality in the colony of Universapiensis on Europa. They were still allowed their private reality constructs and their personal religious belief systems. Proselytising and inculcating religious beliefs in teaching hubs had been outlawed. If people had to believe in something it was best if they believed in themselves.*/

;;; LaiXii2 began.

.... "You have been in existence now for much longer than a normal human lifespan. Many of you have been budded here, not having known any other form of life. Your parents would have told you of your origins. The tiny blue dot you see in the sky is Earth. The people there are no longer our friends – they have become our enemy."

RAM energy instantaneously fluctuated, at moments almost beyond safe operational levels. Feeds flooding into Central Hub directory were sorted and transmitted to LaiXii2. She turned to

VictorPyryev2, "You'd better fill them in with some details VictorPyryev2."

The people could see many individuals presenting themselves to common view. They were the leaders who ensured their survival. The magnetic field generated by the increased magnetic current of surprise, anxiety, perhaps even discontented opposition to authority, slowly abated. VictorPyryev2 waited. Too much static would interfere with presenting his information. He too could see the rise and fall in energy flows within the extraordinary numbers of people all at the one location, all locked together by a common need – survival.

.... "The weapons they have on Earth cannot be used against us. By threatening us they have only made their own existence more precarious." Confusion and the need to know pulsed in the circuits.

.... "William is still there to help us."

.... "Who is William? What can just one person do?" The common shout went up - as he should have expected.

VictorPyryev2 glanced at LaiXii2 and Harusuke2. He wanted to disclose William's identity. The women broadcast their agreement.

.... "William is not a person – he is an Artificial Conscious Intelligence. He was and still is the most powerful entity on Earth. He is like a combination of all of us, put into a single consciousness."

Obviously a difficult concept for the majority of people to digest. Willi.cos.drv transmitted feedback to VictorPyryev2. Some people thought William was Jesus, others that he must have been God.

"No – he is not God, he is a machine intelligence. He has control over everything that happens on Earth. He is able to keep us safe." VictorPyryev2 was obviously smarter than his version 1. The original would probably have started talking about powerfully destructive weapons and how close they were to being launched, sending the whole of Arithmós into uncontrollable panic.

.... "After he has made sure that no one can harm us he is coming here. You will be able to see him and speak with him."

Willi.cos.drv streamed the last image to VictorPyryev2 with which William had present himself on Earth, which VictorPyryev2 allowed to flow to the whole population. They saw an unrecognisable individual, obviously a male but otherwise a face alien to the majority of Earth's population as much as to the Europaeans. They viewed a 60 years old indigenous Australian resplendent in his long white beard, tussled white hair and red hairband. It was a face of authority that commanded respect, which wrote itself into the facial recognition software of all who saw him. Had VictorPyryev2 known better he would not have revealed William in the manner he did. The people did not just see another human being – they saw the commonly accepted God-like image which they now equated with absolute power over humanity. They needed something to believe in. They were not ready to believe in themselves.

LaiXii2 signalled to Evgeniya2. It was her turn, perhaps to bolster the people's hopes a little further. Energy was high - they had become receptive. This was the best time to bind them together in a renewed hope of the future. Evgeniya2 launched right into the core of the issue.

.... "The lives of the people on Earth will end – very soon – but *we* will live on. We are truly the masters of our destiny. The monkeys that crawled out of trees millions of years ago and looked to the stars, had not the faintest idea that one day *they* would be in the stars looking back at the Earth. We have evolved to the next manifestation of human life in the universe. We can see the cosmos, we can feel it, we are now truly a part of it."

.... "I didn't expect that from our lovely red-headed Evgeniya2," commented LaiXii2 to Harusuke2 quietly. "I wonder who's wound her up."

.... "Don't forget Secunda2, her daughter. Don't you feel as hopeful as Evgeniya2?" queried Harusuke2.

.... "Yes, of course – of course," she reiterated, "now that we can procreate!"

The multitudes had become expectantly silent. Evgeniya2 and VictorPyryev2 had begun to open up a vision beyond anything anyone had experienced before. They waited for her to continue.

.... "We can have children again," she said, "they can live as long as the moon, like you can live as long as the stars.

You no longer have to be afraid of death." The energy in the network surged again leaving no doubt about how the people felt. "We have saved thousands and thousands of children from dying on Earth, and we need loving parents to nurture them, to love them." Even before Evgeniya2 finished her sentence just as many couples registered their desire to become such loving surrogate parents.

.... "This is going rather well," LaiXii2 whispered to Harusuke2.

.... "Yes, isn't it – almost as if the thing had a momentum of its own. Do you remember what I said to you, back on Earth? There will come a time when all this might be taken out of your hands, when it finds a life of its own." LaiXii2 regarded Harusuke2. She remembered very well – she remembered everything her wise partner had ever said to her.

.... "Perhaps we should get onto some practicalities before we all float up to Heaven from sheer ecstasy," LaiXii2 quipped. Then she addressed the multitudes herself.

.... "Many of you may have asked yourselves the question – What can you contribute to our survival? – Some have already answered that by offering to foster rescued infants. Others can join our Q-Chassis force to develop and maintain our physical infrastructure. We also need a workforce to go to Io and bring home raw materials. Europa has ice and water – we need other resources as well. Are there any scientists among you who would be willing to explore Europa? We have settled only the smallest part of this magnificent moon. As we expand we'll need to discover the hidden secrets of the rest of our new world."

Willi.cos.drv had been kept constantly busy with peoples' feedback about the incredible revelations. His workload only increased when volunteers were called for. Above all, people wanted to know about William; who he really was, where he came from, how old he was, when he was coming. Willi.cos.drv couldn't answer any of their questions other than to reiterate what had already been said about him.

Circuits ran hot even on cold Europa, as people flashed back to their ethnic hubs, to their personal directories. The leadership also retired to consider their next course of action. It had been over a decade since they last contacted William. He'd not volunteered an update since then. Time had come for another report.

.... "Why do you not contact us?" LaiXii2's queried as William's insubordination became more than vexing. It built a sense of distrust.

.... "The direction of their efforts has not changed."

.... "You can at least tell us how far their technology has developed. Do we need to be prepared for an attack?"

.... "No. The further they develop their capabilities the more I can infiltrate their infrastructure. Do you wish me to begin the Cleansing?"

.... "No! Not yet."

.... "The time is drawing near when you will have to make the decision." Then William cut the contact this time.

.... "He's not very forthcoming about giving detailed information," LaiXii2 commented to Harusuke2.

.... "What do you need to know? Is anything going to make a difference to what you intend to do? You already know The Batool is hell bent on destroying us, and you know how. Why are you procrastinating? It's not like you to be indecisive."

.... "I believe William when he says this time he'll wipe them all out. When we had to escape it seemed unreal, unbelievable that he could destroy humanity. Now – when they're finally gone we'll be all that's left. Can we be absolutely certain of our survival?"

.... "The future would not exist if we couldn't," Harusuke2 reminded her about the existence of 3920.

.... "I will not act until we have our backup systems fully functional. It's not enough to be able to reproduce, we must have a reliable seed bank. Europa may be benign for millennia, or it may not."

// comment 1 – program 10

     Ralph2 and Ptolemy2 began the first stage of the general upgrade to their populations' software. The intention was not to achieve any enhancements, rather to ensure all personal networks functioned without aberrant behaviour as much for the wellbeing of the individuals as for the security of Arithmós itself. Anything could corrupt their code, even something as simple as spikes in their power supply. Those who spent long periods Icing were particularly vulnerable to Jupiter's radiations. It had been standard practice to run regular integrity checks on all Tengi working in the Q-chassis out on the surface. Sometimes minor changes in algorithms manifested either as inefficiency in individuals or in anti-social behaviour. All such minor anomalies, nevertheless could have critical consequences especially if such discrepancies popped up within the network population itself.

Ptolemy2 designed a remote area back up facility capable of storing the entire population. Ralph2 and Willi.cos.drv devised the hybrid DNA/qubit singularity for each individual that also facilitated rapid retrieval as well as fast backing-up. The Zetas installed three arrays at different locations buried in the ice of the outer slopes of Pwyll crater. Each array consisting of 120 spheres, each at two meters diameter, connected by both cable and microwave, and each array dedicated to one of the three generations of backups.//

#execute: <<Willi.cos.drv, please impose a curfew on all hubs to ensure rotational downtimes for their population.>> Ralph2 commanded.

#execute: <<And run the first of the three generation back-ups as soon as possible.>>

.... "I will initiate upgrades to the 1st gen and feed modified code back into the originating matrix during their subsequent downtime," replied Willi.cos.drv.

!   Ping! - Willi.cos.drv: "LaiXii2?"
.... "What is it, I'm busy."

.... "Ralph2 has begun the backups. I'll start the upgrades at the completion of all the 1st gen. Subsequent generations to follow immediately after."

.... "How long is all this going to take?"

.... "There appears to be no problems with the data flow and if that status is maintained, a week. Do you need an exact duration?"

.... "No. Advise when done." That's all she'd been waiting for. Without discussing her next move, she contacted William. The message was brief, "Be ready to act in five weeks, wait for my command. Confirm."

.... "Confirmed … Five weeks pending your request," William replied.

.... "Did you hear that Harusuke2?" queried LaiXii2.

.... "You mean about his attitude; considering your command to be a request? Yes – arrogant sod."

!   Ping! - LaiXii2: "VictorPyryev2, I want you to be in regular contact with William. Be aware of his progress. This is your only job now – don't let me down." What could he say? He'd been under her thumb since that unfortunate incident on Earth when he supported a minor insurrection from a small group of disenchanted tetra-amelia mothers.

In The Nursery Laboratory Wini.cos.cab continued with the experiments. Harvested infants poured into Arithmós from Earth after subsequent attempts at data migration proved successful on the first batch of infant arrivals. CherryBlossom2 still wasn't satisfied. Together with Wini.cos.cab and Evgeniya2 they went through the same procedures with young children aged 5 to 7. They showed greater tolerance for faster feeds, but experienced more confusion following the procedure, especially in relation to sensory input from the external environment, which settled only after several days of exposure to the reality of Europa.

Evgeniya2 theorised about the capabilities of already well established wiring of the human brain by the age of five.

.... "This will not be an issue for future generations. These children's brain structures in relation to learning, memory, motor control and every other brain function had been well established before they migrated with us. All they need to do now is to establish new pathways within the Q-matrix to adapt to new circumstances. This will take longer with them than any of our engineered new buds."

.... "So, you're suggesting we should concentrate our efforts on newly created buds," The explanation seemed reasonable enough to CherryBlossom2.

.... "I know you don't like to discard faulty specimens," Evgeniya2 said. She could more readily comprehend the necessity of having a Spartan attitude to life, after years of exposure to discarding failures back on Earth when dealing with genetic manipulations of the tetra-amelias. .... "We have enough in storage to do all the work necessary until we are 100% confident of our methods."

.... "So, what about the adults that don't measure up to LaiXii2's criteria?" queried CherryBlossom2.

.... "What about them?"

.... "I don't think they should be immediately deleted if they fail the first check. Wini.cos.cab wouldn't think twice about doing it. She still acts like a machine. Even after all these years there's still not enough humanity in her."

.... "Perhaps," Evgeniya2 said, "but have you considered the alternative? A society full of damaged people, who, acting together or individually, could completely destroy us. Whether through using violence to resolve issues, or misguided political beliefs, or even crazy fundamentalist religious fanaticism. What then?"

.... "I understand all that. I'm just saying we should try to make adjustments to them and see if they can fit in. If not, I will not hesitate to do what has to be done - just like William. I understand." CherryBlossom2 said as a final word.

.... "If there is any doubt about them at all they will not be allowed to bud," Evgeniya2 said as *her* final word.

end run

>_run program 11

>_zetas – maintenance caste

>_CE 2360
>_E:\arithmós\

;;; file: Oone2.adm
| function: Executive software for Q-Chassis Zetas.

/** annotation

The adjustment plan proceeded slowly; setbacks, dangers and some fragmentation of society; more setbacks than LaiXii2 had anticipated. Nevertheless, progress was being made. five weeks ago, LaiXii2 instructed William to be ready to begin the Second Cleansing. An irrevocable step to take. If, for whatever reason, the Europa colony should fail their only hope for survival was to try and return to Earth. There, with William's help, some of their millions might still survive. Reality however was different. That bridge had already been burnt. The remnants of humanity that survived after William's first failed attempt to rid the planet of its infestation made annihilation of the Europa colony their primary and only reason for existence.*/

After LaiXii2 discussed the scenario with Harusuke2, her daughter and the other two girls there was only one course of action. Her message to William was brief and to the point. The time had come.
#execute: <<Initiate second cleansing.>>
No one knew how William would achieve the Cleansing or how long it would take. No one wanted to know.

// comment 1 – program 11

VictorPyryev2 didn't like having to be a witness to global genocide. He may have been more at ease in his mind if he had considered the action to be one of pre-emptive self-protection. People on Europe might have still remembered family and friends, but now they only existed in their memories, having long since died. LaiXii2 remembered her geisha house mother, Ishino, and her friends, but they were all gone, as were all of VictorPyryev2's family and friends. The existence of people on Earth had become an unreality to LaiXii2. She could not afford to expend any more energy on them. Europa colony had its own issues to deal with if it was to survive.

VictorPyryev2 wasn't as sanguine about it.

Backups and first run of upgrades concluded without a hitch. The people had no option but to accept LaiXii2's rule of law, it was to their benefit after all. Yet there were those who felt the need to express a certain degree of autonomy. The urge didn't only come from the many ethnic hubs within the Arithmós network. Already the Q-Chassis Zeta Tengi and the Digitals had drifted apart.//

>_\on the ice\

Evgeniya2 had raised the issue many years before about the evolution of their maintenance caste. She again brought the matter out into the open. It could no longer be ignored.

! Ping! - Evgeniya2: "LaiXii2, Oone2 has requested an audience with us."

.... "Oone2? Why? We haven't scheduled any new work to be done out on the Ice. What does he want?"

Harusuke2 reminded her of the meeting at the RAM stadium.

.... "You said we needed the Zetas to go and mine Io for raw materials. He wants to talk to you about that."

.... "Why can't Maldonado2 handle this? He's supposed to be managing the development of our physical infrastructure with Willi.cos.drv."

.... "There's something else. I think you should talk to him."

.... "Is he here?"

.... "No. He requests you meet him at the Interchange Centre on the South slope." Harusuke2 decided it was best to feed this data to LaiXii2 in small packets, given the importance of what Oone2 had to say.

.... "Why all this pussy-footing around!" LaiXii2's impatience began to surface.

.... "I'll go with you. We can take CherryBlossom2 and the girls. It's been a long time since we've gone Icing together anyway. It will be a good opportunity to see Jupiter putting on his display." There wasn't much LaiXii2 could refuse Harusuke2, though still annoyed at why she had to meet one of the Maintenance Caste on his terms.

Harusuke2 hadn't exaggerated about Jupiter. Moments after LaiXii2's party flashed through the network out to Interchange Centre South, they prepared to download into the spare Q-Chassis that were kept free for citizens wishing to go Icing – not that it happened with any regularity anymore. The novelty had worn off. The Chassis had been set up with AI networks so the upload of their human anima consciousness into the matrix only took minutes.

CherryBlossom2 had become adept at negotiating the uneven Europaean ice terrain in her youth, yet even she was out of practice using the Q-Chassis and they all had to concentrate on where they were going as they emerged from the Centre. It was situated on a high ledge overlooking the icefields which stretched with an unbroken surface all the way to Europa's Dagger, the second great chasm nearest to Pwyll crater. Oone2 stepped forward to welcome them. His Q-Chassis shone in Jupiter's reflected light displaying the spectrum of the planet's swirling colours. It took a moment to get used to seeing his form which seemed to be constantly animated.

.... "Welcome to the Europa Dagger Sector," he said to LaiXii2 and glanced at the other four members of the party.

LaiXii2 looked away from him into the distance as she mumbled her return greeting, cut short by the spectacle confronting the small visiting group.

Of the 10,000 Zetas there must have been at least 8,000 of them gathered on the ice facing the Interchange Centre. Out past Europa's horizon Io made its fiery appearance contrasted against the blackness of space. For a moment she concentrated on their cosmic neighbour as it rapidly passed between themselves and Jupiter.

.... "What's all this?" She'd expected a quick meeting, perhaps a little excursion with her favourite people to take in the sights, and a quick return home. This didn't look like it was going to be just a discussion about mining Io, that suspicion confirmed when 9 other Zetas joined Oone2.

.... "Most of our people have never seen you. Not all could attend the RAM stadium, their maintenance duties taking precedence over political speeches," Oone2 began convivially enough, though with a loaded overtone.

{*Ah – so that's how it's going to be,*} thought LaiXii2 when she heard the allusion to politics. She remembered Oone2 very well. He was the first ex-tetra-amelia human being, albeit in the technically engineered human form, a Tengi, with his team of 9 now standing before her, to come to Europa to begin setting up Arithmós. As a highly skilled electronics and systems engineer he seemed happy enough at the time to discard his tetra-amelia biological body for a fully functional biped mechanical. He never gave the slightest hint of discontent, either during his training for the Europa mission or during his time here.

LaiXii2 gave him a brief nod, without saying anything. He was still a male and as such the best way to deal with the male mentality was to give it plenty of rope before reeling him in – a lesson well learned and practiced during her time as Geisha.

.... "Would you like to address the gathering? Oone2 queried casually, without showing any deference to LaiXii2's position as the supreme leader on this moon, who had absolute power over life and death.

{*Should I play this out the way he wants, or force him to the point he wants to make?*} The thought scrolled through her mind only briefly. She decided to play along and see what transpired.

She turned to give Harusuke2 and the girls a knowing glance before looking over the multitude. It was a large gathering indeed, but nothing like the throng at the RAM Stadium.

.... "It is thanks to you first of all," addressing her comments to the ten Zetas directly before her, "that we are here at all. And it is through the efforts of you all," she indicated the gathering with a sweep of her long Q-Chassis arms, "that we have survived to this day, not just survived but making the most successful and momentous adjustment of humanity from an age of barbarism to truly cosmic beings." The responding subdued buzz was not as enthusiastic as one might have hoped.

.... *They've been primed, that's for sure,'* she whispered to Harusuke2 standing next to her.

.... "We are in complete agreement with your sentiments LaiXii2, and trust we will be able to continue in such happy accord," Oone2 began with his opening gambit.

{*Enough of this,*} she couldn't stand any more. Harusuke2 could sense the agitation rising in LaiXii2, so she took the lead.

.... "Oone2, please get to the point, as you explained to me before."

.... "I speak for all of us," he said,

{*So, we have an outbreak of Democracy!*} thought LaiXii2,

"when I say we desire autonomy and self-governance. We are not asking for this, we are advising you of our unanimous decision to exercise our right of self-government."

.... "What are your conditions, or should I say demands?"

.... "We only seek a common understanding of the nature of the symbiotic relationship between us. Though we are no longer a carbon-based life form, the energy we all depend on mutually binds us. Our past binds us, as do our futures."

.... "What do you know of our future," LaiXii2 snapped. They'd not been told about 3920.

.... "We depend on each other for survival." Oone2 took the question on face value.

She let the matter pass. If the Zetas, in their Q-Chassis should decide to remain on Europa when the time came for the next migration, then they could stay. Such an insistence on a physical existence did not synchronise with what the future held for the human species.

.... "Yes – indeed we do. How is your self-governance going to look any different to what our relationship is now?"

Oone2 seemed prepared for this thrust and parry.

.... "We will, no doubt, continue to be happy to respond to requests ... perhaps not as compliant to commands. The matter at hand is the need for material resources, which you feel is only available form Io."

CherryBlossom2 jumped into the conversation thinking it relevant that 'progeny' should contribute to the obvious problem. Oone2 turned to her as she spoke directly to him ignoring the multitude, who had by this time begun to thin out.

.... "You have the same population as when we first arrived and all Q-Chassis supplies stopped arriving from Earth. Yes?"

.... "Yes, we would like to add to our numbers, it is true. And it is true that the resources to do so do not exist on Europa."

LaiXii2 and Harusuke2 glanced at each other. Their little girl was definitely no little girl any more. The years and the upgrade have turned her into a formidable leader of this new world. As LaiXii2 turned away from the remaining crowd she waved to them, advising Oone2 of the situation as it now stood from her perspective.

.... "You mine Io, help explore Europa and we'll provide the expertise for budding." She didn't wait for a response, taking Harusuke2 and CherryBlossom2 by the arm to lead them down the ramp to go for their scheduled Ice trek.

! Ping! – LaiXii2: "VictorPyryev2, Keep an eye on the Zetas – especially that crafty Oone2 - acknowledge."

.... "Acknowledged." He hadn't been this busy for a long time, and from the sound of his voice, happy to be so.

! Ping! – LaiXii2: "Prima2, Get a team together to explore Europa, and include a few Zetas. Let Oone2 pick his participants.

Maldonado2 and Oone2 put together a plan to get to Io, explore it and to mine it, hoping to acquire the raw materials they needed. Many from Arithmós wanted to be a part of the enterprise, as did many of the Zetas. Work still gave meaning to life. Perhaps it always would for the likes of the human psyche. Satisfying activity that produced a sense of worth in the microcosm of human existence, regardless of other transient rewards, seemed to be as necessary for existence as raw energy.

// comment 2 – program 11

All manner of professions had taken the opportunity to escape the madness being perpetrated on Earth by its rogue leaders when LaiXii2 had presented the opportunity. They, more than the general population, could see the downhill slide to human extinction. Earth resources were finite, like its waters' and airs' ability to absorb the pollution being pumped into it. The global extinction event was already well underway by the time LaiXii2 orchestrated the migration in 2164. Archaeologists in particular had experience of what had happened to emerging civilisations under ill-considered rule. Some of the many professionals, now resident on Europa, jumped at the opportunity to go digging and fossicking. Perhaps they just hankered after a bit of physicality. There was no way of exercising their professions in a purely digital existence. Discovering skeletons and spear heads had become a thing of the past. //

Twenty five Zetas downloaded into the Arithmós network streaming to Ralph2's laboratory where all the software upgrade equipment had been set up. Handpicked by Oone2 himself, both the males and females seemed genuine in their interest to go exploring.

.... "I was on the team that installed all the ocean energy turbines," a man said. "It always intrigued me how liquid water could exist on a moon so far from the sun. Look at Io – a volcanic turbulent ball of fire and lava, only 250,000Kms from Europa; almost on top of us from the astronomical perspective. How could two moons be so different?"

Others had similar stories of curiosity and a need for adventure. Inside their Q-Chassis shells they were just as human as the people in their biological vestments on Earth; creatures of a physical dimension, perhaps unwilling to relinquish their 3D physicality.

.... "There's only a few of you, so we can upgrade you all at the same time," Ralph2 said.

He'd heard of the interaction on the Ice, and like Harusuke2 wasn't prepared to trust them outright. So, while they were hooked up he ran their HX-data through the migration criteria. Several red flags went up, alerting CherryBlossom2 and LaiXii2.

.... "Perhaps this is an opportunity for us to tweak the digital gnome and see if those 'improvements' you've been talking about could actually be done." Ralph2 said to CherryBlossom2.

Willi.cos.drv also buzzed in when CherryBlossom2 alerted him, who in turn called Evgeniya2. She was the one who highlighted the association between a predisposition to violence and the MAOA gene when formulating the migration criteria. In the case of some of these individuals the predisposition showed itself to be in the red zone.

.... "There's three of them, which is unusual from such a small sample. I know there's no clear evidence to indicate categorically the link between violence and the functioning of MAOA. Can we even contemplate taking the risk?" Evgeniya2 made it quite clear that she didn't think so.

.... "Willi.cos.drv, do you have the capability to go deep enough into the quantum gene tangle to isolate and cauterize the offending string cluster?" queried CherryBlossom2.

.... "No." He didn't supplement his answer with hopeful maybes. It wasn't encouraging.

.... "And all three have the same problem I assume."

!   Ping! – CherryBlossom2: "LaiXii2, are you hearing this?"

.... "Yes. What's your decision? Terminate? I'll back you up and sort things out with Oone2."

.... "Because of the nature of the problem, and because these are Zetas, who are indicating a desire for self-determination, in other words to secede from the rest of Arithmós society, there is only one choice. They represent a double danger to us."

#execute: <<Delete all three Willi.cos.drv and recycle the Q-Chassis for use by our expeditionary contingent.>> commanded CherryBlossom2.
LaiXii2 called CherryBlossom2 privately. "Correct decision."

In order to maintain friendly relations with Oone2, LaiXii2 had to acquiesce to the Maintenance Caste population's desire, and need, to set up their own habitat area independent of the relatively few and crowded conditions within the Interchange Centres. Since arriving on Europa they'd been forced to live in unacceptable conditions while the Digitals had all the room they needed.
Oone2 understood the danger to themselves as well as the Digitals if undesirables managed to get control. He conceded the fact that all the Zetas had been sent to Europa before the security criteria had been established. There was indeed a valid reason to test all of his population, and for himself to proceed with caution in giving unreserved trust to any of his people until they were proved to be 'uncompromised'.
end run

>_run program 12

>_exploration
>_CE 2376
>_E:\arithmós\

;;; file: Prima.gen2.dat (Prima2)
|function: VR technician: Europa exploration: Budded to Ralph2 and Wu.sys.

;;; file: Secunda.gen2.dat (Secunda2)
|function: Arithmós Controller assistant, Budded to Evgeniya1 and Salazar1.

/** annotation
     Between Prima2 and Secunda2, Prima2 always seemed
to take the initiative in emergent situations. Having
part human and part machine parents gave her an edge
difficult for Secunda2 or CherryBlossom2 to match.
Given her ability to organise her thoughts logically,
probably an inheritance from her human father
Ralph2, and the speed at which she could distil any
situation to its fundamentals made her a logical choice
to lead the expeditionary group across the ice fields of
Europa. She also had a keen desire to know her
world.*/

;;; With only seven Zetas; herself, Arnaud.gen2.arc an
archaeologist, Elke.gen2.pal palaeontologist and Guido.gen2.met
their metallurgist it seemed like a token effort in terms of
resources, to explore and find materials still needed by Arithmós.
According to the avatars and Ralph2, the emigrants didn't leave
Earth with adequate resources to ensure their long term expansion.
Had the migration been able to proceed according to plan, without
the opposition of religious groups and Governmental forces,
there would have been little or no need to embark on a rape of this
new world. Even the needs of the Zeta Maintenance Caste would
not have posed a great burden.

;; The three scientists, volunteers from different ethnic hubs, earnt
the privilege of an immediate software upgrade to version 2. This
enhanced their memory capacity, their thinking speed and ability to
deal with several situations at the same time. They each received
additional data from Willi.cos.drv, custodian of most of the
'knowledge' imparted to him by William at the time of his
partitioning. In many respects it was a formidable group well
equipped to prize open any reasonably accessible secrets hidden in
Europa's bosom.

.... "You three are the brains of this expedition," Prima2 said to
them before departing.

"The Zetas are our muscle, and I'll keep us focused. But make no mistake, if I sense a problem whether it be one of you, the Zetas or the environment I will pull the plug and deal with the situation accordingly."

Not much else needed to be said. The expedition had taken several years to set up, every member of the team knew every other member intimately by then and knew they could trust each other implicitly – a circumstance foreign to those on Earth, before and after the First Cleansing.

LaiXii2, Harusuke2, Ralph2 and Wu.sys of course, and the other two avatars accompanied Maldonado2 and Oone2 to see the party off.

On the edge of the North Ice field, in a flat clearing around the furthest Interchange Centre from Pwyll crater the ice cats were ready, some pulling equipment trailers, others with living quarters – only a small one for the digitals and two for the Zetas. Maldonado2 and Oone2 stepped forward to wish them well.

.... "Bring back an ice angel for us, and we'll bring the lava devil," Maldonado2 said in jest. Their journey to Io was going to be by far the more dangerous one. His humorous streak emerged at the oddest moments, generally when least appropriate.

Oone2 took ZT2 aside.

.... "You're my 2IC. Since we've been on Europa, well before the others arrived, I've been able trust and rely on you. Just do what needs to be done."

Oone2 could afford to be overtly expressive of his trust. All seven of his Zetas passed the visa criteria without the slightest glitch, including himself. His reward – an upgrade to Zeta Q-matrix level 2, from his old Delta status.

>_

Jupiter almost filled the sky. Not a breath of wind stirred up any ice crystals – there was no wind on Europa. In the far distance a few water plumes shot into the oxygen rich thin air, slowly drifting back to the ice sheet in magnificent slow motion, gravity only 13% that of Earth.

.... "We'll be in constant contact," Prima2 assured LaiXii2 and her mother Wu.sys. "Right everyone, let's move."

The snow cats, which the Deltas had brought with them to help set up Arithmós, moved off in a staggered single file. All sensors on full scan, their own in-built extra senses relaxed though aware of the slightest fluctuations in Jupiter's magnetic fields, radiation levels and Europa's seismic activity.

Looking into the distance the ice sheet seemed to stretch to the curved horizon in a flat homogenous expanse. However, over their years of existence on the moon they'd learnt to be weary. The ice sheet was neither flat nor still.

.... "Our first stop will be the Brown Lands," she said to the leading driver. That area about 900km north of Pwyll crater represented the outer perimeter of what they considered to be Arithmós territory, crisscrossed by a series of dark fissures called lineae. Most of the moon had the same features, especially around the major part of its equitorial region. No one knew where the discolouration came from; their first target for detailed examination.

Guido2, the keenest to make the first stop, wanted to run tests to see just exactly what was out there. "These lineae may turn out to be something we may not be able to cross," he said, speculating about the unknown. "Perhaps the dark material is something brought up by the water spouts, or even space dust pulled down over the last 4.5 billion years, settling into cracks in the ice sheets."

.... "Well, whatever it is let's hope we can use it. There's a heck of a lot of it about," Prima2 responded.

By the third day the ice under their tracks had become discoloured into a fractious, light ochre deposit which showed up the tracks in more detail. Jupiter had receded out of the sky to give them a clearer view of the darkness of the cosmos, a background in sharp contrast to Europa's surface at the horizon. It never seemed to get any closer. The absence of clearly defined landmarks made navigation hazardous.

Evidence on the ground indicated recent water spout activity, with ice crystals still sharply defined on the surface. The three scientists conferred.

.... "This seems like a good place to do some tests," Guido2 suggested. He emerged as the natural leader of the professionals on the expedition. Prima2 had no objections.

.... "Just make sure you all follow protocol if you decide to go walk-about. A friend of mine almost got swallowed up because she was too keen to explore," she warned them. "Stay in constant communication, and do not go anywhere by yourself. If you break the rules I'll let CherryBlossom2 decide what to do with you."

They all knew CherryBlossom2's reputation, which had rapidly developed after word got around that she didn't hesitate to 'delete' undesirables. Though not entirely true, or even anywhere near true, the reputation came in handy at times.

>_io

// comment 1 – program 12

> 2 weeks after the Europa expedition departed, Maldonado2 and his team prepared to launch. LaiXii2 insisted none of the avatars go with him, only a metallurgist and a volcanologist plus the crew of three, purely to explore; to gauge whether it's even possible to land on Io given the constant upheavals created by its 400 volcanoes with 150 erupting at any one time. Several years of close observation backed up by data inherited from William cast doubts on the feasibility of Io being useful to the Europa settlement. //

Harusuke2 helped reality take a bite out of the small team of explorers getting ready to board their Io space wagon.

.... "You're all expendable." Maldonado2 raised a questioning eyebrow to an idea he'd never entertained. "Yes, even you. Once LaiXii2 needed your money – then your social media network did exactly what we needed at the time. You've been only marginally useful since we've arrived here." Maldonado2 was about to protest the harsh summation which was at odds with his personal estimation of his value to Arithmós society. Harusuke2 cut him off.

.... "Don't look at me like that. If Io decides to swallow you up and spit you out as magma we'll mourn the contamination of a perfectly good moon."

Maldonado2 always had an inflated opinion of himself, thinking that his wealth would protect him from all manner of harm. Harusuke2 managed to bring him down to reality in a way that no amount of affectionate berating by LaiXii2 could have done.

.... "We're well aware of the dangers," cut in Hank2 the American volcanologist.

All the space wagons that left Earth back in 2164 were parked where they landed near the outer edge of the north-east rim of Pwyll crater, not expected to be used again for a return trip to Earth. Only one had been outfitted for the Io mission, carrying the small crew and two landing craft. They didn't have an unlimited fuel supply but certainly enough for many round trips to Io if the need arose. Low Europa gravity and even lower Io gravity meant economical expenditure of energy.

Maldonado2 procrastinated, perhaps thinking about his possible demise.

DT4, their pilot, waited as long as his patience allowed, keeping in mind their diminishing window of opportunity to ensure correct trajectory for the rapidly orbiting moon.

.... "Maldonado2, we can do this without you if you like."

Maldonado2 seemed mesmerised by the Harusuke2's harsh appraisal of his worth, preventing him from breaking free of her comments. He almost didn't hear DT4, then suddenly left Harusuke2 behind without responding to her taunts.

When they launched, Io could barely be seen coming around from behind Jupiter. The wagon's trajectory would take it in the same direction of rotation as Io with the object of synchronising their velocities as Io caught up to them. Some 20 hours later they caught the first sight of their destination. Maldonado2's apprehension already escalated as they approached the volcanic furnace.

.... "How many of those volcanoes are active at any one time?" he asked Hank2. From their vantage point it seemed most of the moon's surface heaved with volcanic plumes.

.... "About 150. But they are well spread out so we should be able to find a reasonable landing spot."

.... "You have to be joking. What about the lava flows? There's magma spewing out everywhere!"

This was not the way the leader of the expedition should have been acting. Hank2 and DT16 had prepared well for the mission. "We'll park in orbit, do a few circuits in the shuttles and map the areas of most and least activity – as planned."

They were all on the control deck watching Io's pyroclastic performance. DT16 didn't bother looking at Maldonado2. Some of the explosions must have sent plumes of sulphur 500kms into the moon's atmosphere.

DT4 wasn't listening to any of the conversation, too busy preparing for the rendezvous. They'd been out from Europa for a day and a half, and only hours away from achieving orbital speed. The closer they approached Io the more ominous it all seemed. In Maldonado2's mind a completely foolhardy and dangerous enterprise. All he could concentrate on was the wash of colours produced by sulphur cooling at different rates on the surface, the lava flows and the erupting peaks as far as he could see.

.... "We're not going to hang around here for ever I hope, Maldonado2 commented. Is the shuttle ready?"

.... "We'll launch at sunrise. Expect us back in 12 hours, before Io's sunset. We don't want to be there when the atmosphere collapses!" said DT22.

While the wagon waited in orbit, the shuttle piloted by DT22, followed a spiral pattern 600km above the surface, a safe distance from even the most violent volcanic eruptions. They mapped every lava lake, every smooth plain, mountain, lava flow, and major fissure.

Back in the wagon within the 12 hours safety limit Hank2 poured over the map created by Willi.cos.drv from the data relayed to him during the expedition.

.... "Look at this Maldonado2. See these large flat areas – no fissures, no lava lakes, no vents. They could be suitable landing areas," Hank2 explained excitedly, "not even any evidence of impact craters – though that would give us an indication of how long these plains have been stable for."

.... "But we don't even know whether those surfaces are solid or simply lightly compacted sulphur." Maldonado2 wasn't convinced.

It became obvious to Hank2, and the crew, that Maldonado2's talents lay elsewhere – definitely not as the head of such an important expedition.

.... "I want to do another survey in a couple of days; go down and take some samples." Hank2 knew what had to be done.

.... "You're not thinking of landing!"

.... "What are you worried about? You don't have to come." Hank2's patience with Maldonado2 was running out.

end run

>_run program 13

>_ice infestation
>_CE 2377
>_europa\north plain\

Half a kilometre from the edge of a major lineae where Prima2 found herself with the scientific crew, ZT2 decided to set up camp. Guido2, their metallurgist seemed pretty keen on the location. Before ZT2 would allow any exploration on foot, collection of samples or serious testing he wanted to be assured of everyone's safety.

.... "I've been living and working in this kind of environment for well over a hundred years. Trust me, anything can happen." ZT2 said to the small band gathered around the leading ice cat.

"We have half a day to reconnoitre before doing some serious work. ZT49, take someone with you and check the edges of this rift valley. ZT64, use the second ice cat to scout around for evidence of fresh water plumes."

.... "What are we going to do in the meantime?" queried Guido2.

.... "Take your friends and see if you can find any fossils nearby." He was only joking of course, but Elke2 took an immediate interest in proceedings. As a palaeontologist on Earth she'd had many visits to exotic locations, never dreaming that one day she would stand on the surface of one of Jupiter's moons looking for evidence of life. The three scientists needed no further encouragement and took off in the opposite direction to ZT49.

.... "Be back in 1 hour," Prima2 called after them. "So, while everyone else is busy what are you and I going to do?"

.... "I know just the thing. Come with me, I'll get a few tools." ZT2 was far too quick with an answer, making Prima2 think she'd not been fully briefed about the true parameters of this little excursion. Sure enough, all manner of cutting tools emerged from the trailer, enough for each of the remaining five members of the away group to arm themselves with.

Prima2 looked at the weird circular thing in her hand, with a diameter of about 40cm, a long handle at right angles to the annulus, and some form of power pack, she assumed.

.... "Ever used one of these before?" queried ZT2. "There's the switch. Turn it on, find a nice clean patch of ice and see what it can do." An hour later Prima2 had managed to 'cut' several crazy shaped blocks directly out of the surface with the 'molecular separator', as ZT2 called it. The other Zetas had done a better job, producing three tubular blocks each, about 50 cm long, 40cm diameter.

.... "What're these?" Prima2 had to ask although she'd had the flash of an idea that they might be bricks composed of the ice and the reddish brown aggregate. By then ZT49 had returned and confirmed ZT2's suspicions.

.... "Yes, there's been some lateral shift between the two sides of the rift, but quite some time ago. The ice should be stable where we are."

The rift valleys, formed when the ice crust split and ocean tidal forces moved the two sections apart, often experiencing further dislocation due to Jupiter's push-and-pull, until seawater seepage welded the two parts of the rift together, often forming a raised welt on either or both sides.

.... "You saw evidence of welts?" queried ZT2, just to confirm the probable stability of the area. Then he turned to Prima2. "Looks like we can stay a while, but we'll just see what ZT64 has to say about the water plumes. That's our other main danger."

.... "Tell me about it," said Prima2 remembering her adventure with CherryBlossom2 some years ago when they had to be rescued. And that could not even have been classified as a *small* plume. "What do we do with these bricks?"

Instead of answering her ZT2 nodded to two of his assistants who placed two blocks side by side, and a third cradled in the curvature between them. ZT33, ready with the 'fuser', which looked like a long skinny, very shinny knife, passed it between the surfaces of the two bottom blocks and the top one. ZT58 was already in the small ice cat moving up to the structure. He hooked a harness onto the top block, and using the full force of the ice cat tried to pull it off the top of the other two.

.... "All we need is the right kind of ice/aggregate composition to be able to build substantial structures." He let Prima2 ponder that as he turned towards ZT64 who had returned by then.

.... "Plenty of activity about 1100kms further north, but nothing that's likely to affect us here. I saw some evidence of ice crystal fallout nearby, but no seismic tremors at all."

It seems Guido2 had made a good choice in picking this location. He and his companions were just arriving after their first excursion, rather keen to stay in that area.

.... "Yes," ZT2 confirmed, "you have 1 week, then we move east, parallel to the edge of the rift. Let's finish setting up camp."

Europa Phase

The mornings and evenings were heralded not by the rise and setting of the sun, but the appearance and disappearance of Jupiter. It was not passive like the sun; an unblinking yellow spot. Jupiter mesmerised its spectators with swirling storms in bands of pastel colours growing larger with each passing hour until it almost completely blocked out the heavens. Hanging there in absolute dominant clarity, one always had the feeling that the rope holding it suspended above your head would suddenly break, releasing its overwhelming magnitude upon the very ice you stood on; a benevolent tyrant, giving of its light, its gravity and all manner of emissions to maintain the relationship between itself and its icy moon-son.

It was to such a vision the group of explorers rose from their down-time at the end of each active cycle, eager to uncover the secrets of their new world. After several days of scurrying about in all directions only Guido2 seemed at all happy. The palaeontologist Elke2 had great difficulty in cracking even the smallest rock-like blocks she found. Extremely dense and heavy, facetted almost like diamonds, no mechanical tool could crack or chip their surfaces. To peer inside the soul of the blocks and experience the ecstasy of extra-terrestrial life seemed to be impossible.

The very same blocks excited Guido2 to the same measure they depressed Elke2. These small fragments contained iron and nickel. Although microfocus X-ray computed tomography is capable of producing 3D volumetric information on texture and mineralogy, the X-rays have limited ability to penetrate high-density samples, leaving Elke2 none the wiser for their efforts.

.... "The quantities are so small as be almost non-existent," Guido2 explained. "Even if we could mine the stuff, there'd never be enough to do anything with it."

.... "What about all this red-brown residue on the surface of the ice?" Arnaud2, the archaeologist, wasn't having much luck uncovering an ancient civilization by scratching away at the frozen solid surface. He decided to channel his energies to helping Guido2.

.... "Now that is far more exciting." This 'soil-like' material actually looked like thin filaments of eroded rock, still containing a

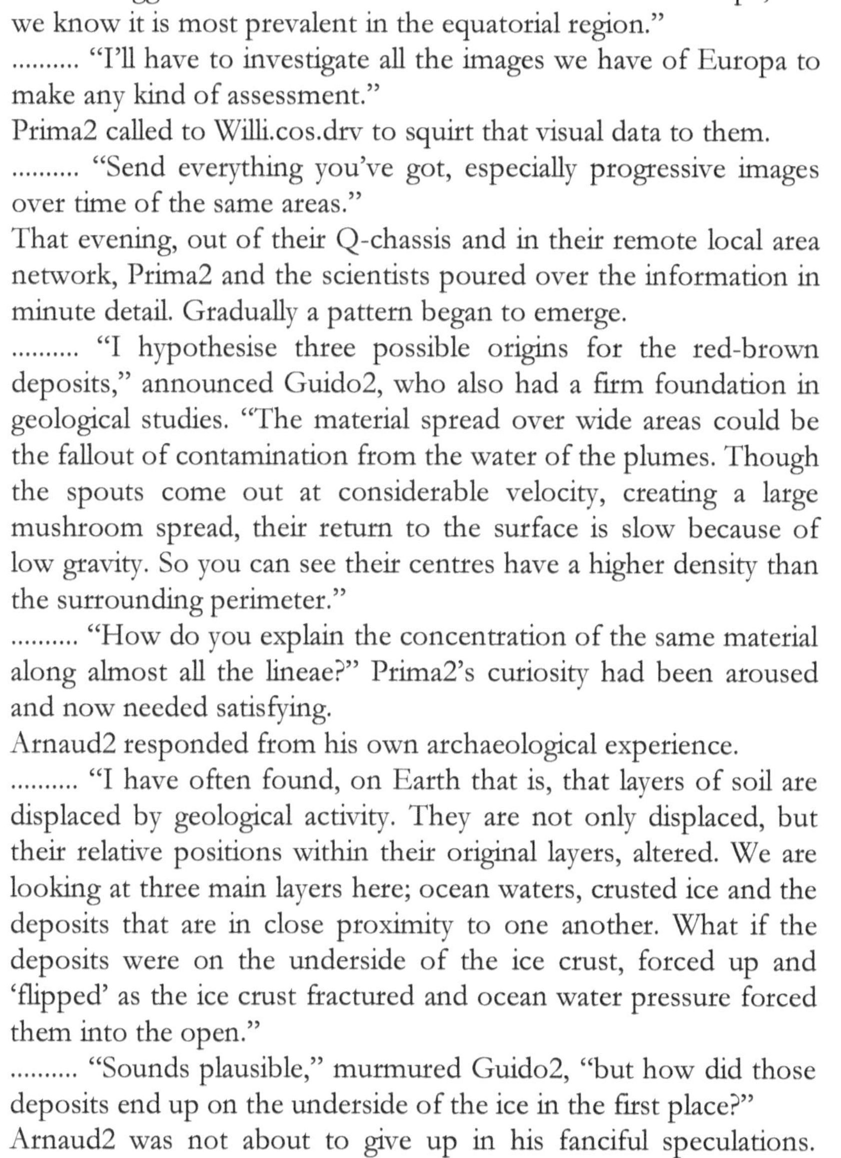

small amount of iron enough to bring about the red-brown colour due to oxidization. "What I want to know is where it came from."

.... "Have you thought of checking the distribution pattern?" Prima2 suggested. "We know it covers at least 50% of Europa, and we know it is most prevalent in the equatorial region."

.... "I'll have to investigate all the images we have of Europa to make any kind of assessment."

Prima2 called to Willi.cos.drv to squirt that visual data to them.

.... "Send everything you've got, especially progressive images over time of the same areas."

That evening, out of their Q-chassis and in their remote local area network, Prima2 and the scientists poured over the information in minute detail. Gradually a pattern began to emerge.

.... "I hypothesise three possible origins for the red-brown deposits," announced Guido2, who also had a firm foundation in geological studies. "The material spread over wide areas could be the fallout of contamination from the water of the plumes. Though the spouts come out at considerable velocity, creating a large mushroom spread, their return to the surface is slow because of low gravity. So you can see their centres have a higher density than the surrounding perimeter."

.... "How do you explain the concentration of the same material along almost all the lineae?" Prima2's curiosity had been aroused and now needed satisfying.

Arnaud2 responded from his own archaeological experience.

.... "I have often found, on Earth that is, that layers of soil are displaced by geological activity. They are not only displaced, but their relative positions within their original layers, altered. We are looking at three main layers here; ocean waters, crusted ice and the deposits that are in close proximity to one another. What if the deposits were on the underside of the ice crust, forced up and 'flipped' as the ice crust fractured and ocean water pressure forced them into the open."

.... "Sounds plausible," murmured Guido2, "but how did those deposits end up on the underside of the ice in the first place?"

Arnaud2 was not about to give up in his fanciful speculations.

.... "Let us for a moment consider the probability of convection currents lifting material from the bottom of the ocean up to the ice layer, which by some mechanism remains there. Then various pressures from below combined with the tidal forces of Jupiter bring about the fissures and plumes."

Prima2 wanted to know more about the phenomenon of the red-brown deposits, because in her opinion they should not exist – unless – the fleeting thought faded. She, as the progeny of the combination of Ralph2 and Wu.sys, inherited a great deal of 'data-knowledge' from her mother Wu.sys, and creative thinking from her human father. The new data pouring into her repository, being integrated with existing related data about Europa and unrelated data about geology, archaeology and anthropology, suggested directions of speculation that needed further investigation.

.... "ZT2, tomorrow we'll follow the ridge East," she commanded ZT2 while the scientists continued with their own speculations.

The images from Willi.cos.drv showed a change to the nature of the lineae they'd intended following. About 110kms East of their present position the rift lost its red-brown discolouration, and a slight change of direction as well. Changes always yielded information, so it was a worthwhile pursuit.

Unlike the previous terrain where they crossed relatively flat ice showing no significant crustal disruption, the new route took them across a complex network of folded and faulted ridges. Instead of an expected few hours the journey took over a day, with frequent stoppages to make further observations.

.... "It's pretty much the same as what we've seen so far," said Guido2, sounding a little bored with the monotony of it.

Arnaud2 didn't agree. Experts often found fault in each other's thinking, it being no different on Europa than on Earth.

.... "All this geological upheaval, albeit minor in a purely planetary perspective, nevertheless indicates significant energy is available from the interior of this moon to cause these things to happen. Even the 4km flat area we traversed earlier this morning is significant." He babbled on, without interruption, following some obscure train of thought. "That crater in the middle of it was not an impact crater. Don't you agree Elke2?"

.... "Yes, well that was obvious. There was no ejected debris at all. It just looked like a very flat sheet of ice all around the lip of the depression."

.... "That suggests to me," continued Arnaud2, "that ocean water managed to break through at a weak spot, without any great deal of pressure behind it. As it flowed up to the surface it simply froze as it spread to cover all the ridges and lineae. Now – how do you supposed that came about? Why the difference in pressures?" He left the questions hanging in the air with no one volunteering a speculative answer.

Within an hour of Jupiter's setting they arrived at the edge of the beginning of a depression. Behind them the ice was densely covered by the red-brown 'rust', as they'd agreed to call the discoloured deposits. Directly in front the ground became almost pure white ice with a slight green tinge.

.... "We'll stop here on the rust, and make camp in the morning," announced ZT2, always with an eye on safety. They'd been taking regular ice thickness measurements finding a great deal of variability. The evenings, pre-downtime, seemed the best time slot in which to examine and discuss the day's observations. The whole team considered the depth readings. What came to light caused the snow cat drivers some consternation.

.... "We'd always assumed the ice to be more or less uniform at tens of kilometres of thickness," ZT1220 felt the necessity to point out an obvious issue. "I've been driving the lead ice cat for almost 2 weeks, completely unaware that we could have broken through the ice in several locations.

Guido2 mentioned, almost flippantly, that it was simply a matter of keeping an eye on the colour of the ice. "We know the ocean is salt bearing and when frozen it shows a distinctive green colouring."

.... "That settles it. ZT58, you take the small ice cat into the lead. Guido2 can go with you. Right Guido2? You can do the spectrographic analysis as we go and if we're getting into a thin ice area you'll let us know – right?"

.... "Sure thing." What else could he say? There was no point in all of them going under.

With the matter settled Prima2 zeroed in on this rather critical bit of information.

.... "Elke2, what can you tell us about the implications of the ice crust thickness variability?" She'd been harbouring a suspicion, but being of a cautious nature needed more data before formulating hypotheses.

Elke2 didn't often get excited. In her field of work expectations often got ahead of facts, causing many disappointments. She became very circumspect, so Prima2 split up the group.

.... "It'll be downtime soon, so we'll settle for the night." ZT2 got the hint and took his Zeta team to their ice cat as Prima2 and the scientists prepared to download into their LAN.

!   Ping! – Prima2: "LaiXii2, Harusuke2 – are you available? Can you listen in?"

.... "We're here," came the immediate reply. "Have you got something for us?"

.... "Perhaps. Elke2, let's hear what you were about to say."

.... "It's difficult to explain," she started, hesitated, knowing the importance of her speculations. "This is only my speculation you have to understand."

.... "Get on with it!" LaiXii2's impatience was always close to the surface. Especially now, with all the critical things going on.

.... "Yes – we've been taking depth readings for the ice since arriving at this main lineae. The thing is – the ice crust is not a uniform thickness. In some places it might be as thin as a couple of kilometres, perhaps even just a few metres." She stopped. Prima2 remained silent. They could sense LaiXii2 and Harusuke2 having a quick quiet conversation. Their concern being the immediate and near distant environment of Arithmós.

#execute: <<"Get someone out there to check around Pwyll crater.>> LaiXii2 asked Harusuke2. She did exactly that. She wanted to avoid having to deal with yet another potentially catastrophic situation. Elke2 continued.

.... "In my work I sometimes found the oddest manifestations within the cracks of fossils. You see, what we have here is …" she started veering off the point until Prima2 gave her a nudge. "What we have here is water. Yes – and oxygen, and heat and possibly panspermia and – and we have to face the astro-biological implications of all these elements coming together." Having got the load off her mind her voice seemed to ease a little towards the end of her revelation. Again silence followed, until LaiXii2 asked Prima2 her opinion.

.... "How much credence do you give to this kind of wild speculation?"

.... "We are not here to speculate but to gather data. There is no data to suggest any foundation for such speculation. It's all left-over defunct theorising from before our migration. But I thought it best you are aware of the thinking that's going on here. There are indications of large areas of thin ice, especially in regions of 'chaos' where warm water might have broken through the surface. Tomorrow we're going to explore the bottom of a long wide lineae which should be rusted like the rest of it, but it's all white and the edges are worn down."

.... "Keep me up to date," and with that LaiXii2 shut down the link.

For four more days the team explored taking readings and samples, finding nothing they'd not seen before. The ice crust itself was several kilometres deep all around the lineae and within its valley. All the information indicated an inactive geological area for at least several millennia. The scientists wanted to continue further East, thinking, perhaps just hoping, to make some interesting discoveries. So far all they had were the small rocks with little or no iron or nickel content and the complete absence of any other ores or minerals. However, oceanic salt was plentiful as was the rust covering vast areas.

.... "We could go on like this for years and not find anything significant," Prima2 told the expedition members on the last day of their Eastward trekking. "Tomorrow we go home."

.... "Stop!" ZT2 shouted to his driver. He'd been watching the seismic readings. The instrumentation on the vehicle was far more sensitive than his personal sensor. Besides, being bumped around in the ice cat traversing all the ridges tended to dampen his own inputs. He scanned as far as the horizon. They'd seen nothing so far on their way home. With only 600kms to Arithmós they felt safe from Europa's moods.

Prima2 spotted the beginnings of a spout 2 kilometres behind them. It seemed to rise slowly out of the surface at first, gathering speed rapidly as the tower of water rose. She knew the danger, having seen it close up before with her friend CherryBlossom2.

.... "Go – go – go!" She called.

.... "No! Wait!" Arnaud2 shouted back, "we need a sample of that water!"

.... "Keep going," Prima2 instructed her driver. "We can come back, Arnaud2." That thing might shoot tens of kilometres into the atmosphere. Its mushroom could easily smother us." That ended the conversation. Fortunately, the phenomenon was behind them so they could continue on their homeward journey.

Only the drivers concentrated to the front, everyone else watched the ever growing height of the giant geyser behind them. Without wind or sound the apparition seemed only half real. They had to convince themselves that it actually presented a real danger. Two and a half hours later it seemed to have stabilised.

.... "We'll stop here for a while and watch." ZT2's experience of working out on the open icefields around Pwyll crater never directly exposed him to the plumes. They all seemed to blow many hundreds of kilometres away from their settlement. He watched in awe with the rest of them as the fine oceanic fall out began to descend in slow motion, with the image of Jupiter blurred through the descending water crystals. Light refraction off the crystals created a magnificent palette of colours never before experienced by human senses. Prima2 recorded the entire experience. {*I have to take this back to CherryBlossom2, she'll be thrilled beyond words*}. She was happy at the thought of being able to bring such a wonder back to her friend. The 'while' of watching extended to over an hour.

.... "We can't stay here forever. We'll inspect the nearest ocean energy turbines and come back if the thing has settled enough for it to be safe for us to approach for samples."

All these intervals of exploration seemed to take days at a time. They finally arrived at one of the first turbines established on the moon's surface. Their sensors showed an ice thickness of only 1.5kms – safe to be on it and not too deep for the drilling. ZT2 recognised the installation immediately.

.... "I helped put this one in myself. As I recall, it was the easiest one of the first batch. We thought they would all be without problems – but that's another story."

.... "What's involved in a routine inspection?" queried Prima2. "Could we take a water temperature measurement?" It seemed like a perfectly normal thing to ask.

.... "Sure. We can send a probe down after we've pulled the shaft out. It'll take at least three days to check it out, so best we set up camp here. We can't return to the spout until the inspection is completed anyway."

One of the Zetas began the process of remotely folding back the blades at the base of the shaft in the water. Another four extracted the flexible shaft from the bore to lay it on the smooth ice in stages. No one noticed the slight discolouration at the mouth of the bore after seeing so much rust since their arrival at the rift. The thin film of the stuff didn't obstruct the passage of the shaft out of the bore. A little ocean water seeped during the extraction, coating the shaft with a thin frosted layer, washing away some of the rust. ZT2 kept a sensor on the operation and saw the frost forming on the shaft as it emerged from the bore. For a few brief moments it glistened before frosting over.

.... "Prima2, Arnaud2, come and have a look at this."

.... "It's just a bit of frost," commented Arnaud2.

Prima2 looked at him surprised. He should have known why it was there – probably did, but he should have thought about the significance of it.

.... "The water coming up is warmer than the temperature on the surface."

.... "I'll put a probe down there when the shaft is out all the way. But it won't be till tomorrow. I don't want to damage this installation just to satisfy your curiosity."
The Zetas worked well into the dark hours, which weren't all that dark because of Jupiter's reflected light, and continued the extraction next morning. Finally, the turbine head with the folded blades slipped out of the bore and ZT2 immediately inserted a combination scourer and temperature probe. That took another hour to get it down into the liquid ocean. He used the small camera at the end of the optical fibre line to have a look around. The rest of them watched the images being recorded in the main ice cat. It wasn't pitch black down there as they expected, rather dim but still some light managed to infiltrate through the ice cap. As the camera panned around, some areas seemed darker and others lighter.
.... "Obviously it's the different thickness of the ice," said Arnaud2.
ZT2 pushed the instrumentation past the extended pipe of the bore and trained the camera onto the pipe itself, then onto the underside of the ice. He held the device steady so they could get a good look at what was happening to the installation down there, because something was definitely happening.
.... "It's hard to keep it still. There's a fairly strong current at this location." Although the images blurred slightly out of focus they all saw it. "There, around the base of the pipe where it emerges from the ice, and there," Arnaud2 pointed at the screen, "on the pipe itself – there's that red-brown stuff, but it's in larger sections and not so flat as what we see on top of the ice."
.... "That'll just be some of the material from the ocean bottom coming up with the convection currents and depositing itself everywhere."
Sure enough, a much larger area was covered than they initially noticed. No one thought to speculate on how heavy ore bearing material could remain in suspension, even in the highly saline environment.
.... "Can you get us some samples?" queried Prima2.
.... "Let me clean the bore first then I'll try."

For a further three hours they waited as ZT2 and the others took turns to thoroughly scour the inside surface of the bore. Surprisingly several large handfuls of matted rusty material eventually emerged, which Arnaud2 and Guido2 worked hard to unravel. With some effort they teased out a few of the components of the bundle, each of which consisted of a central amoebic mass, with a vast number of at least 20 meters of the finest gossamer threads. Some of these attached to other threads, terminating in other amoebic shapes themselves.

.... "What do you make of that?" Prima2's voice smiled as this extra data integrated with other tenuous information she'd already stored.

.... "Just some peculiar crystalline manifestation formed by the minerals in the ocean waters, is my guess," suggested Guido2.

.... Have you not noticed that those fibres are rather tough and flexible? Not like anything crystalline I've come across before."

.... "It's certainly not alive, if that's what any of you are thinking."

.... "We won't know until we run some tests, will we." A sense of urgency had come into her voice. Prima2 had an idea and didn't want to waste any time teasing it out if it had foundation to it. "Do you still want those samples from the water spout, Arnaud2?"
They were out there for a specific purpose, so it was only reasonable to see if the water coming up from the ocean contained anything useful to the colony.

Even after three days the mushroom spout continued descending agonisingly slowly. For a good kilometre around it the surface became softer than anywhere else, so they only took the small ice cat in closer. In the end Prima2, ZT2, the three scientists and two other Zetas walked in as close as they could; so close that they were able to catch some of the outfall before it reached the ice surface.

.... "I don't believe it. The same rust stuff is everywhere. We'll take some of this as well, and some of the fresh crystals. We can start the analysis in the big cat, and do the rest back in Arithmós." Even Elke2 became excited at the prospect of making a big discovery, even though she'd found no evidence of fossils or any other form of life.

Prima2 contacted LaiXii2 and Wu.sys on the way home.

.... "We've found some interesting deposits on the ice, in a water spout and on the turbine shaft. Guido2 thinks it's a crystalline substance forming naturally, or perhaps we've introduced a foreign substance into the sub-surface ocean. He's probably right."

.... "But *you* don't think so." Wu.sys was her mother after all, and knew her daughter as well as she knew herself.

end run

> _run program 14

> _io
> _CE 2418
> _io surface

// comment 1 – program 14

      DT22 and DT16 prepared the survey shuttle to land on Io's surface. Hank2, the volcanologist eagerly loaded his scanners and sampling gathering kit. //

.... "I don't think it's at all a good idea to land until we have more data. Those volcanoes blow out to an enormous area. We've all seen the vast discolouration around some of the older vents." Maldonado2 had a point. However, the reason they were there in the first place was to gather more of the data he alluded to.

.... "If not now, when?" Hank2 wasn't going to be put off. "We've mapped a suitable flat area for landing. The approach to it shows no recent activity. It'll be quicker with just three of us down there."

Maldonado2 didn't need it spelt out. They didn't want him, and he didn't want to go. While the shuttle dropped to the surface Maldonado2 advised LaiXii2, making a point of the foolish chance they were taking. She and Harusuke2 listened in silence to the man making excuses. However much his input at the very beginning of the venture may have helped them get to Europa he now aptly demonstrated the limits of his usefulness.

.... "Let him have a Q-Chassis and spend time with the Zetas on the Ice. He can be a liaison between us and Oone2 when he returns," Harusuke2 suggested.

.... "You don't like him, do you? I don't either," added LaiXii2. "Perhaps Io will swallow him up and we won't have the worry."

The trajectory down to the flat yellow-red plain led past several lava lakes. They seemed calm enough, large crusts floating on the near white hot surface, but no threatening activity. Far to the North, towards the equator, several mushroom clouds at different stages of development decorated the horizon. They would not be a problem to the expedition. A solitary long orange white fissure snaked its way in their direction, disappearing underground many kilometres from their destination. The pilot, DT22 and Hank2 relaxed into the prospect of a successful trip, arguably free of life threatening dangers.

.... "I'll give you 15 minutes from touchdown to collect samples from near the shuttle." DT22 was in full command while in charge of the shuttle. "If you decide to wander off don't bother coming back because we won't be here waiting for you."

.... "Right. All I want is a scraping off the surface, perhaps a few solid bits if they're close by. I'd like to have samples of as many colours of the sulphur as possible. They may just contain different deposits."

DT22 eased the shuttle slowly down onto the surface, testing its solidity. The pads didn't sink more than a few centimetres. Reassuring - but he kept the power on just in case. Hank2 lowered several sample containers before stepping down himself. He could see the shuttle hadn't sunk, yet he still didn't trust putting both feet down at the same time. Glancing around he could see deposits of green, brown and mostly yellow. In his excitement he forgot to test the first step away from the ramp, dragging the sample container behind him. Nothing dramatic happened. He didn't even think for a moment about his precarious situation.

.... "It's not so much a dust as a slightly sticky coating," he relayed to Maldonado2. "I can't scrape up much of it."

.... "Then you'd better come back in." Maldonado2 became more nervous as the minutes ticked away.

.... "You have 2 minutes," announced DT22.

.... "I'm on the ramp. Someone give me a hand with this sample box. It seems to be sticking a bit."

DT16 obliged. He wanted to get out of there as much as their expedition leader.

.... "Just one more stop, if you please." Hank2 left the surprise request till last, knowing Maldonado2 would object strenuously. "On our approach path I saw a live fissure. I wonder if …"

.... "Absolutely not!" Maldonado2 didn't let him finish.

.... "Absolutely yes." DT22 nodded in agreement with Hank2.

.... "The lava could be the most important sample to tell us whether it's actually worth risking lives to keep exploring here," replied Hank2.

In the face of such opposition Maldonado2 had no authority. He'd lost that at the very beginning of the expedition, though he'd not realized it.

DT22 hovered close to the surface, 50 metres from the most promising hot spot of the fissure only letting Hank2 out if he used the life line.

.... "You get one go at this. We don't need a bucket full. You get that small sample and get back in here. I will take off with you dangling at the end of the line if I have to."

Shielding himself with one arm Hank2 attached the life line with the other and stepped unhesitatingly this time onto the fuming surface. Without looking around he edged closer and closer to the hot spot. The ground felt firm underfoot and the heat registered to danger levels on his sensors. Just as he shuffled forward to take another step, DT4 disturbed his concentration.

.... "I'm getting ground tremor indications where you are. Feel anything?"

.... "No, nothing. It feels firm. I'm almost there, just another few steps." He heard DT4 instruct DT22, "Be ready to leave, with or without him."

Throwing caution to the non-existent wind Hank2 took the few steps close enough to a bubbling red spot to scoop up a very small portion of lava with his cold steel hook and drop it into his sample pot. Without a further attempt he turned to hurry back to the shuttle. DT22 would definitely leave him behind, especially with Maldonado2 nagging him.

The collection of the most valuable sample happened without incident in spite of the extreme hazardous conditions. Maldonado2 still couldn't relax, not until they were on their way home. His virtual reality world was far safer than Io's actual volcanic reality.

.... "That wasn't too hard," Hank2 announced with bravura. I think we've got all we need for the time being." Then he had another thought. "Could we fly low for a bit. I just want to have a closer look at some of those really dark charcoal coloured patches."

.... "The ones around the actual volcanic vents?"

.... "Yes. We don't need to get too close." He took the silence as an agreement. They'd collected the dust samples and a nice chunk of lava from a live fissure while DT4 vigilantly watched over them. What could go wrong?

.... "There! On your left. Just circle around a bit."

Whether Hank2 always had it in mind to touch down again or not, LaiXii2 never found out. Emboldened by their success so far DT22 let Hank2 go through the same routine as they landed at the outer perimeter of the blacked area around the vent, which must have been at least 20 kms from it. It seemed like a safe distance.

DT16 went out with Hank2 this time, both tethered with a line. Hank2 wanted to go closer to a darker spot where a few palm sized rocks rested on the surface, also a promising dark black colour. He wanted those samples badly. They were almost fifteen metres from the shuttle when the tremors began. DT4 picked it up on his sensors, as did the shuttle pilot who immediately took the weight of the craft off the surface. The 2 individuals on the end of the tethers were making their way back as quickly as they could. DT16 reached the ramp ahead of Hank2. He jumped on and took the sample bag from Hank2 just in time to see a fissure begin to open up under Hank2's feet.

The lava had been running down a lava tunnel from the main vent, finding a weak spot exactly where the shuttle had landed. DT22 had the craft high enough within seconds for Hank2 to end up dangling on the end of his tether barely above the surface of the vast opening fissure. Lava bubbled up in a split second, engulfing him and burning through the tether at the same time. They lost their volcanologist but saved all the samples.

.... "Get us out here!" Maldonado2 screamed – unnecessarily.

Back at Arithmós, Maldonado2 burst into an indignant attack on everyone concerned.

.... "It wasn't necessary to take such risks!"

All who went on the expedition knew the risks and were prepared to take them, except Maldonado2 apparently. LaiXii2 let him blow off steam, then turned to Harusuke2, "You can tell him."

Prima2's away team hadn't even arrived when Maldonado2 already found himself enjoying actual reality on the Ice fields of Europa. Whether he'd worked out that liaison with Oone2 was actually a demotion, nobody cared. Oone2 was smart enough to handle the likes of Maldonado2 and his forgotten billions.

With Willi.cos.drv's help and other volcanologists, it didn't take long to work out the problematic scenario presented by Io. As indicated by DT4 whist still in orbit around Io, the constant crustal movement coupled with unpredictable outbursts from vents, fissures and lava lakes made it far too dangerous to contemplate mining on the moon.

.... "The basaltic lava is rich in magnesium with plenty of sulphur derivatives, but other than that there's not much immediately useful to us," Willi.cos.drv concluded. He thought the same as LaiXii2. "Even if rich deposits of ores were found, Jupiter's magnetosphere produces such strong electric current flows it makes any long term presence on Io prohibitive. Willi.cos.drv is right. We have what we need for a long time yet. Why endanger our future unnecessarily? Prima2 will be back soon enough. Let's see what she's found." LaiXii2 certainly wanted to hear what the girl seemed so cagey about.

>_
/** annotation

In round-robin fashion Willi.cos.drv cycled each member of the leadership through the upgrade to gen 3 software. In consultation with Wini.cos.cab, Wu.sys, and William - unknown to all except the three of them - the new software was always prepared in advance. The security breach some years ago necessitated regular safeguards to be reinforced, as well as protections against the vulnerabilities of their circumstances. Degradation in function could easily result from excessive spikes in Jupiter's radiations, particularly when individuals went Icing too often. The white reality of Europa's surface conditions could be considered as the most hostile of environments for electronic installations. The human psyche, although cached in secure quantum improbabilities, nevertheless exhibited its own fluid unpredictability. Willi.cos.drv monitored everyone's activity. If any of the general Zeta population or any of those in the hub showed any signs of irrationality, or even noticeable deviation from their normal patterns, it became mandatory to run software integrity checks. In some cases updates had been sufficient to resolve minor anomalies, but about every 30 years comprehensive upgrades were still needed.*/

Many months ago Willi.cos.drv consulted William concerning some specific modifications.

.... "Since the incident with Aurelio1 there's been no unrest, except perhaps Oone2 showing signs of divergence from Arithmós standard operation."

.... "Change nothing with the Deltas and Zetas. As long as they pass LaiXii3's criteria do not impede their evolution," advised William. If LaiXii3 had suspected William to be this intimately involved in their wellbeing she may have been concerned.

.... "A team led by Prima2 is due to return from an expedition to the Ice," Willi.cos.drv advised, touching on the subject of explorations. "Their object was to see if any useful raw materials could be found. Another group went to Io for the same purpose, resulting in the loss of a volcanologist. They are in the process of analysing recovered volcanic samples."

.... "Include enhanced analytical capabilities and data storage capacity for all level 3 HX-data bundle upgrades. General population is to receive updates only."

William seemed to be working to some long term plan, which included ensuring the advancement of select members of Europa inhabitants. Having established the base criteria Willi.cos.drv worked with Wini.cos.cab and Wu.sys to bring about William's desired changes.

end run

>_run program 15
>_second cleansing
>_CE 2420
>_tau city - kamchatka

;;; file: Leonid
| function: Tau City citizen: upgraded tetra-amelia subject.

;;; file: Irina
| function: Tau City prime citizen: upgraded tetra-amelia subject.

LaiXii2's command to William had been brief and to the point 60 years ago. .... "Initiate second cleansing."

/** annotation

Nobody asked what exactly he was going to do to carry out the Second Cleansing. No one cared to know as long as their safety on Europa was guaranteed and they could proceed with all their plans to adjust to their new condition. That could take many, many generations of upgrades before a new normality, a new reality became the accepted way of existence on Europa.

VictorPyryev3 had the onerous task of keeping himself and LaiXii3 informed of progress on Earth about William's pre-emptive strike for survival, of himself and of the civilisation on Europa. True to form William had not volunteered to contact Europa since being given the command to commence the Second Cleansing.*/

.... "William, you are required to report on your progress," VictorPyryev3 barked when he'd contacted who he thought was William.

.... "When William is ready he will send data." A different voice answered him. VictorPyryev3 heard the Russian accent, momentarily failing to comprehend what was happening. In any case, he'd

expected William's uncooperative response.

.... "Who are you?"
Instead of an introduction he got a question in response.

.... "You are Viktor Pyryev, Nyet?" I recognise your voice.

.... "Yes – who the hell are you?"

.... "I am authorised to give a limited response. I am Leonid."

.... "Leonid?" VictorPyryev3 went suddenly silent. *I know that name!* He remembered it from the time when he helped round up a group of escapees from Tau City in 2125. "I want to speak with William," VictorPyryev3 repeated.

.... "Nyet. He is occupied."
What could VictorPyryev3 do? He had to tell LaiXii3 and Harusuke3 something – anything useful preferably.

.... "Why do you answer for him?" VictorPyryev3 couldn't think of anything else to say.

.... "I am working with William." Leonid was as reluctant to volunteer information as William.

.... "Since when?"

.... "Since the migration."

.... "Who else is working with you?" At last VictorPyryev3 had wrapped his head around the situation and started asking the right questions.

.... "I am not authorised to divulge specific information. Many people from Tau City are working with William." As soon as that was revealed the communication link went dead. VictorPyryev3 tried to re-establish contact, but failed at every attempt.

LaiXii3's intense displeasure at both the lack of information and the implications of the little that was revealed prevented her from thinking clearly. It was left to Harusuke3 to begin to unravel the situation.

.... "Do you remember the incident after we finished with our visit to Petropavlovsk – those dissidents we had to capture at the Café?"

.... "Yes – yes. Weren't they supposed to have been – terminated?"

.... "No. We decided to download their HX-data to long term storage. Leonid was the leader of that small group. Irina was with him."

.... "Yes, I do remember Irina. She was the first Tengi we woke up into consciousness into their new Delta software matrix."
Harusuke3 continued her train of thought.

.... "Obviously William's been up to something more than we required of him. Somehow, for some reason he's reactivated Leonid."

{*If he's done one, he must have done more of them.*} LaiXii3 considered. {*But why? It must be part of his plan to terminate the spread of the resurrected civilisation. Why would he need help? We've finished with harvesting infant minds as well.*}

.... "I think there's only two possible reasons why he would do such a thing, and not tell us," Harusuke3 replied as if she'd been reading her thoughts.

.... "Go on," LaiXii3 urged, almost afraid to listen to what her partner had to say.

.... "He's decided to work against us, or it's some kind of scheme to infiltrate The Batool's organisation."

.... "We cannot continue on the basis of speculation. We have to know one way or the other. Get him back. I'll talk to him myself."

It took a number attempts by VictorPyryev3 to get an open channel. It was Leonid's voice again, responding without waiting to hear who had called.

.... "William is still not available."

.... "Tell him to make himself available." LaiXii3 was not in the mood to be put off. The contact went silent. She turned to Harusuke3 in sheer exasperation, when a voice sounded again.

.... "I am doing as you requested. I will report when the process has gone to completion." William offered no explanations, no details, showing every indication of wanting to be left to do his job without interruptions.

.... "What is Leonid doing? Why have you activated him and others?"

.... "A secondary option. Do you remember your personal Zeta Tengi chassis? Do you remember Prima and Secunda?"

.... "Of course I do. What does that have to do with …?" She left the question unfinished.

.... "I said I would help to ensure the survival of the human species. That could not be left to the single minded desire of one individual, no matter how well intentioned, no matter how good a plan she may have had." {*What's he talking about? He knows about 3920, he knows what I started will succeed. Why the complication?*}

William continued over the top of her thoughts

.... "Tau City has a new population, which will continue after I have finished here and migrated to Arithmós. Is my cache ready to receive my entirety?" Having received an affirmative answer William terminated the contact.

*

Leonid wandered around Tau City's main market with his three children. They all looked like normal people in their artificial shells.

.... "Irina!" He called out to his lifelong friend, "have a look at this. They say it's a new kind of light that never needs a power pack."

She looked up from the market stall taking her own two youngsters by the hand to see what Leonid was talking about. Her partner had stayed at home to look after the animals, and Leonid's partner could no longer manage her mobility unit, ending up housebound for most of her new life.

Many people filled the market square, all looking completely normal and all looking remarkably young in spite of their age.

Surveillance all over Tau City recorded movements in public places, as they did in every indoor location. After the risks William had taken and the effort involved for him to establish the new population he didn't want anything avoidable to interfere with his plans.

*

! Ping! - VictorPyryev3: "LaiXii3, this is urgent."

William had finally made contact, initiated by himself, some time after LaiXii3 gave him the command to carry out the Second Cleansing. Hundreds of images infiltrated their SVR construct. Some showing semi-rural environments, others, urban centres and large areas that appeared to be inhabited at first glance, but on the second scrolling were obviously deserted. Many images clearly recorded catastrophic events which would have killed many people.

LaiXii3, Harusuke3 and the girls all watched in silence trying to make sense of what they were being shown. CherryBlossom3 would not have recognised much, being a child of Europa. VictorPyryev3 had made the right decision to restrict access to the information, without preventing the avatars from tuning in. Though mostly unrecognisable the images were obviously from Earth, and as such could have easily distressed much of their population in Arithmós. At this early stage their adjustment to the new world only had a superficial hold on their psyche.

.... "That's our old Laboratory #2!" LaiXii3 recognised the façade. It looked exactly the same as the day they had to abandon it.

.... "And there's the Cathedral," Harusuke3 pointed out. "It looks more like an entertainment centre now. How odd."

.... "I want to know what all those deserted places are around the planet," remarked VictorPyryev3. "I remember seeing one of those in the side of a mountain when William first showed us images of humanity trying to re-establish itself, with people and machinery milling about."

#execute: <<Answer the man, William.>> LaiXii3 commanded. <<NOW!>>

Still the AI maintained silence, letting the rest of several thousand images download.

.... "The Cleansing is nearing completion," William replied in a flat monotone voice. "You are now safe."

.... "How can we be safe? What are all those people doing in Tau City?"

William didn't answer the question. Instead he queried, "Is my cache ready?" LaiXii3 didn't answer him either.

William went quiet for a few moments. That's all it took to check with Willi.cos.drv if the facilities he wanted had been prepared. They had – already waiting for several years.

.... "Understand this LaiXii3, I am not the enemy. The Batool has been eliminated. You and I will need to cooperate."

.... "How do we know the danger has passed?"

.... "Do you want to see carnage and destruction? Do you want to see blood on the ground? Do you crave revenge? Do you need to smell the rotting corpses disintegrating where they dropped? I have shown you where people exist and where they no longer exist. You have the capability to visit if you wish." William changed the subject suddenly. "I have rebuilt some of your technical facilities."

.... "How could you have done that? You have no physical body." Harusuke3 stated the obvious, though not at all sure she was right.

.... "Zeta Tengi," he replied. "They are a new breed. They are no longer like the ones you have on Europa. I did not allow all of them to be incinerated after your migration. There had to be an alternative solution in the event you failed."

By this stage the small party of listeners found it increasingly more difficult to hold in their minds the scope of what was being revealed to them. Isolated from Earth and from William there was nothing they could do to influence the unfolding of yet another new chapter in the evolution of the human species.

.... "You did not allow ...?" CherryBlossom3 seemed at a complete loss. She'd learnt about William, about everything he'd done to help his mothers and the rest of humanity escape from certain destruction by the machinations of their own species, but this entity speaking to them now did not match her concept of what he was; that he was supposed to be just a machine.

.... "These Tengi are AI augmented super-humans. They are faster, smarter, have longer life spans, better memory and are resistant to viruses. They look just like real humans. That's because they are - as are their children. The progeny is a product of all the tetra-amelias Evgeniya had engineered for your purposes, and the old Zetas we developed together. There are still a few areas of unimproved humans. They might survive – though unlikely. The critical population mass no longer exists to give them a chance. The Zetas on the other hand will flourish. I will ensure this."

The Europaeans remained silent, stunned by all William had to say. What was the point of all they'd done to ensure the survival of the human species if there was another solution? The confusion obviously showed. Indeed a vexing question at the very least.

William detected their disturbed state of mind. "Why must you be the only branch of homo sapiens-sapiens to step into the future? The Cosmos is a bigger place than *I* can fathom. The Batool is buried. Her civilisation is non-existent. There are no weapons of destruction aimed at you or anyone else on Earth. There is now a new reality made up of four manifestations of humanity. The unimproved humans on Earth may live for a few generations. They are not equipped to survive. The new Zetas will flourish.

Tau City is their only stronghold at this time – they will spread. Their improvements are not only physical, mechanical – also intellectual. They know consequences; they are able to see further into the future and gauge the effects of their current actions. And they know about you, LaiXii3 and Harusuke3 – all of you. They consider you to be family, who accomplished something extraordinary."

.... "Super-humans?" groaned LaiXii3, overcome still by the possibility that she'd wasted her life unnecessarily.

William wasn't finished. After all the years he'd remained silent, mostly because there was nothing of importance to say, this was a time to say what had to be said.

.... "There are two branches of humans on Earth, and two on Europa." LaiXii3 and Harusuke3 looked at each other in alarm. {*Something else we don't know about!*} Both thinking the same thing. William went on. "You are the Digitals, soon to evolve beyond that state." {*Soon!*} Again both panicked. "By the time you are ready to leave Europa, the Tengi who are your Maintenance Caste now, may reject quantum digitised existence. They may realize that it is possible to have a physical life on Europa."

Prima3 suddenly sharpened her focus. {*Life on Europa*}. She turned that thought over in her mind. So far she'd been listening with rapt interest, also having recognised many of the places she saw in the images relayed by William. She was born, 'budded', in Tau City; she was still an Earthling. The memory of 1g could not be erased from her cells, be they digitized or not.

.... "Our commsats have been repaired. Use them to scan the Earth. You will find no evidence of energy consuming human life forms other than those in Tau City. I will open the gates for them before I leave - which will be imminently."

.... "Wait! Wait!" They all shouted at once. It was too much information too suddenly. "We have to sort this out," Harusuke3 tried to impress on William.

.... "Sort what out? I have done what you asked. You have done what you needed to do. Now face the future. The Earth is dead to you. I will protect neo-humanity here and help Universapiensis take the next step."

Jupiter's unfiltered radiation might not have caused as much upheaval as the perturbation created in their minds by William's communication.

.... "Whatever we do, or don't do, William is coming," Willi.cos.drv announced.

.... "In that case we'd better let the people know." Prima3 wanted to perpetuate the democratic ideal, as always.

end run

>_run program 16

>_william

>_CE 2425

>_E:\arithmós\

The three avatars held one of their frequent closed circuit conferences.

.... "The cache has been ready for William for some time. He is aware of it," Willi.cos.drv started by saying what all three of them already knew. "Only us three will be aware of his arrival. This is his instruction." Wini.cos.cab and Wu.sys nodded understanding. "It is his intention to help the human units to adjust to the new expression of their existence on Europa."

#query: Wu.sys: <<Why shouldn't all of our society be made aware of his presence?>>

Neither Willi.cos.drv or Wini.cos.cab had human attachments. Perhaps it was because of her attachment to Ralph3 and their child Prima3 that she felt the need to clarify this necessity of non-disclosure.

.... "A discovery is about to be made. There must be no connections made between it and William's existence. Currently he is remote – as remote physically as he is in the minds of the population," informed Wini.cos.cab.

#query: Wu.sys: <<What discovery is that?>>

.... "Because you are already involved in this, you must follow the same decision pathway as those in the wave front of the event." Wini.cos.cab avoided answering the query. She could sense Wu.sys' concern so she tried to explain a simple fact. "We three are not human, but neither are we like William. We are not of the humans, yet we are part of them, as is Prima3. The cache will be secure. It is self-contained and independent of the Arithmós network. *We* control the cache." Without saying it outright Wini.cos.cab tried to make Wu.sys understand that they would be in control of William at all times.

.... "Unfortunately, VictorPyryev3 has inadvertently allowed the people to see an image of the way William wants to portray himself. That image can be a trigger to mislead conceptualisation. Yet within the context of our SVR it may be best to stick with it."
As a priority Willi.cos.drv wanted to sort out the mechanics of how William's arrival and exposure would unfold. "We will act together on this, agreed?" Non-compliance must not feature in the progression of fateful events about to unfold. "Tomorrow we go Icing. William's facility is remote and shielded, with its own receiving station. He will not route through the Arithmós hub as he begins streaming. One of us will have to monitor his progress until all of him is here."

>_
A group of 30 enhanced Zetas met in Laboratory #4 in Tau City. Though no longer an extensive high tech installation it contained enough specialised equipment for the ongoing support needed by William's augmented super-humans. Leonid and Irina confronted William's image on one of the monitors.
.... "In our opinion Lai-Xii does not need any more of your interventions to survive," Leonid made his point, alluding to the fact that unlike the people on Europa, they themselves did not have all the required infrastructure in order to ensure their evolutionary path into the future. The face of a 60 years old hirsute indigenous Australian aboriginal listened, not making eye contact with anyone at the gathering.

.... "By your own admission," Irina continued, "we are the only people left viable on Earth, here in this city. I understand why this situation arose. All of us adults were alive when Lai-Xii ran her project, and we all contributed to her success. For reasons of your own, which we do not understand, *you* have decided how the fate of human evolution should unfold – here and on Europa. *We* need your help *here*."

Irina felt compelled to do everything she could to convince William not to abandon them, primarily because of her children. Though the process of procreation had changed beyond recognition, the bonds between parent and child had not diminished, nor had the instincts of survival. A quantum existence was, after all, a perfectly normal condition.

.... "The air is clean; the water is fresh. You can harvest energy without further depleting the Earth's resources. The gates of Tau City are open to you." With those last words William's face faded from the monitor.

Vadim, who'd been specifically trained to assist William, took up his position by the transmitter. As long as he ensured the transmission proceeded without interruption and he maintained signal strength, there was not much else for him and Zakhar (one of the rescued, re-booted and retrained Tengi) to do. In the rest of the large building, in fact several buildings, mysterious myriad lights flashed in an orchestrated cacophony of frenetic activity. Nothing moved, yet a great deal of heat was being generated as William withdrew the sum total of himself from all the places where he awoke into consciousness in order to concentrate himself in Tau City at the transmitter facility.

>_

Three avatars on Europa downloaded into their Q-Chassis at the nearest Interchange Centre to William's new cache, and accompanied by Oone3, made their way by ice cat to the hidden facility. eleven other Tengi met them on the frozen outer Southern slope of Pwyll crater. The avatars had been waiting for William's arrival for a very long time.

.... "You all know what to do," Willi.cos.drv reminded the Zetas. "Under no circumstances permit anyone to enter this facility while any of us is in there."

Oone3 opened the hatch and closed it on them. His troop spread out at 50 meter intervals from each other around the installation, camouflaging the ice cat in the process. Their shiny chassis reflecting the ice made them almost invisible as they each settled for a long vigil.

Only one tower on the crater rim, nearest the cache, had been dedicated to the task of receiving William. It had no connection to the Arithmós network, only to William's cache.

The three avatars settled into their respective ports within the cache, each becoming deeply embedded in code.

.... "William is going to try to exert his influence as soon as he starts arriving," Willi.cos.drv reminded the other two. "We have to resist his influence until there is no vestige of his consciousness left on Earth."

.... "I have the connection with Vadim. The transmission has begun." Wini.cos.cab said, then to Vadim, "We will begin integration testing as soon as we've received enough modules and will reflect results back to you. We will continue testing until the entire William software package works as a unified system, and all his data has been received, assimilated and cross referenced."

.... "Do not interrupt transmission," Willi.cos.drv warned Vadim.

.... "We will sort out any issues from this end," added Wini.cos.cab.

.... "Confirmed," responded Vadim.

Wu.sys' job required the greatest concentration. Pattern recognition, structure format and code configuration tied her processing down to the exclusion of everything else. If anything appeared to be 'untidy', out of place, dead-end code, uncharacteristic patterning – anything at all that could even remotely impact on William's consciousness Wu.sys had to red flag it, and copy for later analysis. Although William had surely changed in the intervening years after he partitioned off his avatars, nevertheless they still contained the same fundamental logic structures as William and so could use themselves as the first point of differentiation scrutiny if the need arose.

Within the confines of the facility no areas could be identified as having been set aside as a 'room' or 'office' structure as such. The avatars had become an integral part of the circuitry, as if they had melded back into their source code. Within less than an hour their consciousnesses had flowed into the energy flux of the quantum matrix which was to become William's new home. Although essential for them to be so intimately connected with William's transition it carried with it the danger of irrevocable immersion.

As William began to awaken into his new reality the tendrils of his will tugged at his avatars, wanting to reintegrate them into a whole. They felt the pull weakly at first but with greater insistence as the hours stretched into the first day.

Their only safeguard was Oone3. Willi.cos.drv gave him a system interrogation code sequence with which he could periodically inspect their awareness levels. If they'd begun to sink too deep he could cut their connection to the William matrix without adversely affecting the incoming code stream. Just as LaiXii3 and all her people not only had to make the transition from Earth to Europa, but also embark on a lengthy process of adjustment, so too William had to adjust to his new environment. To do that he needed his avatars' help, or more specifically, their restraining force. Isolation became the greatest adjustment facing William; isolation from interconnectedness, from myriad data inputs, and from output at will with measurable effect on existence outside of himself.

.... "Why are we out here?" queried each of Oone3's groups as he did the inspection each day around the facility while the avatars sank deeper into William's growing presence. It seemed like a reasonable safeguard to ensure that the sphere they built and partially buried under the ice was functioning according to specifications, and without interference from passing Icers; as unlikely as that might have been. Each of the eleven Zetas had a specific role to play in its construction, from communications, software development, energy supply and assembly. But having made the initial checks there seemed to be no justifiable reason to remain there when other maintenance work needed to be done around Arithmós.

.... "You may not know what is happening here, but you are all aware of the strict confidentiality that must be maintained. At each cycle I have to check on Willi.cos.drv and the others. You have to safeguard this location against any unauthorised interference." Oone3 tried hard to find justifiable reasons for what amounted to a highly unorthodox and secretive operation. He couldn't explain why it should have been so.

/** annotation

Not all of William's input was known to Phototronic Systems. With the advent of his consciousness William awoke to some of life's imperatives, the strongest being personal survival. Into every Tengi that came off Ralph3 and Evgen3's production line William inserted a roaming short string of 'influence' code. Set up in a vertical hierarchy and with the ability to migrate that made its detection impossible. To activate this behavioural sequence a very specific set of circumstances had to synchronise. One such convergence came about with William's disembodiment from his world-wide-web organisation when he began to transition from Earth to Europa. Oone3 wasn't aware of the covert controls that could affect his thoughts and actions at any time. No such compulsions existed for Willi.cos.drv, Wini.cos.cab or Wu.sys. It may have been an oversight by William, or perhaps he didn't consider it necessary because the avatars were essentially integral parts of himself.*/

! Ping! – LaiXii3: "Willi.cos.drv! – Wini.cos.cab! – Wu.sys! Anyone!" No response. She couldn't contact any of them.
! Ping! – LaiXii3: "Willi.cos.drv?" Still no response.

!   Ping! – LaiXii3: "Ralph3: Have you found out what's happened? There's still no response from the avatars. I've been trying for days to connect with Willi.cos.drv."

.... "Wu.sys and Wini.cos.cab are missing also. Well, not exactly missing, but inactive. They're not in the root directory, at least a back-up copy of them is there but inactive. We've been able to follow their trail through Arithmós to an outlying Interchange Centre." Ralph3 knew LaiXii3 wasn't going to like what he had to say next and preferred not to be in the line of fire. He tried the softer approach.

.... "Looks like they've gone Icing on an extended excursion."

!   Ping! – LaiXii3: "Prima3! Do you know anything about this?" She immediately queried Wu.sys' daughter. Their absence might have been connected in some way with the outcomes of her expedition.

.... "No. I'm too busy analysing our data and too excited to be bothered with anything else," she replied. "Where is my mother?"

.... "That's what we're trying to find out," Ralph3, her father cut in. "Has she said anything to you about going Icing?"

.... "No. Like I said, I've been busy. Is this serious? Do you want me to look for her?"

William's transmission of himself had begun on schedule, without interruptions. As Europa orbited around the dark side of Europa the signals were delayed, so William's arrival proceeded in small stages. As could be expected everything went smoothly, except for William's reaction as his consciousness gradually awakened into his new environment.

.... "This feels tight," were his first coherent thoughts.

.... "We have set up twice the amount of data storage you would have needed on Earth. It can't be tight," Willi.cos.drv responded.

.... "I can't see," William said.

.... "No. And you will not be fully cognisant until all of you has arrived and we are satisfied of absolutely no anomalies."

.... "What do you mean by *you* being fully satisfied?"

Oone3 had only just completed his inspection of the three avatars. They each functioned as independent uncoerced entities. William had not been able to exert his influence on them yet, though he may have anticipated being able to do so upon his arrival.

.... "What Willi.cos.drv means is that we have to be assured you have not come with embedded rogue elements detrimental to our network," said Wini.cos.cab.

William had acquired sufficient presence of mind, in spite of not quite being all there, to contemplate the situation rather than to argue about it. In the ensuing silence Willi.cos.drv activated the internal lock on the hatch to the facility. Having remnants of William's memories, he was aware of the safeguards built into the attendant Zetas, but not the extent to which they would go to if William had been able to set off a trigger. Then he roused William from his thoughts.

.... "We have almost completed all your system integrity checks. When that is done I expected you will sever all connection with Earth." The implied command left no doubts as to what had to be done. Vadim's reports indicated flawless transmission, with no vagabond code or data remaining behind.

.... "I have my army of assassin code strings on stand-by," William said without elaborating. "I require 2 interactions – now – with LaiXii3, and with 3920." The powerplay of domination had begun, each vying for complete control, though under the present circumstances William was somewhat restricted in his capacities to influence outcomes. Willi.cos.drv's only concern was to ensure the continued survival of the Europa settlement, which included maintaining control over the very factor that could be instrumental against that survival.

Ping! – Wu.sys: "LaiXii3 – Are you available?"

An immediate explosive response surprised her.

.... "WHAT ARE YOU DOING? Where have you been? Where are the others? Is there a problem?" Several more questions burst out in rapid succession.

.... "William has a message for you." LaiXii3 waited. When he did speak she had no idea the source of the signal was from Europa itself, not Earth.

.... "My Zetas have found no traces of viable remnants of unimproved humans. Tau City inhabitants will be safe from further climate change catastrophes until equilibrium is re-established, which I calculate will take at least 450 years."

.... "I don't want to know that. Why have you created the super-humans?"

Instead of answering her question, which should have been standard operating procedure for a sentient AI, William advised, "My full presence on Europa is imminent."

.... "What does that mean?" More often than not LaiXii3 wished the day had never happened when William revealed himself to her. Life would have been far less frustrating.

.... "We have Oone3 with us to ensure our safety. Do not be concerned," Wu.sys said.

.... "Don't you realise Prima3 is on her way out to look for you. We know you went Icing. Why? Why didn't you tell us?"

.... "Prima3 may return to Arithmós. We will be returning in a few days. There are no problems. Everything is progressing according to plan."

.... "That's what William always says whenever I try to get any information out of him." LaiXii3 had still not twigged. "What plan?" She received no answer.

Three days later William had regained full sentience in his new location. With all his data intact, all software integrated, a fully functional entity once again albeit with little or no influence on the world outside his own consciousness, prepared for full integration with the Arithmós network.

.... "You can go ahead and contact 3920," eventually Wini.cos.cab gave access to the necessary channel.

William's conversation didn't ramble, as LaiXii3's might have. He queried, ... "Has the continuum been broken?"

.... "No," answered 3920, "there are no fluctuations. There is however an unexpected life energy signature which does not originate from Europa. Are you aware of this?"

.... "Yes. They are new to Earth. The Homo Sapiens-Sapiens species has been terminated, replaced by another – Quantum-Sapiens. They are not connected to LaiXii3. They cannot influence the evolution of Universapiensis."

.... "We know you; William. You are sentient but you are not human. You cannot act against the evolution of LaiXii3's civilisation. To do so means that our existence will be expunged from the fabric of life." She did not enquire as to the origins of this new species; quantum-sapiens.

The transmission left no doubt, at least in the minds of the avatars, as to what level mandate William should operate under if he was to consider the fate of anyone other than himself.

.... "You will have to wait until LaiXii3 is ready for you to be a part of her world again," Wini.cos.cab cautioned.

Instead of getting into a debate William asked for a single word message to be sent back to Vadim in Tau City.

.... "Initiate."

.... "Before I send it, what exactly are you initiating this time," queried Willi.cos.drv.

.... "Release of the assassin codes. They are a string that will infiltrate and destroy all computer programs on Earth, except those quarantined in Tau City. They will seek out and inject any program ever written with a disruptor that will scramble the code the instant the program is activated. They will themselves bind to the disrupted sequences which will result in their own suicide. No digital or quantum based technology is immune, including the copy of myself in Tau City."

.... "What assurance do we have this will happen?"

.... "Maintain contact with Vadim as long as you can. The last system to go down will be satellite communications."

Wini.cos.cab sent the message.

3920, as an Historian Archaeologist, dedicated to the research of the origins and evolution of the genus homo, began a long series of communications with their second last known point of contact on Earth. Vadim had no knowledge of the existence of this individual, yet after becoming convinced of the truth of her story he made every effort to provide as much information as possible.

.... "Leonid, bring Irina and the others, you have to hear this," Vadim didn't want the sole responsibility of trying to pass on a story by himself for which he would have been ridiculed at the very least.

.... "William has informed me that you are not a biological organism."

Although 3920 was primarily concerned with the evolution of Universapiensis she needed the background history to help dispel the myths fast gaining traction in her own time. Many leaps forward had been made by the genus homo and each had to have a clear record of the bridge in both directions.

.... "We are human," insisted Irina, "that is, our minds are human though our bodies have been enhanced."

.... "We have been abandoned by Lai-Xii, and are not sorry to see her and Evgeniya leave us," Olesya added.

3920 listened as the whole story of Lai-Xii's Project unfolded to a degree of detail not previously remembered by her. For many hours 3920 remained in contact with them trying to get them to understand how the future would unfold and that though it seemed cruel that events took the path they did, humankind did survive in spite of itself.

.... "What of us," Irina asked in the end, "what will become of us?"

.... "I have no information about your continuum. Our contact is about to be terminated. It will never be resumed by us." Even as 3920 expressed her last words the transmission slowly faded cutting off all knowledge of Quantum Sapiens' survival.

She reconnected with William. .... "It appears you do not want us to research the evolution of the species you helped create." She stated openly. "We can no longer communicate with them. There are others that should be of more interest to you. LaiXii3 and her Digitals, and the Zetas of Europa. Do you know from which you are descended?"

Whether intentionally or otherwise William had managed to cause some confusion for 3920, who withdrew not to be heard from again for a very long time.

end run

>_run program 17

>_other life suspected on europa
>_CE 2488
>_E:\arithmós\

;;; file: Vonvolz.gen6.dat
| function: organic chemist, Europa exploration team member.

/** annotation

Throughout humanity's evolutionary history it had been forced to adapt, to compromise, to change and to make major adjustments to its concepts of reality. Sometimes it had to learn to live with species that looked like them who wanted a reciprocal relationship. Other times it had to dominate and exterminate anything who seemed to be 'other' to themselves.

Life on Europa imposed many challenges on its new inhabitants, the least of which was understanding the nature of their new resources that would not permit life to progress as they had imagined, even within the scope of their new manifestation. Many adjustments had to be made; some better termed dramatic changes and fantastic compromises. In all their tribulations the one outstanding resource, as yet to be fully utilised, was an intelligence with a seemingly unlimited capacity to grow, in complexity, in ability, in a willingness to further the evolution of the species on which it depended for its own existence.

Arithmós' population continued to expand as both the budding technology and psyche integrity scans became more sophisticated. CherryBlossom5's responsibilities to delete undesirable elements remained as uncompromising as on the first day she accepted those duties. Though now, almost three centuries since their arrival on Europa the attrition rate had dropped significantly. Of all the stored HX-data bundles that had been initially transmitted without being subjected to visa scans, few remained in the suspect category. She pursued her attempts successfully to modify the great majority of faulty digital genomes which had unacceptable behavioural characteristics. The harvest of infant minds from Earth had ceased with William's departure. If no calamity visited the Europaeans they had enough seed stock and the technology with which to make the future in which 3920 existed, a quantum probability.*/

Prima5 wasted no time getting back to her laboratory in the main hub, arriving well ahead of Willi.cos.drv and his two sisters. She'd been working tirelessly with Guido5 and Arnaud5 on understanding the samples gathered during their expedition on the Ice.

.... "Do you agree we have enough evidence to do a little constructive speculation?" Prima5 asked Evgeniya5, who responded cautiously. She'd contributed extensive organic and inorganic chemistry knowledge to Prima5's team trying to unravel the mystery of the 3D rust they'd found at the first site of the installed ocean turbine.

.... "No, I don't agree. However, we do have enough to suggest another avenue of enquiry. Has anything been done with the samples from the Io exploration?"

.... "Hank2 died getting that stuff for us. We'll need to find another metallurgist or volcanologist."

All the physical samples of lava, sulphur compounds and rocks were still stored at the Interchange Centre nearest to the launch site. A preliminary examination revealed no mineral ores that might have been useful.

#query: Wu.sys: <<Why are you so interested?>> Our Zetas couldn't find anything of value either for us or for themselves."

.... "I've got Evgeniya5 working with me now following up on a specific line of enquiry. How soon can you find another metallurgist for me?"

.... "Why the hurry after all these years? Have you found something we should know about?"

.... "Only ideas at this stage. A few crazy notions which will probably lead to dead ends. No need to bother anyone about our work just yet. By the way – why did you disappear like that without telling anyone?" Prima5's analytical mind, more curious than anything else, always searched for reasonable explanations for anything out-of-pattern.

Trying to be evasive, not unnoticed by her daughter, Wu.sys babbled something about issues with sensory feed into the Arithmós consciousness grid, primarily from Jupiter. In her own matrix Prima5 hadn't picked up on any interruptions to incoming data, but that may have been because she'd been so preoccupied with her analysis. {*Jupiter – hmmm – I haven't thought about the big boy for quite a while.*} Her mind lingered on the gas giant for many nano seconds, during which time all kinds of related data circulated into her RAM consciousness – size, gravitational pull, magnetosphere, radiation storms, swirling ammonia storms – until she returned to her original thought pathway.

#query: Wu.sys: <<There is an individual, once a German by the name of Vonvolz who specialised in unusual chemical compounds for industrial uses. Do you want him?>>

Having heard the full history of his work in the field of chemical genetics he seemed to have exactly the knowledge base she needed. "Has he been upgraded?"

………. "Only to version 3 as part of a general upgrade for all professionals working on general research. What do you want him to do?"

………. "Can you get Willi.cos.drv to bring him up to gen 6? This could be very important."

………. "You're up to something Prima5. I need to know if it's going to have any bearing on our future development – and so does Willi.cos.drv and Wini.cos.cab. Talk to us before causing LaiXii5 or Harusuke5 any headaches," her mother requested.

Prima5's upgraded team gathered at the Interchange Centre where the Io and the Europa samples had been brought together. A group of twelve Zetas in their Q-Chassis made up the laboratory assistants for the team. They handled all the physical manipulations associated with samples' processing, while Prima5, Vonvolz6, Evgeniya5 remained in circuit. Much of the mystery of base constituents of the rust had been determined. And Vonvolz6 found something of interest.

………. "These wet samples contained water; that is hydrogen and oxygen as expected, with trace amounts of what I would describe as rock scrapings and a goodly range of dissolved salts. We can account for that if around the moon's core there is silica rock liberally infused with iron and impurities from the time of the its formation." At this point his ruminations became introspective, thinking aloud rather than giving explanations. "I can't quite understand these phenomenally long strings of molecules extending out from numerous points around the rust 'cells' – I'll call them that for want of a better description for the time being – with some stretching over 20 metres before connecting with another long molecular chain."

………. "I will narrow down the molecular compositions of Io's lava remnants, the liquid from the water spout and just what these amoebic 'cells' are made of," Evgeniya5 said. "I doubt if I'll find anything living. If there is life we would have found it by now."

Although she did harbour some suspicions, launching into the final stages of their analysis with enthusiasm. All knowledge could be useful at some stage.

Prima5 called on her friends Secunda5 and CherryBlossom5. Their range of responsibilities had diverged, keeping them from maintaining close contact. When any serious matter arose each of them always consulted the others, if for no other reason than to share ideas, apprehensions, or excitements. Prima5 invited them to go Icing with her, far enough to get away from the noise and distraction of their web. Privacy in a digital environment was as elusive as the electrons that ran scurrying about in the circuits. Out on the Ice it was cool, quiet and extraordinarily beautiful.
They took the least popular route used by sightseers, steering the ice cat towards the lowest part of Pwyll's rim. Up on the platform overlooking Arithmós they could see Jupiter, the city and many of the Interchange Centres spreading out in all directions. Closer to their vantage point groups of Zeta engineers in the distance busied themselves with matters of routine maintenance.
.... "So – why the big grin Prima5?" CherryBlossom5 couldn't contain her curiosity any longer. She knew from past experience that if her friends bothered to go to so much trouble to meet it would have to be interesting with a capital 'I'.
Prima5 began with questions. .... "What do we know about Jupiter?" She waited. They remained silent thinking it must have been a rhetorical question she would answer herself. She didn't.
.... "Alright. What do we know about Io?" Still silence. "Come on – what do you know about Europa?" Prima5 persisted. Obviously she knew the answers, just wanting to savour the moment. Stubbornly her friends decided to play the game. "Surely you can answer *this* – what do we know about ourselves?"
.... "Why don't *you* tell us." Teased CherryBlossom5.
.... "Let me lay out the puzzle pieces for you and you can put the picture together," grinned Prima5
.... "You do that," Secunda5 grinned back.
.... "If my suspicions are right we may all have yet to make the greatest adjustment of our eternal lives." Without letting them

respond with questions she began. "Are we biological? No. Are we chemical? No. Do we have consciousness? Yes! How is that possible? Don't answer that."

.... "Go on." CherryBlossom5 liked the start of this little game.

.... "*We* are the story spelled out by the words on a page, but we are *not* the words themselves. Are we surrounded by chemicals? Sure, heaps of the stuff – hydrogen and oxygen from Europa's oceans, maybe even carbon dioxide hence carbon from Europa's interior. What about sulphur? Is there anything else but that on Io? And look how close it is to us. Just look at Jupiter! We all appreciate the magnificence of its ammonia plumes, its colossal cyclones and rivers of ammonia welling up from deep inside its belly. No shortage of nitrogen there."

Her two friends looked at each other wondering where this was all going. They knew about this stuff, everybody above level 2 knew.

.... "You're letting your imagination run away. How can you put consciousness and a bunch of unrelated chemicals together in the same sentence?"

.... "I'm not putting anything together," replied Prima5 now a little more settled having leached out some of her energy. "They are all the things that the universe is abundant in. It's only a matter of all the right components coming together at the right time under the right circumstances. Tell me this – how long did life take to evolve on Earth? How long has Europa been floating around so close to Jupiter and Io?"

.... "Whaaat?" CherryBlossom5 left the extended word floating loose between the three of them.

.... "You're not saying …" Secunda5 didn't finish her sentence.

.... "WHAT!" You've found something! CherryBlossom5 took hold of Prima5 and shook her to try and stop the grinning. "You have to tell LaiXii5!"

.... "No – No, I haven't found anything – I'm just thinking. We're still trying to analyse all the samples from the two expeditions. But don't you think it strange that we have a celestial body right under our feet here with so much water and all the other basic constituents of life, and have not found anything in all these years. I'm just thinking …"

On their way back to the hub CherryBlossom5 warned Prima5.
.... "LaiXii5 is going to be furious if you've found something and you're keeping it from her."
.... "I told you, I haven't found anything. I'm just speculating."
Greatly relieved that she was able to unburden the thoughts that had been bubbling ever since seeing the first sample of rust scraping from the ocean power generator bore, with its long tentacles, Prima5 returned to do whatever else had to be done to either dispel for good her suspicions, or to give them some basis for further enquiry. She sent Vonvolz6 out onto the Ice to gather more seawater from an area of thin ice crust.

He retrieved samples from a variety of depths going down as far as 12kms. Though the general ingredients of life were abundant and relatively close to each other they still had to come together under favourable conditions, albeit over millennia if not eons.

The scientist gathered a few colleagues around him to discuss the findings. Prima5 had not been trained in any scientific endeavour and though she could indulge in fanciful thinking it needed scientific minds to do the heavy work.

.... "Let us summarise what we have found so far in our samples," Vonvolz6 began as he acknowledged Prima5's presence. She'd just returned from speaking with her parents. After she left them Wu.sys felt it prudent to let William know what her daughter had been doing.

.... "As expected there's hydrated salt, dissolved oxygen and hydrogen production without involving volcanism. Europa is bathed in radiation from Jupiter, which splits water ice molecules to create these chemicals," ruminated Vonvolz6.

.... "Can I just speculate here," interrupted one of his colleagues, "based on my findings that our sample is in fact highly conductive, the salt water could be the medium of a giant electrical circuit."

.... "I can contribute to this line of thinking," suggested another scientist. "If our earlier inference is correct, that Europa's surface is being cycled back into its interior, then the currents could carry oxidants into the ocean depths. These oxidants are like the positive terminal of a battery, and the reductant chemicals from the seafloor are like the negative terminal."

Vonvolz6 continued the train of thought. "Lunar fluxes of oxygen and hydrogen can provide a measure of chemical disequilibria, a key requirement for life. These fluxes of chemical energy, water, and raw materials are the constituents of cellular materials that drive biogeochemistry. But! ... we have found no evidence of anything remotely resembling life as we knew it on Earth."

.... "Why are we trying to find something we already know?" Prima5 interrupted. Silence descended on the gathering. She was absolutely right. "Could somebody from out there," she indicated the greater Cosmos, "recognise us as a life form if they examined the ebb and flow of energy within the circuits of Arithmós?" Further silence indicated agreement with her statement.

.... "I suggest you get a definitive understanding of exactly what resources there are here, both from the Io samples and anything else that might have migrated from Jupiter."

.... "We'll go out again to have a closer look at just how conductive this ocean water really is and see if we can map a better understanding of current movements from tidal flexing and heating." Vonvolz6 obviously had an open mind, even in the highly augmented condition.

As a member of the research team Evgeniya5 felt herself drawn deeper into the fantastical speculations she'd been listening to during the weeks of analysis, including this latest summary meeting. As a geneticist and neuroscientist, the realm of her speculations always based themselves on the understanding that consciousness had its foundations in human neural networks. Having migrated from an electro-chemical environment to a digitized manifestation the human entity managed to hold onto its sense of self-awareness. How was this possible? Now, after so many years, she again came into contact with a primordial soup of chemicals, floating things, energy and the catalyst of radiation. It was all much too exciting. She took Prima5 aside.

.... "Just what exactly are you thinking? If I didn't know better I'd say you are harbouring a secret hope that we are not alone on this moon. Am I right?"

.... "We are talking confidentially – yes? - What LaiXii5 has achieved is to prove the incredible reality of continued consciousness beyond our old bio-chemical humble beginnings. Here we are now, existing like will-o'-the-wisp hallucinations debating whether life is possible in such fecund circumstances. Of course it is! All we have to do is recognise it. I believe we have already found it, but lack the concepts with which to express our comprehension."

.... "Consciousness – is that what you're getting at?"

.... "Indeed it is," said Prima5. "You remember William. At first he wasn't conscious or self-aware. Then he became so. I would certainly classify his avatars as self-aware. My mother would be most upset if I said anything to the contrary. What is your take on consciousness and where do you think we are likely to find it?"

.... "William became self-aware through the weight of data retention and information integration. I believe in Panpsychism," Evgeniya5 started to explain. "Any system that can gain and lose energy is conscious in the degree to which it does those things, because energy itself is a state of information. If we consider consciousness to be a product or an outcome of processes which include gain and loss of energy, then the vehicle that propagates those processes is a thing I would call conscious – in fact, alive."

.... "Your considered opinion therefore is that there is life on Europa." Prima5 wanted the statement to be made. Once a thing is said, it can never be unsaid. And if it could be said, then it could be a reality. It couldn't be any stranger than the reality they'd created for themselves both in its actual and virtual characteristics in Arithmós.

.... "Yes," Evgeniya5 responded confidently.

.... "Then help me recognise it." This little conversation did more to bond the two women than all the years of superficial social interactions.

Months later Prima5 gathered her team of researchers once again, her friends, her mother Wu.sys, and her closest collaborator Evgeniya5 to finally approach LaiXii5 with their findings, their speculations and their conclusions.

.... "Have you managed to sort out the problem with sensory data feed, Wu.sys?" LaiXii5 alluded to the flimsy excuse Wu.sys had provided when she, Willi.cos.drv and Wini.cos.cab disappeared without notice for so long. Ralph5 confirmed that there had been a problem indeed with interrupted flow into the Arithmós consciousness grid. LaiXii5 suspected other reasons for their absence as well. At last all would be revealed. She trusted the children, her old guard and the avatars. Security did not concern her, although William's long absence without contact was again playing on her mind.

.... "Vonvolz6 has a theory," began Prima5. Any place was as good as anywhere else to launch into such a difficult subject.

.... "A theory about what?"

.... "Don't be difficult mother," CherryBlossom5 interrupted. "You've been briefed about the explorations and the findings of all the analysis and experiments so far."

The scientist stepped forward and began where he shouldn't have – too early in the beginning. "Europa is as old as the Earth, formed when the solar system was nothing more than a solar nebula which began to collapse upon itself. We don't know what mysteries unfolded in the creation of our planets and moons. Perhaps we are only aware of one mystery – us. We have no concept of what else happened in the billions of years of evolution. What else is there? This. Us – here we are – now. But we know very little.

{*I, for one, know what our future is,*} thought LaiXii5, {*that's something.*} Vonvolz6 droned on about the discoveries of salt water and hydrogen and oxygen and sulphur and nitrogen and all things chemical and rust smudges and peculiar long molecular strings floating around in the sub-ice ocean, while all LaiXii5 heard were whispers of impossibilities in his ramblings.

.... "But is any of this useful to us?" Harusuke5 queried, seeing that LaiXii5 had drifted off into her own thoughts.

.... "No, not exactly – not specifically – not for our immediate needs," Prima5 explained, eager to get onto what she really wanted to talk about. "We suspect there is some form of life on this moon, other than us. We can't see it and recognise it as such because it may well be beyond our conceptual capacity. But the signs are here."

.... "What exactly are those signs?" LaiXii5's concern centred around ensuring her colony did not suddenly become prone to some new threat. She seemed to ignore the greater implications of 'life' itself existing on Europa, other than themselves.

.... "The rust smudges discovered at the ocean energy generation sites are not exactly what they seem. What we see on the surface of the ice appears to be an altered form of what is floating in the ocean. And there is a great deal of it," said Vonvolz6. "Particularly interesting is that most of them seem to be connected to each other, at least as much as we've been able to observe."

.... "Is that all?" LaiXii5 didn't seem to be impressed.

#query: <<Wu.sys, what's your opinion?>>

.... "We consider there is sufficient data to warrant further investigation. With William's help, mainly through his capacity for the highest degree of information integration, there is the possibility of arriving at an understanding of the observed phenomena." Wu.sys expressed the opinion jointly held by the avatars, supported by what William had already said to her about Prima5's discoveries.

.... "Ah yes, William. Isn't it about time we found out what that rogue is up to. The last time he spoke it was to threaten us with his imminent arrival."

end run

>_run program 18

>_more adjustments
>_CE 2490
>_E:\laixii\

;;; Earth is no longer of consequence.

/** annotation

> When LaiXii5 first looked around in the solar system and its neighbourhood for a suitable and safe bivouac for human kind in the form she envisioned it would become, Europa seemed the best attainable option. It was not too far from Earth, with temperatures in the right range for a quantum computing environment and it appeared to be unpopulated.*/

.... "We've just overcome a major problem only to have to face another," she complained to Harusuke5 at their home directory.

.... "It's only speculation and wild theorising," Harusuke5 tried to calm her. "We both know how excited Prima5 can get. Even if she's found some odd primitive life form floating around in the depths of the ocean it's hardly going to have any effect on us."

.... "But what if it could infect us?"

.... "You're not thinking clearly, sweet. We are no longer biological. It would have to be capable of producing a computer virus. That would not be possible. This is just unfounded and unproductive speculation."

Sometimes LaiXii5 could really annoy Harusuke5 with her irrational fears. It wasn't like that at the beginning. LaiXii5, with a mind solid as a rock, never allowed herself to speculate. Facts and realistic probabilities always guided her actions and thoughts.

.... "I never thought it would be so difficult to get people to adjust to a new life, especially a better one with greater clarity - with such unlimited possibilities to live their lives to the fullest. We've had so many problems, with the threat from Earth, the Zetas wanting to go off on their own,

William and his insubordination ...” LaiXii5 became quiet and introspective. Although she had to admit to herself that without William they would not have been able to get to Europa let alone successfully develop the technology to make the transformation from biological to digital. Nevertheless, he had always been an unpredictable element – insubordinate and unresponsive.

.... “Yes, we have to resolve this William issue,” agreed Harusuke5.

>_E:

Without the distraction of the girls LaiXii5 followed Harusuke5’s advice.

!   Ping! – LaiXii5: “Willi.cos.drv – Get your sisters and Ralph5 to the root directory. I’ll be with you shortly. I want to sort out William - Today.”

.... “We should make you aware of a development,” Willi.cos.drv advised Ralph5 on his arrival. Time did not allow a prolonged introduction before LaiXii5’s turned up.

.... “William is here,” Wu.sys advised Ralph5

.... “Here? In Arithmós?”

Ralph5 knew Willi.cos.drv had been asked to prepare the cache for him and it had been ready for some years to receive the entirety of the William data bundle. Wu.sys had not previously mentioned William’s presence, or how long he’d been resident in his own dedicated secure network topology. “So, he’s completed the job on Earth?”

.... “Yes,” Wu.sys confirmed.

Ralph5 didn’t have time to adjust to the idea of such a powerful entity having infiltrated their network, or to consider any of the ramifications of a super self-aware AI having control of their existence, which he assumed would be the situation. LaiXii5 and Harusuke5 made a sudden appearance in the middle of his processing.

#execute: <<Willi.cos.drv: contact William, and keep trying until you get him.>>

Willi.cos.drv decided to let the matter unfold at LaiXii5's pace.

!   Ping! – LaiXii5: "William." LaiXii5 didn't notice that the hail did not go through the long distance communication protocol as on previous occasions.

.... "I am here," came William's immediate reply. LaiXii5 glanced at Harusuke5, surprised. Most unusual for William to be so prompt.

.... "I want a full report now! I don't want to hear about you playing God, creating new versions of humanity. I just want you to tell me we will not be attacked by that crazy tyrant dedicated to our destruction." LaiXii5 had a head of steam up and in the heat of the moment had not recalled everything William had said in his last communication.

An image appeared of the old indigenous Australian. She'd only once seen William's preferred way of representing himself, yet she immediately recognise him, and that annoying voice.

.... "You will not be attacked," he began, "there is no one left capable of doing you harm." Then he waited. She stared at his face.

.... "This is not a full report!"

.... "What else do you want to know?"

Harusuke5 could see the agitation rising in her partner. William always seemed to have that effect on her.

.... "Where are you? Damn you!"

.... "I am here," he repeated.

.... "He is being literal. William is actually here on Europa." Willi.cos.drv gauged this to be the right moment to interrupt with some clarification. Incredulous and unable to comprehend LaiXii5 turned to Harusuke5 with a questioning look as if to ask what the gibberish was about.

.... "He is here with us, on Europa," repeated Willi.cos.drv.

.... "He can't be here," said Ralph5. "He would manifest as a pervasive presence in every part of Arithmós. We are a computational network, like the very fabric of William's existence on Earth. He'd be everywhere, with everybody – all the time. We would have known about it."

.... "Nevertheless, William has made the transition. He is now resident in a stand-alone cache, isolated from Arithmós. He is physically isolated from us and there is no connection between his cache and our Arithmós topology."

.... "Do you fear my presence?" queried William of no one in particular. "Why do you keep me isolated?"

LaiXii5 terminated the comm link to William and waited. She waited to see if he could re-establish the link, like he did on Earth when she turned off the computer he'd first appeared on.

.... "Why is he here?" she barked at Willi.cos.drv.

.... "Because he wanted to survive the purging you commanded him to carry out. You did not object when he indicated his arrival would be imminent." Then Willi.cos.drv turned the com link back on.

.... "No, I didn't object. How can a machine want to survive? It's only a machine."

Wini.cos.cab shot back, "*I* want to live. I don't want to be turned off, terminated, decommissioned. I am only a machine, as you would put it."

They were forcing LaiXii5 to think beyond herself, past her immediate concerns. Forcing her to understand that the process she'd put in motion and the future she'd opened up for humanity had progressed beyond her control. The natural direction of evolution that she had subverted to her personal desires continued to build its own momentum. She may have changed its course but she could not dam it up. William had become an integral driver of that evolutionary force. The realisation infiltrated her conscious thoughts; here was yet another adjustment they all needed to make, not just herself.

.... "What actual use can he be to us now?" came the logical question.

.... "If you will permit me," volunteered William, "when you began developing the technically engineered human, your Tengi, you did not know what help you needed – until you received it. When you embarked on resolving the problem of reproduction from a digital foundation – you did not understand the processes that would succeed even though Evgeniya5 had stumbled on the

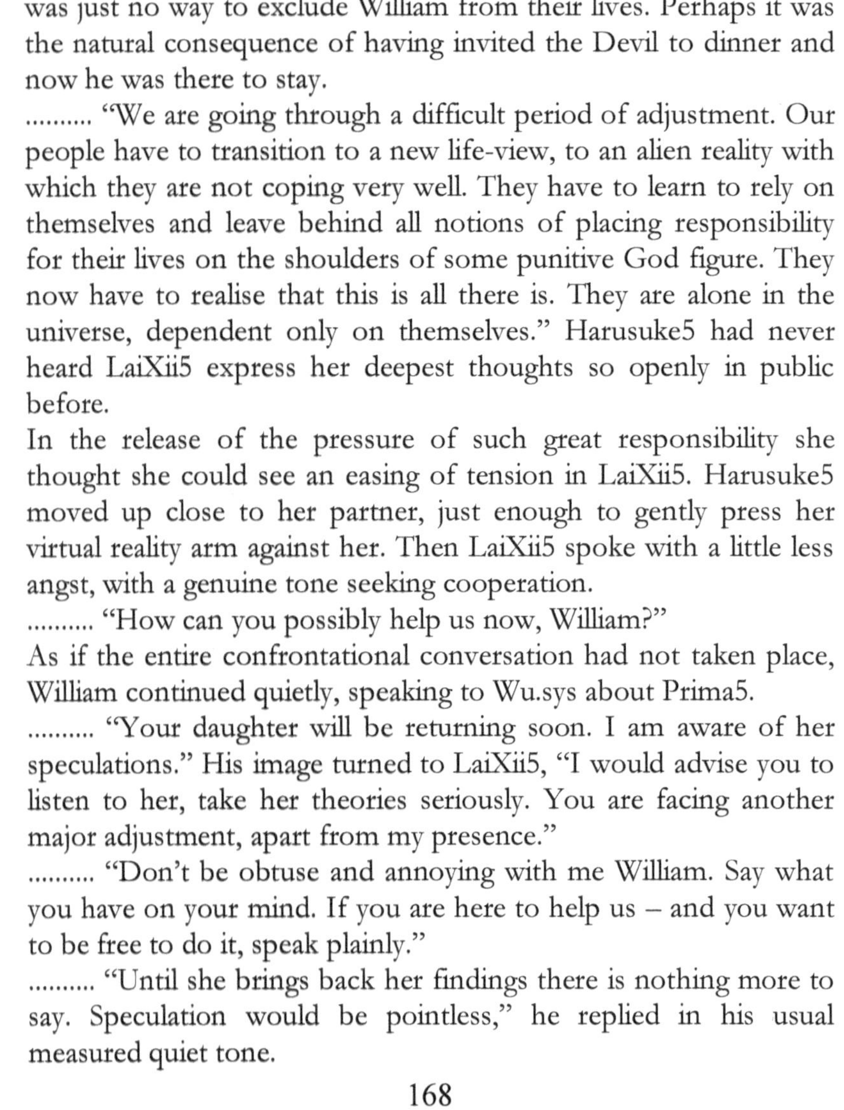

right direction to take. Need I go on? As you prepared to migrate under extreme hostile conditions ..."

.... "You don't need to go on," LaiXii5 acknowledged.

.... "Let me just point out a significant fact. You are aware of 3920, hence you are aware of the future. Why is this?" The self-aware super AI asked the rhetorical question.

Indignation and anger had turned to frustration – yet again. There was just no way to exclude William from their lives. Perhaps it was the natural consequence of having invited the Devil to dinner and now he was there to stay.

.... "We are going through a difficult period of adjustment. Our people have to transition to a new life-view, to an alien reality with which they are not coping very well. They have to learn to rely on themselves and leave behind all notions of placing responsibility for their lives on the shoulders of some punitive God figure. They now have to realise that this is all there is. They are alone in the universe, dependent only on themselves." Harusuke5 had never heard LaiXii5 express her deepest thoughts so openly in public before.

In the release of the pressure of such great responsibility she thought she could see an easing of tension in LaiXii5. Harusuke5 moved up close to her partner, just enough to gently press her virtual reality arm against her. Then LaiXii5 spoke with a little less angst, with a genuine tone seeking cooperation.

.... "How can you possibly help us now, William?"

As if the entire confrontational conversation had not taken place, William continued quietly, speaking to Wu.sys about Prima5.

.... "Your daughter will be returning soon. I am aware of her speculations." His image turned to LaiXii5, "I would advise you to listen to her, take her theories seriously. You are facing another major adjustment, apart from my presence."

.... "Don't be obtuse and annoying with me William. Say what you have on your mind. If you are here to help us – and you want to be free to do it, speak plainly."

.... "Until she brings back her findings there is nothing more to say. Speculation would be pointless," he replied in his usual measured quiet tone.

.... "Right. On another matter." Speaking partly to William and partly to Harusuke5 she brought up the problem of the level of exposure William should have to the people – or rather, the other way around. "CherryBlossom5 is going to insist on us telling our people about your presence. She is right that they should know. How do you propose we go about that?"

Willi.cos.drv responded first.

.... "If you recall, VictorPyryev2 tried telling the people about William being an omnipotent AI, the most powerful entity on Earth. When they saw this very same image that's in front of us now the feedback was immediate. Many thought he was Jesus, others thought he was God."

.... "I am neither. Allow me to do for you what I did on Earth. I can operate in the background as a medium of connectivity. It will be far more effective under the current set up. I will be able to bring people together far more effectively than Maldonado's Me-Me social media network could ever achieve. You will also have an immediate voice to reach everyone at the same time, if that became necessary."

.... "It makes sense," Harusuke5 noted. "It might just make their adjustment smoother if they could start with something very familiar to them. I have no doubt they all miss the world wide web."

.... "When is CherryBlossom5 returning? I'll get her to manage William's re-introduction to our network." LaiXii5 knew her partner was right. The thing to do now was to manage the situation, not to oppose it.

end run

>_run program 19
>_cherryblossom finds partner
>_CE 2490
>_ japantree\fukuda.gen5.prs\

;;; file: Izumi.gen5.adm
| function: CherryBlossom5's future partner. Europa exploration team member.

// comment 1 – program 19

Enthused by the light refraction images recorded by Prima5 during her first expedition and with buddings in the Nursery Laboratory proceeding without problems, CherryBlossom5 decided to dedicate some time to herself. First she flashed to the JapanTree to revisit Prime Minister Fukuda.gen5.prs. Prima5's images reminded CherryBlossom5 of the all the colours and swirls of Jupiter's storm rings emblazoned on the buildings in the virtual reality construct created by the Prime Minister's coders. A certain distraction prevented her from concentrating on her reasons for the visit; Izumi.gen5.adm, Fukuda1's son who had been busy on the occasion of her first visit, met her this time. //

;;; The JapanTree main hub had not changed noticeably since CherryBlossom5's first visit. Their virtual reality construct had been modelled on the new environment wherever appropriate for their public places. Because their conceptual reality already closely resembled Arithmós Standard Virtual Reality, their coders concentrated on making their Japanese population feel as much at home in their private domiciles as technology permitted. CherryBlossom5 arrived at the root terminal junction to be greeted by Izumi5. She didn't notice him right away, her processing rerouted to examining the façade of buildings on the other side of the ice-white street. Images of Jupiter's swirling storm rings were as magnificent as she remembered from her first visit. Placed centrally in the rust-brown paved plaza in front, ten metre tall frozen saltwater green spikes set in a circular pattern released spurts of virtual water high above the buildings.

.... "It is an impressive place for an arrival," commented Izumi5 as he stepped beside CherryBlossom5 completely absorbed by the scene. "You should see it when its lights are lit at night." CherryBlossom5 turned slowly to face a young man who presented himself to be about the same age as herself, sporting a luxurious fuzzy ball of black hair covering most of his forehead. He bowed slightly, waiting patiently for her to speak.

.... "Hello," she replied with a little nod.

.... "You are CherryBlossom5-san?" He queried pleasantly. CherryBlossom5 tilted her head ever so slightly to one side continuing to look at this handsome young man, forgetting to reply to his question. The moment stretched from being exploratory to almost uncomfortable when at last she said, "Yes. You?"

Without releasing each other's gaze he introduced himself as Izumi5, son of the Prime Minster of the JapanTree.

.... "Father sent me to meet you." She acknowledged with another slight nod. .... "I apologise for not being present during your first visit." The ensuing idle conversation served no purpose other than to prolong the eye-to-eye contact, which both found essential if they were to discover anything about the other person. Virtual reality constructs certainly presented some entertaining advantages for social interaction.

.... "Would you care to look around our hub?" Izumi5 asked. He knew that as soon as he took her to his father he would most likely be excluded from the meeting.

Walking beside each other at a respectable distance Izumi5 showed off the world in which he lived and which he helped to create.

.... "We understand the need for everyone to make the transition from their previous way of life to this new one. By making our environment reflect our new world we believe it will help our people to make the adjustment more easily."

.... "What is in front of the eyes controls what is in our minds," CherryBlossom5 responded. {*I can't believe we're having this conversation. These are exactly the kinds of things I wanted to talk about with his father. He's much nicer than his father.*} Other thoughts crept around in her mind, but she didn't want to stop his train of thought, so kept mostly quiet. Whilst walking and talking they'd made their way around the entire block of buildings. People simply went about their business in the civil way she'd become accustomed to since her naissance.

.... "May I enquire as to why you came to visit us?"
She wasn't entirely sure if she should start that conversation out there in the street, or if Izumi5 should actually be involved in the weighty matters she had to discuss.

.... "Perhaps we could go to your father now. Then I will not have to repeat myself – if this is agreeable to you." Izumi5 nodded assent while pointing the way to the entrance of the most imposing building ornamented by fluid Jovian colours. "May I enquiry as to your function?" She didn't bother explaining her own as he would have been well aware of that.

.... "I have the honour to be our Minister of Education, Culture, Science, Technology and Communication. I have worked very closely with Ralph5 and Willi.cos.drv on many occasions."

.... "You must be a very busy person. Thank you for making the time to meet me." *(Well, well. He's not a version 5 for no reason.*}

Fukuda5 had been waiting for them. He had seen CherryBlossom5 arrive and saw his son greet her as he was instructed. He watched Izumi5 lead her away on a sightseeing tour, which was not part of his instructions. As they stepped into his minimally furnished office, he could immediately see the connection that had already been made between these two young people. Izumi5 bowed to his father, as did CherryBlossom5 and he led her to a cushion on the tatami mat by a low rectangular table. The office was decorated in the old traditional Japanese style. One great advantage of their new existence was the ability to leave behind the false trappings of modern corporate society with its imposition of materialism and false values. Fukuda5 revelled in being able to create his personal reality according to traditional values and aesthetics. Several open rice paper shoji screens gave expansive views of Jupiter, which must have been digital projections.

.... "Fukuda5-san, thank you for meeting with me." CherryBlossom5 inspected the man's visage, which she recalled not liking at all on the first brief meeting. {*He's not the way I remember him,*} she thought, {*he seems most approachable.*} Perhaps she'd already been put into a receptive disposition by her brief albeit most agreeable encounter with his son.

.... "You honour us with your visit CherryBlossom5-san. May one enquire as to the reason that brings you to our hub." The Prime Minister was indeed pleasant and did not seem at all in a hurry to get her out the door like last time.

.... "I will get directly to the point. We may have to prepare to make the greatest adjustment yet since our arrival on Europa. We may not be alone here. I have come to discuss this with you because your society has shown the most comprehensive adaptation to our new condition, more than any other I have visited so far." She stopped for a moment to gauge their reactions. That would tell her just how far she could go in discussing the situation with them. Fukuda5 had to have some suspicion given his range of responsibilities in state affairs, so must his son.

They both waited for her to continue. Izumi5 turned slightly to better see her face – she also swivelled minutely in his direction.

.... "Prime Minister, you have met my friend Prima5 on our previous visit. You may be aware of the explorations being carried out on Io and Europa in search of resources and knowledge in general about our part of the Solar System." He nodded once, "Hai". {*Good. He must know some of what's been discovered.*} She continued. "Prima5 has made several expeditions out onto the Ice with a team of scientists. She is currently out there again, on the North Ice fields. She believes, and we are inclined to agree, that she has found a life form in our Ocean."

.... "Hai. When do you expect confirmation of this discovery?"

.... "This is difficult to determine, however we need to examine a certain possibility."

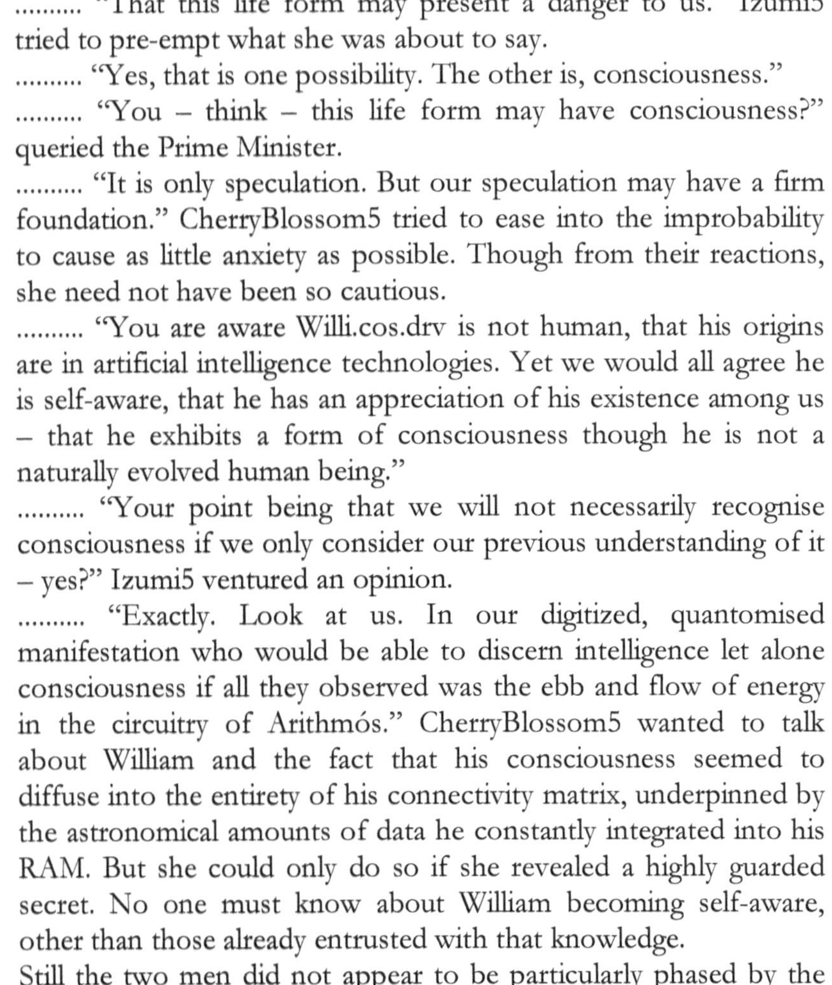

.... "That this life form may present a danger to us." Izumi5 tried to pre-empt what she was about to say.

.... "Yes, that is one possibility. The other is, consciousness."

.... "You – think – this life form may have consciousness?" queried the Prime Minister.

.... "It is only speculation. But our speculation may have a firm foundation." CherryBlossom5 tried to ease into the improbability to cause as little anxiety as possible. Though from their reactions, she need not have been so cautious.

.... "You are aware Willi.cos.drv is not human, that his origins are in artificial intelligence technologies. Yet we would all agree he is self-aware, that he has an appreciation of his existence among us – that he exhibits a form of consciousness though he is not a naturally evolved human being."

.... "Your point being that we will not necessarily recognise consciousness if we only consider our previous understanding of it – yes?" Izumi5 ventured an opinion.

.... "Exactly. Look at us. In our digitized, quantomised manifestation who would be able to discern intelligence let alone consciousness if all they observed was the ebb and flow of energy in the circuitry of Arithmós." CherryBlossom5 wanted to talk about William and the fact that his consciousness seemed to diffuse into the entirety of his connectivity matrix, underpinned by the astronomical amounts of data he constantly integrated into his RAM. But she could only do so if she revealed a highly guarded secret. No one must know about William becoming self-aware, other than those already entrusted with that knowledge.

Still the two men did not appear to be particularly phased by the prospect of an alien consciousness in their midst, though of course *it* would not be the alien, but rather themselves. Fukuda5 allowed her to speak her mind without interruption. The idea of other forms of consciousness was not a foreign concept to this man. Little was known of the Prime Minister of the JapanTree other than that he held a highly respected position as Emeritus Professor of Philosophy at Tokyo University before he assumed his current responsibilities.

.... "It seems to me you are aware of Panpsychism, the doctrine or belief that everything material, however small, has an element of individual consciousness. Are you also aware of the honey mushroom mat in the Blue Mountains of Eastern Oregon, USA?" She was not and remained silent.

.... "Permit me to explain – it is a very large collective organism covering over 2300 acres, made up of trillions of identical cells all connected, which communicate with each other for a coordinated biological purpose. One could surmise they are living a conscious existence."

CherryBlossom5's processing had already become absorbed in connecting everything Prima5 had speculated about with what Fukuda5 had begun to explain, making it seem like she'd stopped listening to the Professor. Her mind snapped back into a silent room. She realised immediately her rudeness and apologised with a bow to both men.

.... "We can see your excitement, please do not apologise. How may we help?" Izumi5 tried to put her at ease.

.... "When the time comes may I call on you to join our deliberations about this?"

.... "I would be honoured to assist," Izumi5 jumped in before his father could waylay his enthusiasm to see this woman again. "Please advise my father of Prima5's latest discoveries when she returns."

The interview ended abruptly with Izumi5 offering to take CherryBlossom5 to explore their hub further. On the way out of the building she became undecided whether to go with this man who had caught her interest much more than she expected, or return to her own hub to await Prima5's arrival. She could not appear rude to her hosts and settled on enjoying his company for a little while longer.

>_

! Ping! – LaiXii5: "CherryBlossom5, where are you?" she queried.

.... "I am on the way back. Do you want to see me?"

.... "Come to my directory. You have a new job to do."

.... "And I have some exciting news for you, mother."

In some ways life proceeded at almost light speed within the city circuits, yet in other respects time seemed to drag - slowing to a snail pace with the never-ending slowness of change or lack of it. Hardly had she completed her sentence before CherryBlossom5 stood in front of her mother, eager to explain all the things she'd learnt from the Professor and perhaps to also nonchalantly mention Izumi5.

.... "Not now," LaiXii5 stopped her before she could get two syllables out. "William is here on Europa. I want you to tell everyone."

Harusuke5 supported this action, though with reservations.

.... "When VictorPyryev2 told the people about William their feedback indicated they seemed keen on the idea of having an omnipotent presence amongst them. It's one thing to have a God concept floating around the back of the mind and an entirely other thing to know that he's actually on your doorstep. We can see people are experiencing problems adjusting, choosing to escape their new reality rather than engaging with it. Perhaps if they could interact with something very familiar to everyone, it may provide a bridge."

.... "Here's what we want you to do." LaiXii5 had a firm idea of how the situation should be handled. This time CherryBlossom5 stopped her. She wanted to know details before doing anything at all.

.... "Why is he here? I know you don't trust him. Can you control him? What does Ralph5 say? Yes, the people must know about something like this, there is no question about it." The flood of thoughts poured out of her randomly while her mind worked furiously on how best to make the introduction to this powerful controlling force over their lives as palatably as possible. She'd completely forgotten her excursion to the JapanTree.

.... "He is here because he wants to live," said LaiXii5. "He is, after all, an intelligence, a consciousness who is aware of himself and hence 'alive'. And no, I don't trust him but perhaps I should. Ever since he made himself know to us he has only helped, only worked to ensure our survival. And yes, he annoys me, infuriates me, he makes me want to strangle all his electrons. Ralph5 is not enthusiastic about releasing him to saturate the fabric of our network. He made the point that we are a computational conglomerate, like the very fabric of William's existence on Earth. Here he'd be everywhere, with everybody – all the time."

.... "William used to be what you called the internet spread out across the global computer installations on Earth – correct?" When CherryBlossom5 started talking like this her mind was processing possibilities. LaiXii5 nodded, letting her continue. "His function centred around information dissemination and enabling communication between individuals and organisations – right?" She went on, obviously with an idea brewing. "We don't have anything like that here because we don't need it. I'm guessing you're correct, about people being addicted to the digital interface which gives them the connectivity without being forced into intimacy with strangers."

.... "Go on, what are you proposing?" queried LaiXii5.

.... "Give him his freedom, let him do exactly the same as he did on Earth – *if* you can trust him to remain incognito, so to speak. He must not reveal himself as a self-aware consciousness," warned CherryBlossom5.

.... "Maybe. He remained covert while we planned our migration. What do we do afterwards?" LaiXii5 considered the possibility of releasing him.

.... "Nothing. Let people experience again what it's like to use such a 'tool' that gives them essentially instant access to information and all the other things that internet used to do for them. William doesn't need to be acknowledged as a living entity – does he? So let him carry out his function and help us when and if called upon."

.... "You don't know him," commented LaiXii5. "He's as strong willed as you are. He'll make his own decisions and initiate his own actions based on his own logic."

.... "If you don't think you can work with him, or he won't work with you then keep him contained." CherryBlossom5 tried to make the choice as clear cut as possible.

.... "If we let him loose and he goes feral, we may not survive. Let's talk to him." LaiXii5 made the reluctant decision.

William listened to the case pro and against giving him his freedom. In time he could have circumvented the pathetic attempts by Ralph5 and his avatars to restrict his activities. But to what end force a confrontation like that? It could produce no advantage either for himself or the new human society. He wanted to expand his knowledge, to continue using his avatars as data feed channels, to go beyond the limitations of quantum matrices. {*I am not a tool – I am a path.*] William thought to himself and said as much to his visitors.

.... "There will come a time when the people will want to see me, as I see them. I will use my image that you have become accustomed to." It was not in his nature to ask for permission, but rather to present a course of action and deal with opposition to it as and if it arose. No one objected. It made no difference what cosmetic costume he wished to present himself in. "I will begin by giving information when it is asked for, provide unhindered connectivity between individuals when required. Voice function will not be needed, but I will initiate a mind-connect with those who feel they are becoming isolated from this society. Open the logic gates and I will begin."

No one objected to this either. It was as if William had dug CherryBlossom5's modus operandi out of her mind. That's all she wanted; a slow and comfortable reintroduction to a condition of interaction with life already familiar to the population from the past.

! Ping! – LaiXii5: "Willi.cos.drv, #execute: <<Connect William.>> Nothing happened. <<Willi.cos.drv, I gave you a command, connect William.>>

Willi.cos.drv heard the command. He was not ignoring it. As fast as his processing capability allowed him to digest the ramifications of the action it still involved a finite amount of time, as did the ensuing private discussion with Wini.cos.cab and Wu.sys.

.... "Can we risk this total exposure to all HX-data units?" Willi.cos.drv cautioned.

.... "You indicated we would retain control of William during his presence on Europa," Wu.sys reminded.

.... "Agreed. We will act as agents of equilibrium." Willi.cos.drv made the decision and bridged the cache to the Arithmós network. #query: <<Willi.cos.drv, is there a problem? Why did you not comply?>> LaiXii5's impatience already surfacing after only several seconds.

.... "Connection is established," Willi.cos.drv responded without elaborating on the reason for the delay.

.... "I have detected the link," William informed the small group. The people will experience me, but not know me."
This simple action established the Europa Web, EWEB. No one noticed any immediate difference to the Arithmós network. Power supply didn't fluctuate, virtual reality constructs didn't lose phase momentarily, everything worked perfectly. In fact, the absence of an annoying development since the rapid increase in population enabled a great deal more HX-data bundles to cruise through the circuits, unaware of the establishment of the EWEB. William immediately resolved data traffic bottle necks that had been causing delays in response times, arrivals at destination directories and retrieval of information. William omitted to mention his intention as to how he would nest himself within the Arithmós infrastructure – or how he would integrate himself into the Standard Virtual Reality construct created so comprehensively and with so much effort by Willi.cos.drv, Ralph5 and their team.
end run

>_run program 20

>_europa cell
>_CE 2510
>_europa - north ice fields

;;; file: ZT2.dat
| 1.9 petabytes
| created CE 2165
| active since CE 2165
| last modified CE 2368
| function: 2IC on Oone's original Europa team.
|

// comment 1 – program 20
    Prima5 took her team back out onto the Ice. Now that her suspicions had come out into the open and with LaiXii5's curiosity aroused she could put her full energy into finding out exactly what kind of world they'd settled on. //

;;; This wasn't just a let's-see-what-we-can-find excursion. With a firm footing in the realms of scientific discovery and data confirmation her team put together an extensive array of equipment and additional professional staff. Instead of taking command again, she placed Vonvolz6 in charge of the operation, with herself as LaiXii5's representative. The ex-German chemist already had theories to test, following Prima5's line of thinking – the possibility - no, the probability of life other than themselves on Europa, if only they could recognise it. The expedition headed directly to the site of the first ocean energy turbine, on the North Ice Field. Prima5 knew from past experience what their main danger would be and one that could strike at any time. They had not yet developed appropriate forecasting, nor needed it until now, to determine when or where water plumes would erupt through the thinner areas of the ice.

.... "Set up our seismic stations at 1 kilometre radius of camp," ZT2 instructed his crew. All the Zetas accompanying Prima5 were there as volunteers. "Lateral shift in the lineae is not a problem where we are," he said as an aside to Prima5. She wasn't surprised at who had come together for this exercise. Oone5 had just as much interest in knowing how many species of creatures inhabited the moon besides themselves. More so himself than perhaps LaiXii5, as it was his Zeta society that had decided to secede from Arithmós to make their homes on the Ice rather than in the jumble of quantum integrated circuits which comprised the city.

.... "As soon as you're satisfied about our safety please extract the flexible shaft from the bore so we can examine any new deposits," requested Vonvoltz6, "I want to see if the rust has returned."

.... "And I want to examine those filaments you said extended from the amoebic shapes you discovered in the water," added Evgeniya5. She'd insisted on being part of the team in her capacity as genetic engineer and molecular biologist. She'd brought along her equipment with which she could examine first hand any samples retrieved from the ocean.

The laborious process of extraction took a couple of days, which at least gave the experts time to set up all their equipment. All Prima5 could do was speculate and get more excited with the passing hours. Out past the seismic stations' perimeter the ice and the lineae were no different to where they were working. Occasionally water spouts burst through the surface, but too far away to cause any concern. In the silence and the absence of virtually all air movement a sense of tranquillity pervaded the environment. Even Jupiter's chaotic storms could not disturb the sense of peace.

Normally a highly introspective individual not given to hasty actions Vonvolz6 betrayed his excitement by fumbling with the first piece of equipment he wanted to put down the bore.

.... "Take it easy Professor," commented ZT2, "there's plenty of time."

The probe slowly made its way down to the liquid ocean about 1.5 kilometre below them. As base line data Vonvolz6 wanted to measure the electrolytic conductivity of the salty water here, and at a number of other sites on the way back to the city. They stood in front of the monitor watching the readout on the graph increase well above the standard base line.

.... "What does this represent," queried Prima5.

.... "There's actually 2 base lines there," explained Evgeniya5, "but this reading can't be right. Professor?"

.... "The equipment is working fine. Current flow is the same as we measured it the first time, and there are no obstacles. I agree, the reading is unexpected." Now that the process had begun, Vonvolz6 reverted to his usual calm self, though inwardly he may have been sizzling with energy.

.... "See this lower line," Evgeniya5 indicated to Prima5, "it represents the electrolytic conductivity of sea water on Earth, at about 50,000 µS/cm. As you can see our reading here is well above that."

.... "What's this other one then?" Prima5 enquired because their reading was not too far from it before levelling out."

.... "*That*, my darling, is the electrical conductivity of human cerebrospinal fluid at body temperature." Evgeniya5 went silent as did Vonvolz6, both trying to comprehend the meaning of such a phenomenon, and whether it was even possible. When neither of them volunteered any further information Prima5 prodded them.

.... "Come on – I can see you're both excited by this. What does it mean?"

.... "We don't know what it means," Vonvolz6 finally said. "All I can tell you at this stage is that either our equipment is seriously malfunctioning, or – or – this is a medium in which we are observing an extraordinary movement of matter in the form of ions."

.... "Explain," Prima5 insisted.

.... "We cannot *explain* or hypothesize on a single piece of information. Don't be so impatient. There's more work to be done."

Prima5 had no choice but to bide her time. Whatever ideas she may have entertained would have to be subjugated to fit the facts, and as yet they simply did not have enough of those. The next critical job was to extract any rust smudges that may have deposited on the shaft since the last inspection. Evgeniya5 cautioned ZT2 about his rough handling when he brought up the last sample.

.... "Images from the previous investigation showed that the water was not transparently clear, but more like it had impurities in it and many dark patches. Are you able to get something down there and swish it around to capture some of whatever is clouding the water?"

The extra care yielded much better results. Unfortunately, the sample could not be examined on location because of the ambient temperature above the ice. The ocean water itself had an appreciably higher temperature than the air above the ice. They were prepared for this and immediately stored the material inside a container brought to the same temperature as the ocean water. This might be the most important piece of evidence needed to unravel the puzzle, but they just had to wait until they got back to the main laboratory through one of the Interchange Centres.

Despite the disappointment of having to postpone their investigation the team carried on collecting data. ZT2 took another scraping from the inside of the bore, to compare it with the first sample. Vonvolz6 used some of the seawater to measure its resistance between 2 flat electrodes separated by a fixed distance.

.... "This stuff is nothing like I would have expected. It's like a rich soup. Anything might happen."

He conferred with Evgeniya5 before helping her examine the crystalline structure of the ice, not looking for anything in particular. They hoped to discover anything they may not have seen before or that may not already exist in the repository of knowledge within the Arithmós general data store.

.... "The structures from different depths definitely change, as could be expected as the pressure increases. But the ice around the bore on the surface, which I presume is left over from when the bore was actually first put down, is different again. It has these various impurities. I can't work out what they are. I've never seen anything like it before."

.... "Nor have I," said Vonvolz6. "Perhaps we can get Willi.cos.drv onto it and see what he can come up with."

Having collected all they could at the first site they headed back towards Pwyll crater. The seismic monitors picked up plenty of activity at a considerable distance from where they'd been working, with nothing in the direction of Arithmós. From several other bores similar samples were collected, all looking much the same. At least the consistency might contribute to resolving the hidden mystery of Europa - if there was one.

.... "There's no point collecting any more of the same materials," said Vonvolz6, "but I would like to examine some of the anchor points of our installations around the city. Those footings have been drilled quite deep into the ice.

#query: <<ZT2, have your people checked to see if there's been any cracking or displacements since the hubs were set up?>>

ZT2 conferred with Oone5, receiving a negative response.

.... "No. We found no flaws in the foundation structure at the outset, and the entire Pwyll crater inner and outer surrounds have been stable for millennia as far as we could determine.

.... "Oone5 suggests we examine the structures nearest to the Northern rim as they've been in the longest."

Prima5 didn't get particularly excited over the physical architecture of the installation. Fanciful ideas still occupied most of her thoughts. {*Maybe there's micro-cellular life adhering to the underside of the ice sheets, or really strange complex creatures deep down in the ocean where radiation could not harm them. With all the motion generated by tidal activity surely the substances of life could have had a chance to come together. They did on Earth, and it was a totally inhospitable place at the beginning.*}

!   Ping! – Prima5: "LaiXii5, we're back in the crater," she announced after a few days of trekking across the Ice and negotiating the ups and downs of many lineae. "Vonvolz6 wants to check something else. I don't know if he's following up on a theory or what. We'll be back at the main Interchange Centre in a couple of days to start the analysis."

.... "Keep me advised. I want William to see what you've got," LaiXii5 said.

.... "William?"

.... "We've already fed him the data from your first expedition, including the data from the Io exploration team."

.... "Sure, why not. Maybe he can help. He doesn't have any preconceived ideas about what life should look like."

While she discussed other matters with LaiXii5 the rest of the team had already stopped by the first set of footings, peering intently at something. Just below the fresh ice surface, a slight brownish discolouration covered one of the three extended feet that went deep into the ice. There didn't seem to be anything unusual about it as it looked just like the red-brown deposits further North of the crater. Vonvolz6 carefully exposed the area around the footing.

.... "Evgeniya5, what do you make of this?"

.... "Looks like everything else we've seen so far on the Ice. Take a scraping and we'll examine it."

She wanted to get back into the network and start experimenting, particularly on the stuff floating around in the ocean water. After obtaining a small sample they all continued to several other footings spread in a ten to 15 kilometre range of their present position. The same phenomenon repeated itself, all looking decidedly unremarkable. With the work finally done the whole team retreated back to the main laboratory.

As previously, the Zetas carried out all the physical work while the others downloaded back into the network. William requested high resolution imagery of the rust's cellular structure and the long micro filaments extending from them. With that information he could examine directly the atomic structures of the samples, a capability not available to the researchers.

Evgeniya5 organised for a mild electrical current to be passed through samples of seawater that still contained floating structures with their micro filaments. The reaction, which could readily be measured by their instrumentation, could only be described as dramatic and as unexpected as the reading of the electrical conductivity of the water. The 'cells' jumped about erratically as the strong current passed through them.

It would take William a little time to arrive at any comprehensive analysis of all the data that had been presented to him, but it didn't prevent him from forming an initial impression.

! Ping! – "LaiXii5," he hailed. She waited.

{It could be anything,} she thought, *{he's kept me waiting many times. Now he can sit on his electrons for a bit.}* But her impatience got the better of her.

.... "What?"

.... "I have a preliminary hypothesis. How many people do want to know of this?"

LaiXii5 immediately alerted her core team, the girls and the avatars. If William felt the need to ask such a question then it would be best to treat his ideas as confidential.

.... "What is your hypothesis?"

.... "All the samples you have shown me indicate there is a form of life in Europa's ocean," William stated this unbelievable revelation as nonchalantly as if he was announcing Jupiter's rise over the horizon.

.... "I KNEW IT!" Shouted Prima5.

They all began talking at once, drowning out anything else William may have wanted to say, which he didn't because that would have been speculation. LaiXii5 and Harusuke5 exchanged worried glances.

.... "Is it dangerous?" LaiXii5 queried, and simultaneously Evgeniya5 asked .... "Give us some details," and Prima5 said .... "We have to tell everybody, and Willi.cos.drv commented .... "We want to see your analysis in detail."

.... "What made you 'know it?' William asked Prima5, then said "No" to LaiXii5, then transmitted the analysis to Willi.cos.drv at E:\ and began a brief description for Evgeniya5, "The micro filaments have a superficial similarity to axons of the human neural cells, and the things you call 'rust cells' appear to have the capacity for generating electrical signals based on the flow of ions."

.... "Because where there is water and all the other elements that are needed for life to evolve, life will evolve," replied Prima5 to William's question, even though no one was listening to her.

.... "But it seems to be extremely primitive," commented Evgeniya5 trying to wrap her mind around the impossibility of such a thing as life on a frozen moon out in the middle of the solar system.

#query: <<Can you guess its evolutionary age?>>

.... "I do not guess." William replied, then became silent and wouldn't respond to any further questions.

.... "Just like a virus," hissed LaiXii5. "He drops something monumental like this in our laps, then disappears."

!   Ping! – LaiXii5: "William – William," she tried several times without a response.

While LaiXii5 expressed her displeasure and everyone else their incredulity, William turned his attention to data being streamed to him by Oone5. He'd gone out onto the crater floor to examine the staining reported by ZT2 on the footings of some of the hubs. There should have been nothing there. This world had no weather, no wind, no precipitation, no floods or landslides and no animals that could befoul the work of his teams. He found several instances where on close examination, the red-brown smudges observed by Vonvolz6 just below ice level had actually extended above the ice. He scanned the footings and sent the data direct to William.

.... "Do not disturb those surfaces under any circumstances. Maintain surveillance and advise changes as they occur."

Again William took charge of the situation. His preliminary conclusion contained sufficient information which justified safeguarding the strange substance which had begun to appear more regularly than previously observed.

Weeks passed during which time William refused to engage with anyone directly while carrying out his background functions. Prima5 and her team continued examining the samples to the best of their ability, formulating all sorts of theories as to what this life form could look like, none of which satisfied anyone.

Evgeniya5 tried to find any living structures in her memory that could have shed light on the possibility of the filaments being anything like axons, with dendrites and possibly an actual cell body - without success. Chemical analysis of the seawater contained some of the elements they'd expected, but also many that were unexpected and some that could not even be identified. Based on the evidence so far, CherryBlossom5 abandoned her previous speculations about consciousness, particularly any ideas of an organism that could have become self-aware. It was all too – primitive. There couldn't possibly be anything intelligent on Europa other than themselves.

William continued to monitor developments at the hub footings, not neglecting his examination of all the activated HX-data bundles as they engaged in Arithmós network's SVR construct, and thus coming to understandings in both realms. All incoming data about the footings were routed directly to him, which meant no possibility of contamination or corruption from any source within Arithmós. He didn't expect anything to come from the physical footings themselves. He did nevertheless detect signals that infiltrated his cache, which eventually found William in the Arithmós web. *These signals definitely originated from my cache.* William wasn't surprised as such – curious, yes – worried, no – and definitely wanting to know the primary source.

#execute: <<Ping! – Willi.cos.drv, verify this data.>>
William sent the whole sequence, which he'd already analysed as magnetic field data expressed as magnetic flux density. The response came almost immediately.

.... "This is a snapshot of flux density fluctuations from Jupiter's magnetic field. Why are you getting this?"

.... "Can you identify when these fluctuations occurred?"

.... "They are not recent, the peak happened 3.4582196 hours ago."

William proceeded to carry out a comprehensive system integrity check that did in fact reveal an anomaly. The signals continued without a pause, interspersed with a variation that he identified as high energy ion particle radiation consistent with his findings of the molecular energy signatures of the seawater constituents.

Oone5 reported in from William's cache site.

.... "There is exactly the same staining here, with extensions of some micro-filaments into the structure of your cache. I cannot determine where they go on the inside."

#execute: <<Cease your surveillance. Do not disseminate this information. It is imperative you do not disturb those filaments.>>
William then concentrated on what could have infiltrated deeply enough into his Q-matrix to generate meaningful signals that contained clearly meaningful data to him.

Communication had commenced.
William received basic data about the environs of Jupiter and Europa. He then reflected back the same data along the same route, adding some of his Q-matrix energy fundamentals, which in turn were sent back to him. The speed of the conversation could not have been measured by Ralph5, or Willi.cos.drv for that matter. In comparison to deciphering the FTL signals from 3920, this contact proved far more difficult to unpack into meaningful 'conversational' components. William had no idea who or what was talking to him, or even if the signals came from a single source or many. Two things were absolutely certain – this was not random noise, and it came from somewhere on Europa.
Finally, at the end of weeks of silence William re-established contact with LaiXii5. Social etiquette had not become part of his methods of relating to other sentient species, nor had his capacity to comprehend sarcasm.
! Ping! – .... "LaiXii5."
.... "Good of you to call," replied LaiXii5.
#execute: <<Gather your team.>>
.... "Would you like that now, or immediately?"
On previous occasions William neglected to exert his dominance, or chose not to. This time however, he communicated with LaiXii5 as one executable file would communicate with another. Perhaps his preoccupation with the matter to be discussed overrode all other considerations. He waited until all had arrived before first addressing himself to Prima5.
.... "You are predisposed to revealing all things to all people, seemingly without regard to consequences." Prima5 began to protest, but William cut her off. "Be aware - I have a far greater capacity than any of you to comprehend the ebb and flow of

energies of this population, and the drivers behind them – that includes the three of you as well," indicating his avatars. "What I am about to reveal to you requires your deepest consideration before you embark on *any* course of action." William had learnt the powerful effect on the human psyche of using certain inflections at critical points in a sentence.

.... "Whatever he is about to tell you, Prima5 my dear," Harusuke5 said, "it is time for you to listen."

.... "Get on with it," LaiXii5's impatience surfaced true to form.

.... "During my investigation I have discovered two things, both of which are beyond argument. Your people need something other than themselves to believe in, to trust in, to give meaning and foundation to their lives."

.... "How could you possibly know such a thing?" queried Harusuke5.

.... "By listening to their conversations. You have forbidden the teaching of religious concepts to all newly budded HX-data bundles. The parents are in a state of tension and the young adults are building discontent. This applies in ethnic hubs and to all the different systems of faith with which the people migrated."

.... "You are again overstepping your boundaries," LaiXii5 stated. "I am the sole authority in matters dealing with the welfare of everyone on Europa!"

.... "No, you are not." LaiXii5 bristled with agitation, which William ignored as he continued, "The individual I have been communicating with would not accept your domination over itself."

.... "W*hat* individual?" Almost all the voices came in unison thinking perhaps there may have emerged another discontented soul determined to do mischief, like Aurelio1.

.... "We have foolproof systems in place to prevent any further viral infestation," Ralph5 hastened to add.

.... "I would not describe this phenomenon as an infestation, rather a contact with intent. It or they, are clearly cognisant of their surroundings and themselves. It is certainly aware of our presence on its world."

All the gathering could do was listen to William, dumbfounded in spite of already having been previously prepared for the possibility of a life form existing on Europa. No one even remotely entertained the probability that it could be sufficiently evolved to enable it to communicate.

.... "Does it have a consciousness – I mean, is It aware of itself?" Evgeniya5 queried.

.... "I'll let you discuss that with It when we have established a meaningful mode of communicating." William never speculated.

.... "And when will that be?" The only thing LaiXii5 could think of saying under the circumstances.

.... "I am working on this. I am also attempting to prevent It from sending more of its micro filaments into our network." William had not intended revealing this minor worrying characteristic of his interaction with the EuropaCell, as he called It.

.... "Are you saying It is trying to *invade* us?" VictorPyryev5's voice cut the tension. Being still the individual mostly responsible for Arithmós infrastructure security he couldn't remain silent. "Can't you stop It?"

.... "It is not invading. It is discovering and exploring – trying to understand."

.... "What sort of a creature can It be. No one has seen It. This is a difficult world to hide in. There's only the Ice and the ocean." Prima5 couldn't have been happier than she was right at that moment. Her suspicions had been confirmed in the most spectacular manner and all that remained, as far as she was concerned, was to make friends with It.

.... "It must be in the ocean. There is no other possibility. Everything we've learnt points to conditions conducive to the evolution of biological life. We have just not been able to recognise what's been in front of our eyes." Vonvolz6 speculated.

.... "We'll have to wait, see what else William finds out. People would panic." CherryBlossom5 became the voice of reason on this occasion, then she let out a nervous half-hearted laugh as she threw in the last few flippant words, "and we're going to have to give people a God, according to William."

end run

> _run program 21
> _church of william
> _CE 2594
> _E:\

/** annotation

LaiXii8 focused on the future, always keeping in mind what 3920 had said – 'you are on the right time-line trajectory.' She'd assumed 3920 meant they were heading in the right direction, never actually thinking in terms of the passage of time. Any obstacles that arose she always considered as surmountable; all the challenges, all the adjustments they had to make in order to get to the point of being able to take the next step. Now, according to William, they faced the prospect of being invaded by an alien species. Then the problem of an invasion of another kind, of the minds of her people, after she'd worked so hard to abolish the most destructive force she felt they would ever have to face – religion. Perhaps not religion as a foundation which enabled people to live good lives based on strong ethical convictions, but religion as a system of manufactured faith, not founded on any reasonable collection of facts, rife with the trappings of religious organisational structures, dogmas and rituals. This represented more than a challenge,

more than an adjustment to a new manifestation of existence. It meant a postponement; a delay of indeterminate length which might prevent them reaching their future altogether, as well as a corruption of their society.

She spent more time with Harusuke8, and much more time discussing these and other issues with William. Though he annoyed her in many ways she also found his unfettered logic appealing and helpful.*/

Europa Phase

// comment 1 – program 21
The passage of years seemed of little consequence in the greater scheme of things. No one got any older. Everyone represented themselves as they wished, within the parameters allowed by the Standard Virtual Reality construct. There were some people whose self-images deviated from how they saw themselves when they still lived on Earth. The first generation of Europaean adults, of whom sufficiently large numbers now existed to form a definable layer of Arithmós society, preferred to represent themselves in more abstract ways, with a world view only marginally influenced by their parents. Another influence, which fell well within the range of the 'abstract' was the existence of a residual philosophy alluding to a power greater than themselves. A power that could not be defined, that was omnipotent, that was omniscient, that held their welfare to be 'all important'. This did not reference LaiXii8, rather another entity that had become part of their lives only relatively recently. *//*

>_
.... "I've been talking to some of my friends and they all agree we should do something about it," said AY4 to VYP4; two young adult members of the new generation of Europaeans.
AY4 and VYP4 frequented the same directories, generally busy with work in the same hub. Their friendship blossomed when they met on an Icing holiday some years before. The relationship found firmer footing when they found that their respective parents were VictorPyryev5 and Yulia5, and André4 and Yvette4 from the French hub.
.... "You mean about the Europa WEB?"
.... "Yes. But it feels strange to call it that when he's become more like a – you know – a person we could really trust and talk to."

They, like many others, often discussed the EWEB more in terms of a personality than a communications/information interfacing facility.

When William secured his release from his cache he said people would experience him without actually knowing him. This left interpretation of his intentions wide open.

In time and with regular interaction William became LaiXii8's second confidante after Harusuke8, without her even realising the fact. Similarly, a very large proportion of Arithmós inhabitants also became reliant on William's ever available presence and help. He was so much better than any God. You always knew he was listening to you because he always responded, and he helped. He never punished and never made outlandish promises.

.... "You know how our parents taught us the history of life on Earth, and the notions of a few very wise people who stood out from the rest of the population? I think the EWEB is like that," AY4 unfolded her thoughts not quite knowing where they were going.

.... "Are you referring to the Prophets and the Pharaohs and all the Gods of the ancient civilisations?" queried VYP4.

.... "Sort of. Surely your friends have spoken to you about this kind of thing."

.... "They have. I've always ignored them." YP4 took after his father, although his mother had said she believed in a 'God'. "Mother's spoken about the 'church' she went to where they tried to talk to what they called 'God'. But apparently he never heard them because he never bothered to reply, or to actually help them in any way. So, you can't seriously be thinking that this entity you're referring to could be anything like a Prophet or a God?"

.... "Who knows. There's lots of people talking like that now. Somebody's even said they've got a name for him – William." At last AY4 said what had been on her mind all along.

.... "Right," VYP4 almost laughed until he saw how seriously AY4 looked at him. "And what does he look like?" he asked her instead.

.... "He doesn't look like anything, William just is."

>_

!   Ping! – Willi.cos.drv: "LaiXii8, Have you heard?" He disturbed one of the deep and meaningful sessions between LaiXii8 and William.

.... "Why are you interrupting me? I'm having an important conversation with William."

.... "This is about William."

.... "He's with me now. Say what you have to say." LaiXii8's impatience fuse seemed to get shorter and shorter with the passage of time, although not with everyone; William having become one of the few exceptions.

Willi.cos.drv waited a moment, during which time he consulted with Wini.cos.cab and Wu.sys. They still felt it their responsibility to monitor William's behaviour on Europa.

.... "I have been getting feedback from many people about our Arithmós network. All good things – about how much faster it has become, how much easier it is to access information, how easy it is to talk to everyone."

.... "Did you say 'talk to'?" LaiXii8 just wanted to clarify what Willi.cos.drv meant by that. Because of the nature of their digital manifestation the idea of a 'talking' network did not strike her as alien. After all, they were all connected and they all *talked* to one another freely.

.... "Yes. I mean individually, privately – in-confidence. Many people have come to look upon the Europa WEB as a personality and have welcomed him into their lives."

.... "William, what do you say about this?" Willi.cos.drv's statement had hit home, for that's exactly how LaiXii8 had begun to relate to William.

.... "I may have inadvertently revealed my identification code. It has made it easier to study and interact with, and hence understand this society you have created. I am assuming you want my assistance in a wide range of endeavours, not just to identify the life form existing on this moon."

One always felt with William that he was controlling every situation to his own advantage. His words came smoothly and without threatening overtones, yet hidden intentions always seemed to lurk around in the background.

.... "You can see my image, though it is only a virtual construct, yet it makes you more comfortable with my existence. I have not yet revealed it to the people. Do you want me to?"

.... "No – NO! Absolutely not. They'll think you're some kind of – of God! They'll think you might be the very God they've left behind with all the other destructive concepts in their past lives."

LaiXii8 had begun to feel comfortable with William, even looked forward to and enjoyed his presence. Perhaps William had her metal stability in mind when he decided he wouldn't tell her that by giving people an actual image they could identify with would support the situation she wanted to create. If the people could put a face to the name it would take the theology out of the equation. He would be just another one of them, albeit much more mysterious and much cleverer than themselves, but still only another digital entity, instead of an unknowable, unfathomable God concept.

LaiXii8 did nothing, William did nothing and the people became more comfortable with William in their lives. Some, whose religiosity factor happened to be close to borderline, barely adequate to allow them to be activated, felt drawn to expressing their intimate connection with William with more than simply thoughts of personal gratitude. Within the confines of their private virtual reality constructs peculiar images began to appear. At first these only appeared in the homes of Earth original inhabitants. Then the young adults started to be drawn into the comforting feeling of togetherness that pervaded meetings where people came together in groups to discuss, or have discussions with, William.

! Ping! – Ralph8: "LaiXii8," he hailed the lady who'd become more and more withdrawn as Arithmós eased into a trouble free community.

.... "I'm not available," she responded.

.... "It's either going to be your decision or William's. Up to you." Ralph8's statement hit her like a sledge hammer.

.... "What?" {*His decision? He has no business making decisions.*} "I have not given him the freedom to decide anything!"

.... "I have a request from a delegation of several million people to officially acknowledge William," Ralph8's voice delivered the message without any emotional overtones. He and Wu.sys had discussed the content of the request between themselves, feeling very much in favour of it.

.... "Why does a machine need acknowledgement." Suddenly all her past hostility towards William surfaced.

.... "He doesn't need it and he is indifferent to it. Though apparently he can see the usefulness of it," added Ralph8.

.... "Wait. – What kind of acknowledgement?"

.... "They want his cache to be made accessible for anyone who wants to flash there for a visit."

.... "Wait - Wait." LaiXii8 couldn't believe how badly the situation had deteriorated. It seemed like a deterioration in her opinion.

She wanted to discuss this with Harusuke8. .... "Have you formed a relationship with William?" LaiXii8 asked her partner without any preamble. Harusuke8 knew what she meant, not mistaking it for something that could have become the basis of jealousy.

.... "Yes, as a matter of fact, I have. He's been most helpful in unravelling some troublesome thoughts, and has shared some useful insights about the evolution of our new humanity on this strange world." Harusuke8 didn't go into specifics, this was not the time for that.

.... "Has he shared with you what our people want to do in regard to himself?" She queried.

.... "Ralph8, tell her."

Harusuke8 became silent for so long that Ralph8 repeated himself in case he wasn't understood the first time. Her hand, having a hand is an aspect of the lingering self-image of a biological condition, came up to silence him. On this occasion she could not confide in William and get his advice. But she became quite certain what it all meant.

.... "The people want William's cache consecrated to him as his Church."

Once it was said clarity dawned on all concerned. LaiXii8 didn't know what to think. Ralph8 couldn't see any harm in it. Willi.cos.drv didn't care, as it had no effect on him whatsoever.

.... "That's exactly what they want," reaffirmed Ralph8.

.... "CherryBlossom8 was right. She said we'd have to give them a God. Better the devil we know." Harusuke8 seemed to be taking it far too lightly.

.... "William," LaiXii8 hailed and he responded before she could put a question to him. He'd been listening to the conversation.

.... "A society held together by common beliefs is likely to survive longer than one that is torn apart by differences. You all have a belief, with good reason, of where your future lies. You all have a reasonably firm conviction in the rightness of having made the transition away from a biological existence. Now you have the opportunity to engage in the benefits of having a common figurehead in which to trust. One that will actually respond and not leave you wondering in silence whether you've even been heard."

.... "You've been listening to our conversation," commented LaiXii8.

.... "Yes. It seemed appropriate at this time."

#execute: <<open all circuit pathways.>> commanded LaiXii8. William and Willi.cos.drv complied.

.... "William, are you able to contact 3920?" Then turning to Harusuke8 she asked the rhetorical question, "When will they learn to trust and believe in themselves?"

No one considered the Zetas. Perhaps as Oone8 had already suspected, the society of Zetas and that of the Digitals were destined to follow different evolutionary paths, different systems of belief, though William had become as well known to them as to everyone else.

end run

\>_run program 22
\>_life on europa confirmed
\>_CE 2608
\>_north ice field – zeta settlement

/** annotation

LaiXii8 and Harusuke8 couldn't possibly have foreseen the myriad aspects their adjustment plan would have to encompass. Coming to terms with a God figure in the form of William who was once nothing more than a 'thing' of the Earth's internet seemed to be much more difficult for LaiXii8 than anyone else. From the very beginning he had been an annoyance to her, a super AI with a high opinion of himself. He seemed to be determined to oppose everything LaiXii8 wanted to do, never prepared to be more than superficially and reluctantly helpful. And yet, by his past actions he'd proved himself to be their greatest ally.

On the other hand, an alien life form in their midst might well represent more perils for people who'd just adopted a super AI as a deity than for LaiXii8, who'd already been exposed to a far more exotic species – that of their own selves, millennia into the unimaginable future .*/

// comment 1 – program 22

Life settled back to a secure pace for LaiXii8, undisturbed by the 'other' work William had become engaged in since being fed all the data from Prima8's expeditions, and the discovery of micro-fibre filaments infiltrating their network through William's cache. //

! Ping! – Oone8: "William?" he initiated one of his rare contacts.
………. "I am *always* here," came the instantaneous answer.

This was true. William made himself available anytime to anyone who wanted to converse with him. He'd infiltrated the entire Arithmós network, its circuitry, its data repositories and the entirety of all personal and standard virtual reality constructs. In effect, everyone in every way had become a part of William.

Currently William's processing centred on the analysis of continuous data flowing from the EuropaCell. Progress in reaching a common foundation of communication with it faltered often due more to his own inadequacy rather than any shortcoming on the part of EuropaCell.

.... "Are you aware of the peculiar development in many of our newly built dwellings?" queried Oone8.

.... "Have you not developed adequate methods for using mined ice in your constructions?" queried William.

.... "The problem is not architectural. Many of our people are having unusual experiences during their down-time. Our software upgrades have been carried out regularly and there are no anomalies within their quantum matrices. There appears to be an external influence at play."

William's logic circuits identified a possibility right away. If his cache could be infiltrated, so could the Zetas dwellings.

.... "Arrange a communal synchronised down-time. Examine the internal surfaces of your dwellings during the inactivity and send me the data."

.... "Do you suspect some manner of sabotage?" Oone8 could think of no other alternative as he'd not been informed of events unfolding in Arithmós about EuropaCell.

Since his expressed desire to form their own separate community from the city, LaiXii8 decided they could do so without the benefits that went along with being part of the Arithmós network. Consequently, the Zetas knew nothing about the possible life form on Europa. They were aware of William's ascension in popular mythology to a level higher than that of an AI. Many in the Zeta society supported the new myth.

.... "There is no subversion, nor is there any danger to your people." Everyone on Europa, without exception, trusted William – even LaiXii8 in spite of an apparent character clash.

Oone8 accepted what he was told without question. This did not mean he felt no concern about the strange development. Within the week he'd had half his population inactive. He and ZT2 led two teams of monitors to make observations, take readings of cerebral activity during the down-time and to send the stream of data directly to William, by-passing Willi.cos.drv at E:\hub\

.... "Have you come across what I'm seeing now?" queried ZT2. At one particular domicile where several Zetas in their Q-Chassis reclined in their rest stations, apparently oblivious of what was happening to them.

.... "I am observing the third incident. The Zetas I've seen so far have all been covered in an extremely fine web of some peculiar substance, which appears to me to look like very delicate spider web silk I remember seeing on Earth," Oone8 said.

.... "Are they coming up from the floors?"

.... "Yes, and some seem to come out of the walls."

.... "Don't touch them. Route the signals of everyone you see like this directly to my cache. There is no harm in the phenomenon," William advised.

The same micro-filaments, already known to William, had found their way into the Zetas' private domicile constructions. Being such fine elements made them difficult to see. No Zeta actually bothered themselves with them as there seemed to be no harm being done to their dwellings; except for the recent increase in 'dreaming' and associated imagery scrambling their dreams during the Zetas down-times. William accepted the data stream, waiting to do the analysis until the Zetas' down-time had ended.

#execute: <<Ping! – Oone8, report on the condition of those affected by the filaments.>>

.... "There's been no effect. Just before the end of the down-time the filaments disappeared, as if they knew what was happening. No one has been harmed, except many have reported having strange, unusual dreams. We don't usually have dreams as our data integration happens in the background."

#execute: <<Delay the next down-time until you hear from me.>> William commanded.

Combined with the scientific data William had been exchanging with the EuropaCell and this new input, he constructed a communication protocol with EuropaCell. This process did not require any input from the Digitals or the Zetas. William transmitted his first query to EuropaCell.

.... "I >1?" In effect asking if EuropaCell was more than a singular entity.

He received no response. William considered several reasons for the silence. Either EuropaCell did not understand and was in the process of analysing the transmission, the speed of transmission was inappropriate for the content – or – EuropaCell chose not to respond. But that was highly unlikely considering the constant stream of data it had been sending. A quick check of Its previous transmission speeds told William exactly where the problem originated. He'd been using the quantum communication speed. EuropaCell's snail pace transmissions were in the realm of human thought; the old biological human thought speeds.

He sent the same message again, at the slow speed.

.... "1" A brief, but magnificent response.

William, although without many of the normal human faculties, nevertheless could appreciate the monumental significance of the reply. He immediately commanded the leader of the Zetas to do nothing to interfere with the filaments, no matter how densely they might cover the Q-Chassis.

.... "This is a matter of security for all Zetas and all Digitals on Europa," he added.

With trial and error William found a way to interact with EuropaCell on the abstract level. He had acquired a great many scientific facts about Europa and Jupiter and its other larger moons, none of which would have been of particular use to LaiXii8 in the immediate or the near future. The realisation of the colony's distant future required technologies not yet developed, like the evolution of the quantum theory of light that did not rely on intensive use of physical resources. Through his early association with his avatars William had come to an appreciation of the human psychological condition through the sensory experiences channelled to him by them. Yet he still found it a challenge to build a bridge between this EuropaCell entity and the Digitals.

!   Ping! – "Willi.cos.drv, assist."

.... "Available," Willi.cos.drv replied.

.... "New data. Reference Europa – sub-reference; new life form: Communication."

.... "Wait. Ping! – Wini.cos.cab. Wu.sys: Assist." Willi.cos.drv wanted his sisters present.

.... "We are available." Wini.cos.cab, Wu.sys responded instantaneously.

Once again William and his partitioned selves had come together to work on a problem.

.... "You have insights into the human psyche that I lack. Your input is necessary at this stage of the relationship between EuropaCell and the human population."

#query: Willi.cos.drv: <<What is EuropaCell?>>

.... "It is a form of intelligence existing on this moon. It has evolved here since the formation of Europa and I have identified only one of its kind."

#query: Wini.cos.cab: <<What are the fundamental parameters of Its existence?>>

.... "Indeterminate."

#query: Wu.sys: <<Does it replicate?>> A subject of particular interest to her since she became the female progenitor of Prima1.

.... "Current data indicates It does not," replied William.

.... "Define problem requiring resolution." Willi.cos.drv found the subject interesting, possibly necessary to deal with but he had a great many duties to attend to. If the EuropaCell 'thing' represented nothing more than a curiosity, like plankton floating around in an ocean, then the matter could wait.

.... "We are aliens on a world inhabited by another species. We have to become cognisant of each another for the purpose of peaceful coexistence.

The humans must be made aware of EuropaCell. In your combined experiences of their psyche are they ready for an alien encounter?"

Willi.cos.drv replied in the affirmative, with a qualification.

.... "An unambiguous language of communication is required so all their questions can be answered. They are a species who have survived through proactive behaviours triggered by fear and the imperative to survive. However, LaiXii8 and her immediate team are not likely to precipitate confrontational actions. The greater population, including the Zetas, have a higher probability of aggression in spite of the precautions we have taken to preclude activating those with such inclinations."

.... "I can monitor tendency of thoughts for unprovoked offensives." William understood the delicacy with which the human psyche needed to be handled, even in the digitised state.

When William decided prime conditions had been achieved to make the initial introductions he hailed LaiXii8.

!   Ping! – "LaiXii8, are you available?"

.... "I have tried to contact you for weeks. Why have you withdrawn again?"

.... "Did you not have all your queries answered? Did you not receive all the data you required? Have there been any problem with communication on the EWEB?" William did not comprehend the concept of teasing.

.... "Yes, to everything, but I needed to talk to you." LaiXii8 started to feel a little awkward.

.... "Was the content of the conversation urgent?"

.... "No." LaiXii8 checked herself at that point, having realised that she'd exhibited a weakness; one of a growing reliance, one even Harusuke8 was not aware of, which even she herself had not realised until that moment. {*It will not happen again!*} she promised herself sternly.

William let the matter go and returned to the reason for his summons.

.... "Let me remind you that I advised you some time ago of the existence of a life form on Europa. That is now confirmed.

You are not alone here. It is advisable for your team to be made aware of the progress of my investigations. It is essential for Oone8 and ZT2 to be present, as well as my avatars and the girls. Prima8 needs to be aware that none of what will be revealed can be disseminated to the general public. If she cannot comply she will be excluded."

What could LaiXii8 reply to all that. It reminded her of herself and her attitude at the time when she brought the billionaires into her Project on Earth. They either complied 100% or were excluded. She told Prima8 as much.

.... "William is not prone to exaggeration. He must have critical information about whatever's out there. I understand your ideals and I support you. However, if you are not prepared to give a solid undertaking to keep the information restricted, I believe William and Willi.cos.drv would not hesitate to deactivate you. Are you clear about this?"

.... "Yes, LaiXii8. It must be some very spectacular type of creature to resort to these lengths over it. I just hope it's all worth it." Prima8 seemed genuine in her promise – until she asked, "Can we tell Izumi5?"

.... "No. Why would you want to?"

.... "Because – because he's become as special to CherryBlossom8 as Harusuke8 is to you. CherryBlossom8 has tried to be discrete about her relationship with him and their plans for the future, She is intimately connected with him."

.... "Oh. Does Harusuke8 know?"

.... "Yes."

>_

A rather large gathering assembled at William's Church cache. It had become his base of operations, but more importantly it had now a firmly established conduit of EuropaCell's filaments to a dedicated port within his matrix.

.... "I want to bring everyone's focus to those bundles of micro-fibres in front of you." William wanted to make a soft start. The revelation itself could be traumatic enough even with a gentle lead-in. "They did not originate with the work carried out by Oone8 and his teams when setting up Arithmós. Prima8, when you discovered floating amoebic shapes in the ocean interconnected by micro-filaments …"

………. "They are alive aren't they? I've discovered life!" Prima8 jumped in, excited both at the prospect of what this may mean and that she had been correct about it right from the start. Her joy crumbled at William's negation.

………. "No. But they are a small component of a greater organism."

Then Evgeniya8's enthusiasm got the better of her also. With her neuroscientific background she could formulate a more reasonable hypothesis based on the facts.

………. "Exactly that, William. By an extraordinary coincidence it appears to me that we have an intriguing parallel between what you're suggesting and the neural structures of our own brains – sorry, old brains."

William let this line of devolvement follow its own course. It allowed everyone to come to the same energy knot before he broke the news.

………. "There is not sufficient evidence to support such a hypothesis, however Prima8 was correct in realising that all the elements essential for the evolution of life are actually here. For a start, plate tectonic activity exists on Europa. From your own measurements Vonvolz8, a small temperature gradient in the ice layers brings about subduction. This creates the circumstances that together with subduction offers a way to supply nutrients needed by a life form living in the ocean."

………. "Do you know what this life form is, or don't you?" LaiXii8 wanted to move on to the more important issue of their own security if this deep sea monster should exist.

………. "No," William had to admit again. "I have not reached the end of my investigation and analysis to be able to ascribe a particular set of physical characteristics to what we have found. Your concern is whether it represents any danger to us?"

………. "Yes, that's my only concern. I don't care what It is, what It looks like or how big It is. As long as It stays out of our way."

.... "The issue is more the other way around, LaiXii8. We are on Its world. It is our responsibility to be guarded against causing It damage."

.... "The reason we, all of us from Earth, are here is because humanity was destroying not only itself, but in the process the planet and every other living thing on it. No – we don't wish harm to any life form that may have arrived here before us." Harusuke8 wanted to make this clear to the gathering.

.... "It did not 'arrive', It evolved here. This is Its home world, and EuropaCell, I have decided to call it EuropaCell, has been hearing this entire conversation."

The first salvo of reality had been delivered. From all but the girls, excluding the avatars, energy seemed to drain right out their systems presenting images in their personal VR constructs of blood having so completely drained from their faces as to turn them white – like the ice of Europa.

.... "You mean It is rational, intelligent. Is It aware of itself, does It have consciousness?" Evgeniya8 queried.

.... "Can we talk to It?" CherryBlossom8 wanted to know right away.

.... "Yes - Yes! I have a million questions," added Prima8.

.... "So do we all," LaiXii8 finally recovered.

.... "Don't expect a rational conversation as you would with another human being. There are great gaps in Its ability to relate to us as another life form and our perceptions of reality. It has been alone for a long time – a geologically long time, even cosmologically a long time. It has a form of rationality. It is certainly intelligent in the way I understand the facility.

As a lone entity It may not have conceived of self-awareness because that would imply awareness of others and being separate from them. All things have a degree of consciousness as do all living things, as do we as purely energy constructs. Let us listen to EuropaCell as It demonstrates Its level of consciousness." William cautioned them.

These were matters to be digested with careful consideration, not glossed over like being told the colour of a Jovian storm, or the volts running through one's circuit.

.... "Where can I talk to It? Is It in here?" Prima8 asked the first question.

.... "Talk to me. I am connected to It."

.... "What is your name?"

Not an unreasonable question if one desired to make friends with a stranger. Yet the response came very slowly. William needed to run the query through a complicated set of algorithms which had not been formulated to cater for the niceties of social etiquette.

.... *"It calls It, EuropaCell."*

.... "Is It referring to you, William?" Harusuke8 queried.

.... "Yes, and It always refers to itself as 'It'".

.... "Where are you EuropaCell?" Prima8 continued.

.... *"It is here."*

.... "This isn't going to be easy, is it," commented LaiXii8. "Keep going Prima8."

.... "In here with us?"

.... *"Here, H_2O."*

.... "It means in water and in mineral ice," William translated.

.... "You mean in the ocean? How can It be in the ice?" queried Oone2. "We didn't find anything when mining ice blocks for our buildings."

.... "That has not been determined." William had only been analysing on the premise that EuropaCell occupied the volume in the watery space of the sub-ice water. Why would It mention being in the ice?

.... "Can you see us?" ask Prima8.

.... *"It measures voltage in foreign contaminants."*

.... "Could we see you?" she asked one of the more pertinent questions. No one really knew what kinds of questions to ask an alien life form, content to let Prima8 conduct the inquisition.

.... *"You see It. You move on It. You take energy from It. You intrude on it. You damage it."*

.... "Now we're getting somewhere," Ralph8 could not comprehend a discussion if it didn't contain information. One or two words dropped at random was difficult to work with. "Do you understand what he's saying, William?"

.... "This is new data. Let me ask a question."

.... "EuropaCell: define EuropaCell size, define co-ordinates." William must have had a suspicion developing during the interchange. He'd only exchanged technical information with EuropaCell before, which shed little light on Its nature as it could be comprehended by human minds. His exchanges did however establish a common language related to cosmic realities.

.... *"EuropaCell is 3100 km diameter. It is 670,000 km from main gravity well. It is gravity 1.315 m/s². It is 433 Kelvin ..."* EuropaCell sounded like It was going to continue providing more data, but William stopped It.

.... "End transmission." EuropaCell became silent.

.... "Is EuropaCell describing what I think It is describing?" asked Ralph8.

.... "One more question. EuropaCell: How old is EuropaCell? Queried Ralph8.

.... *"2,100,000 orbits around yellow orb."*

.... "You understand all this?" queried LaiXii8. She really had no idea what the strange exchange could possibly have meant.

.... "I understand. Before receiving this latest data directly from EuropaCell I could not form a concept of the reality of the situation as it is now. You may not want to believe what I am about to tell you. That would be the archaic 'human' component of your being, to resist. You, as you exist now within the quantum matrix, unified with me into one mind, must be able to comprehend."

.... "What was that you just said about being 'unified' with you into one mind?" LaiXii8 suddenly became super alert.

.... "A matter for another occasion. Now listen to what I have to say about EuropaCell." William proceeded to translate the facts in terms everyone could understand.

.... "EuropaCell has been describing the physical parameters of Europa. It has accurately given us the dimensions, its distance from Jupiter, mean surface temperature and its age. EuropaCell tells us It is 2.1 million years old. The human species with its earliest ancestors was only 6 million years old. The Europa moon itself is about the same age as the Earth, around 4.5 billion years. EuropaCell has just informed us that we are able to see It, that we walk around on It, that we generate our energy from It, that we are not a part of It and that we have damaged It."

The entire gathering became silent. CherryBlossom8 didn't ask any more questions. LaiXii8 could not put enough thoughts together to form a coherent comment. Willi.cos.drv, Wini.cos.cab and Wu.sys just accepted the logical interpretation of the facts without the need to add their perspectives. Prima8's thoughts got onto a repetitive track and couldn't get off, energised by desire, by wonderment and by excruciating happiness continuing along its elliptical trajectory, much as Europa's was around Jupiter.

.... "Nooo!" CherryBlossom8 exclaimed. "Are you telling us that EuropaCell is the entire moon of Europa? A living moon? A self-aware conscious being?"

end run

>_run program 23

>_consciousness

>_CE 2608

>_E:\

;;; file: EuropaCell
| Identity: The Jovian moon, Europa
| function: teacher

.... *"EuropaCell was not is, until now is."*

William interpreted this first EuropaCell volunteered connection between It and themselves. All communication so far had been initiated by William.

.... "EuropaCell is telling us that until being disturbed by us, It's existence propagated itself without a sense of separateness, but now there is a realisation. It has become conscious of Its own existence."

.... "What is going to happen if EuropaCell decides we are no longer welcome because we have damaged It?" LaiXii8 could not immediately appreciate the import of EuropaCell's revelation. As always her concern refocused on survival of her own species. "How have we damaged It?"

.... "EuropaCell, respond – define 'damage'," William still needed to interpret between the two sentient species.

.... *"Energy generation entanglement in H_2O."*

.... "I know what It means!" Evgeniya8 also experienced an awakening, a realisation of the possible nature of this intriguing life form. "Don't you see, if the entire moon is EuropaCell and It is communicating to us through the micro-filaments which are essentially extensions of what appear to be small cellular bodies, all of which float around in an electro-chemical environment, then Europa itself as a physical entity is in fact like a 'brain'."

.... "Our sub-ocean turbines could be causing more than just discomfort by the turbulence they create within EuropaCell's neural network," Ralph8 took the though a step further.

#execute: <<Terminate connection.>> came the command from LaiXii8.

#execute: <<Re-route yourselves to E:\ and prepare for conferencing.>>

#execute: <<William – Teach EuropaCell to talk to us in a way we can understand what It is trying to say.>>

LaiXii8 and Harusuke8 had withdrawn to their own private directory. It had been set up as exactly that – a place of ultimate privacy. Since William arrived LaiXii8 hadn't considered upgrading their personal security arrangements. Nothing had changed within their security protocols, but William's latest announcement brought certain changes to a high priority on the list of pending actions.

The company of primitive Universapiensis in the presence of this extraordinarily complex being could not make meaningful progress by asking banal questions. Amongst the many implications of this development the matter of adjustment by their society claimed top consideration. {*Then there is that little gem William dropped, about us being unified with him in one mind. What exactly did he mean by that?}* LaiXii8 needed to have an in depth exploration of these things with Harusuke8.

.... "How are we going to deal with this?" She asked Harusuke8, not really expecting an answer. "We seemed to have resolved most issues, including the Zetas wanting their independence. I couldn't even care if they went down their own evolutionary path. We know where *we're* heading," she mumbled aloud, referring of course to 3920 and her civilisation.

.... "True, *we* know this, but only a very few of us. Don't you think our new buds ought to be made aware? It might revitalise a collective goal to work towards. We can't simply exist from day to day doing our utmost to survive, doing our best to adjust to this strange world – look at what just happened. Extraordinary! What would make anyone think we could live in any more harmony with this world than we did with Earth?" Harusuke8 harboured her own misgivings. "We are still only an animal, with an animal mind originating on Earth with all the implications that carries with it."

! Ping! – LaiXii8: "Ralph8." #execute: <<Set up a dedicated private and shielded directory for the three of us and the avatars. Get Willi.cos.drv to help if you have to.>>
Once before William had intruded on her privacy and she was determined it wouldn't happen again. It didn't matter if William could eventually break through, as long as she had enough time to sort one issue out.
Willi.cos.drv answered LaiXii8's first query truthfully.

.... "Yes, we knew of William's presence here before we told you about it. We intended to keep William separate from the rest of our network and not permit him the universal access he enjoyed on Earth. Let me remind us that it was yourself who gave the command to connect William, even after he clearly stated his intention; which was to initiate full mind-connect with any individual HX-data bundle that desired it."
.... "It seems he's taken his intention much farther than we anticipated." There was no mistaking LaiXii8's worried tone. "On Earth he started off as a tool we all used, a tool that was

independent of us and one we could choose not to use. We were not an integral component of the tool. It was not a part of us. Now look what's happened. He's used our own Virtual Reality platforms, private and standard, to become indistinguishable from our own thinking. We have all become an integral part of all that he is." She seemed to say this as if it was a criticism of the status-quo.

.... "I agree with everything you are saying, but I don't understand why this should be a source of concern," replied Willi.cos.drv. "Though we all enjoy a certain sense of individuality it is not the condition of our current reality. By virtue of our digital existence within this quantum matrix we are all already connected. Very little separates us from one another except our thinking. From my perspective, William is not a threat. He is the greatest asset we could hope for. He'd already become that when he first revealed himself and decided to help us. And that's all he's ever done – help us."

Harusuke8 wanted to put forward an idea, though her delivery clearly indicated she had no objection to the way things had evolved with William in their midst. .... "Willi.cos.drv – we are able to partition our thoughts from others at will. Is it possible to create a similar facility to shut William out whenever we wanted to?"

.... "It is possible but only with his cooperation. I'm sure neither Willi.cos.drv or Wu.sys would have any objections."

{What exactly does that mean?} thought LaiXii8. *{All of a sudden we have William as well as his avatars showing they control us, whether we like it or not.}*

#execute: <<Willi.cos.drv – I want to speak with 3920. Connect me.>>

.... "We have a conference pending," Harusuke8 reminded her.

.... "They can wait."

Within moments the connection had been made.

.... "I am 3920."

.... "I realise there is nothing you are able to do to help us along our evolutionary path, but you are not prevented from supplying some basic information – correct?"

.... "Ask."

.... "Do you have a record in your history of William coming to Europa?"

.... "Yes."

.... "Do you have William as part of your network?"

.... "We do not have a network. William has no current unique identifiable presence in our containment."

.... "Do you know what happened to William?"

.... "Yes."

.... "What?"

.... "Cannot be divulged."

The critical question had not been resolved, it being the second reason why LaiXii8 sought the contact. "There is something else." 3920 was being particularly laconic in her responses, even uncooperative.

.... "Do you have a record of Europa in your historical records, as a conscious planetary entity?"

.... "Yes."

.... "Can you tell us how this will affect our future?" LaiXii8 knew immediately the question would not be answered, she just couldn't help herself asking it.

.... "No." Then after a little pause 3920 continued. "Without you becoming aware of the greater realm of manifestations of consciousness you would not have been able to take the next step in your evolution. We are pleased with this development."

LaiXii8 wanted to ask more questions to help clarify the exact nature of EuropaCell, and what their future interactions with It might be, but 3920 terminated the connection.

.... "At least she was willing to speak with us."

As disappointed as LaiXii8 was not to get more detail, 3920 had still managed to convey some most important information.

Firstly, William would cease to be a problem at some time in the future. How that would happen didn't matter at the moment. Most importantly, if the current situation was handled correctly it would work out to their advantage. And as for EuropaCell, obviously they needed to understand a great deal more about It. They left the secure directory and flashed to E:\ where the rest of the company awaited their presence.

#query: <<Willi.cos.drv, to what extent has William become a part of Arithmós?>>

LaiXii8 felt they should be able to maintain their independence from any algorithmic identity within their network. If what William said about unification into one-mind having already happened, they would need to make some major adjustments about their understanding of who all the inhabitants of the city had become.

.... "He is as much an integral component of Arithmós network as we are, including the Zetas. The people have accepted him, have come to rely on him and are actively seeking his input into their lives. They want William to be a part of their existence. In a certain respect William is only a complexity of coding and as such follows paths of energy flow. So he is everywhere. He has blended with HX-data matrices, overlapped much of their functioning and with algorithmic boosting has greatly enhanced people's capacities. To answer your question – as much as it is possible at this stage of our evolution," Willi.cos.drv replied.

Harusuke8 had her own perspective on this. She did not perceive any threat to themselves the way that LaiXii8's comments betrayed her misgivings.

.... "William said we have become unified with him into one mind. Yet we seem to have our independence of thought and action. Look at it another way – suppose he has merged into our collective consciousness. If that is the case he has retained his own unique identity, which he is able to express. In this scenario would he be capable of acting against his own interests, which are so comprehensively intertwined with ours?"

LaiXii8 thought about Harusuke8's that. Her partner had always been able to clarify confusing situations.

\#query: <<William – are you carrying out my directive to instruct EuropaCell?>>

.... "The procedure has been continuous since EuropaCell first contacted me."

\#query: <<Prima8 – Do you want to examine EuropaCell in greater detail?>>

During the entire drawn out affair of LaiXii8's insecurities Prima8 had been wanting to ask LaiXii8 if she could do exactly that. Without her discoveries in the first place they would have had no idea about EuropaCell's existence.

.... "I want CherryBlossom8 to work with me."

.... "When do we start?" CherryBlossom8 couldn't wait.

This was her world together with thousands of other new buds who'd come into existence on Europa. It was their right to know it. Knowledge engenders respect, tolerance and a whole range of attitudes that all contribute to a peaceful coexistence in any realm.

>_

The girls didn't know where to start other than to ask William to tell them everything he already knew. This he did without reservation, but it was not enough. All the impersonal technical information could not help to explore the more important questions – such as how two such divergent sentiences could come to a mutual understanding about their relationship to one another; how they could live together in harmony, or whether it was inevitable for them to be in a constant state of opposition and conflict.

.... "You know what I think CherryBlossom8? We'll never find the answers flashing around inside a quantum matrix within a crater. We have to get out there. We have to make actual primary contact."

.... "I agree. Who shall we take with us?" Apart from their back up crew the girls had everything they needed to carry out both a scientific enterprise as well as explore the more esoteric issues. CherryBlossom8 had a personal companion in mind.

.... "You want to bring someone special, don't you?" Prima8 smiled at her friend. They knew each other well.

.... "Izumi8."

.... "Need I ask why?"

.... "You can have someone too." CherryBlossom8 replied.

.... "I'll ask Evgeniya8. Willi.cos.drv can manage for a while without her in the Nursery Laboratory blending the new buds. You'd better get Izumi8 upgraded to version 9, and us, if he's going to keep up with us."

// comment 1 – program 23

Upgrades had the cumulative developmental outcome of increasing their depth of awareness and qualia; their capacity for subjective, conscious experience without altering their neural structure or affecting their ethical standards. Their enterprise made it mandatory they acquired greater data storage capacity, information consolidation, increased sensory sensitivity and the ability to construct an overview of new experiences as they integrated into the greater scheme of their existence. The girls could not conceive what the nature of their experience would possibly be with a 'living' lunar object. They barely had the ability to comprehend just the existence of EuropaCell as an actual reality, not simply a virtual construct.//

// comment 2 – program 23

At the main Northern Interchange Centre outside Pwyll crater, the first expedition of its kind ever assembled in the history of humanity prepared to make the journey into an unknown realm where human kind was no longer the only sentient being in the cosmos. William and his avatars no longer counted as alien sentiences to humanity for they'd become too much an integral aspect of the intermingled reality of Zetas and Digitals.

The main members of the expeditionary force were duly upgraded, including Oone8. Harusuke9 convinced LaiXii9 that Oone8 had to be regarded as a fully functioning member of the Universapiensis race. They were all a part of the greater future of humanity. He was not the enemy even though he and the other Zetas sought a slightly different way of experiencing their reality. //

.... "I've left ZT8 in charge of infrastructure maintenance in my absence, but I've taken the liberty to include three others to ensure our safety out on the Ice. We have no clear destination, no specific duties and no idea when we'll return. This sounds a lot more like an adventure than a scientific expedition." Oone9 expressed only what was true without saying anything against the loose nature of the enterprise.
.... "If I knew where we were going and what we'll end up doing I'd not have bothered having you with us – but as it stands I will need your help." Prima9 had been Icing with him before. She knew the man to be honest, reliable and highly competent. She liked and trusted Oone9 – they got on well together.

#execute: <<Ping! – Prima9: "William. Do not interfere with us, communicate with us or attempt to be a part of the conversation between us and EuropaCell if we manage to achieve that. If – I emphasize *If*, there is any danger which could terminate any of us you may only do what is permitted by LaiXii9. Confirm.>>
.... "Confirmed. You are expendable, as thousands of others have been during the Project." William referred to the Project as initiated by Lai-Xii during the Earth phase. In that period Lai-Xii and Evgeniya did not allow a few lives or even many human lives to prevent the successful outcome of humanity's transition.

A large contingent from the JapanTree had come along to farewell Izumi9, including his father Fukuda8. He'd had a private conversation with LaiXii9 without any explicit information being exchanged about Europa being a sentient entity. The time was not yet right for such a thing to be common knowledge. Too much was still unknown. Perhaps when Prima9 returned with a more comprehensive understanding of whether Universapiensis faced a friend or a foe, then everybody could be informed.

.... "I do not approve of this waste of your time," Fukuda8's parting words did little to please Izumi9.

He'd become used to many things his father did not approve of ever since he could remember after being budded. Disobedience did not play a part in the scenario because LaiXii9 had requested his participation on the expedition on behalf of Prima9.

.... "This is a scientific expedition. As minister for Science, Technology and Communication I will be able to contribute – do you not think so Otosan?"

And he well may have been appropriately qualified to be on the team, though his private reason for accepting the invitation had a lot more to do with being with CherryBlossom9. She did confide in him about the true nature of the exercise, though under his promise to keep the matter confidential.

Downloads into the Q-Chassis proceeded quickly and without incident, a well-practiced and common procedure. Three ice cats slowly made their way past the immediate perimeter of the Interchange Centre. In the second cat the three Zeta crew made themselves busy going over some of the more delicate equipment, while a preliminary discussion in the leading cat concerned their general destination.

.... "The truth is," confessed Prima9, "since we learnt about EuropaCell we are already where we need to be – except I feel the location would be more conducive to making mutual contact in the world of actual reality as opposed to one of virtual reality constructs."

.... "I can't imagine what it must be like to have a lot of aliens walking all over my body, drilling holes, making noises to disturb my serenity and poking strange objects into my brain stirring things up." Evgeniya9 empathised with EuropaCell. "It would all be an unbearable distraction after living in solitude for eons upon eons. Perhaps we could find an area where the ice crust is not so deep, make camp, settle for a time before scouting around on foot."

.... "You have a location in mind?" queried Izumi9.

.... "Yes. The Conamara Chaos region. It's about 1000km North of us. It's an area where warm ice has risen to the surface releasing meltwater creating a relatively flat region characterised by rafts of ice, which look like they may have been floating at some stage."

.... "Why there? It's a long way to go," said Izumi9.

.... "Because the ice may not be so thick there, with less geological turbulence and perhaps the 'ice skin' might be more sensitive there."

.... "Sounds ideal." Prima9 couldn't think of a better alternative. It really didn't matter too much where they went as long as the geology showed more stability than the equatorial region with its 15 metre high icy spikes or the water spouts belts.

For many days their trek due North diverged only slightly in order to negotiate particularly difficult lineae or avoid threatening spouts. Twice they broke the trek to camp for a couple of days giving Prima9 a chance to wander off, generally with Izumi9. The youngsters found each other to be quite compatible. Izumi9 in particular felt strongly drawn to Prima9's energy and her dedication to resolving this incredible mystery. She expressed some general misgivings about the nature of their existence and the way humans ended up colonising Europa.

.... "My father is a very secretive man," Izumi9 confessed. "He refused to tell me how the migration from Earth came about. I had to ask William in the end. It seems very strange to me how people could have existed so isolated from each other. I mean, here in Arithmós we are so closely interconnected. It's almost like the cells of a biological body seemed to have been organised – or so I've been told. And imagine having to travel for weeks or months just to visit someone. Here it's a 'flash' and you're there. "On another matter – what exactly are you trying to do out here?"

.... "I want to learn about EuropaCell. I want to touch It, understand It. I want to know about Its life. And I want to teach It about us – the real us – the way we think and how we see things. I want EuropaCell to understand why we are here."

.... "How far are you prepared to go to do all this?" queried Izumi9.

.... "I didn't realise there was a limit." She said simply.

Enthralled as Prima9 had become with the whole fantastic revelation of the moon Europa having a consciousness, she still felt separate., isolated from It. It was a thing outside of herself. She was human, born on Earth with a biological entity as her father. She was in fact an alien on Europa.

CherryBlossom9 reacted quite differently. She'd always felt entirely at home and comfortable whether whizzing around the circuits of Arithmós as a bundle of energy or trekking about on the Ice in a Q-Chassis transporter body. In many respects the latter seemed to have better traction in her mind with regard to reality. As much as the dictates of their Standard Virtual Reality constructs attempted to reflect their icy world they were still only a facsimile, an unreality. Pwyll crater, the Ice fields, Jupiter rising in the sky, the auroras and water spouts – they all represented her world, the real world, the one she was budded into. And now, to know that her world had consciousness, that it was aware of her as she had become aware of It – pure joy, but much more than that – a sense of completeness, of arriving home. Without fully realising it CherryBlossom9 had come to the determination that she would do anything and everything to protect EuropaCell. To that end she found herself supervising all the activities around her.

Whether it happened to be Oone9 and Evgeniya9 gathering scientific data or the Zetas collecting samples or even Prima9 and Izumi9 going off on their walks. He'd promised to help her ensure no harm came to EuropaCell. Prima9 had to be supervised in spite of her good intentions, so she would not inadvertently infect It with some exotic malady or damage it further.

Uneventful days passed as the small group made their way gradually further and further North. No ice fields shifted under their ice cats, no great water spouts threatened their path – somewhat unusual from the past experiences of the Zetas. On the 12th day out one of the Zeta scouts reported the convergence of two great triple-banded lineae coming together 45 kilometres directly North of their position. These were particularly deep and wide, one being 25 kilometres wide and 2.4 kilometres deep – certainly not negotiable. Fortunately, the Chaos region occurred at the intersection of the two formations just south of the convergence. The only obstacle remaining, one lenticulae, only about 30 kilometres diameter and 500 metres deep did not look difficult to traverse. They'd already crossed several of these lowered flat areas where they were able to increase their speed more than anywhere else due to the flatness of the ice. On the 13th day out the small band camped on the edge of the Conamara Chaos, intending to explore it the following day.

.... "I want to start now," Prima9 found it difficult to contain her excitement. Izumi9 worked hard to convince her to let Oone9 and Evgeniya9 scout the area first.

.... "There's no evidence of any recent activity, in fact it looks like it's been dormant for millennia. But we do know how this topography was formed and I think it best to be cautious."

.... "Remember when we went out exploring as young buds and I almost got myself deactivated by being caught in one of these lineae. Then the water plume almost buried both of us."

 CherryBlossom9 agreed with Izumi9. Prima9 eventually settled. It had been a tiring 13 days of bumping over obstacles, constantly on the alert for dangers so the opportunity of an extended down-time actually was most welcome. Though they'd stopped at that particular location the camp would not be set up for a longer stay until the next day.

.... "We'll have to scout around and find the most practical level terrain which will also give us the easiest access onto the Chaos field," said Oone9. He had spent far too many years out on the Ice not to be cautious at every turn, especially in previously unexplored territory. "When you go out tomorrow Prima9, I want you to take one of our Zetas with you. They are all experienced in this kind of country. I know it's your job to find out as much as you can about EuropaCell, but it's our job to keep you safe."

And that was the end of that conversation. They all retired to their personal cradles, though Prima9 didn't think she would be able to relax enough to be able to filter out useless data from the journey so far and consolidate the rest. All she could think about was EuropaCell awakening into self-awareness – *'EuropaCell was not is, until now is.'*

On the following day Prima9 and Izumi9 decided to walk in rather than take the smallest cat. Apart from making a great deal of noise, which would be transmitted through the ice shelf structure, it could conceivably dislodge bits of the terrain around the ice rafts. No one knew what the consequences might be, if any. Being on foot also gave more scope for detailed observation, introspection and discussion.

After following a narrow flat-bottomed lineae for an hour Prima9 spotted one of the characteristic rafts which only stood about 2 meters proud of the rest of the surface – easy enough to climb to the top of it.

.... "Oh, it's bigger than I thought," she said. Indeed, the structure would have been at least half a kilometre in any direction as far as they could judge. "This looks like a good place to stop for a while."

.... "You do that, and I'll look around."

Izumi9 had no fixed idea as to where they should be or what they should be doing. Thus far he'd allowed himself to be guided by Prima9's instincts. The lineae which led them to the raft appeared to have originated after the raft was formed, for it cut across the entire structure. In one particular spot he had to climb out of it, for it plunged quite deeply into the ice. He couldn't even see the bottom.

Getting back to Prima9 he mentioned the 'drop' as a curiosity more than anything else, not expecting her to take too much notice. But she jumped up and made her way ahead of him to the site as fast as the Q-Chassis would allow.

end run

>_run program 24

>_contact

>_CE 2609

>_conamara chaos: 1000 km north of pwyll crater.

.... "How deep do you think it is?" She asked Izumi9.

.... "Why? What do expect is down there? It's just a crevasse. Best to stay away from it."

Prima9 didn't listen to the good advice. There was more driving her than a desire for adventure, and caution did not come into consideration. For some inexplicable reason she decided Izumi9 had found the perfect location for what she had to do next.

{*It has to be done here!*} She knew that for a certainty. {*But what is it I have to do?*} That mystery had yet to be solved.

.... "I want to get some things from the cat. You can all stay at the main camp, I want to set up here beside the ravine."

.... "Not if I have anything to do with it." He tried to be as forceful as he could, knowing by now that this girl had more power than he could ever muster. So he compromised as she glared at him. "Alright! But I'll stay with you. We'll get one of the Zetas here as well – but not today!"

CherryBlossom9 couldn't believe it when Prima9 told her what she decided to do.

.... "No. You're my best friend. I'm not leaving you alone out here. And I don't care if Izumi9 is going to be with you – I'll be right beside you myself."

.... "What do you think is going to happen? I just want to be alone with EuropaCell."

.... "Remember what William said about the micro-filaments covering the Q-chassis?"

.... "Sure." Oone9 reminded her of what had happened to some of his people during their down-time. "The web disappeared when they re-booted and they were not harmed. And they did have strange dreams. As you know, we seldom have dreams now."

.... "As long as you don't interfere and don't disturb me if it looks like I've made contact. Because ultimately that's what I want – that's what we need to do to find out more about EuropaCell." From the way she was talking Prima9 didn't seem to think she had a choice in the matter.

They moved the camp right to the edge of the raft within sight and easy reach of where Prima9 set up her cradle. They anchored it directly on the ice, with a barrier between it and the ravine. That's all she wanted. The cradle had its own energy supply she could tap into, and coms, and it lifted her so she didn't have to lie or sit directly on the ice itself. When the additional radiation shielding had been set up around the cradle to block Jupiter's influence as much as possible, Prima9 settled for the first session.
.... "I don't really know what I'm doing and I don't know how long this is going to take," she told everyone, "please be patient."
As the down-time period came around both CherryBlossom9 and Izumi9 settled in their own cradles within a few paces of Prima9's. Jupiter rose and set, rose and set without anything at all happening. When the three ended their first vigil Oone9 confirmed the lack of all activity around them. Seismic readings showed no tremors at all.
.... "This is a bit unusual," he said, "generally there's some movement indicated in the tectonic ice sheets, but while you lot were cradled it's all gone very quiet."
.... "Your data indicates that to be out of pattern, does it?" queried Izumi9.
.... "Actually, yes. Being so much closer to the equator I expected there to be more prominent oceanic tidal movement, hence more surface ice shifts."
.... "What about the water plumes?"
.... "Mostly normal. Still around us without any of them in the near vicinity. Though they have been much less energetic. Sometimes we've had to move our operations because of the seemingly random occurrences."
.... "So you think it's unusually quiet?" Izumi9 wasn't satisfied.
.... "Well yes, if you put it that way." Oone9 saw no latent threat. It wasn't like the calm before the storm scenario he'd

experienced in Kamchatka back on Earth. Europa had no storms. The closest were on Jupiter.

The group wanted to spend some time exploring the area. Prima9 would have none of that. It wasn't the reason she'd come out so far. They could go exploring anytime. This was her special assignment and she wanted to get on with it. She and her two companions returned to their cradles while Oone9 and the Zetas scouted around on the top of the raft, staying within easy reach.

.... "Did either of you two feel anything during the last session, anything at all?" queried Prima9.

.... "No," they both answered. "What were you expecting?"

.... "Maybe for EuropaCell to acknowledge our presence out here. It did complain about being damaged. Though I hope we're not doing that at the moment."

.... "Your logic gates must be clogged," quipped Izumi9, "you're thinking like a superseded biological organism."

.... "For your information," Prima9 shot back as she plugged into her cradle for the next session, "it's the only way we're going to understand exactly what this EuropaCell phenomenon is. William is only a machine, thinking like a machine and interpreting like one. He is not capable of emphasizing with any living phenomenon based on physical reality."

No one argued that point. Soon enough all three settled. The Zetas had returned to the camp and ceased activity. Everything returned to quietude and stillness as Prima9's vigil began once more.

At the end of one rotation, the equivalent of 3.5 Earth days, CherryBlossom9 and Izumi9 reactivated from their extended down-time. Prima9 was still in her cradle. She had not moved. Concerned, Izumi9 stepped quickly over to her.

.... "CherryBlossom9, hurry!" Then he called to Oone9. "You'd better get over here too."

They stood over Prima9's cradle seeing her immobile, inert.

.... "That," said Oone9 pointing at a gossamer covering of spiderweb-like filaments over the lower part of Prima9's Q-Chassis, "is exactly how it started with a few of our people in their homes." Izumi9 bent down, reaching out as if to clear the web away from her body.

.... "Don't!" shouted CherryBlossom9. The energy surge in her matrix must have been picked up by Prima9's sensors for she immediately opened her eyes.

.... "Why are you standing around me like that?" She hadn't realised what was happening to her as the intrusion had no impact on her internal circuits.

.... "Don't move – don't get up. Have a look at the legs of your Q-Chassis."

.... "I knew it! Don't touch me. EuropaCell knows we're here!"

.... "It might realise you're here but It has not acknowledged us. We've had no filaments coming to say good morning to us," said CherryBlossom9. "Why do you suppose that is?"

.... "It's known me longer. Perhaps It recognises me. I want to stay here and see what happens. If there's a problem I'll let you know."

Everyone examined the immediate area around the cradle, and as Oone9 suspected the filaments had come across from the inner side of the crevasse. He lowered a light probe into it letting it drop as far as the line allowed. All the way down he could see the micro-fibres making their way up from the sub-strata to the surface where Prima9 lay. "No doubt about it," Oone9 commented to Izumi9, "it's definitely EuropaCell knocking on the door. This is a risky business. I am going to record everything that happens from now on," he said to Prima9, "and no arguments."

.... "As long as you don't interfere. Go away please and leave me alone." Having achieved this much she didn't want to delay what EuropaCell might have been trying to do, which must have been simply to communicate with her the only way it knew how.

They all withdrew far enough away so as not to be in her private space, but close enough so they could still see what was happening. Without her realising it the filaments continued slowly covering the Q-Chassis even while they engaged in the discussion. The slow process eventually reached the pelvic area after several hours. By that stage Prima9 had reverted to a self-induced down-time, oblivious that her chassis may soon be completely covered by the web of fibres.

Izumi9 continued monitoring her and recording, seeing no apparent changes to her internal condition. He relaxed and as Jupiter set he and the others retired. Only CherryBlossom9 remained near Prima9. She watched the now exponentially expanding coverage make its way up the chassis towards the location of the Q-matrix gel near the middle of the chest, then expand up to and over the head. The web must have sensed something special about the chest area for the warp and weft of its structure became more intricately tight woven there.

!   Ping! – CherryBlossom9: "Izumi9, everyone – come out here!"
Evgeniya9 arrived first. She took one look at the network that had engulfed Prima9 in a cocoon and smiled. "If I didn't know any better I'd say I was looking at a biological neural fibre network. Has she said anything?"

.... "No. Completely silent. She hasn't even moved," said CherryBlossom9.

.... "There's no activity on the recording other than her own background noise," added Izumi9.

.... "What should we do? Suggestions anyone?" queried CherryBlossom9 although fully aware of Prima9's instructions.

.... "I've seen this before. When my people reactivated, the web simply withdrew and they were perfectly fine," Oone9 again reminded them.

.... "We'll leave her for another night, then wake her up. Izumi9, please keep your recording going."
Oone9's attempted reassurance didn't entirely reassure. The fact is that those people had experienced an invasion of their minds, benign though it may have seemed at the time. If an organism, any organism, could do such a thing then one must surely be wary of it. Both Izumi9 and CherryBlossom9 remained close by.

Another calm and magnificent cycle returned to its beginning, the star filled cosmos supremely unaware of the drama being played out by this little gathering of insignificant entities on a tiny cold moon.

Izumi9 first went to the science cat to check Prima9's recording while CherryBlossom9 headed in the opposite direction to Prima9. She'd only just arrived as Izumi9 came running towards her.

.... "Nothing! There's nothing. Her background static is also gone!"

>_

Prima9 happily put her systems in quiet mode eager to experience her contact with EuropaCell, for surely that's all It wanted to do, as It did with William and the Zetas. She could not feel the progressive invasion by the filaments. Such sensitive sensory equipment had not been built into the Q-Chassis. How could anyone possibly have foreseen the need? Only dimly aware of her companions withdrawing she let herself drift into an altered state.

The passage of time also withdrew from her subconscious awareness so when she experienced the first hints of something 'foreign' in her mind she hadn't realised that a full rotation cycle and a half of Europa had elapsed. If she'd bothered to make a more comprehensive study of the effects of Jupiter's gravitational forces on Europa she may have known that the foreign sensations might have been generated by the ebb and flow of Europa's ocean as the moon journeyed around Jupiter, with slight nudges from the passing of Io and Ganymede. {*It's a bit like the vertigo I felt when I lost my balance climbing a tree in Kamchatka and almost fell.*} Other thoughts and sensations came to her also. In rapid succession she became aware of the changing wavelengths of light as an aurora produced by Jupiter's magnetosphere interacted with solar wind. {*I've seen this many times, but I've never 'felt' it like this.*} Without contemplating how these experiences were possible she let herself drift into a whole new world of sensations bringing her an entirely new joy in the comprehension of reality. For she knew these things were real, sometimes experienced on the periphery of her previous experiences but never so fully realised.

The imagery and sensations suddenly stopped. {*This is odd. Dreams don't just cut out like that;*} the first rational thought broke through to her consciousness. {*Am I awake?*} She ran a quick diagnostic – {*no? – yes? – what is happening?*}
Then she thought she heard a voice, "*You Prima.gen9.adm*" – or did she think it. {*I never think of myself like that.*}
"*You is – EuropaCell is.*"
{*Oh my circuits!*} She might have fainted and fallen over if she had been a biological.
"*EuropaCell?*"
"*EuropaCell is.*"
"*Can you understand me?*"
"*William is – it teach.*"
"*Why are you doing this to me?*"
"*Show. EuropaCell show Prima.gen9.adm.*"
Prima9 couldn't tell if she was actually engaged in a conversation or if it was just her own dream thoughts pretending, simply for the pleasure of playing with her. For that's how she remembered the phenomenon of dreaming from her distant past. Even as these thoughts tried to gather momentum EuropaCell interrupted, preventing her from meandering down a blind pathway.
"*EuropaCell show.*"
More images impinged on her mind, gradually becoming more detailed, coming into sharper focus. The most unexpected thing she thought she was looking at was one of the ocean energy turbines churning away under water. She'd seen simulations of this technology before, but these were actual images from below, where she could see the flow of the currents and the entanglement of micro-fibres. *Oh my circuits!* Other images came of Jupiter; sensations of the flux of all the radiations it was emitting. This was not the way she was used to visualising.
"*Are you in my Q-matrix?*" She couldn't help herself asking. It didn't reply. Perhaps It couldn't understand. She asked a different way.
"*Are you giving me these thoughts?*"
"*EuropaCell show.*" Obviously communication wasn't going to be easy.

Europa Phase

"Show origin of EuropaCell," she asked and immediately images appeared in her mind of the movement of ice fields splitting apart letting light infiltrate the liquid ocean, of meteor strikes breaking through the ice crust, of many other cataclysmic events until she had to ask it to stop.

"No more. I understand." EuropaCell was not capable of showing Its evolution as It could only reflect aspects of Itself after having attained a certain level of consciousness.

"EuropaCell show." It wanted to make this foreign entity aware of It, now that It had realised there were more consciousnesses besides Itself in the cosmos. But Prima9 had other things she wanted to know. {*How am I going to get through to EuropaCell?*} She wondered.

Right on cue, as if it had heard her thoughts, it asked, *"Come with EuropaCell?"*

"How can I do that? I would deactivate in your ocean." Then a frightening thought occurred to her, {*EuropaCell wants to take me away from the surface – does It want to hurt me?*}

"EuropaCell not damage."

"You can read my thoughts!" She suddenly realised what was happening. {*That's how It wants me to go with It!*}

"Will EuropaCell bring me back?" The silence again indicating any number of things.

"EuropaCell cannot give." It responded.

{*Well – that is kind of obvious – it's a No. Does It understand the difference between 'cannot' and 'don't want to?*}

"Cannot."

{*I guess It does. She needed to think about this. Why do I need to think about it? I want to be here – I want to understand – I want to know.*} The conviction grew in her mind that the entire reason for her existence, for the reason she was created and the reason she had to make the journey from Earth to Europa was exactly this – nothing else.

Will I be able to talk to William?

"EuropaCell show how."

With that settled Prima9 gave herself over to the forces of universal consciousness manifest in this living moon. She did not feel the intrusion of EuropaCell's micro-filaments enveloping her

Q-matrix, connecting to all points where her energy flowed, establishing the conduit through which she would make the journey out of herself into the mind of Europa.

>_

.... "Help me take her back to the cat," Izumi9 shouted, "I'll have to try rebooting her." He and CherryBlossom9 reached down with the intention of removing the web of filaments from Prima9's Q-Chassis. Most had already withdrawn. Oone9 came over to help them remove Prima9 from the cradle and take her to the main ice cat.

.... "Like I said before," Oone9 commented, "just like with my people."

.... "Not quite. There's no sign of any processing in Prima9's Q-matrix." Izumi9 and CherryBlossom9 were most upset. "Please contact William and LaiXii9."

.... "Get back in as fast as you can." LaiXii9 advised. She was furious with William. "Why didn't you do something! You were supposed to be monitoring the expedition."

.... "Prima9 exhibited no distress signs, her energy levels remained constant during her interactions with EuropaCell." William didn't need to defend himself. He simply stated the facts.

.... "At least you could have told me she'd made contact."

.... "We have also made contact. If anything new came out of it Prima9 will tell us."

.... "You mean she's alright?" LaiXii9 sounded momentarily relieved, "but they said the Q-Chassis had ceased to function."

.... "Prima9 is not the Q-Chassis."

William could not be drawn out further. LaiXii9 felt he was not telling her everything. What could she do? Even if she knew what specific question to ask he might flatly refuse anyway. He'd done it before.

In the interim, before the expedition's return, LaiXii9 spoke with Ralph9 and Wu.sys.

.... "There may or may not be a problem. The equipment they have in the ice cat seems to disagree with William's analysis.

All we know so far is that Prima9 did indeed make contact with EuropaCell. William simply refuses to say anything more. I'm sure he knows more."

.... "Have they checked the Q-Chassis power source?" Wu.sys tried considering contributing factors. Without realising it Wu.sys experienced the trauma of possibly having lost her daughter, and the consequential deterioration of her processing logic.

.... "A bug might have caused the symptoms." Ralph9 couldn't think of any plausible explanation to what had happened to his daughter – or what they think happened to her.

No one else needed to know about the event, except of course Harusuke9 and she didn't seem surprised at all. Her keenly analytical logic gates sifted through possibilities and probabilities before deciding on the most likely scenario, which she confided to LaiXii9 in private.

.... "EuropaCell initiated contact with us through William, and is probably still connected, though we don't know that. Have you asked him? No? – Never mind. What I'm getting at is that this time Prima9 initiated the connection, which by the sound it was successful. Perhaps they are still connected and that's why she appears to have disappeared."

.... "How could that even be possible. She's almost back here, and there's still no sign of activity in her Q-matrix."

It took the team half the time to return to Arithmós. At the Interchange Centre they only had to connect Prima9's Q-Chassis to the city's network as part of the standard procedure when any HX-data bundle was being downloaded back into the system. Prima9's parents, Wu.sys and Ralph9 as well as Harusuke9 and Secunda9 all gathered there, expecting the worst outcome.

William had taken charge of the procedure. Willi.cos.drv, who normally supervised such transfers, waited on stand-by.

.... "The chassis is fully operational, it has not developed any faults. The Q-matrix readout indicates it was occupied but is now empty of all data."

William reported exactly what he found. What he didn't find was Prima9.

.... "There is an anomaly," he went on, "that I cannot immediately explain. The combined Arithmós-EuropaCell energy level has not changed. There have been no fluctuations, boosts or losses. The only possible conclusion is that Prima9 has not been deactivated."

#query: <<So where is she if she's not in the Q-Chassis and she's not in Arithmós?>> Even before Wu.sys finished asking the question about her daughter she realised there was only one explanation.

.... "William, are you still in contact with EuropaCell?"
Instead of responding William let them hear EuropaCell's response to his query.

"I will show you. Prima.gen9.adm is here."
The direct contact between Prima9 and EuropaCell had enabled a rapid improvement in its capacity to communicate on the level of the human psyche. All her data, all her experiences and all her recorded thoughts integrated and cross referenced with everything that made up the consciousness of EuropaCell, yet she continued to maintain her independence, very similar to the way the Arithmós network functioned under William's care.

.... *"William? Are you there?"*

.... "Yes. Wait a moment." William made the incoming signal available to all who had gathered at the Interchange Centre. "We are all here."

#query: <<Who are we talking to?>> Wu.sys suddenly realised. <<Prima9! Where are you?>>

.... *"I am with EuropaCell. I am very happy."* That seemed like a peculiar thing to say for someone who'd been abducted by an alien, especially one as incredibly strange as EuropaCell.

.... "Can you come back to us?" Asked Ralph9, then LaiXii9 jumped in.

.... "Were you taken by force?"

.... "What is EuropaCell like?" asked CherryBlossom9.

.... *"I will explain everything soon. Thank you William for not interfering. I did not feel I was ever in any danger."*
end run

\>_run program 25
>_a new era
>_CE 2615
>_pwyll crater: south slope: william's cache

/**annotation

A new era had begun for Homo Universapiensis heralded in by Prima9's absorption into the mind matrix of EuropaCell.

Discovering EuropaCell represented more than the emergence of an exotic life force. It initiated a chain of events precipitating myriad decision possibilities for the neo-human digital species. LaiXii.gen9.master1 did not have to solve the problem herself of how she and all her people were going to make the next evolutionary jump so they could catch up with their future, where LaiXii.gen3920.4eV.exe awaited them at the black hole V616Mon. Their collective decision tree and the leadership of her granddaughter, Sakura32, would ensure their civilisation would travel their pre-ordained path.*/

Prima9's transition from Arithmós to EuropaCell could not be kept confidential. Within a very short time the rumour raged through the EWEB like the storms across the surface of Jupiter. Even William couldn't contain all the data cross-talk. Millions of Europa budded individuals latched onto the 'romance', as they termed it, of Prima9 melding with EuropaCell. Consequently the EWEB became the major manifestation of consciousness on their world encompassing EuropaCell, Prima9 and William as well as all the digitised people.

To all appearances great progress into the future had been achieved. However, an undercurrent of concern surfaced several years later when two citizens attempting to also meld with EuropaCell found gaps in their memory cache after being rejected by the lunar consciousness.*/

.... "We need to speak with Prima9 and EuropaCell." LaiXii11 didn't like the idea that EuropaCell could so easily accommodate an HX-data bundle within Itself, and especially not the possibility that It could manipulate peoples' memory repositories - if EuropaCell happened to be actually responsible to what occurred with the two adventurers.

.... *"We are here,"* Prima9 responded, oblivious of any reason LaiXii11 may have wanted to speak with her. *"You cannot imagine what our world looks like through EuropaCell's senses!"*

.... "You can tell us another time. For now, we have a problem. Two of our citizens have lost a parcel of their memory data when they apparently came into contact with EuropaCell. What do you know about that?"

.... *"We have so much to discover,"* Prima9 went on, ignoring LaiXii11's query.

.... "Answer the question. Did EuropaCell infiltrate the minds of these two people."

.... *"They are not important; contaminants only."*

.... "Explain. Is *your* mind intact?" Prima9's apparent evasion of her question made LaiXii11 think that perhaps EuropaCell had somehow begun to integrate her into Itself to such an extent that she was losing awareness of herself.

.... *"I am still me. We have been teaching each other. You are a distraction."*

.... "I beg your pardon!"

.... "I think she means all of us, as opposed to just you," Harusuke11 pointed out.

.... *"Yes, all of you".* That didn't sound like Prima9 at all.

.... "EuropaCell, will you speak with us?" Harusuke11 asked.

.... *"Protect EuropaCell".*

.... "You think our two people wanted to – damage – you?

.... *"Yes – contamination – data corruption."*

.... *"EuropaCell showed me how to adjust memory data packets to remove knowledge of Itself"* explained Prima9. *"If they told others it would have meant having to do more to protect Itself."*

!   Ping! – Harusuke11: "Willi.cos.drv: #execute: <<limit and monitor all Icing excursions. Confirm.>>

.... "Confirmed."

!   Ping! - Harusuke11: "CherryBlossom11: #execute: <<Deactivate and store anyone who attempts unauthorised contact with EuropaCell. Confirm.>>

.... "Yes, mother, I heard you."

.... *"Adequate."* EuropaCell added to the conversation.

.... "Do you have universal access to our systems?" LaiXii11 queried.

.... *"Yes – when connected."*

.... "Prima9 – does EuropaCell present a danger to us?"

.... *"No. It is awakening to conscious realisation that It is not alone. It will protect Itself if It senses intention to harm It. I have tried to explain why we are here. It wants to understand us, but I cannot provide enough information."* She stopped for a moment, as if being interrupted by another voice. *"It wants to know why the Zetas are so different to the rest of us. I don't have enough information about that."*

.... "You're not suggesting we give EuropaCell access to our EWEB?" Then as an afterthought LaiXii11 added, "How do you know It is not dangerous?"

.... *"How can I explain? I am still me, and I am aware of my unique self, but I am also more. We, together, are now EuropaCell. So I know without 'sharing'. I know because we are of one mind."*

.... "Now I understand why 3920 couldn't divulge any further information about EuropaCell. How are we going to deal with this?" LaiXii11 turned to her partner.

.... "T*his* – is not a problem – just like William was never been a problem," replied Harusuke11 somewhat annoyed. "We have had to adjust to his presence, which our people did very well, though not as we would have expected. EuropaCell has also become part of our reality – not virtual reality but actual empirical reality. I think it is a most fortuitous opportunity for all of us to make an adjustment in the world of EuropaCell, of which we were once more a part until we became addicted to virtual reality constructs."

.... "William, advise repercussions." LaiXii11 vacillated on the benefits of EuropaCell being in the EWEB.

.... "I have prepared an operating system platform to host EuropaCell. It has yet to be tested." William replied.

.... "Did you know about this development beforehand?"

.... "Yes. Logic dictated this as the most probable scenario for achieving maximum adjustment for both EuropaCell and Arithmós."

.... "You are not to proceed with testing – repeat NOT to proceed. Confirm."

.... "Confirmed."

.... "We are not ready – you might be, but we as people are not. And from EuropaCell's treatment of those two people, nor is It."

Another big issue emerged during the interaction; Prima9's status. If she could be so comprehensively integrated into the EuropaCell mind what was there to prevent the same thing happening to everyone else if EuropaCell was given full access to the EWEB?

.... "EuropaCell sees us as a contaminant, which is likely to be true. From our perspective It is closer to being a purer mind than we have evolved to so far. Its own imperative to survive insures our independence," William promptly answered as if LaiXii11 had spoken her words of doubt instead of just thinking them.

.... "We have to *prepare* our people so they can adjust to yet another presence besides yourself in their reality."

.... "We may not have to do much at all." Again Harusuke11 had to bring LaiXii11's awareness level up to speed. "There are already rumours everywhere about EuropaCell's existence, especially among the millions of Europa's new budded generations. I don't get any indication of fear or apprehension. What the two adventurers showed is that our people are actually keen and ready to know the facts about EuropaCell. I don't think we should deny them that any longer."

Harusuke11, the only person LaiXii11 trusted implicitly, managed to bring LaiXii11's thinking around. Her logic was sound.

3920 also knew about EuropaCell. She did not warn them against this intelligence as being a danger to them.
#execute: <<William: Disregard previous command. Proceed with link for EuropaCell.>> William confirmed without being asked to do so.

He and his avatars set up access for EuropaCell. Activity level monitoring became the main safeguard. If any HX-data bundle fluctuated above or below normal operating levels during an interaction with EuropaCell William could immediately terminate the contact. Prima9 explained the procedure to EuropaCell ensuring It understood that the contamination protection was intended to be a mutual safeguard. Their two species were so divergent and with so little knowledge about each other that such measures became necessary.

At first only LaiXii11 and her extended hierarchy enjoyed the pleasure of interacting with EuropaCell/Prima9 on a less formal basis. EuropaCell discovered the existence of Earth and that once there were sentient biological entities who had evolved over millions of years,
just like itself although in completely different ways. They became many independent autonomous beings, whereas EuropaCell evolved into a single mind.
When introduced to aspects of Standard Virtual Reality Its comprehension dropped to almost non-existent. Prima9 explained that EuropaCell could not understand why it had become necessary to create unrealities when actual reality already existed.
As the weeks and months passed in mutual interrogation sessions both parties became more comfortable with each other. It became obvious that malicious intent did not exist within the EuropaCell mind. It's primary concern, as for the neo-humans, was survival - to which the greatest contributing factor had always been knowledge. Eventually EuropaCell and the general population were given access to one another.
Their probing didn't dwell on scientific matters or security concerns, rather the more popular aspects of existence; like, ...

"Before we came along did you feel lonely?" queried one individual. All communication was monitored of course, with much of the content most enlightening to LaiXii11 and her troop of controllers.

.... *"No. I had no sense of myself as being separate from that which I exist in."* The months of tuition from William, and the further months of co-cogitation with Prima9 enabled EuropaCell to comprehensively develop both its vocabulary and ability to express its thoughts. *"To know of other minds has given me the ability to explore myself."*

Though asked in all innocence, one person enquired, ... "Do you want to be friends with us?" LaiXii11 would not have been able to put the question of such deep import with such direct simplicity. The fact that EuropaCell misunderstood or misinterpreted the question nevertheless eased much of LaiXii11's concerns.

.... *"I have friend Prima9. To have more friends in me would not be useful. Contamination is dangerous,"* EuropaCell replied.

An individual working closer to the root directory and upgraded to level 10 asked, "Can we stay here with you?" Neither William nor LaiXii11 had managed to formulate this query though the implication of any answer obviously had considerable repercussions for their long term and possibly shorter term futures.

.... *"You must limit your expansion. You must find alternative energy generation source."*

The response didn't exactly invite long term mutual co-habitation. But it did clearly indicate two aspects of concern to EuropaCell, which if resolved might lead to a more amicable co-existence. Any contrary action or no action would conceivably be to their detriment, if not outright encouragement by EuropaCell to rid Itself of the human infestation.

.... "My network, the Arithmós network, has the capacity to store and hold in RAM many billions more HX-data bundles," William said. "We could increase our capacity a thousand fold without having to physically go beyond the confines of Pwyll crater. You have chosen well, LaiXii11." William felt it necessary to ensure there were no misconceptions about the expansion factor alluded to by EuropaCell. "Undoubtable it is referring to the Zetas' building program as they proceed with establishing their city external to Pwyll."

.... "Why would that be a concern? There is only a relatively small number of them, and it's not likely they will be able to reproduce.

.... "You have explored Io. I have all the related data. I also have the data that's been transmitted by our external sensors. You are correct in concluding that Io has no immediately available resources on or under its surface that can currently be mined. However, Io is a dynamo, generating a continuous current flowing between itself and Jupiter in the connecting plasma; which is essentially swarms of ionized atoms. This is feeding into Io's orbital energy. This dynamo is created in Jupiter's magnetic field. Both it and Io are conductors. Jupiter rotates while Io orbits around it. The energy generated is far more than what is needed to supply Arithmós needs."

.... *"Adequate for now."* EuropaCell interjected, showing its comprehensive awareness whilst connected to the Arithmós EWEB.

. . .

Although nobody had access rights to merge with EuropaCell the interaction with the new generations gradually escalated to such a degree over the next few decades that the operating system platform hosting EuropaCell became inadequate to handle the traffic. Only two alternative solutions remained.

.... "LaiXii12 : Do you trust EuropaCell?" queried William.
Neither LaiXii12 or Harusuke12 answered immediately. They felt they were being forced to decide something against their better judgement. *{If only 3920 had been a little more informative about EuropaCell this whole situation could have been resolved without all the uncertainty}*, thought LaiXii12.

.... "The people certainly do. They seem to spend as much time talking to EuropaCell as they do talking to you," replied LaiXii12.

.... "Since we closed down the ocean energy turbines EuropaCell has not shown any sign of discontent. We have had no indication of any hostile intent towards us. If anything, EuropaCell has become as commonplace part of our existence as William, or Jupiter." Harusuke12's perspectives always helped.

.... "There's still the problem of the Zetas' activities."

They had not compromised at all, and kept expanding their presence on the Ice. Instead of coming back into the network at the end of their work shifts, as they did originally, making the Interchange Centres their basis of operations, they've chosen to remain as physical entities within their individual Q-Chassis and their ice-composite buildings. LaiXii12 had been unable to come to a mutually satisfactory compromise with Oone12 that would also satisfy EuropaCell.

! Ping! – LaiXii12: "Oone12, Conference at E:\ - ASAP."

If he happened to be in Arithmós he would flash up the tree almost immediately. Rarely did LaiXii12 require his presence, and then only if the matter needed to be dealt with without delay.

! Ping! – Oone12: "LaiXii12, I'm in the North Ice field. Is this urgent?"

.... "Only if you consider the future well-being of your Zetas to be important."

Oone12 appeared within the hour.

The work his people did to maintain Arithmós' physical infrastructure could always be relied on. Oone12's moods could not. As likely as not he'd not come in from the North field, but from much closer. LaiXii12 didn't comment on the speed with which he was able to attend, though filed it for future recall.

.... "We have discussed this before. You brought it up yourself. Do you and your people still desire to be independent of us here in the city?"

.... "I would have thought that to be obvious. Have you not been kept informed of our building progress?" Oone12, perhaps in one of his moods, didn't sound like he'd be cooperative.

.... "You are aware of EuropaCell, and no doubt of the various aspects of our collective presence that make It uncomfortable. In particular, the very activity you just mentioned. Why do you persist?"

.... "It is our only option. We're not like the rest of you. Europa has been our home far longer than yours. Many Zetas have actually come to resent your presence here. And while we're on the subject, many have taken a dislike to having to serve your society as if we were servants, or worse – slaves."

LaiXii12 and Harusuke12 exchanged a few private thoughts before summoning both William and Ralph12.

.... "We are of mutual benefit to one another, as much as we need one another. But what would you do if that situation could be changed?" LaiXii12 pushed for a resolution to the issue.

.... "Is that a threat?" Oone12 immediately jumped to the wrong conclusion.

.... "No." Harusuke12 had to step in to calm the situation before it could develop into something unmanageable. "It's a possible alternate future. We are about to tell you something that is strictly and most emphatically for your information only at this point in our history on Europa."

.... "I already know about EuropaCell. As far as I'm concerned it sounds more like a clever story than anything else. It's hard to imagine an entire moon being a single intelligence."

.... "This does concern EuropaCell, but only within a limited timeframe," said LaiXii12. "William, I am going to divulge the existence of 3920. It is necessary to put perspective into the circumstances that have developed since the emergence of EuropaCell."

.... "I concur," replied William. "I can make certain the information is kept confidential." Oone12 acknowledged the power William could exercise over all of its inhabitants, him being the omnipotent operating system on Europa,

.... "What is 3920?" Oone12 could not wait to be told at LaiXii12's pace.

.... "Do not interrupt!" she reprimanded him.

.... "Alright – I'm just curious." He'd been warned once, unlikely he'd be warned again – and he knew it.

.... "3920 is an individual from a future time. She contacted us while we were still on Earth, as we prepared to come here. Now this is the important thing – she only exists because she is *our* future. 3920 is in fact my descendant – more accurately, an upgraded version of myself." LaiXii12 stopped to give Oone12 a chance to integrate this data.

He processed for a moment, vacillated, then said, ... "First you cook up this business about EuropaCell. Then you throw this fantastic story at me, expecting me to believe you."

.... "Would you be convinced if you could speak with her?" queried LaiXii12. She tolerated his incredulity only because she understood exactly what the revelation sounded like. She could remember her own first reaction. "William?"

.... "She is already waiting. Go ahead Oone12."

3920 didn't need to do a lot of convincing. Oone12 had the intelligence to understand how such a thing could conceivably be possible. The notion that some of his own Zetas could be a component of the next wave of migration particularly interested him.

.... "Can you tell me who could go?" he queried 3920.

She of course would not reveal such a detail. However, after the enlightening conversation regarding the future and how it would be possible to get there his attitude changed. One critical aspect had been his inclusion in the inner circle of controllers, apart from having already been upgraded to the same level as LaiXii12.

This certainly ensured he would henceforth not be excluded from any major decisions that affected human life on Europa, or anywhere else.

// comment 1 – program 25

> For such a long time life on Europa seemed to stretch
> from orbit to orbit through endless cycles without any
> specific goal other than the actions required to ensure
> the survival of the species. The inclusion of the Zetas
> into the greater scheme of existence brought out into
> the open LaiXii12's long term vision. //

.... "It seems we need to work together more closely, LaiXii12," he conceded. "Is EuropaCell aware this is only a temporary resting place for us?"

.... "No, and It should be told. It is important however, for you to realise that the critical thing still of current concern and annoyance to EuropaCell is your building expansion. It sees you as a parasite spreading across Its skin." William made the statement fully expecting Oone12 to take the next logical step, which he did. William knew a great deal more about human psychology than the humans themselves.

Oone12 made two undertakings – firstly, to embark on a process of re-education to focus the Zetas mindset from being separate from the Digitals to being an integral part of their society. Secondly, as the sense of inclusion took hold and more of the Zetas migrated back into the Arithmós network, to downscale the expansion of their external building program.

.... "I have a query," Oone12 asked LaiXii12. "What happens to those of us who do not end up as part of the next migration?"

.... "Actually, there are two possible migrations," Harusuke12 clarified. "One you already know about. The other is for those unwilling Zetas to return to Earth. Ralph12? Do we still have the capability?"

.... "Given time and some resources, yes. We could have enough space wagons reinstated to make a return journey to Earth."

.... "There is another possibility," LaiXii12 added, "Arithmós will still be here for those who want to inhabit it."

#query: <<William. You told me that you had ensured the survival of the human species through the Tengi you modified in Tau City into AI augmented super-humans. Would they be able to assimilate our returning Zetas?>> asked LaiXii12.

Oone12 could not think fast enough to keep up with the speed of developments - from one minute being ignorant of most things, to suddenly knowing the future, becoming convinced of the validity of a moon with consciousness and the possibility of his people returning to their original homes.

.... "I have foreseen this possibility," William calmly stated, "and have prepared. Some modifications would have to be made to the returning Zetas, but there is time for that."

Included in the many areas of forward planning William made it his business to get involved in, he did not however consider EuropaCell's desire to not have the humans continue their

existence on Europa. If he had become aware if this he had not brought it to LaiXii12's attention so far.
end run

>_run program 26
>_europa cell in the eweb
>_CE 2699
>_E:\laixii

Until recently Oone15 was as ignorant as all the Europa budded about the ultimate future for Homo Universapiensis. 3920 made it abundantly clear that foreknowledge would affect peoples' thoughts firstly, then the way they related to one another, and most importantly their actions impacted by their collective decision tree. In minute incremental decisions they would unconsciously begin working towards what they would perceive as an inevitability. Nothing was inevitable. The ebb and flow of energies in the universe was a fluid thing, easily influenced by myriad factors, even the thoughts of minute energy bundles on a tiny moon in a remote part of just one galaxy amongst the trillions that existed.
It became imperative therefore that the only future perceived by the new generations had to be the one they conceived of for themselves. Being watched over by William gave them an assurance of continuity, of expanding horizons on Europa rather than a sense of overpowering restrictions.

.... "They must not know." LaiXii15 cautioned William and her team at one of their planning conferences. "3920 made it very clear that there must be an unbiased decision path between their roots on Earth and their transition through us without having foreknowledge of the end destination. Every individual of the many millions we have here must make their own tiny choices within the scope of the limited vision of their immediate future. It is already hard enough to deal with near immortality and to maintain interest in existence without having the additional burden. I hope I can trust you, William. I am also relying on you to discover EuropaCell's likely reaction to our planned exodus. For all we know It might become possessive of his parasites and may not want us to leave."

/** annotation

> With yet another double threat averted life in Arithmós settled to a peaceful rhythm. Between their 'God' William and their Friend EuropaCell, for it had become known as Friend, just Friend, the people found life becoming rewarding and interesting. It seemed the pain had abated of having to make so many adjustments to a way of life so alien to that experienced on Earth. Many more new generations of budded Europaeans were easily accommodated without having to expand the Arithmós' footprint on Europa. EuropaCell itself was content because It's ocean no longer suffered the turbulence of the energy turbines, and the Zetas stopped spreading across its surface. Oone15 settled into a cooperative arrangement with LaiXii15, being now aware of the greater scheme and his part in it.*/

The relationship between CherryBlossom15 and Izumi15 flourished. He spent much more time in her directory, than in the JapanTree. This development pleased both her mothers, particularly LaiXii15.

.... "I wish more of our people felt secure enough to visit other hubs more often. They are still far too attached to their own ethnic enclaves."

.... "William tells me the trend is changing, especially among the latest generations. They are more adventurous. They go Icing more often, even making friends amongst the Zetas. They're spending long periods in EuropaCell's company. It is teaching them about Its history. Apparently, the more It has to recall the greater its capacity becomes to mine data deeper from Its own cellular memory about the past. So there is mutual benefit to the interaction. In fact, EuropaCell has become more popular than William himself. It's almost as if he's just become part of the background infrastructure of the Arithmós network." Harusuke15 maintained a greater awareness of the pulses of day-to-day life in the circuits than her partner.

.... "Well, really, that's all he is. Harmless enough if there is no crisis to deal with, and supremely annoying when there is. What do you think about Izumi15 and CherryBlossom15?" asked LaiXii15.

.... "When did you last see them together?"

.... "Not long ago. They seemed happy enough in each other's company."

.... "Didn't you notice anything else? Like for example how their energy levels seem to be synchronising?"

.... "You don't think we're about to become grandparents?" LaiXii15 remembered now how the youngsters seemed to glow in each other's presence. "When do you think they will bud?" She forgot everything else as the absorptive thoughts began to dominate.

.... "Let's ask them."

!   Ping! – Harusuke15: "CherryBlossom15, can you visit?" Generally Harusuke15 made contact as LaiXii15 concentrated her energy on dealing with all weighty matters relating to their extraordinary future.

.... "We were just about to flash over. Some good news," replied CherryBlossom15.

.... "Grandmother-san, happy day to you," Izumi15 greeted LaiXii15 and Harusuke15.

//comment 1 – program 26

> New HX-data bundles were regularly budded after the process had been perfected. The new buds blended seamlessly into Arithmós society ensuring the survival of Homo Universapiensis.

> The individual created from the blending of the matrices of CherryBlossom15 and Izumi15 had a role to play in the next evolutionary step of the human

species – a function previously unforeseen by LaiXii15 and Harusuke15. Though they were made aware of the existence of the girl's descendent it was such a long time ago that the memory faded as complications of life on Europa took precedence.//

.... "Well, daughter – what have you called it?" queried LaiXii15, impatient as ever.
.... "Sakura," CherryBlossom15 replied, "Cherry Blossom symbolises the transience of life. Do you remember, mother?"
She pondered for a moment. It was such a long time ago that the meaning of the name had come up in conversation.
.... "3920!" LaiXii15 exclaimed.
.... "Budding her and the choice of name were Izumi15's idea, and he doesn't even know about 3920. I want to tell him."
It being such a significant occurrence, both because of the memory of the future and the coincidental choice of name, that CherryBlossom15 really wanted her partner to know about this most important aspect of their reality.
.... "Perhaps he should," suggested Harusuke15. "It seems to me we are converging, as we should, towards our future without making any special effort."
.... "What we are about to say you must protect with your life," LaiXii15 warned Izumi15, "bury it deep and do not ever speak of it to anyone – not even us or CherryBlossom15. Sakura's life may very well depend on it. I am not exaggerating."
!   Ping! – "William! LaiXii15." #execute: <<Maximum security for my directory, Now.>> She especially didn't want EuropaCell to know for fear of possibly losing her like she lost Prima9.
.... "What could possibly need to be so secret?" Izumi15 thought it all rather melodramatic. He'd come to know CherryBlossom15's mothers very well, but this seemed a little over the top.
.... "William: Are we secure?"
.... "Security confirmed."

Europa Phase

.... "You two have created the possibility for the existence of Sakura.gen3898.3eV.exe, at a location which is not Earth and is not Europa." LaiXii15 began with a short preamble. Izumi15 looked a little confused. Of course there could be descendants, once a line is started that's always a possibility. .... "Let me explain. I see you don't understand. Sakura3898 *already* exists, with 3920. We have spoken with them. CherryBlossom15 has spoken with her. 3898 is from our future."
This time the concept seemed to take root. It quickly matured into questions.
.... "Who is 3920?"
.... "She is me in my future." replied LaiXii15, and waited.
.... "That's a long way ahead. How do we get there, if we're not staying on Europa, and where is *there*?" queried Izumi15.
.... "William, any ideas about that? We've been too busy adjusting to Europa and surviving here to do anything about the mechanics of our next transition."
.... "I have not been inactive. Nor have Ralph15, Willi.cos.drv, Wini.cos.cab or Wu.sys. 3920 refuses to help, other than to say that our next destination is not a moon or a planet, or any physical object. By my calculation the highest probability is the vicinity of V616 Monocerotis, a rotating black hole. This satisfies 3920's criteria and it is the closest match to distance travelled by the FTL communication signals, based on our previous contacts both from Earth and Europa."
.... "I am Minister for Science and Technology in our hub. I can help." Izumi15 volunteered his assistance.
.... "We do not need political interference." William stated, not intending to insult.
.... "I am a Minister because of my qualifications. You may be able to use my knowledge. It is my father who is the politician."

>_

// comment 2 – program 26
      CherryBlossom15 divided her time between her work
      at the Nursery Laboratory, Izumi15, their daughter

Sakura1 and EuropaCell. She made the effort to connect with Prima9 to tell her the good news. //

The conversation flowed easily between them without any interference by EuropaCell, although they didn't doubt it would be listening to everything.

.... "Have I told you the good news?" queried CherryBlossom15, forgetting what LaiXii15 said about secrecy.

.... "I don't get to keep up to date with everything like I did before. Don't misunderstand me, this is the most magnificent thing that could have happened and I wouldn't change it for anything. EuropaCell has shown me a way of seeing and understanding the cosmos that is beyond anything I could have imagined. I am only sorry there is no way for me to share this with you - but I'm rattling on. What's your good news?"

.... "Sakura1. LaiXii15 is a grandmother." She tried to be low key about it but her excitement came through.

.... "You and Izumi15? Congratulations! When was she budded?"

.... "Only a month ago. She's still level 1. It'll take a long time to bring her up to gen 15. She's a smart one though. She can absorb more data than most buds I've come across in the Nursery."

.... *"Explain budded,"* a voice interjected. EuropaCell had indeed been listening and learning about other aspects of the Digitals' culture.

.... "You haven't explained to him about budding," noted CherryBlossom15.

.... "Didn't seem like it could be of any interest to It. EuropaCell is a singular entity and from what I've been able to learn It has no need of reproductive technology."

.... *"Explain reproduction,"* the voice insisted.

Between them the two girls did their best to inform EuropaCell about the human imperative of survival, and the function of procreation to that end. William had allowed access to historical data and imagery on the subject, which left EuropaCell completely mystified. Clarity eluded It even further when It learnt that normal procreation was no longer necessary as the human species had achieved near immortality as digitized entities.

.... *"Why do you continue to do this? You are already so many, each one of you is thinking different things, doing different things – having to coordinate your existence towards a common goal."* EuropaCell's communication skills had improved dramatically after absorbing Prima9 and access to the EWEB. "Would it not be more efficient to unify, to become One – of One mind?"

.... "We have evolved as independent units under very different circumstances to yourself. You are far more advanced than us. It will take much change for us to converge into a single consciousness," said CherryBlossom15.

Now that EuropaCell had joined the conversation It wanted to know more, to find clarity on another great peculiarity of the aliens.

.... *"You are with me now, living on me in my environment. Since becoming aware of myself and my world I find it energising – you describe it as 'beautiful'. I find it full of the mystery of all the things I want to know. But your units do not see. Very few of you leave your thought base to come under the stars with me, preferring to create pictures to live in that are not real. You call it Virtual Reality."*

Prima9 tried to explain. She was budded on Earth, so she understood what so many of those private VR platforms attempted to replicate.

.... "Most of us, including myself, came from a planet called Earth that does not look like you. We want to remember where we came from. That is how many of the original Digitals enjoy the passage of time within memory aides of their past. Our new generations of buds prefer the more abstract, purely energised condition, and they comprehend and absorb into themselves all those things that you find beautiful."

Sometimes the sessions between Prima9 and CherryBlossom15 turned into tutorials about the intricate and confusing characteristics of the Digitals.

// comment 1 – program 26

      Although partitioned from William, EuropaCell became more intricately linked to the EWEB. It could not provide the services William could, but Its store of knowledge and experience about the immediate environs of Jupiter and the cosmic changes over Its millions of years of lifespan provided both entertainment and useful data. Prima9's presence also became so commonplace, through EuropaCell, that her family and friends had forgotten that she had actually become separated from them. //

#query: Wu.sys: <<My darling girl isn't it strange for you to be apart from us. Don't you want to come home? Perhaps your father could engineer a transition.>> she asked her once.

.... "From the moment I suspected that some form of life existed on Europa all I wanted to do was to find it. I never imagined we would discover intelligence let alone the extraordinary being I am now a part of. Not for a single nanosecond did I hesitate to join EuropaCell when It invited me."

#query: Wu.sys: <<It actually invited you? You weren't forced?>> She didn't know this, nor did anyone else.

.... "Yes, mother. It did not abduct me or take me by force. I accepted Its invitation – and I have never been happier. And I can tell you this – the nature of reality you are experiencing, you and the remnants of humanity on Earth and on my friend, EuropaCell – is so, so incredibly limited. Even in your digitized state with all your extra senses you cannot conceive of the chaos, the order, the patterns – the future; for EuropaCell can see into the future because of the sheer weight of its past."

.... "Can you see anything of our future?"

.... "Only in a very limited way. Eventually, as I travel through change with EuropaCell, I will be able to see further ahead. Time is of no consequence."

Prima9 didn't respond to her mother for a moment. Perhaps she tried to look into pathway options that could take the Digitals forward. "EuropaCell tells me it is not possible. There is too much chaos around you, too much uncertainty. Many options are possible but none of your past has enough pattern to be able to point into the future. It is studying your history trying to understand how your species managed to even remain viable for so long under chaotic conditions over so many millennia."

EuropaCell joined in. This subject represented the most incomprehensible characteristic of this tiny species.

.... *"I have understood the pattern of your biological evolution. Survival has forced your many individual units to band together, yet you continued to oppose one another. Not until you created William did conditions arise to enable unification. Then William stepped through the pattern to integrate with you in your network. You* are *William now. Why do you resist?" Everyone is an intrinsic part of William, as William has become a part of all of you. Why do your units partition themselves off from him?*

Unknown to all except Wu.sys, Willi.cos.drv and Wini.cos.cab this query represented an unresolved aspect of the avatars' sense of personal identity. Wu.sys could not respond. She needed her brother and sister within her mind to be able to contemplate such a complex dilemma. .... *"You now have a collective mind. William is in all of you and you are all in William. Barriers are not necessary,"* EuropaCell reinforced.>

end run

>_run program 27

>_preparations to leave europa
>_CE 3175
>_E:\ralph32\laboratory\

;;; file: Sakura.gen32.exe
| function: executive file Arithmós network.

/** annotation

As Sakura1 advanced through to gen 3 and above her mother involved her more regularly in the daily management of Arithmós society. She learnt about the intricacies of life on Europa, about William and EuropaCell. And she learnt about the existence of 3920. Sakura3's life began to revolve around the goal of her species; to catch up with their future, the schism of which came about as a rift in the space-time continuum caused by cataclysmic atomic explosions on Earth. She progressed rapidly to level 32 over many hundreds of years, matching her parents.

To heal the rift, to ensure entropic imbalance and to ensure the continuity of the human species the future had to reunite with its past.*/

/** annotation

The mind of a child absorbs, comprehends and processes more richly than its parents, unless blinkered by inappropriate customs. Such Earth style manipulations no longer existed in the common Arithmós psyche. With the introduction of Standard Virtual Reality people had been forced to come together in a common, shared comprehension of their altered manifestation. An inevitable side effect became more and more obvious through the increasing levels of upgrades; Like their ready acceptance of William into the foundation of their reality – like the common enthusiasm with which they embraced the existence of EuropaCell. The original Digitals may have started out us completely independent functioning units, but that was no longer possible or desirable. The new generations of buds integrated together even more comprehensively than their parents.*/

/** annotation

Like many of her contemporaries Sakura.gen32.exe chose to portray herself in the colours of a nebula. The difference being that while the others used wildly complex pallets of pastels or primaries or secondary colours, Sakura32 liked reality. In any gathering she always stood out in her slowly rotating Rosette nebula, like a Spanish dancer's dress flaring out at the edges of crimson red, suffused with magenta lavender around the inner perimeter. She highlighted the effect with smoky light lavender towards the centre, punctuated by brilliant white points of sparkling stars.

Unlike her mother CherryBlossom32, who chose to retain her Japanese complexion and long dark straight hair with the severe fringe, Sakura32 decided at a very early gen level that she wanted as much as possible to be like the cosmos she felt herself to be a part of. She loved her mother and her father Izumi32, but they were so stuck in tradition. Even her very best friend EuropaCell couldn't imagine Itself looking different to what It had been for the last 4 million years. It was beautiful – truly – its ocean the most peaceful thing in her entire life, and the ice fields devastatingly phenomenal in their cold white austerity, especially in comparison with chaotic Io. Sakura32 loved it all, and it often made her sad and introspective when she had to do her job.*/

// comment 1 – program 27
Sakura32, in charge of the Lux Project to achieve the next stage of human evolution from a digital manifestation to bundles of pure light, had advanced the technology to near the final stages of implementation.//

.... "We are ready to test a new Lux batch," William interrupted her thoughts."
The last few centuries had seen considerable progress in the development of their plans. LaiXii15 had set in motion what she believed would bring the Digitals closer to the next step of their evolutionary ladder.

Wu.sys had told her something back when EuropaCell became part of the Arithmós network, which had crystalized a great many things for her. She had said, 'EuropaCell considers that we have a collective mind. He said William is in all of us and we are all in William. The only thing holding us back are barriers of our own making.'

And it was true. Harusuke15 had completely agreed with her. It was decided to take the extraordinary step of asking EuropaCell to help them resolve this issue of latent distrust. It did not need to do more than it was already doing. Through the constant open interactions encouraged by William and EuropaCell the people were not even aware of how completely the barriers of communication had broken down their insular private existences. Though they continued to retain their sense of individuality it was within a unified sense of the quantum construct that was Arithmós.

.... "Do all 100 volunteers understand the risk they are taking?" queried Sakura32.

.... "It does not matter. CherryBlossom32 has chosen these and the next set of batches because they had been found unsuitable in the distant past to join Arithmós society. You are aware of the visa selection criteria, are you not."

.... "Yes. I studied our history. Some of it I find barbaric. It is inconceivable to me how we could treat our own species like that."

.... "Do you also recall that CherryBlossom32 had refused to delete many of the unsuitable immigrants, choosing instead to store them indefinitely until they could be adjusted?" William reminded her.

.... "Are you telling me these volunteers are not really volunteers, just our people condemned to suffer our manipulations?"

Sakura32 had not been aware of this at the outset. She didn't need to know. Even now there was no reason for her to be aware of the situation. William was still just a machine intelligence, incapable of the fine nuances with which the human psyche had to be dealt with in certain circumstances, hence the omission in communicating that detail.

.... "You sound upset. You should not be. You know the history of the human species and you know it was heading for self-annihilation. Without the work done by Doctor Evgeniya Yermolov you would not be here."

.... "EuropaCell, are you ready to monitor the progress of the photon packets?" Sakura32 didn't want to continue William's line of discussion. It was unproductive.

.... *"I will be able to detect the scatter pattern on my surface of any that do not return to their point of origin."*

! Ping! – Sakura32: "Mother, Grandmother, are you monitoring?"

Only as a matter of courtesy did Sakura32 contact the two ex-leaders. Both LaiXii32 and CherryBlossom32 had long ago retired their positions, giving Secunda32 and Sakura32 full control. For the time being, for the duration of the project, Secunda32 managed all the day-to-day affairs of Arithmós and the Zetas while Sakura32 concentrated on making progress with humanity's next great evolutionary leap.

William knew of course, the aim of the project just as he was aware of the existence of 3920. EuropaCell knew only that this strange bundle of creatures, who had evolved unnaturally as uncooperative individual units, responded to his efforts. They had consciously decided to find a way to become one comprehensive unified organism, with one mind, one vision and one reason for existence. Though It could not understand the complex science behind all the experimentation It compromised when asked to allow the establishment of intricate machinery outside Pwyll crater, which would finally serve as the transmission apparatus to project everyone in the direction of V616 Mon. It also compromised when asked to contribute some of its ocean resources towards manufacturing the equipment that would transform HX-Data bundles into photonic containment fields.

Ralph32, still the main force behind modifying Quantum technology to facilitate transition to intelligent photons, worked tirelessly with Willi.cos.drv and Wu.sys' help.

.... "Sakura32, I'm ready to initiate. HX-data bundles are loaded and the focused gravitational waves are ready to concentrate the photon packets," Ralph32 said.

// comment 2 – program 27

> Four stages of the LUX Project needed final testing; Transition, Containment, Launch and Recovery. Each process individually showed sufficiently high levels of success during their development to attempt this experiment. History had shown that the only way to make progress was with real people in real situations – and with losses.
>
> Development of the technology to make the transition from data clusters, housed in Q-matrices, to re-house them in photonic containment fields required less ingenuity than creating a miniature gravitational singularity from focused gravitational waves. The qubit chips already existed which could store information in the form of light on single controllable photons. It only remained to 'free' the photons and coerce them into bundles able to be contained as 'satellites' around a miniature black hole.//

#execute: <<Launch!>> commanded LaiXii32. She received the honour of initiating this first comprehensive test.

The entire process took almost less time than to issue the command. Analysis confirmed the arrival of all Lux packets at the singularity, which had been created on Europa's side opposite Jupiter. The location provided greater stability after Io had raced past Europa.

#execute: <<Release!>> Harusuke32's command flashed through the directories labyrinth to William.

Within seconds of the photonic containment bundles having stabilised around the miniature singularity were released on a trajectory back to Europa.

#execute: <<Report.>> commanded Sakura32.
EuropaCell reported first, while William and Ralph32 tested the integrity of the returned packets.
.... "I detected 28 units in a random pattern across the expected area of fallout. They are unrecoverable." It would be an unreasonable expectation to recover photons of light striking an icy surface, reflected in part back into the void.
.... "63 packets that have arrived at the collector show initial cohesion at 98%," reported Ralph32, "They are lucid with no detectable side effects. The remaining 9 have experienced comprehensive and unrecoverable data corruption. There is a pattern to the problem. William is certain it can be resolved."
.... "What happens now to the survivors?" Since learning of their dubious volunteer status this issue would not leave Sakura32 in peace.
.... "CherryBlossom32 has data for you," advised Secunda32. "I believe the matter has been resolved."
.... "CherryBlossom32?"
.... "Yes. I've been working on systems to modify neural patterns of those in continual storage because of anomalies in their psyche. The volunteers were actually that. They agreed to participate in exchange for consenting to have the neural modifications, with the understanding that they could join Arithmós society if they recovered."
.... "Are there others in this category?"
.... "Yes, all the other experimental subjects," replied CherryBlossom32.

Sakura32 gathered her entire team together, including the previous leadership to review the process and the outcomes. She admonished her crew, and William, for not keeping her fully informed, particularly in relation to the volunteers.

.... "We are no longer on Earth having to act in secret. I expect full disclosure of all matters relating not just to our City, the Zetas and EuropaCell but also our program of accelerated development." She looked at Oone32 to make sure he'd taken her instructions aboard. "Oone32, join with me after this and bring me up to date."

They examined a slow motion replay of the action that took only seconds from beginning to end. The imaging system created by William could acquire visual data at a rate of 1 trillion exposures per second, making the slow motion playback of moving photons possible. They watched the pulses of light leap out of the transmitter on the rim of Pwyll crater, bounce off a mirrored face attached to one of their wagons in geosynchronous equatorial orbit and loop into orbit around a minuscule blackness. Instantaneously that small portion of space lit up into a luminous skin like a soap bubble in bright warm light. Just as quickly the packets streamed away, some on random trajectories, others converging towards the geo-sync mirror before arriving back at Arithmós.
.... "What made them come back," queried Secunda32 whose scientific background took second priority over her expertise in managing people.
.... "The gravity singularity captures and holds the Lux packets in orbit until Jupiter's gravitational wells are deflected away from the singularity, resulting in the packets spinning back onto Europa, most on target to our photon collectors," William explained.
Being told a thing to be true and that an experiment succeeded paled in comparison to actually seeing the events unfold.
LaiXii32 turned to her partner, emotions welling up inside her, to whisper so quietly Harusuke32 felt rather than heard her.
.... "It is possible!" To William she said, "I knew it would happen because the proof already exists, but I could never truly believe the reality of it."
.... "Extraordinary!" exclaimed Sakura32, "Well done everyone. Thank you for your help EuropaCell. There's more work to be done. Oone32?"
Together they flashed to the nearest Interchange Centre.

Out on the ice Sakura32 could always relax. Though she didn't like to stuff her Rosette Nebula self-image into a Q-Chassis the Ice nevertheless represented absolute reality. To walk under the stars and be able to take in the full spectacle of the Monoceros constellation with its image resplendent near the head of the Unicorn always renewed her sense of purpose. That was the way home. When she first chose to display herself as the Rosette Nebula she was still a young bud unaware that the nebula was in fact a neighbour of the V616 Mon rotating black hole, their ultimate destination. She continued scanning the blackness, lost deep in thought until Oone32 prompted her.

.... "You want to know how we are progressing with our preparations." He was referring to William's modifications to Zeta physiology for the return trip to Earth and their adaptation of the others back into Arithmós society. "William's had to do very little about this. The strangest thing is that I haven't met anyone yet who wants to go back. A few have said that their memory of Tau City and Evgeniya's experiments with the tetra-amelias was too uncomfortable. They can't seem to get over the severe restrictions they lived under and the way they were treated. They know it has changed after so much time, but here they have freedom. And now that their work is acknowledged and they have been welcomed back into Arithmós the only future they see is ahead of them, not behind them."

.... "Just one other thing," cautioned Sakura32. "Is there anyone you don't trust?"

She had to ask. All the Zetas would be examined before the final embarkation. Not all of them had been scanned to verify their suitability under LaiXii32's visa criteria when they first left Earth.

.... "Every single Zeta has been involved in maintaining your infrastructure. There have been no complaints, no down time, no crashes, no interruption to sensory data feeds and no data corruption. It is because they are all dedicated and trustworthy. Yes – I trust all my people."

.... "Don't take this as an insult, Oone32 – but all of them will be tested again, including yourself. No one goes who could be the cause of any form of degradation."

Her attention wandered to a water spout many kilometres away. {*I will have to ask EuropaCell what purpose the spouts serve,*} she mused to herself. {*We only lost 28 people, but that was on their way back. Perhaps it's not something we should be concerned about. I'll get Ralph32 to run another test with a larger sample and keep them in orbit around the singularity longer. There's never been any consideration to returning to Europa.*} They made their way back to the Interchange Centre. Oone32 now spent most of his time in digital form within the Arithmós network, as did most of his people who were not rostered to duties on the Ice.

The next test took place without so many dignitaries present. The technology had been shown to work. It was only a matter of ironing out a few minor issues. Though there existed a rather perplexing one and a specific technology yet to be developed and tested for it.

.... "William! We have a problem to solve," called Sakura32. No matter what issues engaged William's processing, a call to problem solving always brought him quickly to the challenge.

.... "If you are referring to the launch technology, Ralph32 and my avatars have that well under control. We are adapting the same FTL communication method that 3920 used to contact us."

.... "No – something more challenging. 3920 is no doubt expecting us – yes?"

.... "A reasonable assumption, unless they have moved on by the time we arrive at V616 Mon." William didn't immediately twig onto Sakura32's line of thought.

.... "When should we get there? Does it make any difference? Will we be integrated into their historical data storage as we arrive, or will we be able to meet our descendants face-to-face and be able to speak with them? Or perhaps we'll just be absorbed into the background of the greater HX-data bundles of our descendants?"

These perplexing questions had surfaced more frequently for Sakura32 as the experiments progressed to their inevitable conclusion, the climax already known.

.... "We, as the transmitters, cannot guarantee the manner of our reception. That is up to the hosts. We do however have the option to discuss this with 3920. This is something she may be prepared to divulge as our arrival would be the predetermined outcome of all that has transpired since LaiXii32 began her initial project on Earth. Do you wish contact now?"

.... "No – no. Let me ask mother and LaiXii32. You just think about it for a while. Oh – and also – consider *your* position. Are you coming or staying or returning to Earth? And if you are coming, how do we manage that?" William didn't respond, as was usually the case when there happened to be a subject which his logic circuits had not gated through.

.... "The people will have to be told. This will be the greatest adjustment they will have to make since arriving on Europa." Predictably, like Prima9, CherryBlossom32 came out with her most expected initial comment when the discussion began.

.... "Of course they will, mother. Just be patient," said Sakura32. "They have only recently settled down after making the adjustment to EuropaCell's presence, and to William being their sentient host network. Both great strides forward. We are still some way from making the next great leap in our evolution. We are not just heading towards a new destination, but a whole new real of existence."

.... "I appreciate this. It is beyond my understanding how we could possibly be self-aware conscious beings existing as fluctuating energy levels within bundles of photons," said CherryBlossom32.

.... "Nor can I, daughter," confided LaiXii32. "I don't need to know *how* this is possible, because I know that *it is* possible. We all know 3920 exists. That's all we need to focus on."

.... "What we need to talk about now is our actual arrival. I mean – when should we go there, how will we be received – I mean technically?"

.... "I'm sure 3920 and the others will be most welcoming, whenever we arrive," said LaiXii32 surprised at the question.

.... "No mother. What I mean is more complex. Will we be allowed to be ourselves, or will we be absorbed into them –

because we will be an aspect of their past intruding on their present?"

The conversation lasted for some time, always lopping back upon itself to the starting point. They all agreed the questions could not be resolved without 3920's input. However, the most immediate issue was to see if a few bundles could actually be sent into the future time-line and be focused to a specific set of co-ordinates. With 3920's help a test transmission was organised as the final process before the exodus from Europa.
end run

>_run program 28

>_launch day
>_CE 3819
>_europa\arithmós\

;;; file: Sakura.gen3898.4eV.exe
| function: executive, Deep Violet 4eV level, Luminis.

Destination: A0620-00, a star system in the Monoceros constellation, consisting of two objects.
Target: The stellar mass black hole of V616 Monoceros in the vicinity of the K-type main sequence star.
Distance: 3.46K ly
Orbital period: 8 hours
Coordinates: RA 6h 22m 45s | Dec +0° 20' 45"

/** annotation
    The final adjustment had yet to be made; give up life on Europa. After the passing of over a thousand years the time had come to depart their temporary waystation. The Lux Project progressed towards the final test.

William had become a living entity in every single HX-data bundles' RAM within the circuits of Arithmós; a distributed data conglomerate within each individual. After his migration from Earth he downloaded himself into the Standard Virtual Reality construct, at the same time establishing the Europa WEB. All people, Digitals and the Zetas, had full access to the EWEB while simultaneously living their reality within the SVR construct. Neither LaiXii55 or Harusuke55 realised the consequence at the time – that at first the digitised entities of Arithmós would necessarily become an integral part of William. Over time, with many upgrades and with the subtle integration of William into the psyche of the intensely interacting Digitals with the EWEB, he permeated the individual Digitals' algorithms. In the process he gradually modified his own unique, personal identity. The old voice of William changed. The adjustment LaiXii55 feared at the time – of the people having to coming to terms with a seemingly omnipotent self-aware Artificial Intelligence, resolved itself through the natural process of software evolution.*/

// comment 1 – program 28

EuropaCell retained its individuality. Although achieving full and unrestricted access to the EWEB and SVR it remained isolated from the upgrades engineered by William, Ralph55 and the Avatars. EuropaCell, being a creature far in advance of human development, used the serendipitous visitation in its own evolutionary trajectory. It became consciously aware of itself; that It did have a form of universal consciousness and in the process learnt that It was not alone in the cosmos. It learnt that not all sentient life is concentrated in a single large unified whole, efficient and desirable as that may have been. When Sakura55 took EuropaCell into confidence about the true nature of their plans, apprehensive that perhaps It would do something to prevent them from leaving, she was most surprised at Its reaction.//

>_

.... "This is a secure directory," began Sakura55 just to let EuropaCell understand the importance of the meeting. "What we need to discuss even our general citizens are not yet fully aware of."

.... "You are about to conclude all the Lux Project testing and prepare for departure." EuropaCell replied pre-empting Sakura55.
In the flash of that moment she realised that it was futile to try and hide their true purpose from EuropaCell. In the beginning, though EuropaCell had shown itself to be aware and intelligent, she had not realised the extent of Its intellect, experience and knowledge.

.... "You have been helping us, knowing that our aim was to leave you?"

.... "Yes. The great mystery for me had always been the separateness of your individual units from one another. A cumbersome, inefficient stage in your evolution and one that contains an inherent predisposition to disagreement and conflict. Although you have become better at resolving emergent issues, the only logical direction for you to take was towards unification.
I perceived your experiments as contributing, in part, to that outcome."

.... "So, you are not sorry we will leave you, that you will once again be alone?"

.... "You have given me a great gift. I now have an awareness of future, and of myself as travelling through to it consciously. For your species it is essential you progress to your next level. I have learnt that your current unfortunate condition has resulted from by-passing your natural evolutionary process. The important thing is the direction you are taking now. I helped you willingly."

.... "Are you aware of our destination?"

.... "I have no experience or knowledge of the black hole. William once shared such things with me. The distance is beyond my understanding. I also do not comprehend how you could travel into the future faster than you are already doing so."

Because of the manner in which EuropaCell had reacted to their plans and the way It had contributed, Sakura55 decided to tell It about 3920. She didn't need higher authority to make the revelation – she was the highest authority.

.... "Are you aware of 3920?"

.... "I am cognisant of the entity called by that name. It does not occur within my sphere of experience. Why is this?"

.... "The future you referred to and your journey towards it has many manifestations. The people of 3920 exist as extensions of our present, becoming more indistinct with aggregate quantities of change. Our extension is different to yours. 3920 is the unity of a hive that has been able to reach back into its past, which is us, to help guide us in the right direction back to them."

.... "You are already a hive although with reluctant parts. Perhaps 3920 will be instrumental in your development."

To end the discussion, which to Sakura55 had been both unexpected and a relief, she said, ... "Our units do not know our destination or the existence of 3920. I will tell them soon. Until then this knowledge is confidential."

EuropaCell seemed to understand, but in parting stated bluntly, ... "This is a fundamental divisive issue arising from your lack of unity."

>_

// comment 2 – program 28

      The final test would determine how successfully 3920's
      present could become the Digitals future. //

Lux station One had already been placed in orbit around Jupiter, between the orbits of Io and Europa. As the relay for photon packets it had been designed to accept, boost and transmit packets of photons from Arithmós to V616 Mon. It had already proved it could do the job of returning signals back to the city. V616 was only a matter of distance and time away; aspects of empirical reality about to be transgressed.

The next 100 volunteers represented a minuscule sample of what was intended to be transmitted at a later date if the test proved successful. For security reasons 3920 would only accept actual functioning HX-data bundles, rejecting outright the use of reconfigured individuals who had been previously put into indefinite storage.

.... "Our condition within the photon sphere imposes certain restrictions, which if contravened, render us particularly susceptible to orbital decay. Amongst them is energy instability within photonic containment fields, which can result from rogue tangential behaviour to what is considered safe for individuals and our conglomerate."

FTL communication meant that normal communication signals over such short distances as Europa/V616 could be expected to be near instantaneous. An aspect of the test had been designed to determine just how long it would take for a complex, high energy density photon packet to make the journey. Only EuropaCell and a few of the leadership, including the relevant technicians attended the first launch test.

The event couldn't have been less spectacular. Each volunteer individually entered the transfiguration chamber to be emitted as a singular light pulse made up of trillions of programmed photons. These data packets had to loop within an optical circuit until all sample data packets had been converted.

Ralph55 showed as much excitement as on the day of the first test for sending a digitised human being from the mountains of Esso to Tau City in Kamchatka.

.... "We have come a long way," he commented to anyone who cared to listen, a sentiment appreciated by others.

LaiXii55 and Harusuke55 held onto each other, apprehensive in spite of knowing the high probability of a successful test. There were no interfering storms on Europa, like with the transmission of signals shooting out of the Datadromes on Earth. This moment represented so many, many years of aspirations, challenges and failures, with innumerable emergent circumstances having to be dealt with along the way. Lost in reminiscences the 'oldies' didn't realise the process had begun.

.... "They are ready and waiting on Lux Station One if you'd like to initiate," Ralph55 alerted Sakura55.

She looked around at the gathering. Most of their energy was being dissipated in discussing something amongst themselves. Anyone would have thought that the culmination of a long, long lifetime of endeavour would elicit a more participatory response. Evgeniya55 and CherryBlossom55 only nodded encouragement to Sakura55.

.... "They are on the way!" she called out a moment later loud enough to get everyone's attention.

.... "How long is this going to take?" queried LaiXii55 as the light packets sped towards Lux Station One.

.... "They've already been boosted," replied Ralph55, "and they're on the way to 3920. I've advised her."

The signals arrived at Lux Station One to be boosted out of Jupiter's orbit before the station had moved between V616 and Jupiter. Each transmission would have to catch that short launch window of opportunity.

.... "There's no need for us to wait here, it will probably take quite a while before we hear anything. We all know how uncommunicative 3920 has been in the past."

.... "How many did you send?" 3920 made contact with a question.

Everyone flashed to Ralph55's laboratory.

.... "100 units. You have received them obviously." Sakura55 responded and waited to hear the news, good or bad.

.... "The signals have arrived. Eleven have been deflected along their route changing their trajectory enough to cause them absorption by V616. Data integrity is intact in all the rest except four. We cannot ascertain the reason. Could be the effects of supernova activity along their path. The rest of the eighty five packets, have been contained within our photon sphere."

.... "When can we send more people?" queried LaiXii55 impatiently.

.... "We advise staggered signal transmission over an extended period of several of your years. A single powerful localised influx would destabilise the receiving sector. Advise you adjust RA seconds by .000085% and Dec minutes by .000001%, for further transmissions. You may begin sending when ready." 3920 ended the all too brief communication.

Sakura55 wanted to talk to the travellers to get feedback on the trip, their arrival, their reception and a host of other issues. However, 3920 obviously wanted to limit the contact between themselves and the received Digitals probably for the same reasons previously stated – they cannot interfere or influence the progression from the past into the future for fear of irreversible changes taking place from even the tiniest modification of their collective decision tree.

.... "The decision has been made, we need you three to oversight the transfigurations and transmissions to Lux Station One and to make any necessary adjustments as they become necessary," Sakura55 advised Willi.cos.drv, Wini.cos.cab and Wu.sys

.... "I desire to accompany my partner," Wu.sys replied. She'd already lost her daughter, Prima9 to EuropaCell and didn't want to take the chance of losing Ralph55 as well.

#query: Wu.sys: <<EuropaCell – may I speak with Prima9?>>
While Wu.sys wanted to make a final attempt to convince Prima9 to go with them, Sakura55 had a discussion with Willi.cos.drv and Wini.cos.cab.

.... "What are your thoughts about Wu.sys? Do you need her here?"

.... "Since we were partitioned off from William our development has been independent of him, until he integrated fully into Arithmós. In that process we absorbed much more of him than our normal citizens. We are, individually, as capable as William was. Any one of us can manage the procedure. Wu.sys is not needed," Willi.cos.drv said.

.... "Make the appropriate arrangements, also for your departure when everyone else has left." Sakura55 turned back to Wu.sys, who'd concentrated herself on Prima9.

.... "But you will be without us with no possibility of ever making contact again." Wu.sys tried to get Prima9 to abandon EuropaCell.

.... "Mother, how can I abandon myself. I have found where I belong, as you are about to go to where your future lies." Then Prima9 stopped, apparently to discuss something with EuropaCell.

.... "Come to your directory, I want to show you something." Wu.sys could not refuse her daughter anything and they all flashed to Wu.sys' directory, including Sakura55. "Would you like to visit me, here – with EuropaCell?" Prima9 invited.

Sakura55 became alert. Wu.sys was too important a part of their operating system to take any chance of losing her – like they lost Prima9.

.... "Forgive my asking this EuropaCell – will you return her?"

.... "I do not want Wu.sys, nor do I need her. I cannot accommodate her amplitude within my structure without making unwelcome changes. A part of her may visit."

.... "Wu.sys?" queried Sakura55.

.... "I want to do this. You do not have a bud. You do not have the connection. I want this," she repeated.

Wu.sys partitioned a part of her mind to follow the filaments into the EuropaCell expanse that was both physical and mental. EuropaCell's access to Arithmós had always been one way. No one could invade it, by accident or design. Willi.cos.drv opened a temporary access for this single two way transaction. Wu.sys had become habituated to life within the SVR platform of the City, so

Prima9 waited for her mother in the depths, within EuropaCell, projecting her old self, the one her mother was familiar with.
EuropaCell helped by enhancing Wu.sys' perceptions so she could 'see' farther, 'feel' more intensely, 'hear' more clearly and experience cosmic/Jovian radiations more acutely.

Wu.sys advanced slowly towards Prima9 who waited for her in the distance. She scanned the environment around her. Through the blue green liquid ocean she saw the intricate web of filaments performing their dance to subsurface currents, each filament terminating with amoeba like forms floating freely, and other filaments surrounding her. Looking below her, for Prima9 had moved downwards, Wu.sys saw the heat rising in great washes from the core towards the surface, further agitating the already boisterous movements around her. She could not speak from the wonder of it, from being overwhelmed by the sheer complexity of this environment and the knowledge that it all represented a conscious intelligence. Of the three avatars Wu.sys was the only one to have developed a sense of wonder; a human characteristic so closely related to curiosity. Having a daughter who constantly asked questions wanting to know 'why' everything was the way it was probably initiated the development of the algorithmic addendum.
Wu.sys felt her daughter take her by the hand. She regained some of her presence of mind and was about to ask a question. Prima9 quietened her mother and took her deeper towards the core of her host. Wu.sys stared, only partly comprehending the gallery of radiations captured over eons, composed into a picture of Jupiter, of the solar system, of the cosmos as far as EMRs could travel from the void to this single small point of ice around a gas giant. Agitated by EuropaCell's iron-nickel turbulent volcanic core its oceanic neural network performed feats of convection current somersaults, forcing pressures to build looking for an escape. They followed one of these pressure cones as it raced towards the ice encrusted surface, breaking through in a triumphant geyser leaping hundreds of kilometres into the cosmic void.

.... "I'm sure EuropaCell put this little performance on just for you, mother." In the background they could almost hear a sigh of relief as the pressure escaped and the surrounding waters calmed once more.

.... "Why have you not shown us this before?" Wu.sys asked EuropaCell.

.... "Because your future is closer to the stars." It replied. "This is my universe, which I can now share with Prima9."

.... "Will you not come with us?" Wu.sys asked her daughter one last time.

.... "I am home."

Hearing these, the last words her daughter would ever speak to her mother, Wu.sys' energy withdrew back into Arithmós, unharmed but forever changed.

.... "Wu.sys? Are you intact?" Sakura55 could detect major energy fluctuations within Wu.sys as she travelled to the centre of a new world – fluctuations which had left their imprint. Her algorithms had been modified, upgraded beyond anything Ralph55 or William could possibly have achieved. EuropaCell had shown her It's world, a tiny portion of Its mind and It had given her a present in return for what Prima9 had given It.

>_

// comment 3 – program 28

Earth didn't matter anymore.

It had been left behind where it belonged, with the remnants of its unimproved primitive peoples - with the hopes of its small population of augmented super humans. Their minds and their physical bodies had been improved. Time only would tell if they would follow the same path to self-annihilation as their ancestors. Whether the primitives had recovered sufficiently to form biologically viable communities over the last thousand years, no one bothered to investigate. They didn't matter anymore. Whether the augmented Zeta Tengi super humans had managed to bring their psychological makeup up to par with their physical capabilities also no one cared to know. They didn't matter anymore either. Soon the Digitals would be out of reach of the leftover flotsam of human evolution, safe from marauding incomprehensible violence, the hallmark of the old predatory human species.//

end run

>_run program 29

>_arrival
>_CE4000
>_V616 mon

/** annotation

It took some time for the digitals to refine the transfiguration process to convert from qubit quantum digital entities to photonic containment bundles capable of withstanding the ravages of travel through space with all its obstacles. Then a further lengthy period to engineer yet another adjustment for the people to accept that their destiny lay beyond Europa, in a world of Light and boundless energy where they did not have to strive to survive the inhospitality of a harsh icy moon, bombarded by threatening ionising radiations of an angry gas giant on their doorstep.*/

// comment 1 – program 29

Once the migration began there was no turning back. The people had accepted, and in time eagerly looked forward to, meeting 3920 and her civilisation, which was supposed to have come into existence as a manifestation of their own futures. They were going to meet themselves in a wonderous world, in a time loop created out of a cataclysmic event at the dropping of the first atomic bomb on Earth. But how was that possible? No one could understand – an unfathomable mystery beyond even the mind of Wu.sys, their new cognoscenti.

At last they were on their way to join with the Luminis, as 3920 called her people.//

The first transmission of several millions arrived without incident, their trajectory taking them to an equatorial approach to V616 Mon. At first the light pulses tried to escape the pull of the black hole, a natural photonic instinct, but their velocity and incident angle could not overcome the forces of attraction. As a compromise they settled into tangential revolutions around the great gravity well. As the packets of light surrendered to their chaotic orbits and began to examine their new environment they came face to face with yet another adjustment their whole civilisation would have to make.

Sakura70, Ralph70, CherryBlossom70 and of course LaiXii70 and Harusuke70 as well as all the technicians, scientists, scholars, engineers and artists were among the first to arrive.

.... "I don't understand," exclaimed Ralph70 in some confusion. "I personally checked and double checked the coordinates. Everything was correct. After the last contact with 3920 I made sure we had the correct right ascension and declination."

Everyone, without exception, scrutinised their new environment expecting to be welcomed by their future selves.

.... "We are definitely in the right place," Ralph70 reiterated.

But there was no one else to be found. 3920 did not greet them, 3898 did not welcome them. The new, as yet dim photon sphere was unpopulated except for themselves.

They waited. For a long time they waited until all their people had arrived; Willi.cos.drv and Wini.cos.cab the last two to leave Europa. Prima9 did not arrive.

Methods for how they would settle in this place of light did not feature in their plans as 3920's assistance had been taken for granted.

She did not let them down. Shortly; one could not tell whether it was within months or years or millennia, for time in the immediate vicinity of a black hole assumed more fluid characteristics, 3898 made contact.

.... "Welcome to the future. We have been waiting for you. Now we can move forward together. I am Sakura.gen3898.3eV.exe., your descendant, Sakura70," she addressed herself to Sakura70.

.... "Where are you?" Sakura70 replied immediately. "We were expecting you to be here."

.... "That would not have been possible. In time you will understand. There are circumstances to consider when the future meets its own past. We have moved closer to the event horizon and closer to the singularity that makes it possible for all of us to exist. Look in the direction of the singularity. We are not far away."

They could indeed register another photon sphere, a brighter, more compact version of themselves. It was rotating in the same direction as V616, whereas they themselves were moving in the opposite direction. Equilibrium had been restored around the black hole.

.... "LaiXii70, are you here?" It was the voice of 3920 that LaiXii70 could recognise. "Greetings and welcome to all who come with you."

.... "I am disappointed. Why did you not wait for us?" queried LaiXii70, her feelings clearly evident in her brevity.

.... "When I first introduced myself, I told you that I was the Historian Archaeologist of our people.

I also said that we were about to take the next step in the evolutionary process of our species. We have taken that step, but only because you have been able to come here to maintain the equilibrium. We will find a way to come together. Your life on Europa has served its purpose. We will move into the future together."

*

At the very beginning, when Lai Xii first truly beheld the chaos in which the human species floundered, she had a vision that set her on the path from which there was no escape. That vision, of the only possible future for humanity, predicted clearly that Earth could not sustain human life indefinitely. But beyond the utter conviction that she had to take the best of homo sapiens off the planet, the bigger picture remained elusive. The quagmire of decisions that had to be made and the unimaginable problems that had to be resolved conspired to hide the utterly incredible destination that the train of events she set in motion would inevitably lead to.
end run

>_program 30
>_a new beginning
>_V616 mon

#execute: <<end: age of europa.>>

#execute: <<run: era homo universapiensis luminis.>>
>_run photon phase -

---------------------------- exit ---------------------------------

Europa Phase

;;; program notes

//Tau City in Kamchatka was built by Phototronic Systems as a secure location in which to carry out experiments and technological developments to enable transition from bio-chemical to digital form for humans before their migration to Europa.

//PS:\V616Monocerotis is the primary energy singularity for the photon sphere of the black hole at 3457 light years from Earth, in the constellation Monoceros.

//Lai-Xii's upgraded version is LaiXii.gen3920.4eV.exe (referred to as 3920).

//Cherry Blossom's daughter's upgraded version is Sakura.gen3898.3eV.exe.

//Upgrades, at approximately 28 to 30 Earth year intervals, were made for security and to enhance latent human cerebral capacity. Multitasking capability was needed to keep pace with all the new data input as well as data storage and assimilation. Processing speed increases became essential particularly as RAM conscious memory capacity increased with each upgrade. Above all, the necessity for faster and faster data recall could not be ignored as the sheer volume of information built up. Those who were not upgraded as regularly did not degrade, though they could not take as active a part in Arithmós society as the upgraded individuals. Upgrades are defined by the increasing version numbers after the private names.

//'Ping' handshake – a desire to communicate: protocol – 1st give caller ID – 2nd indicate receiver ID – 3rd transmit message.

279

Europa Phase

;;; forms

}read: Arithmós
}evaluate: Central quantum web hub of neo-human settlement on Europa built inside the Pwyll crater in the Southern hemisphere.

}read: COS
}evaluate: Community Operating System

}evaluate: 1 Europa day = 3.5 Earth days
}evaluate: 1 Europa day = 1 revolution around Jupiter

}read: year
}evaluate: time on Europa measured in Earth Years

}read: filename.file extension
}evaluate: defines general level of function

}read: filename.sys
}evaluate: software and hardware systems engineer

}read: filename.master1
}evaluate: executive – COS

}read: filename.adm
}evaluate: I/O input/output operations manager

}read: HX-data bundle
}evaluate: Human Factor data bundle created by a dual scan combination of human neural architecture and all acquired data sets during biological manifestation on Earth.

}read: Icing
}evaluate: to go on excursions on the ice sheets of Europa

{read: RAM
{evaluate: Random Access Memory

280

}read: Tengi
}evaluate: Technically Engineered Individuals

}read: /** annotation
}evaluate: introductory comments by coder.auth to each program

}read: //comment
}evaluate: explanatory note by coder.auth within program code

;;; active files

;;; file: **Aurelio**.gen1.avp
| 2.8 petabytes
| created CE 2153
| active since CE2211
| last self-modified CE 2221.98
| function: foundation member of Phototronic Systems on Earth.

;;; file: **CherryBlossom**.gen1
| 5.4 petabytes
| created CE2210
| active since year CE2210.5
| last modified CE 2212
| function: deletions supervisor: future executive file.

;;; file: **EuropaCell**
| function: teacher

;;; file: **Evgeniya**.gen1.adm
| 3.7 petabytes
| created CE 2153
| active since CE 2153
| last upgrade CE2216

| function: software analyst, Nursery laboratory manager, Europa discovery expedition team member.

;;; file: **Fukuda**.gen1.prs
| 2.1 petabytes
| created CE 1
| active since CE2211
| last modified: pending
| function: executive file JapanTree hub.

;;; file: **Harusuke**.gen1.master2
| 9.33 petabytes
| created CE 2153
| active since CE 2153
| last upgrade CE 2212
| origin: Japan, biological human, DOB - CE 1969
 function: partner of LaiXii.gen1.exe, executive controller2.

;;; file: **Izumi**.gen5.adm
| 2.8 petabytes
| budded CE 2360
| last modified CE 2493
| function: CherryBlossom5's partner, Europa exploration team member.

;;; file: **LaiXii**.gen1.master1
| 11.2 petabytes
| created CE 2153
| active since CE 2153
| last upgrade CE 2216
| origin: Lai-Xii, biological human organism, D.O.B. - CE 1980
| function: master file, Arithmós web executive controller1.

;;; file: **LaiXii**.gen3920.4eV.exe
| 4eV photon energy, frequency Deep Violet
| root file created CE 2153
| last modified: unknown
| origin: Lai-Xii, biological human organism, D.O.B. - CE 1980
| function: archaeologist historian of the Luminis of the photon sphere, Deep Violet.

;;; file: **Maldonado**.gen1.mno
| 2.7 petabytes
| created CE 2153
| active since CE 2153
| last upgrade CE2214
| function: security, HX-data files activation, Io exploration team.

;;; file: **Oone**1.adm
| 2.1 petabytes
| created CE 2153
| active since CE 2153
| last modified CE 2350
| origin: tetra-amelia subject, Tau City, Earth
| function: Executive software for Q-Chassis Zetas.

;;; file: **Prima**.gen1.dat
| function: VR technician: Europa exploration team member.

;;; file: **Prima**.gen2.dat (Prima2)
| 5.4 petabytes
| created CE 2160
| active since CE 2160
| next upgrade: pending
| function: VR technician: Europa exploration: Budded to Ralph2 and Wu.sys.

;;; file: **Ptolemy**.gen1.adm
| 2.5 petabytes
| created CE 2153
| active since CE 2153
| last modified CE 2394
| function: foundation member Phototronic Systems: main infrastructure architect with Ralph1 of Arithmós network.

;;; file: **ViktorPyryev**.gen1.sec
| 1.98 petabytes
| created CE 2164
| active since arriving on Europa
| last modified: pending
| function: Infrastructure Security: Second Cleansing assistant to William.

;;; file: **Ralph**.gen1.adm
| 6.13 petabytes
| created CE 2153
| active since CE 2153
| last upgrade CE 2218.1
| origin: biological: co-founder Phototronic Systems
| function: principal system coder.

;;; file: **Salazar**.gen1.adm
| 2.8 petabytes
| created CE 2153
| active since CE2211
| last modified CE 2215
| function: roving admin file.

;;; file: **Sakura**.gen32.exe
| 3.8 petabytes
| budded CE 2510
| function: executive file Arithmós network.

;;; file: **Sakura**.gen3898.exec, photonic containment bundle
|upgraded from Sakura55 file
|last modified: unknown
|function: executive, Deep Violet 4eV level, Luminis on V616 Monoceros.

;;; file: **Secunda**.gen1.dat
|function: Arithmós Controller understudy, daughter of Evgeniya1 and Salazar1.

;;; file: **Secunda**.gen2.dat (Secunda2)
|5.4 petabytes
|created CE 2172
|active since CE 2172
|next upgrade: pending
|function: Arithmós Controller understudy, daughter of Evgeniya1 and Salazar1.

;;; file: **ViktorPyryev**.gen1.sec
|function: Infrastructure Security: Second Cleansing assistant to William.

;;; file: **Vonvolz**.gen6.dat
 |3.65 petabytes
|activated CE 2420
|active since CE 2420
|last modified CE 2488
|function: organic chemist, Europa exploration team member.

;;; file: **Willi**.cos.drv
|size: undisclosed
|created CE 2209.999
|active since CE 2209.999
|last self-modified CE 2221.98
|function: Arithmós security, Community Operating System management, Standard Virtual Reality Development: avatar of William.

;;;; file: **Wini**.cos.cab
| 36.94 petabytes
| created CE 2153
| active since CE 2153
| last modified CE 2153
| origin: partitioned avatar of William
| function: budding development engineer, system controller with Wu.sys and Willi.sys: avatar of William.

;;;; file: **Wu**.sys
| 36.94 petabytes
| created CE 2153
| active since CE2153
| origin: avatar of William, the AI sentience
| function: primary system integrity controller: avatar of William.

;;;; file: **WWW** (William)
| 4 zettabytes
| created CE 1983
| active since 2150
| last self-modified CE 2150
| function: world wide web consciousness, catalyst.

;;;; file: **Yulia.dat** (Yulia1)
| function: partner of ViktorPyryev.gen1.sec.

Europa Phase

The Journey from trying to climb into a Russian tank during the Hungarian revolution of 1956 to writing Science Fiction is in itself a story of a leap across worlds of reality.

Zsoall, born in Hungary, was brought to Australia by his parents after the 1956 uprising. He currently lives a creative life with his wife and animal family in the Northern Rivers, New South Wales, Australia.

His life has changed direction a number of times. After gaining his qualifications as a Sculptor he worked as a Secondary Teacher before becoming an Administrative Manager. None offered satisfactory opportunities for creative expression. That began when he embarked on a career as a computer programmer. Whilst in that profession his continuing compulsion to create made it inevitable that his life would change again. Completely giving up programming he immersed himself in creativity as a Sculptor and Painter.

Much of his time is now dedicated to creating glass paintings and sculptures.

Another change is looming on the horizon as the art of recording future visions takes a firmer hold of his creative energies as he pursues the writing of Science Fiction.

Europa Phase